MARS, Inc.

inc.

THE BILLIONAIRE'S CLUB

❖ ❖ ❖

MARS, Inc.

THE BILLIONAIRE'S CLUB

❂ ❂ ❂

BEN BOVA

BAEN

MARS, INC.: THE BILLIONAIRE'S CLUB

Copyright © 2013 by Ben Bova

A Baen Book

Baen Publishing Enterprises
P.O. Box 1403
Riverdale, NY 10471
www.baen.com

ISBN: 978-1-4516-3934-6

Cover art by Stephan Martiniere

First Baen printing, December 2013

Distributed by Simon & Schuster
1230 Avenue of the Americas
New York, NY 10020

Library of Congress Cataloging-in-Publication Data

Bova, Ben, 1932-
 Mars, Inc. : the Billionaire's club / Ben Bova.
   pages cm
  ISBN 978-1-4516-3934-6 (hardback)
1. Billionaires--Fiction. 2. Investment clubs--Fiction. 3. Mars (Planet)--Exploration--Fiction. I. Title.
 PS3552.O84M373 2013
 813'.54--dc23

                    2013033169

Printed in the United States of America

10 9 8 7 6 5 4 3 2

❄ DEDICATION ❄

To the lovely Rashida,
and the future.

MARS,
INC.
THE BILLIONAIRE'S CLUB

Confidence is what you have
before you understand the problem.
—Woody Allen

YEAR ONE

※ 1 ※
SAN FRANCISCO

"Well, somebody's got to do it. The goddamned government isn't going to."

Charles Kahn smiled tolerantly as he reached for his half-finished glass of manzanilla. He had never heard Art Thrasher speak the word "government" without preceding it with "goddamned."

The two men were sitting in a pair of wingchairs in a quiet corner of the Kensington Club's Men's Bar, a haven of restful luxury, leather upholstery, and dark cherrywood paneling. Through the gracefully-draped window beyond Thrasher's chair, Kahn could see the club's lovely little private garden and, beyond its carefully-tended trees, the Bay Bridge arching over the surging waters.

The trouble is, Kahn thought, that no place on Earth is placid or quiet when Art's in it. I should never have invited the little toothache to come here for a drink with me. He's small potatoes, him and his electronics gadgets; he's not even worth a billion. Nowhere near it. Why am I putting up with this aggravation?

Kahn reached for his wine again; the little stemmed glass rested on the elegantly-styled sherry table standing between their two chairs. Thrasher's mug of ginger beer was beside it, untouched. Ginger beer, Kahn thought; how infantile.

Mistaking Kahn's silence for tacit approval, Thrasher continued, "We can do it! You, me, and a handful of others. We can get to Mars!"

"Really, now, Art."

"Really," Thrasher insisted.

The two men were a study in contrasts. Thrasher was short, paunchy, with big round light hazel eyes made even more owlish by his rimless eyeglasses. He wore his sandy hair boyishly short despite his receding hairline. His tan sports coat and darker chinos barely passed the club's dress code, Kahn knew. Instead of a tie he was wearing one of those ridiculous Texas string things. Even sitting in the capacious wingchair he fidgeted and squirmed restlessly, like a little boy yearning to go outside and play in the mud.

Compared to him, Kahn was a monument to calm dignity in his gray three-piece suit and chiseled ruggedly handsome features, the very best that modern cosmetic surgery could provide.

"And just how much would this mission to Mars cost?" Kahn asked.

Thrasher hesitated, rolled his eyes ceilingward, pursed his lips, then finally replied, "About a hundred billion, tops."

"A hundred billion?" Kahn almost dropped his drink.

"That's over five years, Charlie. That's twenty billion a year. Peanuts, really."

Kahn sipped at his manzanilla before replying, "You have a strange concept of peanuts."

"Come on, Charlie, we both know you're making indecent profits. What's the price of gasoline at the pump? Nine bucks a gallon? Going up to ten, eleven here in California, isn't it?"

Kahn shrugged noncommittally.

Thrasher went on, "You and your brother can put up a billion per year, each. You make that much in interest on your holdings every year, don't you? Take it off your taxes as a charitable donation."

"Really," Kahn muttered.

"Think of the publicity you'll earn! The good will! You could use some good will. I hear you're getting death threats on Twitter."

With a sigh, Kahn said, "I have PR people to handle things like that. And security people, as well."

"Give the people Mars and they'll love you! They'll build statues to you."

"There's no profit in such a mission."

"Only the profit of knowing that you've helped advance

humankind's frontier. Mars, for chrissakes! The red planet! The scientists are dying to explore it, find out if there's life there."

"And why should I spend my hard-earned money on such a venture?"

"Come on, Charlie, this is me you're talking to. The hardest work you've done in the past fifteen years is reading *Forbes* magazine to see where you stand on the billionaire's list."

"Why isn't NASA—"

"Because the goddamned government has slashed their budget, that's why! Those fartbrains in the White House have no interest in human space flight anymore."

Kahn said nothing. He had contributed generously to the superpac that had helped get the current president into the White House. And Thrasher knew it.

Scrunching up closer on the wingchair, Thrasher coaxed, "Look, the Chinese are sending a man to the Moon in five years or so. America's going to look like a chump."

"You want to upstage the Chinese."

"It'd be great, wouldn't it? Leave those commies in the dust by going to Mars. Make *them* look like chumps."

"That's what John Kennedy did to the Soviets back in the Sixties," Kahn mused. "He leapfrogged their space efforts by putting Americans on the Moon first."

"And we can leapfrog the People's Republic of China! With private enterprise! Capitalism beats the communists!"

"A billion a year," Kahn murmured.

"For five years."

Leaning back in the warmly embracing wingchair, Kahn eyed Thrasher for a long moment, then said, "Tell you what, Art. You go to New York and see my brother. If you can talk David into doing this, then I'll come along, too."

Thrasher jumped to his feet, pumped Kahn's hand vigorously, and dashed out of the bar. Heads turned as he raced out. Several of he elder members shot disapproving glances at Kahn.

As if I'm responsible for the little ass, Kahn grumbled to himself. Then he reached for his sherry again. Let him talk to David. My brother will swat him like the annoying little mosquito that he is.

◎ 2 ◎
HOUSTON

The flight from San Francisco to Houston took just a tad over three hours, in Art Thrasher's executive Learjet. The plane's interior was luxuriously outfitted with swiveling plush reclinable seats, leather covered bulkheads and a full bar. Thrasher ignored all the amenities and split the time between phone calls and text messaging, while wondering in the back of his mind if he should get himself a supersonic jet.

Naah, he decided. The goddamned government doesn't allow supersonic flight over land. People complain about the sonic boom. As he hunched over his notepad's keyboard, pecking away, he thought: Maybe a rocket, like Branson's flying out of New Mexico. Cut the travel time to half an hour or less.

He cleared his screen, then texted his secretary in Houston to look into the idea. Branson's Virgin Galactic was making money, at last, flying tourists to the edge of space for a few minutes of experiencing weightlessness. Could the same technology be adapted to fly from point to point on Earth at hypersonic speed? That could make as big an impact on commercial air transportation as the transition from piston engines to jets, over a half a century earlier.

The pilot's voice came through the intercom speaker. "Making our approach to Houston, Mr. Thrasher."

Home sweet home, Thrasher thought, tightening his seat belt. But not for long. Gotta get to New York and see Charlie's big brother. They say he's got balls that clank.

Leaning back in the commodious chair, Thrasher thought, I've got to come up with something that'll get him interested. He won't go for scientific interest or national pride; not him. It's got to be something that'll make money for him. Let's see . . . he's into real estate, banking, what else?

As offices of corporate moguls go, Arthur Thrasher's was minimalist. No swanky overdecorated suite filled with underlings and paper shufflers. No airport-sized executive desk to overawe visitors. No art treasures on the walls.

Thrasher Digital Corporation had a modest suite of offices on the top floor of one of Houston's least gaudy high-rise towers. One flight up, on the building's roof, was a helicopter pad. Thrasher made the commute from the airport to his office in half an hour or less.

He hustled down the spiral staircase from the roof to the reception area of Thrasher Digital, briefcase in hand. With a nod to the two young women seated at their desks, he dashed into his suite's outer office. His executive assistant, Linda Ursina, was standing just inside the door with a frosted mug of ginger beer in her hand.

"Thanks, sweetie," Thrasher said as he took the drink from her with his free hand and headed for his private office. "Got me a date with Dave Kahn yet?"

Linda was just a few millimeters taller than Thrasher, with the slim, graceful figure of a dancer. Long legs that showed nicely in her midthigh skirt. The face of an Aztec princess: high cheekbones, olive complexion, dark almond-shaped eyes and sleek midnight hair that she wore tied up on the top of her head, making her look even taller.

"Mr. Kahn says he's free tonight," she replied, in a smooth contralto voice, "but not again until next Wednesday afternoon."

Thrasher grunted as he pushed through the door to his private office. It was large enough to hold his teak and chrome desk, a round conference table in one corner, and a trio of comfortable armchairs, upholstered in burgundy faux leather. One entire wall was a sweeping window that looked out on the city. The other walls held flat screens that showed priceless art treasures from the world's finest museums. Thrasher appreciated fine art, he just didn't want to have to pay for it.

The screens on the walls were showing High Renaissance works from Italian masters: Da Vinci, Michelangelo, Rafael.

His one concession to vanity was a small sculpture sitting on a credenza against the office's back wall. It was bust of Thrasher himself, sculpted by his second wife, back in those early days when he thought she loved him.

Sliding into his padded, high-backed desk chair, Thrasher slammed his mug of ginger beer on the desk's cermet coaster as he muttered, "If I run out there tonight Dave'll think I'm pretty damned desperate to see him. If I let it slide into next week . . ." He snapped his fingers. "Get Will Portal on the phone."

Linda's full lips curved into a slight smile.

"I know, I know," Thrasher said, peeling off his jacket. "Portal doesn't come running to the phone just because I've called him. You just explain to whichever flunky you talk to that this is the chance of a lifetime and it can't wait."

Looking less than impressed, Linda asked, "May I tell him what it's all about?"

"Hell no!"

"Would you kindly tell *me* what it's all about?"

"Mars, what else?"

"Oh, that."

It was nearly seven p.m. when Linda stepped into Thrasher's office and said, "If there's nothing else you need, I'll be going home now."

He glanced at his empty mug, but nodded. "Yeah, sure, go on home, kid."

"Portal hasn't returned your call," she said.

"It's two hours earlier out in Seattle. He'll call."

"You're going to wait here until he does?"

"Yep."

"You'll miss dinner."

He sighed. "As General Grant once said, I intend to fight it out along these lines if it takes all summer."

Linda said, "If I recall my history lessons, Grant didn't win until the following spring."

Thrasher grinned at her. "Go on home, smartass."

The phone jingled.

Linda started for the desk, but Thrasher stopped her with an upraised hand, waited for the second ring, then punched the speaker button.

One of the wall screens flicked from a Renaissance Madonna to the youthful, slightly bemused face of Willard Portal.

Thrasher broke into a wide grin as he said, "Hello, Will. Good of you to call back."

With a lopsided smile, Portal said, "Your message said it's a matter of life and death."

Leaning back in his leather-covered desk chair, Thrasher said, quite seriously, "It is, Will. It is. The life or death of human space flight in America."

"Oh?"

"We've got to put together a human mission to Mars, Will. There's nothing more important, absolutely nothing."

Linda went to one of the armchairs and sat down, fascinated, as Thrasher spent the next hour and a half cajoling another billionaire.

3
HOME SWEET HOME

It was nearly nine o'clock when Portal finally said, "Okay, Art, okay. I'll think about it."

His bolo tie pulled loose, Thrasher tilted his padded chair back and planted his booted feet on his desk top. "Think of the tax break you can get out of this, Will. Think of the publicity and good will."

"I said I'll think about it," Portal repeated, his thin voice rising slightly.

"Fine, wonderful."

"Now can I go to dinner?" Portal's face took on a sardonic little grin.

"Sure," said Thrasher magnanimously. "Sorry to have kept you so long. I appreciate your time, Will, I really do."

"Good night, Art."

"'Night, Will."

The wall screen went back to the displaying the Madonna. Thrasher sighed heavily, then took off his glasses and rubbed his eyes. He was surprised to see Linda still sitting there, her chin on her fists.

"I thought you were going home."

"I am," she said, getting to her feet. "Goodness, look at the time."

Replacing his glasses, Thrasher said, "Just because I work crazy hours doesn't mean you have to."

She smiled. "Have you made any plans for your own dinner?"

"I'll grab something out of the freezer."

Linda gave him a critical look. "You ought to take better care of yourself."

Getting up from behind the desk, Thrasher said, "Yes, Mommy. Now go home."

"Make sure you get some food into you."

"And be back here at eight sharp."

"Right, boss." She turned and left the office.

Admiring her form, Thrasher recognized that Linda was really a very beautiful young woman. What is it the Catholics call it? he mused. Then he remembered, she's a near occasion of sin. A very tempting morsel indeed. He shook his head and said to himself sternly, you do *not* come on to employees. It's very unfair to them. And you could get sued up to your eyeballs.

The intercom buzzed.

"What?" he demanded.

Linda's voice asked, "Should I tell Carlo to meet you in the lobby?"

"Naw. Tell him to go home. I'll stay here tonight."

"You're sure?"

"Stop mothering me, kid. And go home yourself."

A hesitation, then she said, "Goodnight, then."

"Goodnight, already."

Thrasher's home was far out in the posh suburbs, a mansion he had built for his second wife, the sculptress. But he maintained a modest apartment on the other side of the corridor from his office suite. Nothing very fancy, just a couple of bedrooms, kitchen, sitting room, and a book-lined study. Plus a walk-in shower in the master bathroom. He had spent some very special hours, sharing that shower.

But tonight he was alone. He pulled a dinner package from the freezer, microwaved it, then sat at the kitchen counter and nibbled at it while he watched television, switching from CNN to Fox News to MSNBC and back again at every commercial break.

Pouring himself a ginger beer, he briefly thought about adding a dollop of brandy to it. Brandy and dry, the Aussies called it. He decided against the brandy and walked slowly to his study, then out onto the balcony that overlooked the garish lights of downtown Houston.

Can't see the stars, they keep it so goddamned bright, he complained silently. Not like Arizona. Not at all.

His mother had died in childbirth and Thrasher was raised by his embittered father, a dry husk of an astronomy professor at the University of Arizona's Steward Observatory. Dad worked all his life and what did he get for it? Bubkiss. A lousy pension and his name on a couple of boxfuls of research papers.

His father had accomplished one other thing, though. He had instilled in young Arthur D. Thrasher a love of astronomy, a fascination with the grandeur and mystery of the stars.

Not that Art followed his father's footsteps. The chalkdust classrooms and genteel poverty of academic life were not for Art. To his father's despair, Arthur took the university's business curriculum, then won a partial scholarship for an MBA at Wharton. He covered his expenses with the money he'd made from his first entrepreneurial venture: a bicycle repair shop on the edge of the UA campus.

His father died the year Art made his first million. Art married, divorced, married and divorced again. By the time he was worth a hundred million, he had given up on marriage—but not on women.

Leaning against the balcony railing, Art took off his glasses, folded them carefully into his shirt pocket, then peered at the sky. He was farsighted, he didn't need the glasses to see the stars. Farsighted. He laughed to himself. At least that's better than being myopic. His second wife had gotten him to try contact lenses, but Art hated to insert them, felt uncomfortable with them, always feared one of them would pop out at an embarrassing moment.

There was talk of new surgical techniques to alleviate hypermetropia, the medical term for farsightedness. Art shook his head at the thought of it. Maybe after I'm sixty-five and eligible for Medicare, he decided. Let the goddamned government pay for it.

Then he reminded himself that it wasn't the goddamned government's money, it was the taxpayers'. With a sigh, he realized that sixty-five wasn't that far away: thirteen years. Lucky thirteen.

He ducked back into his study for a moment and pulled what looked like binoculars from his desk drawer. Actually, they were nothing more than a pair of toilet-paper rollers, duct taped together. Out on the balcony again, Art put the contraption to his eyes and searched the sky. The tubes blocked some of the glare from the city's lights.

He saw a reddish dot through the glow and smog. Mars? Might be Antares. But no, the dot wasn't twinkling, the way stars do. It was a steady beacon. The planet Mars. He remembered the first time his father had shown him Mars, rising bright and clear over the rugged mountains ringing Tucson. I couldn't have been more than five years old. And the lurid adventure tales set on Mars that he'd read in his teen years; his father shook his head with disdain at his son's choice of literature.

"Mars," Thrasher breathed, staring at the red dot in the sky. Thirty-five million miles away at its closest. But we'll get there. We'll get there.

Why? he asked himself. Because it's there? He laughed. Because we can make money from it? I doubt that. Because I want to show my father that I'm not just a money-grubbing Philistine?

None of the above.

Or maybe, he thought, it's all of the above. And more.

And he remembered his father's dying words, as he lay in the hospital, withering away before Thrasher's tear-filled eyes:

"Make something of yourself, Arthur. There's more to life than money. Do something you can be proud of, something worth doing."

Something, Thrasher thought bitterly. Something you could never do, Dad.

We'll get to Mars because it's worth doing. Something I can be proud of. It's that simple. It's something I can be proud of. Something to make my father proud of me.

◎ 4 ◎
JOHNSON SPACE CENTER

"But I'm a NASA employee, Mr. Thrasher—"

"Art. Call me Art."

Jessie Margulis looked distinctly uncomfortable. Thrasher had driven out to the NASA center specifically to meet the engineer, but Margulis had refused to bring him inside, to where the offices and laboratories were. They sat next to each other in the spacious visitors' center reception area.

Margulis hunched close to Thrasher, his eyes worriedly following every salesman and bureaucrat and engineer that paraded past. He even glanced cautiously every few seconds at the four receptionists sitting behind the big curving desk in the center of the room. Christ, Thrasher thought, he acts like we're planning a bank heist.

Thrasher's chief engineer, Vince Egan, had identified Margulis as one of NASA's top engineers, the man who headed Johnson Space Center's advanced planning department.

"I'm a government employee," Margulis repeated. "I shouldn't even be talking to you."

"Why not?" Thrasher countered, "I'm a citizen and a taxpayer; that makes me your boss, kind of." Then, with a grin, he added, "It's not like we're plotting to blow up the place."

Margulis winced. He's sweating, Thrasher noticed. They air-condition this barn cold enough to put icicles on your *cojones* and he's sweating.

Thrasher went on, "We're just having a friendly little chat about what a manned spacecraft—"

"Crewed," Margulis corrected.

"Crude?"

"Cre-*wed*." The engineer emphasized the second syllable. "We don't say 'manned.' It's not politically correct."

Thrasher nodded. "I gotcha. And besides, we'll have women among the crew for the Mars mission."

Margulis winced again at the word "Mars." He was a bland-faced man in his forties: receding hairline, little fuzz of a goatee hiding a weak chin, a pot belly, shirt pocket stuffed with pens. Put him in a party with six hundred guests and ask any one of 'em to find the engineer, they'd go straight to him, Thrasher thought.

Still, the headhunters claimed he was a brilliant engineer. And more than that, he was a leader among engineers. The rest of them respected him.

But Margulis was saying, "NASA has been directed to shelve its plans for a crewed Mars mission. There's no money in the budget for it."

"And all the work you've done on the project has been scrapped," said Thrasher.

"Mothballed," Margulis corrected. Thrasher thought he detected some resentment there.

"So what are you working on now?"

The engineer tracked with his eyes an older man in his shirtsleeves and a NASA employee's badge dangling from a chain around his neck. The guy glared disapprovingly at Margulis as he walked past.

"What are you working on now?" Thrasher repeated. "Is it a secret?"

"No, we don't work on classified projects. We're completely open."

"So what're you doing now?"

Margulis shrugged. "Robotic planetary probes, mostly. Another mission to Europa. Conceptual studies of a probe to land on Titan."

"That's a moon of Saturn, right?"

"Right."

"And manned . . . I mean, crewed missions?"

"Nothing."

Brightening, Thrasher said, "Well, I've got a crewed mission for you to work on. Mars."

"I can't discuss that with you," Margulis hissed, almost pleading. "I'm a NASA employee."

"You're not allowed to consult with a private citizen?"

"No. That'd be a conflict of interest, in the government's eyes."

"Then quit the goddamned government and come to work for me. I'll double whatever you're making now."

Margulis' mouth popped open, but no words came out.

"I want you to head my Mars project."

"I . . . In another couple of years I'll have put in my twenty. I've got a pension coming, and there's the health-care insurance . . ."

"I'll equal or better it."

"Could you wait two years?"

"No."

Margulis was clearly torn. Tempted.

Thrasher coaxed, "You'll be head of the project, free to run it any way you like."

The engineer blinked twice, then asked, "Suppose I want to use a nuclear propulsion system."

"Nuclear?"

"A nuclear rocket would be a helluva lot better than chemical rockets. More efficient, capable of moving a much bigger payload. But NASA's stopped all work on nukes. Too much anti-nuke pressure."

Thrasher saw an opening. With a shrug, he said, "You're the tech leader. If you think nuclear is the way to go, we'll go nuclear."

"There'll be a lot of opposition," Margulis warned.

"I'll take care of the opposition. You do the engineering."

For a long moment Margulis said nothing. Then, "The problem is . . . Art, your project might go belly-up. You might not get the funding you need. Or the anti-nuke people will stop you. Or the money might run out. With the government, I've got a steady job. I've got security. I have a wife and three kids to think about."

"Jessie, I will personally fund a pension and health care insurance plan for you. Fully fund them both. Put the money into a separate account, where it'll be safe."

"I . . ."

"I want you Jessie. You're the best man to run this project, everyone I've talked with agrees on that. I *need* you."

"I'd have to quit NASA. Leave all my benefits."

"Can't you take a leave of absence? For a year, say? Then, if my project doesn't work out, you can come back to NASA and no harm's been done."

"Maybe . . ."

"You think about it, pal." Thrasher popped to his feet. Margulis remained seated, his expression somewhere between thoughtful and frightened.

At last he got slowly to his feet, too.

"I will think about it, Mr. Thrasher."

"Art."

"Art."

"Double your salary. Full pension and health insurance." Thrasher started to turn toward the door, hesitated, and turned back to Margulis.

"Oh, I almost forgot the most important point of all."

"What's that?"

"You'll be working on a mission to Mars, by damn. A nuclear-propelled crewed mission to Mars. You'll never get to do that as an employee of the goddamned government."

◎ 5 ◎
NEW YORK, NEW YORK

The town so big they named it twice, Thrasher mused as he looked out through the narrow window of his Learjet at the forest of towers blanketing Manhattan.

David Kahn was ensconced in an office in one of those towers. Throughout the rough-and-tumble world of commercial real estate and investment banking, the man was known as Jenghis Kahn. Nobody said that to his face, though. Very few got to say it more than once, even behind his back.

His office was high up in the Chrysler Building, which he owned. An icon of art deco architecture, the building's interior had been completely remodeled, Thrasher saw. High-speed elevators, swift and quiet. Elegant carpeting along the corridors. The walls were hung with photographs of Manhattan scenes: ghetto kids playing in the spray from a fireplug, glittering Broadway openings, the Twin Towers collapsing in smoke and death.

He's a Noo Yawkah, Thrasher realized. Born in Oshkosh, but he's made the Big Apple the center of his soul. Assuming he has one.

Kahn's outer office was larger than Thrasher's entire suite, back in Houston. You could play a hockey game in here, Thrasher told himself as he plodded across the thick carpeting to the desk where a lone executive assistant sat, pointedly ignoring him by keeping her beady eyes focused on her desktop display screen.

She was middle-aged, lean, lantern-jawed, with her graying hair pulled back in some sort of knot. A dragon, guarding the entrance to her master's lair.

As Thrasher stepped up to the desk, the dragon looked up at him.

"Arthur D. Thrasher, I presume." Her voice was a surprisingly smooth purr.

"That's me!"

"Mr. Kahn is on an international call at the moment. Please have a seat. He'll be with you shortly."

Thrasher grinned. He'd seen this ploy before. *I'm so busy and powerful that you'll have to wait before I have the time to listen to your pitiful little spiel.*

Chuckling to himself, he went to the nearest couch and sat down. The coffee table in front of the couch held a scattering of business magazines. Thrasher picked up a copy of *Forbes.* Sure enough, it was the edition that featured the nation's wealthiest people. David Kahn and his brother Charles were tied for fourth place, just ahead of Will Portal.

The minutes ticked by. Thrasher put the magazine down, pulled out his handheld, and checked his phone messages. *Nothing that can't wait,* he thought. *Besides, if I try to make an outgoing call the dragon lady will probably throw a hissy fit.*

He went back to the magazine. One of the articles was about the shaky financial status of the private space-launch business. Four firms, all deeply in debt, competing for the contract to run cargo and people to the International Space Station. Not enough of a market to sustain four companies, the article concluded. Thrasher agreed.

They're at the mercy of the goddamned government, he fumed. *NASA's got them by the balls. The tourist market that they all banked on hasn't materialized. Not yet.*

"Mr. Thrasher."

He looked up.

"Mr. Kahn will see you now."

Thrasher saw that the door to Kahn's private office had magically opened. He rose to his feet, beamed his brightest smile at the dragon lady, and went through.

David Kahn sat behind a massive desk almost as big as a helicopter landing pad. He was an old man, so shriveled and wizened that even his completely bald head was creased like a badly rutted road. He had a hooked nose and narrow, cold eyes. His skin was gray and wrinkled like old parchment. That's what his brother would look like in ten years, Thrasher thought, if it weren't for the cosmetic surgery industry.

Then he realized that Kahn was sitting in a powered wheelchair. Attached to the seat's back was a stack of electronics boxes, beeping softly. For god's sake, Thrasher thought, the man's on life-support.

As brightly as he could, Thrasher said, "Mr. Kahn." He put out his hand, but the desk was too broad for him to reach the old man.

"Mr. Thrasher," said Kahn, his voice a harsh croak. He ignored Thrasher's extended arm and gestured with one clawlike hand to the plush chair directly in front of his desk.

"It's good of you to take the time to see me," Thrasher said as genially as he could manage, while he sat down.

Kahn was in his vest and shirtsleeves. Still he looked almost formally dressed, compared to Thrasher's suede-shouldered western-cut jacket and onyx bolo tie.

"Cut the crap, Thrasher," Kahn rasped. "My brother tells me you want us to put up the money for a mission to Mars."

"Part of the money," Thrasher countered. "A billion a year each, for five years."

"Why?"

"To get to Mars! To put human explorers on the red planet. To fulfill the dream of the ages."

"I told you to cut the crap. What's in it for me?"

Thrasher smiled minimally. "To begin with, you'll get a sizeable tax break."

"We could donate the money to charitable causes here on Earth and get the same tax deduction."

"But not the same publicity. Not the same good will."

"I don't want publicity and I don't need good will."

"The Mars program will stimulate lots of businesses," Thrasher explained. "Aerospace construction, rocket engine development, electronics—"

"Hah!" Pointing an accusing finger, Kahn said, "That's where you've made your money, isn't it? Electronics. Cell phones. Global positioning systems."

"True enough."

"So this is just a ploy for *you* to make more money."

"It's much more than that."

Kahn almost smiled. "I have nothing against making money, you know." Hunching forward and clasping his mottled hands together on the desktop, Kahn went on, "Now, how will this scheme of yours make money for *me*?"

Thrasher leaned back in the plush chair, thinking, Pretty much what I expected. What's in it for *numero uno*?

"Well," he said, drawing out the word, "as this program builds up, we're going to hire lots of engineers and technicians. Mostly in the Cape Canaveral area, I imagine."

Kahn muttered. "Real estate values are very depressed there."

"At present."

"And California? What about the Bay Area, Silicon Valley?"

Looking out for his little brother, Thrasher thought. He replied, "Same thing, pretty much. Houston, too. There'll be a bit of a housing boom there, as well."

Kahn stared fixedly at Thrasher for a long, silent moment. Thrasher thought he could see the wheels turning inside the old ogre's skull.

At last Kahn shook his head. "It's not enough. How many engineers will you need to hire? Not enough to start a real-estate boom."

"But it's not just the engineers," Thrasher immediately replied. "There's a multiplier effect."

"Multiplier?"

"Engineers need technicians. Technicians need warehouse operators, truck drivers, clerks, secretaries. Their spouses need supermarkets, babysitters, car dealers, auto mechanics. And schools for their kids! Teachers, school bus drivers."

"And real estate agents."

"You bet! There's a boom for you!"

Kahn unlaced his fingers and eased back in his wheelchair. "Let me think about this," he said. "And talk with my brother."

"One other thing," Thrasher said. "The banking industry in those areas—particularly the Cape, in Florida—is pretty depressed right now."

Kahn nodded.

"If I were involved with the banking industry, I'd start quietly buying out some of those locals, while the prices are still low. Once we announce the Mars program, prices will skyrocket."

The old man actually smiled. "I've already thought of that."

6
THRASHER DIGITAL CORPORATION

All through the flight back to Houston, Thrasher mused about the possibilities of developing existing rocket technology for hypersonic commercial air transportation.

Big public-relations problem, he said to himself. People remember whenever a rocket blows up. Sticks in their minds. They'll be scared to fly a rocket.

Then he thought, but why should it have to take off like a rocket? Why not a jet plane that carries the bird piggyback up to high altitude, then the bird lights its rocket engine and goes off like a bat out of hell. That's what Branson's doing with his suborbital flights. Tourists pay good money for a few minutes of feeling weightless, as if they were actually in space.

As he rode his helicopter from Hobby Airport to his office, the city below reminded him of an inhumanly busy ants' nest, with cars scurrying madly along the throughways. He pulled out his handheld and called Linda.

"Get Egan to meet me in my office before the day's out," he said.

Her face in the phone's miniature screen looked only mildly surprised. "Egan is in California, meeting with the SpaceX people. Besides, it's almost five o'clock."

"You don't expect to leave at quitting time, do you?"

"Of course not." With a rueful shake of her head.

"Set up a phone link with him for me. I'll be in the office . . ." he glanced at the clock readout on the handheld, ". . . in ten, twelve minutes."

"Right. Oh, Mr. Ornsteen wants to see you as soon as you get in. He says it's urgent."

"Sid?" The corporation's treasurer never brought good news, Thrasher thought. "Urgent, huh?"

"He seemed upset."

"He's always upset. The man's a walking ulcer."

"Shall I tell him to meet you in your office?"

Nodding reluctantly, Thrasher replied, "After I've talked with Egan."

Linda kept a corner of her desktop screen focused on the view from the camera at the helipad, up on the roof. The instant her boss' chopper touched down, she went to the minifridge built into the cabinets lining the back wall of the anteroom and poured a chilled mug of ginger beer. She sniffed at the bubbling brew, wondering why Thrasher liked it so much. It's not alcoholic, she knew. It's sort of like ginger ale, only stronger.

Thrasher came breezing through the corridor door, briefcase slung over a shoulder of his rumpled sports coat, one hand reaching for the mug.

"Egan is standing by in California," she said.

"Good."

"And Ornsteen's on his way up."

"Oy."

Thrasher disappeared into his office. Linda returned to her desk and saw his phone line turn on. She clipped on her Bluetooth earset and listened in for a few moments. Tech talk, about flying rockets from Houston to California. She quietly cut her connection and put the earset back in her top desk drawer as Sidney P. Ornsteen stepped in, looking more worried than usual.

The corporate treasurer was balding and rail thin, anxiety thin. Linda thought he always looked as if he were on the verge of a nervous breakdown, although Thrasher insisted that Ornsteen didn't get nervous breakdowns, he gave them to others. He wore a three-piece suit, dark as an undertaker's, and an expensive-looking patterned blue tie. He might be good-looking, she thought, if he'd only relax and smile once in a while.

Nodding toward Thrasher's closed door, Ornsteen asked, "He's in?"

Linda replied, "He's on a phone call, Mr. Ornsteen. He'll be with you in a moment or two. Can I get you something? Coffee? Soda?"

Ornsteen shook his head and began pacing back and forth in front of Linda's desk.

"Who's he talking to?"

"Egan."

"The engineering guy?"

"Yes, sir."

"Probably pissing more money down a rathole," Ornsteen muttered. Then he looked stricken. "Sorry about the language, Ms. Ursina."

Linda smiled minimally.

"How long—"

Thrasher's voice came over the intercom. "Is Super Sid there yet?"

"He's right here," Linda cooed.

"Good. Send him in."

Linda started to get up from her desk, but Ornsteen didn't wait to be ushered. He bolted to the door and opened it himself.

Thrasher closed his eyes briefly as his treasurer stalked into his office. Ornsteen looked more worked up than usual, he saw. Can't be good news.

"Hello, Sid. Have a seat."

Ornsteen sat on the front three inches of the nearest armchair.

Before the treasurer could say anything, Thrasher asked, "What's happening, Sid? You look unsettled."

"Somebody's making a run at the corporation's stock," Ornsteen announced.

"A run?"

"Buying up a lot of shares."

"How many?"

The treasurer reached into his jacket and pulled out his smartphone. Thrasher noticed his left eye twitched as he tapped at the phone's screen.

"Eleven percent, as of close of business this afternoon."

Thrasher gave out a low whistle and swiveled his desk chair slowly back and forth, thinking fast. He mused, "I left Jenghis Kahn's office just about one p.m., New York time . . ."

"The push started yesterday," Ornsteen said. "It just became noticeable this afternoon."

"His brother Charlie?"

"You think?"

"I popped the Mars idea to Charlie last week. He didn't seem too wild about it, but maybe he was conning me."

"Why would he want a chunk of our stock?" Ornsteen wondered. "All he's doing is driving up the price."

"Eleven percent?"

"And counting."

"Maybe he wants to buy his way onto our board," Thrasher guessed.

"Why would he want to do that?"

"To block my Mars program."

Ornsteen shook his head. "The smart thing to do would be to wait until the value of our shares drops and then scoop 'em up."

"Why would our stock's value drop?"

The treasurer closed his eyes and massaged his brows. Then he said, "Because, Art, once you start pumping money into your Mars thing our net is going to sink like a lead balloon."

"Maybe," Thrasher admitted. "For a while."

"It doesn't make sense to buy now," Ornsteen insisted.

"Any way of finding out who it is?"

"Come on, Art," Orsteen replied sourly. "He must be using dummies. Just what you'd do if you wanted to move in on a company."

"H'mm."

"I can ask around on the Street, see if anybody knows anything."

"You do that, Sid. This could be serious."

"You're telling me?"

Thrasher watched his treasurer get up from the chair and walk stiffly to his office door. Once Ornsteen was gone, he leaned back in his desk chair and tried to make sense of what was happening.

Somebody's trying to buy his way onto my board of directors, he thought. Hell, this might be the first step in an attempt to weasel me out of my own company!

I've got to find out who it is. And what he's after.

7
WASHINGTON, D.C.

Two weeks later, Thrasher sat in the office of his corporation's chief Washington representative, waiting for the man to return from a conference on Capitol Hill. Thrasher Digital's D.C. office was distinctly more sumptuous than the corporate headquarters in Houston. It didn't pay to look seedy in Washington; elegant décor bespoke of money and power. It was a language that political decision-makers understood instinctively.

Thrasher glanced at his wristwatch. After eleven o'clock already. Impatiently, he got to his feet and went to the window. Traffic was heavy down on K Street: cars, taxis, buses inching along in a sluggish clot. Even the sidewalks were jammed with well-dressed pedestrians.

Most of them are employees of the goddamned government, Thrasher thought. They all spend every waking hour trying to figure out how to spend my tax money.

The office door banged open and in breezed Reynold R. Reynolds.

"Sorry to keep you waiting, Artie," he said, grabbing Thrasher's hand in a big, meaty paw, then hurrying to his broad, uncluttered desk. "Big pow-wow with Senator Nicholson."

Widely known as "R Cubed," Reynolds was a large man, tall and portly, who always wore a crafty expression on his fleshy face, a sort of disdainful smirk that seemed to say, "I know more about the ins-and-outs of this town than you do."

Thrasher knew that R Cubed was very knowledgeable, but he didn't know everything. He didn't know, for example, that someone was trying to buy his way into Thrasher Digital's board of directors. And Thrasher had no intention of telling him about the subtle raid his stock was suffering. One word to Reynolds and the news would be all over Washington, and then spread like a tsunami across the business world. For the way Reynolds maintained his reputation for knowing things was by telling everyone almost everything he knew. Almost.

"So what's the chairman of the Senate appropriations committee have to say for himself?" Thrasher asked, sitting himself in front of the desk.

Reynolds took a pipe from the rack on his desk and stuck it in his mouth, unlit. He knit his brow, pursed his lips, and stroked his double chin. "The usual. The Democrats don't care a rat's ass about space and the Republicans are only interested because the Democrats aren't."

"The next NASA budget?"

"It'll grow, but only by the inflation index. One percent, maybe a little more."

"Nothing about Mars."

Reynolds huffed. "Hell, they even canceled the latest unmanned rover project. NASA's not going any farther than the International Space Station, not for the life of this administration. And then some."

"What about that big telescope they want to put into space?" Thrasher asked.

"Barely squeaked through the budget review. It's years late and a couple billion over budget, but it's got major contractors in so many different states that the Congress has to keep it on life-support."

"They're not worried about the Chinese?"

Another huff. "Chairman of the Senate committee on commerce, science, and transportation—that's where NASA's pigeonholed in the Senate's pecking order, in with airline safety and fisheries—anyway, the committee chairman told me, 'If the Commies want to put a man on the Moon, I say, good luck to them.'"

Thrasher grumbled, "Idiot."

"Smart politician," Reynolds corrected. "There's no political push for space. No bloc of votes that can toss a politician out of office if he doesn't vote for bigger space appropriations."

"What about those grassroots organizations? The Planetary Society? The National Space whatever?"

"Small and powerless. Staff people up on the Hill regard them as a bunch of kooks."

"I'm supposed to speak at their international meeting in a couple of months."

Reynolds shrugged. "Might do you more harm than good."

Thrasher nodded. "Maybe."

Hunching forward in his oversized desk chair, Reynolds said, "Look: NASA's being hamstrung. There's no political push for space."

"But companies like Boeing, Orbital Science, SpaceX—they're doing business—"

"Ferrying people and cargo up the ISS and back," Reynolds interrupted. "Running a bus line to low Earth orbit. At prices the government sets. Hell, Virgin Galactic doesn't even go that far, they just sell you a ride up about a hundred miles and then you come right back down again."

"People pay good money for that ride."

"Piffle. Compared to what you're trying to do, it's small change. Nobody in this town has any interest in trying to get the government back into space in a major way."

Thrasher sunk his head. But he was thinking, Good. Good. Keep the goddamned government out of it.

"How good are you at snooping?" Thrasher asked.

Patti Fabrizio looked up from her champagne cocktail. "Me? Snooping?" A sly smile curved her thin lips.

The two of them were sitting in a corner of the Cosmos Club's bar, as far from the entrance as they could get. The darkly paneled room was designed to allow people to hold private conversations, safe from prying eyes and ears.

Thrasher had first met Patricia Fabrizio at an embassy party, so long ago that he had still been married to his first wife at the time. Patti had been a reporter for Fox News back in those days, and a good one. She was regally tall, a bit over six feet, and slim as a marathon runner—which she had been in her college days. Born to old Virginia money, she had gone into TV news when she fell in love with Daniel Fabrizio, who taught journalism at the university she attended. Their marriage endured until Danny died in a train wreck just outside of the District of Columbia. She had never remarried, but she stayed with news reporting. She found that she enjoyed prying secrets out of politicians.

Thrasher was having a drink with her in the Cosmos Club bar before flying back to Houston.

Leaning so close that their heads almost touched, he confided, "Somebody's making a run at my stock. Started a couple of weeks ago and whoever it is is still nibbling away."

She grew serious. "How do you know it's a raid? Maybe your stock looks attractive."

With a shake of his head, Thrasher said, "No more attractive than it was a month ago. And the word's out on the Street that I'm going to be dumping a lot of the corporation's assets into the Mars program—"

"What Mars program?"

Nearly two hours later, Patti knew almost as much about the workings of Thrasher Digital as Thrasher himself did. The bar had emptied of its cocktail-hour customers and was slowly filling up again with more serious drinkers. An aging, pot-bellied Senator towed a low-cut blonde up to the bar, where they sat on display, in full view of everyone.

Patti sniffed at the man's arrogance, then turned back to Thrasher. "So you think somebody's trying to buy his way onto your board?"

Thrasher nodded.

She fingered her nearly-empty glass. It was her third champagne cocktail, but the liquor didn't seem to affect her at all.

"And then kick you out?" she continued.

"I own more stock than anybody else, but not an absolute majority. Whoever it is might be able to build up a coalition—"

"A cabal."

"Whatever. They could bounce me out."

"Or maybe," she said, slowly, "maybe they want to acquire a healthy block of your shares, then dump them. Start a panic. Depress the price of your stock. Ruin your company."

Thrasher felt appalled. "I never thought of that."

"You're too much in love with your company to think anybody could stoop so low."

"But why? Why would anybody want to wreck the company?"

That sly smile returned. "You don't have any enemies?"

"Nobody who's that sore at me. I think. Years ago, maybe, when I was just starting the company. But not now." Again he added, "I think."

"You haven't stepped on any toes? Stolen a woman from somebody, maybe?"

"Me?" Thrasher was honestly surprised at the thought.

"I've heard stories about some of your lady friends," Patti said. "In fact, why couldn't the culprit be some woman you dumped?"

"I don't dump women!"

"Hell hath no fury, you know."

"Jeez, Patti. I'm asking you for help and all you're doing is giving me heartburn."

She laughed heartily. "All right, Artie, all right. I'll poke around a little for you."

"Discreetly," he said, making a shushing motion with both hands. "Quietly."

"Like a little mouse," said Patti.

But Thrasher got a mental impression of a lean, hard-eyed cheetah stalking its prey.

8
INDEPENDENCE, MISSOURI

Margaret Watkins spoke with a leisurely southern drawl. Thrasher wondered whether it came naturally to her, or was an affectation.

She was approaching eighty, Thrasher knew, although she dressed in frilly little frocks designed for women half her age. And weight. She was what was once called "pleasingly plump," short and round. Born to the founder of Watkins Brands, Inc., she had been an adorably pretty little girl when her father made his first few millions, and one of the nation's most attractive debutantes when the old man died, leaving her a cool billion dollars in trust. Maggie turned out to have a good head for business, and now was one of the wealthiest women on Earth. But for each billion she gained, she also put on ten pounds. Or more.

She and Thrasher were wending their way slowly through the Truman Library, early in the evening, after the museum was closed to the general public. Through the long draperied windows Thrasher could see the sunset outside turning the sky flame red.

"So to what do I owe the honah of your visit?" Maggie asked, in her girlish southern accent.

She's trying to sound like Scarlett O'Hara, Thrasher thought. Maybe I should try my Clark Gable impression on her.

Instead, he shrugged and answered in his normal voice, "I just realized it's been a while since we've seen each other and decided to drop in on you. Hope you don't mind."

Maggie gave him a disbelieving look. "And your sudden yearnin' to see me wouldn't have anything at all to do with Mars, would it?"

With what he hoped was a boyish grin, Thrasher answered, "Mars? What have you heard about Mars?"

"That you're sweet-talkin' and arm-twistin' and goin' every which way to raise money for flying out to Mars."

"You're damned right I am," Thrasher said, with some heat.

They started along a corridor lined with photographs from Truman's career. Thrasher especially liked the one of Harry from the morning after election day, 1948. He was grinning from ear to ear as he held up a copy of the *Chicago Tribune* with its famously incorrect headline, DEWEY DEFEATS TRUMAN.

Now they stood at the entrance to the replica of President Truman's Oval Office. As they stepped through, Thrasher realized with some bitterness that the present president hadn't invited him to the White House. Not once.

"What's so special 'bout Mars?" Maggie asked, her baby blue eyes intent.

"Lots of things," said Thrasher. "It may have harbored life once. There might even still be some form of life there, maybe deep underground. It's another world; we have a lot to learn from it."

"How're you goin' to make money out of it?"

"I'm not. None of us are. We're doing it because it's the right thing to do."

Maggie Watkins shook her head slowly. "Hard to raise money fo' that."

"I don't know about that. I think the Kahn brothers will come in on it. Will Portal's in, for sure. Bartlett. Gelson. If you join the club we'll be more than halfway there."

"A billion a year? For five years?"

"You can afford it."

"Well sure, I can *afford* it. But why would I want to?"

Thrasher looked around at the replica of the Oval Office. Hard decisions were made here, he knew. Dropping the atomic bomb on Hiroshima. Standing up to Stalin's aggressions. The Marshall Plan. Korea.

He looked at the sign resting on Truman's desk. *The buck stops here.*

He thought, Damn! If Harry were President today we'd be going to Mars, and then some.

Turning back to Maggie, he said, "We can leapfrog the Chinese and their Moon program. We can get America back into space in a major way. We can open the way to the whole damned Solar System, and then maybe go on to the stars. It's the human race's destiny, Maggie: to expand, to reach out, to explore. That what we do! That's who we are!"

She said nothing.

Pointing to Truman's desk and the sign upon it, Thrasher said, "It's time to put up or shut up. If we don't go to Mars this nation will be giving up its heritage and we'll sink into insignificance. We're a frontier people, Maggie! Your father understood that! He was always breaking new ground."

"An' making money out of it."

"So now you've got more money than you know what to do with. Do something big! Do something significant. Put up or shut up, for chrissakes!"

Maggie broke into a low chuckle. "All right, Artie. All right. I'll put up. Even if it's only to make you shut up."

◉ 9 ◉
SPACEPORT AMERICA, NEW MEXICO

The governor of New Mexico was perspiring. Thrasher could see sweat beading his broad forehead and upper lip. He was a stocky Hispanic, built like a sack of cement. Even in his light gray summerweight suit, he was obviously uncomfortable. But as long as the TV news cameras were on him, the governor beamed a big telegenic smile while he stood beside Thrasher and his other guest at the VIP stands overlooking the rocket launch pad.

It was a bright desert afternoon, with the Sun blazing in a cloudless sky of turquoise blue. Hot. Dry, baking oven hot. Thrasher could feel trickles of perspiration sliding down his own ribs, beneath his short-sleeved shirt.

The viewing stands were more than half empty, despite the governor's presence. Launching rockets from the New Mexico desert had become almost commonplace.

"Five minutes and counting," boomed the loudspeakers on either end of the benches.

The camera crew started to shift their attention to the tall, slim rocket standing on the pad, but the TV reporter—a determined-looking young woman with perfectly-coiffed auburn hair and the buxom figure of a temptress—stayed with the governor and his two guests.

The other guest was Elton Schroeder. It was his rocket standing on the launch pad, a thin wisp of vapor leaking from halfway up its length. The vapor dissipated in the dry New Mexico air almost immediately. A slim gantry tower stood next to the rocket, holding hoses that connected to the rocket's base and upper stage. Thrasher could see a handful of technicians in white coveralls climbing down from the launch platform and heading for a trio of SUVs parked nearby.

With his smile still in place on his beefy face, the governor began to lecture Thrasher, "It's a two-stage rocket, you know. The first stage is jettisoned as soon as its rocket engines run out of fuel. Parachutes bring it down to a soft landing."

"Here at the spaceport?" Thrasher asked.

Waggling one hand, the governor replied, "Well, within the confines of the White Sands range."

Schroeder spoke up, in a strangely harsh, rasping voice, "We retrieve the stage for reuse."

Pointing to the bird on the launch pad, Thrasher asked, "How many times has that one been reused?"

Schroeder thought for a moment, then answered, "This is the fourth flight for that one."

"Four minutes and counting."

Schroeder was trying to look like a cowboy, Thrasher thought. He had the craggy, weathered face for it, but his clothes looked like Brooks Brothers, or at least L. L. Bean. He was wearing brand-new, sharply creased chinos, a monogrammed white-on-white shirt, unbuttoned leather vest and hand-tooled boots. His lean face bore two days' stubble, yet his hair was so light he almost looked like an albino. His eyes were deeply brown, though, almost black, probing. He had hardly spoken a word since the governor introduced him to Thrasher, and he conspicuously avoided the television news crew.

Thrasher noted that Schroeder put his hands behind his back and crossed his fingers. He started to say something about it, but caught himself in time. Don't make fun of a man's superstitions, he told himself. He's got forty million bucks riding on this launch, he's entitled to a quirk or two. Hell, he probably doesn't even realize he's doing it.

Instead, Thrasher said to the governor, "This is a magnificent thing you've done here. A private spaceport."

"It's owned by the State of New Mexico," the governor said, with pride in his voice.

"Plus a consortium of private investors," Schroeder added. His strained voice was almost painful to the ears.

The governor nodded. "Virgin Galactic, SpaceX, your own company, Mr. Schroeder . . ."

"Is it a profitable operation?" Thrasher asked.

"Oh yes," the governor replied quickly. Thrasher saw that Schroeder suddenly looked uncomfortable. If this place is making a profit, Thrasher surmised, it isn't much. Not enough to make Schroeder happy.

The minutes ticked by. Thrasher wished they were inside the sweeping modernistic air-conditioned operations building, instead of baking out here in the sun. The buxom reporter had moved to stand next to him, close enough for him to catch a hint of her perfume. His nose twitched. Musk. The damned stuff always made him sneeze.

"I didn't get your name," he said to the woman. She was really quite pretty beneath her makeup, he thought. Curly auburn hair clipped short. Big baby-blue eyes. The blouse she wore showed just enough cleavage to be interesting.

"Victoria Zane," she said, smiling at him.

Thrasher nodded and turned his attention back to the activities at the base of the rocket. The SUVs were backing away and heading for the operations building, spouting roostertails of dust behind them.

Schroeder, his hands still behind his back, rasped tightly, "They'll be going into the automated sequence now."

"One minute and counting," blared the loudspeakers.

He glanced at the reporter. Her eyes were riveted on the rocket and she seemed to be holding her breath. Too bad, Thrasher thought. She breathes so fetchingly. But he forced himself to keep his face impassive. This is no time for making a pass.

"Ten . . . nine . . . eight . . ."

The rocket seemed to be coming alive. Standing tall and alone against the turquoise sky, to Thrasher it seemed to quiver, to breathe, almost. The hoses from the gantry tower dropped away and the tower itself rolled back from the launch platform.

"Three . . . two . . . one . . ."

Christ, Thrasher thought to himself, this is like having sex! The tension building, building, and then the release. It's like working up to an explosive orgasm.

Flame blossomed at the base of the rocket and it shuddered, then began to rise, slowly, ponderously, as if in no hurry to leave the ground.

The sound came crashing in on them, an overpowering bellowing roar that rattled the bones and sucked the breath out of Thrasher's lungs.

The rocket was rising faster now: up, higher, faster, climbing into the bright sky.

"Go, baby, go!" yelled the governor.

Schroeder brought his hands to his chin, his fingers no longer crossed. The reporter was breathing again, Thrasher saw. Very visibly.

The rocket dwindled into a blazing star, streaking upward. Then a flash of flame startled Thrasher.

"First stage separation," Schroeder said.

"She's on her way," said the governor happily. "Another successful launch."

"Congratulations," said Thrasher, sticking his hand out to Schroeder.

Very seriously, Schroeder took Thrasher's proffered hand in a firm grip. "Thanks."

"Let's get inside," said the governor. "I've had enough New Mexico sunshine for one afternoon."

Thrasher felt grateful.

◎ 10 ◎
LAS CRUCES

Once inside the air-conditioned operations building, Schroeder led Thrasher, the governor, and Victoria Zane to a door marked:

MISSION CONTROL
AUTHORIZED PERSONNEL ONLY

Schroeder pushed through the door and led the others into a small , windowless room filled with a dozen workstation consoles. Only four of them were occupied by technicians hunched over their keyboards, Bluetooth phones clipped to their ears. Three walls were covered with floor-to-ceiling display screens, all of them blank. Thrasher noticed a glassed-in visitor's gallery running along the rear wall. Empty.

A slim young woman in gray slacks and a white blouse that bore a Schroeder logo on its back stood behind the technicians. She turned when she heard the four visitors enter the room.

Making a circle with her thumb and forefinger, she announced cheerily, "On the money, chief. Orbital insertion in eleven minutes."

"The first stage?" Schroeder asked.

"Harry and his team are in the truck, on their way to pick it up."

Victoria Zane asked, "Could I get my camera crew in here for a few shots?"

The governor started to reply, but Schroeder cut him off. "Not while they're working. Later, after the payload's linked up with the space station."

"How long will that be?"

"A couple of hours."

She looked disappointed. "Maybe I can get the crew to hang around that long," she said, more to herself than to Schroeder. "I'll have to call the station." She pulled a cell phone out of her handbag.

"Not in here," Schroeder snapped. "Outside."

Victoria nodded glumly and headed for the door. Thrasher thought, how extravagant, throwing away women like that. It was a line he remembered from an old movie.

The governor clasped one hand each on Schroeder's and Thrasher's shoulders and said, "Why don't you fellows let the people of New Mexico buy you lunch?"

For the first time all day, Schroeder smiled. But it looked as if it hurt his face, Thrasher thought.

The three men rode in the governor's air-conditioned limousine to the Ramada Palms hotel, in downtown Las Cruces.

"Finest eatery in the city," the governor said, as a fawning hostess showed them to a table in the nearly empty restaurant. It was decorated to resemble an adobe hacienda in old Mexico.

"We're between the luncheon and dinner serving hours," the hostess apologized, "but I'm sure whoever's in the kitchen will be happy to make whatever you ask for, Your Honor."

As the governor settled his portly body onto the chair she held out for him, he said, "Just something to snack on. And drinks, of course."

Thrasher figured they wouldn't have ginger beer, so he asked for a Diet Coke instead. Schroeder ordered a Coors Lite and the governor settled for a dirty Martini.

As their drinks were being served, Schroeder asked Thrasher bluntly, "So are you looking for launch services or is this just a tourist trip for you?"

Thrasher leaned back in his chair. "A little bit of both. I'll be looking for launch services soon, but I think I'm going to need a bigger rocket booster than yours."

"Bigger?" the governor asked.

Schroeder pointed out, "We're launching three-man crews to the International Space Station."

Nodding, Thrasher replied, "I'll be able to use that capability, but I'm also going to need a bird that can put ten, twelve tons into orbit."

"What on Earth for?" said the governor.

"Nothing on Earth. It's for Mars."

Schroeder's eyes narrowed. "I heard you were putting together a consortium for a Mars mission."

"A crewed mission," said Thrasher.

"So you need a heavy-lift capability."

"My engineering guys tell me that's the least expensive way to launch the components of the spacecraft."

"You're going to assemble your Mars craft in orbit?"

Thrasher nodded.

"Have you done a cost analysis on using medium-lift boosters? Like mine?"

"My number crunchers have. Looks like I'll have to talk to Boeing. Their Delta IV can carry the load, I'm told."

It was Schroeder's turn to nod.

"You could still launch from here," the governor said. Then he added hopefully, "Couldn't you?"

"Not from what my engineers tell me," said Thrasher. "Unfortunately, the Delta IV's first stage would fall back to Earth outside the confines of the White Sands range."

"Oh."

"Wouldn't want it landing on this hotel." Thrasher said it lightly, but both the others maintained a stony silence. He took a sip of his cola.

"Then you'll have to use the Kennedy launch complex out at Cape Canaveral," said Schroeder. "Let the first stage plop into the ocean."

"Looks that way."

"Isn't there *any* way you could use Spaceport America?" The governor almost whined his question.

Thrasher shrugged. "This is all preliminary, of course. Maybe, once I get my tech team fully staffed and running, they'll come up with something better. I sure don't want to have to lease a launch facility from the goddamned government."

Schroeder took a pull from his beer bottle, then said, "I've worked with the NASA guys at the Cape. They're not so bad."

"I'm sure the technical guys are okay," Thrasher replied. "It's the bureaucrats they work for that bother me. And their lawyers."

"But you'll launch your crew for the Mars mission from here?" the governor asked.

"I'd like to. Unless Boeing and NASA make me a better deal." Before either of the men could react, Thrasher added, "Which I doubt will happen."

The governor looked unhappy, Schroeder thoughtful.

"For what it's worth, we'll have to launch people to assemble the spacecraft in orbit. Looks like there'll be lots of launches."

"And you'll have to bring those guys back, right?" asked Schroeder.

"Right."

Sitting up straighter in his chair, Schroeder said, "We can do that for you. We've brought people home from the space station."

"Landed them right here," the governor added, "on our own airfield."

Thrasher gave them a warm smile. "I'd really like to do business with you."

Schroeder nodded again. The governor said, "And we'd love to do business with you!"

◎ 11 ◎
BOARD MEETING

Thrasher sat at the head of the conference room's long, polished table while Sid Ornsteen droned through his treasurer's report. Board meeting, Thrasher said to himself. It ought to be spelled b-o-r-e-d.

The corporation had rented the conference room from the Marriott Residence Inn in downtown Houston. It was cheaper to rent the hotel facility than to maintain a conference room in the corporate office suite that was only used four times a year.

Ornsteen made no mention of the recent run-up on the corporation's stock. Whoever had bought the shares was apparently content, for the moment. The stock's price had settled back to where it had been before the run.

Who would do that? Thrasher wondered. Why? It didn't make sense.

Looking down the long table at the assembled directors, he noted that every one of them was here for this meeting. That's unusual. Last meeting half of them didn't bother to show up. Is one of them behind the stock run? We'll find when we get to new business, I suppose.

White hair and bald pates. Q-Tips and bowling balls. Which one of you is trying to muscle me out of control?

Thrasher turned slightly to glance at Linda, seated against the side wall, recording the proceedings. She looks tense, he thought. Probably she senses that something's in the wind.

The meeting dragged on. No problems, no arguments, no gasbags giving long-winded speeches to satisfy their egos.

At last he was able to say, "Okay. The last item on the agenda is new business." He made himself smile as he looked down the table again. "Anybody?"

Nels Bartlett cleared his throat. "I'm not sure this falls under the heading of new business," he began in his reedy, nasal voice, "but I think you should tell the board about your plans for a Mars mission. After all, you'll probably want to sink a good deal of the corporation's assets into this."

Heads nodded. Directors fidgeted in their chairs, waiting for a reply. Thrasher made himself smile. So it begins, he thought.

"Yes, what about this Mars business?" asked one of the more prominent Q-Tips. "How will it affect the corporation?"

"Positively," said Thrasher.

"I think you owe the board a more detailed explanation," Bartlett said dryly.

"I'm planning to send a half-dozen human explorers to the planet Mars," Thrasher began. "The goddamned government isn't going to do it, so I think it's up to American free enterprise to step up to the challenge."

Uta Gelson said firmly, "I agree."

"I've already bought into your program," Bartlett said, "but what I want to know—as a director of Thrasher Digital—is how this is going to affect this corporation."

"It's going to soak up a great deal of our assets, in the short term. We're going to be a major supplier of electronics components and communications systems for the spacecraft and the ground-control facilities."

"Without a profit, I presume?" grumbled one of the bowling balls.

"That's right. For the short term, we'll show no profit from the program."

"What about our stock dividends?"

Thrasher fought down the urge to squirm in his chair. "We'll try to continue giving dividends, of course . . . but it might not be possible, for the near term."

"Then why should we—"

"You said for the near term," Sid Ornsteen said, as if this were all new to him. "What about the long term?"

Good boy, Sid, Thrasher praised silently.

All eyes were on him. The boardroom was so quiet Thrasher could hear a chair squeak when one of the directors shifted in it.

"When I said we planned to send six explorers to Mars I misspoke," he started to explain. "In reality we'll be sending a million or more."

"A million?"

"What do you mean?"

"Do you remember at our last board meeting I reported on our virtual reality program?"

"That simulation stuff. It's for kids' games, isn't it?"

"That's only a part of the market for VR. The armed services use virtual reality to train their personnel. Big industries are buying VR rigs to train their people, especially technicians and field crews that have to work in extreme environments. With virtual reality they can *experience* the situations they'll be facing: see, hear, feel what they would come up against in the real world."

"It's a growing market," Ornsteen commented.

"For the porn industry," said one of the bowling balls—with a sly grin.

The woman beside him frowned, then turned to Thrasher. "So you'll use VR systems to train the people who'll go to Mars. "That won't make much of an impression on our bottom line."

Thrasher smiled broadly. "The sale of several million VR sets will affect our bottom line very nicely, don't you think?"

"How on earth—"

"I get it!" exclaimed the woman sitting at the foot of the table. "People here on Earth will be able to link in to the people on Mars."

Thrasher bowed his head graciously. "Through virtual reality, people safe in their own homes—or in gaming arcades—will be able to walk on the rust-red sands of Mars. To all intents and purposes, *they'll be on Mars.* How much do you think that'll be worth?"

"Will they be able to interact with the astronauts on Mars?"

Thrasher shook his head. "The time lag is too long, as much as half an hour most of the time. But they'll see and feel and hear everything the astronauts are doing, just as if they were actually on Mars."

"How many sets do you think we could sell?"

"We'll start doing VR sessions from the spacecraft as it goes out to Mars," Thrasher explained. "The publicity from that ought to ramp up sales nicely. By the time they actually set foot on Mars, we should have sold several million sets, at least."

"How long will it take to get there?"

Thrasher waggled a hand. "Six, maybe eight or nine months. The tech guys will figure that out for us."

"That will be a good time to build up the market, I agree."

"We'll have to ramp up production. Don't want to be caught short-handed."

"That's going to cost a lot, isn't it?"

Thrasher nodded. "Yes indeed. As I said, we'll be sinking a good deal of the corporation's assets into this and the other aspects of the Mars program."

Thrasher's public relations chief, a former anchorwoman for Global News Network, suggested, "We should give VR sets to the major news nets, for free. Good PR."

"And schools!" shouted one of the directors. "Selected schools."

"Major universities."

"Ghetto schools."

The directors babbled on enthusiastically. Thrasher sat back, smiling. But in his mind he was still wondering, which one of you is trying to take over my corporation?

◎ 12 ◎
CHICAGO

The atrium of the Hyatt Regency Hotel looked like a major political convention had taken over the place. It was jammed with people, hundreds of men and women all talking and scurrying around. City of the big shoulders, Thrasher reminded himself. Lots of 'em here, bumping into each other.

Unlike a political convention, though, these people were mostly young. There were plenty of gray heads among them, but somehow even the graybeards seemed more youthful, more vigorous than the typical politician.

This was a major conclave of space enthusiasts, Thrasher knew. A couple of thousand nerdy kids, working engineers, pro-space activists, scientists, teachers—and a handful of men who had walked on the Moon.

For the most part they were dressed pretty decently, Thrasher saw as he pushed his way toward the hotel's registration desk. No outlandish costumes. Nothing for the news shows to poke fun at. From teenagers to oldtimers, these people were serious about their love of space exploration.

Then he saw a twenty-something woman saunter by, wearing a baseball cap that said: AD ASTRA. And right behind her an even younger lad wearing a bright red cap emblazoned with: MARS, INCORPORATED.

His brows rose. Has word leaked out?

Then, as he got into the line for registration, he saw a middle-aged guy who looked like a typical engineer: tweed jacket, blue jeans, loafers. But on the lapel of his jacket there was a button that proclaimed:

THE MEEK SHALL
INHERIT THE EARTH.
THE REST OF US
ARE GOING
TO THE STARS!

Thrasher laughed to himself. *These are my people, God help me.* Then he thought, *Mars, Incorporated is a good idea. Once we get the funding squared away, I'll have to get my legal eagles to form a corporation for the program. Mars, Inc. would be a good name for the firm.*

He had preregistered for the conference itself, but he had to stand in line to register for the hotel. By the time he finally got to the counter he felt tired and irritable. *They ought to have a better way to take your money,* he grumbled to himself.

He went through the tedious routine: credit card, driver's license for ID, signature. At last, with his electronic room key in one hand, and his roll-along travel bag in the other, he squeezed through the milling crowd toward the elevators.

A buxom, auburn-haired woman was among the group of people waiting in the elevator lobby. Thrasher recognized her.

"Victoria Zane, isn't it?" he asked.

She turned, saw who had spoken her name, and smiled at him. Victoria was wearing a navy blue business suit, which complemented her reddish hair very nicely.

"Mr. Thrasher!"

"Arthur," he said. "My friends call me Art. Not like a work of art, though; just Art."

She laughed.

"What're you doing here, Victoria? Covering the convention?"

"Yes, but not for my station. They're not interested in anything outside of New Mexico. I'm on my own here."

"Freelancing?"

Victoria said, "That's what it used to be called. I'm hoping to write an article for *The New Yorker*."

"Do they know that?"

An elevator arrived at last and everyone tried to jam into it. Thrasher tugged at Victoria's sleeve and said, "Let's wait for the next one."

She frowned.

"Better still," he said, "let's go to the bar."

The frown melted. "Always a good idea."

Strangely, the atrium bar wasn't at all busy. Thrasher led Victoria to a table by the high, sunny windows. They parked their luggage and sat down. An overweight waitress came up immediately.

"Chardonnay," said Victoria.

Half-expecting the hotel wouldn't have it, Thrasher ordered a ginger beer. To his surprise, the waitress wrote it on her pad and headed off to the bar.

Casting a suspicious eye at him, Victoria said, "What did you mean when you asked if *The New Yorker* knew I wanted to do a piece for them?"

"Oh, I was just surprised that they'd be interested in a space conference. Doesn't sound like the kind of thing they would do— unless they want to sneer at it."

"I don't intend to sneer at anybody or anything," Victoria said, with some heat.

"Good."

"I've been in contact with one of their editors. He said he'd read my article and if he likes it he'll show it to their editorial board."

"Great," said Thrasher.

The waitress arrived with their drinks. Thrasher took a sip. It was ginger ale, of course. He sighed inwardly.

Victoria toyed with her wine glass. "I've heard a rumor that you want to send an expedition to Mars."

Thrasher thought there were too many blabbermouths in the world to keep his plans secret for long. With a smile he replied, "I had intended to make a public announcement at this conference, but I don't have the funding settled yet."

She smiled back. "Maybe next year."

"I'd rather you didn't put anything about it into your article."

"It might help you to raise money if I did."

With a shake of his head, Thrasher said, "It'd bring out the kooks. I don't need that."

"When do you think you'll get the money?"

"In a couple of months, if things go right."

"How close are you now?"

"No comment."

"Who are you talking to?"

"No comment."

She leaned back in her chair and eyed him carefully. "What are you willing to comment on?"

"I'd like to take you to dinner."

"Tonight?"

"Sure."

"You don't have any other commitments?"

"I'd break them if I did."

Victoria took a sip of her wine, then said, "All right. I'd like to have dinner with you."

"I'll knock on your door at seven o'clock."

"Okay."

"What's your room number?"

She had to fetch her room key from her handbag and read off the number.

Thrasher said, "Right down the hall from me."

"How convenient," said Victoria Zane.

⬡ 13 ⬡
PANEL DISCUSSION

For an early morning panel, Thrasher thought, we've got a good audience. There must be two hundred people out there. Of course, "early morning" meant ten a.m. But after the night he had spent with Victoria, it felt like sunrise.

Tired but happy, Thrasher couldn't suppress a self-satisfied smile as he recalled their gymnastics in bed together. She was still curled up in his bed snoozing contentedly when he quietly left for this meeting.

The moderator was introducing the panelists sitting along a long table draped with hotel-issue white tablecloths. Of the six panelists, two were former astronauts—one male and one female—an executive from Lockheed Martin Corporation, a Congressman from Cook County, a women from NASA's public affairs office, and . . .

". . . and last but not least," the moderator said, "Mr. Arthur D. Thrasher, founder and CEO of Thrasher Digital Corporation."

The ostensible topic for the panel was "How Can Space Advocates Influence the Nation's Space Program?"

Thrasher thought he already knew the answer: Very little, if at all. But he listened patiently as the other panelists ran through all the clichés about grass-roots involvement and political action.

"Congress does listen to the voters," the Congressman was saying. He was fairly young, his hair still dark, his face lean and earnest. "But you've got to realize the tremendous pressures there are on us.

Advocates from every part of the nation, from industrial groups and farm lobbies, from foreign nations, even, are constantly pressuring us to enact laws that will help them."

"So where do we space advocates stand?" the moderator asked.

"You've got to get more voting power behind you," the Congressman replied. "Your influence is directly proportional to the number of votes you can swing your way."

One of the former astronauts, with handsome silver-gray hair, looked down the table at the congressman. "We've got thousands of citizens involved in the space movement. I mean, just look at the turnout for this conference."

The congressman nodded, but said, "Look, I understand that most people like space. They want to see a vigorous American space program. But they want lower taxes, too. And they want jobs, they want their communities to be safe from crime, they want health care—nobody's *against* space, but they just don't have space high up on their priority list."

The discussion surged back and forth. Thrasher listened in silence. He had heard it all before, for years and years.

At last the moderator looked down the table in Thrasher's direction. "Mr. Thrasher, you've been very quiet about all this. How do you feel about it?"

Thrasher straightened up in his chair and reached for the microphone on the tabletop in front of him with both hands.

"I'm more-or-less a bystander here," he began. "I've been a member of several space advocacy organizations for many years. I agree with the Congressman: until we can bring a million marchers to Capitol Hill, Washington isn't going to pay much attention to us."

"That might work for civil rights or some other cause," said the Lockheed Martin executive. "Space advocacy is different."

The NASA woman said, "That kind of populist pressure might actually do more harm than good."

Feeling mildly disgusted, Thrasher looked out at the audience and said, "As long as you depend on the goddamned government, your space program is going to be run for political reasons. Hell, President Kennedy started the Apollo program to take the public's mind off the Bay of Pigs fiasco."

"That's not true!" the NASA woman flashed.

"The hell it's not," said Thrasher. "Okay, we went to the Moon to beat the Russians. Once we got there and planted the Stars and Stripes, Washington's interest in space evaporated."

The Lockheed Martin executive said, "Perhaps interest in *human* spaceflight fell off, but we've done a magnificent job of exploring space with robotic craft."

"But that doesn't get the public excited," Thrasher countered. "That doesn't translate into votes and political power."

"It's important, though."

"Sure it is. But it's not enough." Turning to the Congressman, "You say people are worried about jobs. The biggest boost to the American economy that Washington ever made in peacetime was the Moon program."

"But it cost the American taxpayer more than twenty billion," said the Congressman.

"And pumped *trillions* of dollars into the economy," Thrasher countered. "Computers, medical monitors, new materials . . . the whole cordless power tool industry began when NASA realized they wouldn't be able to run an extension cord from Tranquility Base back to Cape Canaveral."

The audience laughed heartily. Thrasher knew he was preaching to the converted.

One of the astronauts asked him, "So what would you do if you were running the space program?"

"I'd turn as much of it as possible over to private enterprise. Let the goddamned government develop the new technologies, that's what they're good at. For the rest of it, private enterprise."

"We already have private firms supplying transportation to and from the ISS," said the NASA woman.

"Do you think private enterprise could take us back to the Moon?" the moderator asked.

"Yes," said Thrasher. "Or to Mars, for that matter."

"To Mars? Private enterprise?"

"Why not?" Thrasher challenged.

"You've got to be kidding," said the female astronaut.

Hunching over his microphone, Thrasher said, "Look, we know how to build rockets. We've had years of experience of keeping people alive in space, aboard the International Space Station."

"But Mars . . ."

"It's a different order of magnitude, I know. But private enterprise can do it. The goddamned government isn't going to."

The audience roared its approval. They got to their feet and applauded wildly.

The moderator, grinning, waited for them to quiet down, then announced, "I think that's a great note to end this panel discussion. We've just about run out of time."

"No," Thrasher said. "The time for Mars is just beginning."

☼ 14 ☼
REACTION

Thrasher was mobbed as he tried to get down from the platform. Young men and women thronged around him, asking him questions, shoving programs at him for autographing. The two astronauts grinned at him as they shouldered their way down to the floor; the male made an "okay" circle with his thumb and forefinger. The Lockheed Martin executive patted his shoulder as he struggled past.

The NASA woman gave him the kind of look she would give to an impudent little boy. The congressman avoided him altogether.

He worked his way toward the doors at the rear of the auditorium, scribbling his signature, answering dozens of questions.

"Do you really think private enterprise could take us to Mars?"

"Sure."

"But who would put up the money?"

"There are enough billionaires in the United States to finance a Mars mission out of their own pockets."

"You really think so?"

"I really do."

Then Jessie Margulis came out of the crowd, looking almost awkward, almost embarrassed. "You didn't make any friends with the NASA hierarchy," he said, his voice so low Thatcher could barely hear him.

"Yeah, guess not," said Thrasher.

Glancing guiltily over his shoulder, Margulis stepped close enough to whisper, "Is the job offer still open?"

Still edging through the crowd toward the doors, Thrasher said, "Yep."

"Same terms?"

"Yep."

Margulis kept pace with him. "I've talked it over with my wife. We won't have to move, will we?"

"No, you can stay in Houston. There'll be a lot of travel, though."

"That's okay. I . . . I'm going to take a year's leave of absence, like you suggested."

Thrasher beamed at the engineer and stuck out his hand. "Welcome aboard, Jessie."

Margulis took his hand in a quick, limp grasp, then hurried away like a criminal who had just made a drug deal.

Thrasher shook his head. I've got my lead engineer, he told himself. If he doesn't die of anxiety before he signs up.

As he neared the doors he saw Victoria standing there, smiling at him. She was wearing a nubby light blue sweater and darker slacks.

"Good morning!" he said, taking her by the arm. "How long have you been here?"

"I came in about halfway through. You didn't see me, did you?"

"No, I didn't."

They stepped out into hallway, where even more conference attendees were milling about.

"That was quite a performance you put on in there," said Victoria.

"Oh. That. I guess I got carried away."

"For a man who doesn't want me writing about your plans, you sure shot your mouth off."

He grinned at her. "I didn't say anything specific. And the news media won't take note of what's said in this conference. Not unless an astronaut or a NASA boss makes some dramatic announcement."

As they headed toward the breakfast bistro, Victoria asked, "You still think you can keep your plans under wraps?"

With a nod, he replied, "I've got to. For the time being. Until I get the financing nailed down. Then you can have an exclusive, if you want it."

"I want it!"

As Thrasher led her to the bistro, he thought to himself that he'd have to handle Victoria very carefully. She could become troublesome. Good thing she's based in New Mexico. That's far enough away to give me room to operate.

And he knew that his next meeting was the key to all his hopes and plans. Gregory Sampson. If I can bring him into the game, then everything falls into place. I'll have all the funding I need and we can go ahead and formally start Mars, Inc.

If I can bring Sampson into the game. Trouble is, he hates my guts.

Gregory Sampson was a major contributor not only to the incumbent President's political campaigns, but to the campaigns of many other Democratic Party candidates. An archetypical "self-made man," Sampson started with the money his father had made in the retail clothing business—barely a few million—and built it into the seventh largest fortune in the United States, an empire built on banking and the entertainment industry.

He was a gruff old bear of a man, big and burly, with a loud voice and a hard face. He reminded Hollywood people of the old studio tycoons, men who ruled their industry with iron personalities. It was an image he deliberately cultivated. On the desk in his Wall Street office was a plaque bearing a quote attributed to all those old Hollywood tyrants: "Never let that sonofabitch back into this studio again—unless we need him."

Thrasher knew he was one of those sonsofbitches, in Sampson's eyes. Early in his own career, when he was just starting out in the rough-and-tumble competitive world of internet technology, Thrasher had come to Sampson for financing. Sampson was willing, but only if he could control Thrasher's fledgling company. Thrasher took the money, but outmaneuvered Sampson's representative on the corporation's board of directors and held onto his controlling interest.

Sampson dumped his Thrasher Digital stock, which sent the corporation's shares plummeting. Thrasher held on and came through, which angered Sampson all over again. The man did not enjoy being proved wrong. Twice.

So it was with some trepidation that Thrasher flew back to Manhattan for his visit with Gregory Sampson. Thrasher was even more alarmed when, as his executive Learjet entered the landing pattern at Newark's Liberty International airport, he received a phone call from one of Sampson's innumerable assistants.

Even in his cell phone's minuscule screen she looked like a video starlet. Sampson stocked his office with gorgeous, hopeful young women, Thrasher knew.

But she put on an unhappy pout as she said, "I'm afraid Mr. Sampson won't be able to meet you in his office this afternoon, Mr. Thrasher."

"What? We set this meeting up a week ago! I'm just about to land—"

"You don't understand, Mr. Thrasher," she interrupted. "His chauffeur will meet you at the airport and he'll see you at the appointed time, but not in his office."

"Oh. Where, then?"

"Central Park. At the entrance to the zoo."

☀ 15 ☀
CENTRAL PARK ZOO

This must be the old man's version of a sense of humor, Thrasher thought sourly as the limousine pulled up at the curb. Then he decided, no, it's the old bastard's way of humiliating me.

The chauffeur came around and opened the limo door. Thrasher stepped out into a muggy hot afternoon. The dog days in the Big Apple, he grumbled to himself. Part of the treatment.

The chauffeur pointed and said, "The zoo is through that entrance and down the path, sir." His accent sounded Haitian to Thrasher. His skin was ebony, his eyes rimmed with red. He added, "You can't miss it."

Thrasher muttered, "You'd be surprised at the places I've missed."

"Sir?"

Thrasher loosened his bolo tie and peeled off his jacket as he headed for the entrance to the park. A couple of teenagers on skateboards rocketed past him on either side.

Could Sampson be behind the stock grab last month? Thrasher asked himself. Be just like the old bastard to walk me to the monkey house and then tell me he's bought control of my board of directors.

And there he was, standing at the entrance to the zoo, in rumpled shirtsleeves and suspenders, a bag of peanuts in one meaty hand, munching away contentedly. He's putting on the humble billionaire

67

act, Thrasher thought: just a simple man of the people. Yeah, like Ivan the Terrible.

Sampson was looking the other way, not deigning to notice Thrasher approaching him. I should have brought a hat, Thrasher thought, so I could hold it in my hand like a proper beggar.

He looked bigger than ever, and shaggier: he had augmented his thick mop of dead white hair with an equally white and bushy beard. Thrasher felt like a little kid approaching his rich, powerful grandfather—which is just the way he wants me to feel, he realized. Well, screw that!

"Hey, Greg," Thrasher called heartily as he got to within a few steps of Sampson.

The older man turned, smiled with sharp white teeth, and boomed out, "Artie! You found me!"

No handshake. Sampson just loomed over Thrasher and stuffed his free hand into the bag of peanuts.

"Peanut?" he offered.

"Thanks," said Thrasher, accepting the one unshelled nut.

"Come on into the zoo," Sampson said, leading Thrasher through the entrance. "Good place to talk without being interrupted. Or overheard."

So that's why he wanted to meet me here, Thrasher said to himself.

As he sauntered along he curving lane, crowded with visitors and tourists, Sampson said, "You know, Bernard Baruch used to come out here to the park when he had some thinking to do. When he was in Washington he'd go to Lafayette Park, across from the White House."

Baruch was a financier, Thrasher knew, who had advised many presidents—whether they wanted his advice or not.

"The Boy Scouts put up a bench to his memory in Lafayette Park, you know."

"Will wonders never cease," Thrasher muttered.

Sampson turned to follow a sign that pointed to the monkey house. Thrasher followed along, his heart sinking.

"I had a long talk with Dave Kahn a few days ago," Sampson said, lowering his voice a bit. "He says you want to raise money to send people to Mars."

Looking up at the shaggy, munching, smiling old man, Thrasher said as brightly as he could manage, "That's right. I think it's time that we showed the world what American free enterprise can accomplish."

"Very patriotic."

"I'd like you to join the team."

"You want a billion a year for five years?"

"Right."

"From me?" Sampson almost snarled the words.

Thrasher decided to be completely open with the old bully. "If you come in, the Kahn boys and all the others will come in, too."

"And if I don't?"

"Look, Greg, I know you don't like me. I suppose you've got good reason to hate my guts. But Mars is too big for that. We have to do it! If we don't, nobody else will."

"So what? What's so wonderful about Mars? What's in it for me?"

For the first time, Thrasher felt a glimmer of hope.

"You can have the motion picture rights," he said.

Sampson shrugged his heavy shoulders. "A few hundred million. Not much of a return on my investment."

"But we're not doing this for profit, it's—"

"You're keeping the virtual reality rights for yourself, aren't you?"

I should have known he'd know, Thrasher thought. On impulse, he said, "I'll give you half the VR rights to the mission."

"Really?" Sampson broke into a delighted smile. Then he asked, "And how will your board of directors react to such generosity?"

"Let me worry about that."

They had arrived at the monkey house. A gaggle of children, mostly boys, pressed against the guard railing and laughed at the little animals capering inside their cage. Thrasher felt unspeakably sad to see them penned up that way. One of the kids, standing just next to a DO NOT FEED THE ANIMALS sign, threw a handful of peanuts through the bars. A half dozen monkeys scampered to grab the treats.

Sampson turned from the monkeys to face Thrasher. Grasping his shoulder in his big ham-sized hand, the older man said, "Tell you what, Artie. I'm going to come in on your Mars deal. The VR rights will be piffle compared to what I'll have to put into your project, but it'll be worth it so see your corporation go down in flames."

"Gee, thanks," said Thrasher.

"Think nothing of it. I'm going to enjoy this. Mars or bust! We'll go to Mars and you'll go bust!" Sampson laughed so heartily that even the children turned to gape at him.

And Thrasher remembered a line written about Bernard Baruch, from long ago: *Bernard Baruch sat on his favorite park bench, struggling with his conscience. He won.*

◎ 16 ◎
MARS, INCORPORATED

Valentine's Day. Thrasher hurried from his limousine to the entrance of the Marriott Residence Inn, with Linda Ursina scampering along beside him. A Blue Norther was sweeping through Houston, making Thrasher realize the truth behind the old saying that there's nothing between Texas and the North Pole but a barbed wire fence.

"Lord, it's freezing!" Linda said. She was wearing a lined leather coat over her businesslike pants suit, but it was obviously too light for the weather. Thrasher, in nothing but a tan sports jacket and brown whipcord slacks, agreed with a shivering nod.

The first meeting of Mars, Incorporated's board of directors wasn't scheduled to begin for another hour, but Thrasher wanted to be there first, to make sure that everything was set up properly and to greet his directors as they arrived.

The hotel manager was just inside the door, all smiles.

"Sure is cold out there, isn't it?" he said.

"Yep," said Thrasher, grateful for the hotel's warmth. "Is everything set up?"

"Yes indeed," the manager replied, leading Thrasher and Linda to a bank of elevators. "You'll be in the executive suite, on the top floor."

"Good," Thrasher said, thinking, That ought to impress Sampson. And the Kahn boys.

Fifteen minutes before the hour appointed for the meeting, all twenty of the directors of the newly-formed corporation had arrived in the executive suite. The conference room was a little crowded, but Thrasher thought the sweeping view of Houston's skyline would make up for it. That, and the long table filled with drinks and finger foods.

He greeted and chatted with each of the directors as they arrived. Once all twenty were present, Thrasher called out, "Okay, I think we can get started now."

He went to the head of the gleamingly polished table and watched the directors arrange themselves along its length. Sampson sat at his right, of course. The Kahn brothers opposite him. Will Portal nonchalantly pulled out a chair halfway down the table. No pretensions for Will, Thrasher told himself, smiling inwardly. Uta Gelson, Nels Bartlett and the others arranged themselves within a few moments. Linda took up her usual post along the wall, recorder in hand, alongside Francine Timons, Thrasher's public relations director.

Once they were all seated, Thrasher—still standing—wiped his glasses, replaced them on his nose, and said, "I want to thank you all for joining this mission. We're going to make history."

Somebody muttered, "Instead of money."

Thrasher ignored the comment. They went through the agenda with surprising alacrity. Thrasher was elected chairman of the board by acclamation. Sampson was named vice chairman, and David Kahn—after a whispered conversation with his brother—accepted the post of treasurer.

"That fills the legal requirements for forming a corporation in the sovereign state of Texas," Thrasher said. "We're in business."

They broke into applause. Briefly.

Then Sampson asked, "Who's our legal counsel?"

"I'm using the same firm that Thrasher Digital uses: Towers and Towers."

Sampson nodded. "Are you getting a volume discount from them?"

Polite laughter.

After a few more questions and answers, Thrasher said, "Now I'd like you to meet the guy who's heading up our technical team." He turned to Linda and nodded. She spoke quietly into her smartphone.

Everyone turned to face the door as Jessie Margulis stepped into the conference room. The engineer was wearing an actual suit, dark blue, and a Texas Aggies maroon and white tie. He looked uncomfortable as he stood by the door, all eyes on him.

"Ladies and gentlemen, meet Jessie Margulis, the best engineer in NASA—until this past January first. Now he's the chief engineer of Mars, Incorporated."

Another spattering of polite applause.

Margulis blinked shyly and went to the empty chair at the foot of the conference table, next to Vince Egan. As he sat down he pulled a smartpad from his jacket pocket.

"I have a few slides to show y'all," he said.

Thrasher groaned inwardly. Every NASA presentation always begins with, "The first slide, please."

Linda went to the nearest window and touched the control panel. Storm shutters slid slowly down, darkening the room.

The wall above the buffet table lit up and showed: MARS, INC. PRELIMINARY PLAN.

Margulis fiddled with his smartpad and a chart appeared on the wall.

I hope he doesn't bore them to death, Thrasher thought.

"We're going to use the Earth-orbital assembly technique," Margulis said, aiming a laser pointer at one of the boxes. "Instead of building a rocket booster big enough to lift the whole spacecraft and send it to Mars, we'll use existing commercial boosters such as Boeing's Delta IV to lift the craft in segments and assemble the segments in low Earth orbit."

"Won't that be expensive?" Uta Gerson asked.

"Not as expensive as developing a whole new booster," said Margulis.

"How many launches will you need?" Sampson asked.

"I'm figuring on a minimum of six. That includes lifting the propulsion system and its propellant, plus all the life-support supplies."

Will Portal, the only other engineer at the table, asked, "Do you plan to send supplies and fuel for the return flight on ahead, separately?"

In the darkened room, Thrasher could see Margulis relax into a grin. *A fellow geek boy to talk to.*

"You're thinking of the old Mars Express idea," he said to Portal.

"Zubrin's plan, yes."

"We'll be looking into that, of course," Margulis said. "We'll have to do a cost analysis and weigh the consequences of a possible failure somewhere along the mission profile."

"Failure?" piped Charlie Kahn.

Spreading his hands, Margulis said, "Rockets blow up sometimes. Spacecraft go dead. It's a long way to Mars. We've got to factor in the effects of possible failures."

"You mean somebody might get killed?"

Before Margulis could reply, Thrasher said flatly, "It's a possibility. We'll be doing everything we can to make that possibility as small as we can, of course."

"Zero defects," Margulis said.

"What does that mean?"

"It's a program NASA instituted during the Apollo program. Every piece that goes into the spacecraft is examined and tested. Every single weld, every component of every vehicle, every shoelace, even."

"Instead of just taking samples at random and testing them," Portal said.

"Yessir," said Margulis. "Zero defects is our goal. No piece goes uninspected or untested."

"That *will* be expensive," Gelson murmured.

"Not as expensive as a failure," snapped Thrasher.

⚙ 17 ⚙
NEWS RELEASE

Fortunately, Margulis only had a half-dozen slides to show the board of directors, and the last one was an artist's painting of a team of spacesuited people standing on the surface of Mars, bearing two flags: the Red, White and Blue, and a rust-red pennon that bore the logo of Mars, Inc.

Even more fortunately, Thrasher thought, most of the directors didn't have a deep enough technical understanding to ask meaningful questions. They sat there and let Margulis tell them how everything was going to work. All except Will Portal, but he seemed more fascinated with what Margulis was showing than combative.

They even swallowed Margulis' fleeting reference to the main propulsion system without comment. The slide clearly showed the standard symbol for a nuclear facility, but none of them seemed to notice it. It helps to get their eyes glazed over before you flash the zinger at them, Thrasher thought.

Of course, some of the directors around the table had to vent their egos. Both the Kahn brothers asked about specifics of budgeting. Margulis looked at Thrasher.

"Much too early for that kind of detail, fellas. We've just started out, after all. All this is conceptual, not concrete yet."

Sampson stroked his shaggy white beard as he asked, "How do you propose to pick the people who'll go to Mars?"

"They'll all be professional astronauts," Thrasher said.

"Or scientists," Margulis added. "Geologists, planetary scientists, biologists. They'll get astronaut training, like the scientists who flew on the old space shuttle."

"Biologists?" Nels Bartlett asked.

"Yessir," said Margulis. "There's an excellent chance that Mars harbored life, eons ago."

"There might even be life still existing there now," Thrasher added.

"Martians? Little green men?"

"Microbes," said Margulis. "Living underground, perhaps."

"That means you'll have to take precautions not to contaminate them with terrestrial bugs," said Portal.

"That's right."

"Could Martian bugs infect our people?"

"No," said Thrasher.

"We don't know," Margulis countered. "Contamination precautions work both ways, of course."

"Of course," Sampson said dryly.

Thrasher let them prattle on until they seemed to run out of questions. Then he got to his feet, thanked Margulis, and asked, "Do I hear a motion to adjourn?"

The meeting broke up after Thrasher reminded the directors that they were invited to dinner at Gatlin's, a Houston favorite.

"Seven o'clock," he told them. "Authentic Texas barbecue."

Sampson groaned.

As the group filed out of the conference room, Thrasher crooked a finger at Francine Timons. "We need to talk, Francie."

She nodded. "We surely do."

Linda was waiting at the door. Everyone else had left the conference room.

"You go on back to the office," Thrasher called to her. "Then send Carlo back here to pick up Francie and me."

Once Linda departed and closed the door, Thrasher took a seat in the middle of the conference table and gestured Timons to sit beside him.

Francine Timons was a dark-skinned woman who worked very hard to maintain her figure. Not that she was a beauty, by any means, but in the struggle upward from an affirmative action "two-fer" black woman she quickly realized that she needed every asset she could attain. She learned to dress stylishy, and to make the most of her looks. Thrasher had hired her away from Global News to be the PR head of Thrasher Digital.

"You're going to have to do double duty, Francie: I want you to head the public relations teams for Mars, Incorporated."

Flashing a bright smile, she asked, "Do I get a raise?"

"Not just yet. We have to operate lean and mean."

"Can I hire a couple of people? I mean, I've only got a three-person staff as it is."

Thrasher pursed his lips. "Will you really need extra help?"

"To handle PR for Mars? What do you think?"

"Lean and mean," Thrasher repeated.

"Two new hires," Francine said, her long face settling into a determined scowl.

"Two? Can't you—"

"Two," she insisted. "I already know who I want."

"You do?"

"I knew you'd want me to do the Mars operation. You're too cheap to go out and hire somebody else when you can dump the job on me."

Thrasher scowled back at her. "I want you to do the job because you're the best person for the assignment."

"And I work cheap."

"Well, that's a point in your favor," he admitted.

They laughed together.

"Okay," Thrasher said. "Two new hires."

Francine nodded happily. "And we're off to Mars."

"Indeed we are," Thrasher said fervently.

◈ YEAR TWO

◎ 1 ◎
PORTALES, NEW MEXICO

Thrasher had wanted to keep the headquarters of Mars, Inc., as close to his own Houston offices as possible. But Sampson and the Kahn brothers insisted it should be near the New Mexico spaceport, where most of their launches would take place.

Sid Ornsteen broke the deadlock by suggesting Portales. It was more or less halfway between Houston and Las Cruces, had an excellent university, and to clinch the argument, he pointed out that office leases in Portales were less than half the going rate in Houston.

Thrasher reluctantly agreed, although he worried about being too close to Vicki Zane. He thought the distance between Albuquerque and Houston was just about right: close enough for them to get together for romantic weekends, far enough to allow him to keep from getting entangled.

When Linda suggested he rent a condo in Portales rather than taking a hotel room every time he traveled there, Thrasher vetoed the idea. "No condo. I don't want anybody thinking I'm setting up house."

Standing in front of his desk, with the panoramic view of downtown Houston's skyscrapers behind her, Linda shook her head knowingly. "'Anybody' meaning a certain redheaded newswoman from Albuquerque?"

Thrasher grinned. "You know me too well, kid."

Quite seriously, Linda said, "You're what my grandmother would call a reprobate."

"Maybe so," he admitted. "But after two marriages and two divorces you can't blame a guy for being gun shy."

"You need a woman in your life," Linda insisted.

"More than one," said Thrasher. "More than one."

Linda threw up her hands and stamped out of the office.

Thrasher chuckled and muttered to himself, "Women."

The Portales headquarters was hardly imposing or impressive. It was an old warehouse, abandoned by its former owner, an automobile tire retailer who had gone bankrupt—because of gambling debts in Las Vegas, according to the local rumor.

Thrasher had the place cleaned up, and set up movable partitions for offices and work spaces. Best of all, he had converted part of the parking lot into a helicopter pad. The city council had balked at the idea, but Thrasher personally appealed to the zoning board, dropping incredibly broad hints about the job opportunities that Mars, Inc., would create. Several members of the zoning board had teenaged children or kids in college; Thrasher's appeal passed by a one-vote majority.

Now, as he looked out the window of the helicopter as it approached the parking lot at a steep angle, he thought that the zoning board had made a decent decision. The former warehouse was on the fringe of the city, a district of small factories and warehouses; there were no residential areas within several blocks to be bothered by the noise or the danger of a crash.

We could even offer helicopter transportation to the other companies in the neighborhood, he thought as the chopper landed in a swirl of gritty dust. Make a couple of bucks; maybe the chopper can pay for itself.

It felt chilly as he strode through the bright afternoon sunshine to the door that stood beneath a bold red MARS, INC. sign. April in New Mexico, he thought. Still winter, almost. There's still enough snow in the mountains for the die-hard skiers to get another shot at breaking their necks.

The offices inside the former warehouse looked temporary. The bare girders of the ceiling made the place feel like an empty, echoing airplane hangar. And it still smelled vaguely of old tires, Thrasher thought. The partitions of the cubicles were only shoulder high, and most of them were bare, the cubicles unoccupied. That'll change, he told himself.

Jessie Margulis' cubicle was bigger than most of the others, because he had an oblong conference table butted against his desk like the long leg of a T. When Thrasher breezed in, Jessie was sitting at the desk, staring admiringly at a model that looked distinctly ungainly to Thrasher.

It was perched on a wooden base, a bulbous cylinder with a fat wheel attached to one end of it by four spokes.

"That's it?" Thrasher asked, without preamble.

Margulis looked up from the model. "This is it," he said, smiling like a kid who'd just unwrapped his birthday present. "This is the vehicle that'll take us to Mars."

Thrasher pulled a chair out from the conference table and plopped into it.

"Jessie, I've got to tell you, it doesn't look very sexy. In fact, it looks kind of ugly."

Margulis' smile widened. "It's going to be assembled in space. It'll go into orbit around Mars. Never touch the ground, never fly through an atmosphere. It doesn't have to be sleek and sexy."

"It's not going to look good on TV."

"So what? It's going to be home to seven people for just about two years. They're going to love it. And so will you."

"What's this wheel thing?"

"Living quarters. That's where the crew will live during the six-month flight to Mars. It spins to give the crew a feeling of weight."

"Oh?"

Slipping into his lecture mode, Margulis explained, "The biggest problem we faced was the fact that the trip takes a minimum of six months. The crew would be in microgravity all that time."

"Zero gee," said Thrasher.

"The science people call it microgravity."

"They're weightless, like up in the space station."

"Right. But after six months of microgravity, they won't be in any physical shape to go down to the surface of Mars and work there. Their muscles will be deconditioned."

"How bad—"

"People coming back from six months on the space station need a week or more to get back to normal on Earth."

"But Mars' gravity is lighter than Earth's, isn't it?"

"About one-third."

"So is there really a problem here?"

"According to the medical people, the physiologists, yes there is."

"And this wheel thingee will solve it."

"Damned right," said Margulis, fervently. "The wheel rotates at a rate that produces a feeling of Earthly gravity."

"So there's no problem with weightlessness."

"Better than that, Art. Better than that." Margulis was almost gleeful. "As the ship proceeds to Mars, we gradually despin the wheel—slow down its spin rate—so that by the time they arrive at Mars they've been living under Martian-level gravity for weeks."

"You can do that?"

"Damned right we can! The crew can go right down to the surface and start working as soon as they get there. Isn't that neat?"

Thrasher nodded in admiration.

"And on the way home," Margulis went on, "we reverse the procedure. By the time they get back to Earth they're fully re-adapted to terrestrial gravity!"

Thrasher saw that Margulis was as happy as only an engineer can be when he's hit on an elegant solution to a difficult problem.

He nodded graciously. "I've got to hand it to you, Jessie. It may not look like much, but it'll get the job done."

Margulis' face grew more serious. "One problem, though, Art."

"What?"

"We're going to need more than six Delta IV launches to get all the components into orbit."

"More than six? How many more?"

"I'm figuring on nine."

Thrasher winced. "That's fifty percent more than we're budgeted for."

"Plus one, maybe two as backups. In case of launch failure."

"Double the budget, just about."

"The budget was preliminary, you know."

Thrasher sighed. "I know, but still . . . doubling the heavy lift budget. That's a tough proposition."

The engineer asked softly, "You want me to see if we can squeeze by with less? Cut corners?"

"No," Thrasher said. "I'll break the news to Jenghis Kahn." To himself he added, *I'd better wear a bulletproof vest when I do.*

⊚ 2 ⊚
SAN FRANCISCO

Vince Egan rode with Thrasher to San Francisco. Thrasher Digital's chief engineer was on his way to a consumer electronics conference; Thrasher himself had an appointment with Bart Rutherford, the retired genius who had designed the rocketplanes that carried tourists on suborbital flights up to the fringes of space.

"So how's Jessie Margulis working out for you?" Egan asked.

Egan was a wiry, intense forty-something whom Thrasher had met when he'd been a student at MIT. In a school full of the brightest kids in the land, Egan had stood out among his MIT classmates. Thrasher had hired him on the spot for his fledgling Thrasher Digital Corporation and never regretted his impulsive decision.

"Fine," Thrasher answered absently, gazing out the plane's oval window.

Sitting in the plush leather-covered swivel chair facing Thrasher, Egan stared at his boss for a moment.

Then, "Art, when you say 'fine' I worry. Is Jessie giving you problems? Does he need help?"

Forcing a smile, Thrasher said, "No problems. Not really. Nothing that money can't fix."

One of Vince Egan's best traits, Thrasher thought, was that he knew when to shut up. "Okay," he said. "I was just wondering. I could help him out, if he's not working out for you."

Changing the subject, Thrasher asked, "You know Bart Rutherford, don't you?"

For an instant a flash of irritation crossed Egan's face. But it passed before Thrasher could react to it. Egan said, "I've met Rutherford a few times, yes. He's retired now, I've heard."

"I want to talk him out of retirement."

"Hire him for Mars?"

"Take him on as a consultant."

"To look over Jessie's shoulder?"

"No, no. Something else entirely. Nothing to do with Mars."

Egan looked puzzled. "Gee, boss, I didn't think you had time for anything except Mars."

Thrasher grinned back at him. "I'm deeper than you think, pal."

"I'm retired," said Bart Rutherford, kicking off his loafers and stretching out on the reclining chair.

He and Thrasher were sitting on the back deck of Rutherford's home, a deceptively modest-looking frame house perched on a rugged hillside overlooking the blue Pacific. Surf was rolling up to a slim crescent of a beach nestled among the hills. Thrasher could see a gaggle of young surfers riding the waves while slim young girls in bikinis stood on the sand admiring them.

"It must be nice, taking life easy," Thrasher said. He was sitting beside Rutherford, glad that he'd had the sense to wear a leather jacket. The wind coming in off the ocean was chilly, despite the bright sunshine. Thrasher remembered Mark Twain's comment that the coldest winter he'd ever experienced was a summer in San Francisco.

Rutherford seemed impervious to the chill, in cut-off jeans and a baggy T-shirt. He looked like an aging surfer himself: broad shoulders, fuzz-covered barrel chest, long, wavy blond hair speckled with silver, two days of stubble covering his jaw. He was sipping at a tall glass of iced tea. Thrasher wished he had a hot cup of coffee to warm his hands. He could understand why Irish coffee was invented in the Bay area.

"I hear you're running a project to send people to Mars," Rutherford said casually, his eyes on the surfers.

"Jessie Margulis is running the show," said Thrasher. "I'm just the president and CEO. You know Jessie?"

With a nod, Rutherford said, "Top-flight guy."

"I'd like to ask you a question," Thrasher said.

"If it's about Mars, the answer is no."

Then why'd you agree to see me? Thrasher wondered silently. Curiosity? Boredom?

Aloud, he replied, "No, nothing to do with Mars. I was just wondering why somebody hasn't designed a rocket system for commercial air transportation."

"Air transportation?" Rutherford's head turned away from the surfers to focus on Thrasher.

"Point-to-point. San Francisco to Houston for instance. You could cut the travel time to half an hour or less, couldn't you?"

"If you could design a system that works. And works profitably."

"You could," Thrasher said pointedly.

"I'm retired."

Ignoring that, Thrasher said, "I figure you could start from the design you worked up for those suborbital tourist hops."

"Piggyback the rocket to high altitude with a carrier plane," Rutherford mused.

"And then light 'er up and off she goes," said Thrasher. "San Francisco to New York in half an hour."

"Isn't Boeing working on something like that?"

"Not that I know of."

"Or Lockheed Martin. One of them."

"It could be a major breakthrough in commercial aviation," Thrasher urged. "As big a break as the changeover from prop planes to jets, back in the 1960s."

Almost shyly, Rutherford said, "Y'know, I've often wondered why nobody's looked into that. You're right, it could revolutionize air transportation."

"There's a trillion-dollar market waiting."

Rutherford said nothing, but his eyes had a faraway look now.

"How'd you like to look into it?"

"Could be fun."

"More fun than sitting on your back porch and watching the kids surfing."

Rutherford stared at Thrasher with new respect in his eyes. "Where would you fit into it?"

"Me?" Thrasher felt surprised by the question. "I've got my hands full with the Mars program."

"So you're just handing me the idea? No strings?"

"No strings. I couldn't get involved in it, all my money's tied up with Mars."

"There's an old saying about being wary of Greeks bearing gifts."

"I'm not Greek. I just want to stop spending half my life on airplanes. I need to get from *here* to *there* a lot faster."

Rutherford nodded. "I'll think about it. It's an interesting challenge."

"Great," said Thrasher. He got to his feet. Rutherford stood up, too, towering over Thrasher's stumpy form.

Looking up at him, Thrasher said, "Let me know what you think, will you? Maybe we can work something out with Orbital Sciences or Boeing."

"What's this 'we,' white man?" Rutherford joked.

"Aw, I'll keep a finger in the pie, I guess."

Gripping Thrasher's shoulder with a heavy, muscular hand, Rutherford said, "If I get involved in this—and that's a big if—I know enough people in the industry to get a working group going."

"Fine."

"And I'll see to it that you're included, one way or the other."

"Don't expect anything from me except advice."

"Good enough."

Rutherford walked Thrasher through the quiet, neatly furnished house to the front door, where his car and chauffeur were waiting.

"Where are you off to now?"

Thrasher answered, "Houston. Home base. It'll take me damned near three hours to get there."

"Maybe I can do something about that," Rutherford mused.

"I bet you can."

3
HOUSTON

As his executive Learjet winged high above the granite peaks of the Rockies, with scattered pockets of snow melting in the springtime sun, Thrasher phoned Linda, at his office.

"I'll be home in two and a half hours, if our flight plan holds up."

Linda nodded. "We're expecting some thunderstorms."

"That might delay me."

"Likely so."

"Don't wait for me. Go on home at the end of the business day."

"Are you sure? I can wait."

"Naw, go on home. You've got a life, don't you?"

Linda smiled bitterly. "Not much of one."

That surprised Thrasher. He knew she'd broken up with her live-in boyfriend a year ago, but assumed she had plenty of other guys chasing after her. She was bright, intelligent, good-looking. What's wrong with the guys her age?

Breaking into his thoughts, Linda said, "Victoria Zane phoned."

"Oh?"

"She said she's been trying to get you on your cell phone but you don't return her calls." Even in the phone's miniature screen Thrasher could see the disapproving frown on Linda's face.

"You check my incoming calls, don't you?"

"Not the personal ones."

Almost squirming with discomfort, Thrasher admitted, "I guess I ought to call her back, huh?"

"Sooner or later," said Linda.

"Okay, Mommy, I'll phone her right now."

"Reprobate," Linda said, but she smiled slightly as she cut the connection.

Vicki was bubbling with enthusiasm. As soon as her happy face appeared on Thrasher's phone screen, she announced, "They bought it! *The New Yorker* bought my piece about Mars, Incorporated!"

"About Mars, Incorporated?" Thrasher didn't know whether he should be glad or worried.

"It's going to be published in three weeks!"

"I thought you were writing about the space convention."

"No. Your project is much more interesting. And now that you've publicly announced it, you won't mind a piece in a national magazine, will you?"

"No, not at all," he said, silently adding, I guess. Better tell Francie about this; don't want her blindsided.

"I'm free this weekend," Victoria went on. "I could fly over to Houston Friday night."

Thrasher's first instinct was to talk her out of it. But his second instinct—much stronger—was more primal.

"I'll meet you at the airport," he said, surprised at how cheerful he sounded. "Send me your itinerary."

"Sure. And I'll send you the text of my article, too."

Thrasher said goodbye to her and realized all over again that when there's a conflict between a man's brain and his gonads, the gonads almost always win.

By the time he reached his office, no one was there but the cleaning crew. Thrasher trudged to his desk and opened up the message Victoria had sent to him.

Mars or Bust!
THE BILLIONAIRE'S CLUB
A Private Program to Reach Mars
By Victoria Zane

An exclusive, tightly-knit group of twenty billionaires is financing a nongovernmental effort to send human explorers to the planet Mars.

The group, which has formed a private firm called Mars, Inc., is led by Arthur David Thrasher, the founder of Thrasher Digital Corporation, a Houston-based firm that develops electronic communications systems, digital games, and other computer-related software.

Mr. Thrasher, an owlish-eyed Texan of fifty-three who wears bolo ties and scuffed, well-worn cowboy boots, is the driving force behind the project. No billionaire himself, he has recruited twenty of the nation's wealthiest men and women to finance the venture.

The billionaires represent interests ranging from construction and real estate to smartphones and consumer electronics, from banking and investment to retail chain stores.

Why Mars?

"Mars is the frontier," Thrasher claims. "It's the most Earthlike planet in the solar system. And it's close enough for us to reach. It may have harbored life. It might still harbor life-forms of some kind."

Thrasher isn't talking about little green men or sci-fi monsters. He's citing scientific speculations about microbes that might exist deep underground on Mars. The surface of the planet is an apparently barren, frozen desert, where overnight temperatures regularly plummet to a hundred degrees below zero. But belowground conditions might be warmer and more hospitable for primitive life forms.

Why try to bypass NASA and the government's space program?

"The goddamned government has cut all funding for human missions beyond the International Space Station," asserts Thrasher, who apparently cannot speak the word "government" without preceding it with "goddamned."

Can private industry build the rockets and other equipment needed for a human mission to Mars?

Thrasher firmly believes so. "We know how to build rockets, there's no big secret to that. We know how to keep people alive for a year or more aboard the International Space Station. We can do it. And we will."

Thrasher is also driven by a patriotic streak in his hard-driving personality. Pointing out that the People's Republic of China plans to send Chinese astronauts to the Moon within a few years, he maintains that America can reclaim leadership in space by sending a team of Americans to Mars.

Among his billionaire investors . . .

Thrasher read to the end of the article, then looked up from the screen of his desktop computer.

Not bad, he thought. It's not really a hatchet job. If *The New Yorker* actually prints Vicki's piece as she's written it, it'll be pretty good publicity for us.

But then he wondered, Is publicity what we want?

He started to call Francine Timons, then realized it was well after ten p.m., and decided to send the woman an e-mail instead, with Victoria's article attached.

Call me as soon as you've read this, he typed. *We need to discuss the ramifications.*

He leaned back in his chair, took off his glasses and closed his eyes tiredly.

Vicki will be here Friday evening, he thought. For the weekend. Maybe I'll take her out to the house. Might as well get some use out of the place. Eight bedrooms. He grinned. Let's see how many we can use in one weekend.

◎ 4 ◎
CAPE CANAVERAL

Florida is a swamp surrounded on three sides by beaches, Thrasher reminded himself. Almost the entire state has been reworked, transformed from its natural condition into a sort of Disney World of high-rise condominiums, shopping malls, hotels and highways. There's hardly a native species of plant or animal to be found anywhere in the state. The palm trees were brought in from Cuba, the banyans from India. Alligators are becoming an endangered species and the native panthers are on the edge of extinction.

But still, it's wonderful, he thought as he stood in the bright, hot morning sunshine and felt the breeze from the ocean tousling what was left of his hair. Warm and clear and clean. No wonder people come here to retire.

Thrasher was standing at the base of a launch platform. Towering above him was a massive Delta IV booster, gleaming white in the Florida sun. A team of white-coated technicians was busily making last-minute checks at the base of the rocket.

"It has two stages, plus a kick stage at the top for the final orbital insertion," said Saito Yamagata, director of the International Launch Services crew. He was a short, wiry Japanese executive, dressed quite formally in a dark blue business suit. His face was lean, almost ascetic, except for his cheerful ear-to-ear grin. His English was impeccable, with a barely-discernable Oxford accent.

Thrasher had left his jacket in the minivan that the two of them had ridden to the launch pad. He stood with his shirt collar pulled open and looked up the length of the rocket launcher; despite the polarized sunglasses he was wearing, the glare of the Sun made him squint.

"And those are the solid rocket boosters?" he asked Yamagata, pointing.

"Indeed. Four of them, for this launch."

Gesturing for Thrasher to follow him, Yamagata said, "We'd better get back to the control center. This area will be an inferno when the bird lights up."

Thrasher noticed that the men and women in white ILS coveralls were all clambering down from the steel platform and heading for the minivans lined up at the edge of the launch pad.

As they walked to the nearest minivan, Thrasher asked, "How big a payload are you lifting today?"

Yamagata replied, "It's in the twelve-ton range, I believe. Two communications satellites and a geosynchronous one for the U.S. Air Force."

The control center was humming with quiet intensity as the ILS team counted down the final minutes to launch. It was a lot smaller than the sprawling seas of desks and monitor stations that Thrasher remembered from the old Space Shuttle program. Windowless, its walls were covered with display screens. Men and women hunched over their consoles, headsets clipped over their hair.

The place was also air-conditioned to the point of chilblains, Thrasher thought. I should have brought my jacket with me from the van.

Yamagata led him to a row of empty chairs by the rear wall. As they sat down, Thrasher watched the big screen that showed the Delta IV standing tall on the launch platform. Somehow, it looked to him as if it were alive, almost, proud, straining to get going, to leave this Earth and get out into space, where it belonged.

Sentimental twaddle, he told himself. Still, he felt the eagerness and mounting tension as the overhead speakers announced, "One minute and counting."

Forty million bucks riding on that baby, he thought. Maybe more.

Thrasher found himself silently mouthing the last few seconds of the countdown. Five . . . four . . . three . . .

The thunder of the rocket engines shook the control center, even through its solid concrete walls. Thrasher could feel the shudder, like an earth tremor.

"Liftoff," came the laconic voice of the launch team's communicator.

The launch pad disappeared in the billowing smoke and steam. But then Thrasher saw the massive Delta IV rising out of the clouds like a skyscraper on the move, flame spurting from its rocket nozzles, climbing up, up, up. He felt his heart thumping beneath his ribs. No matter how many times I see a launch, he realized, it still gets to me. He wanted to jump up and down like a little kid. With a shock, he realized that he actually was on his feet, straining himself to keep from cheering. And Yamagata was standing beside him, fists clenched, just as excited.

"Wow," breathed Thrasher, as the rocket disappeared from view. "That's something!"

"Indeed it is," Yamagata agreed. He took in a deep breath, then said cheerfully, "Let's have some lunch."

The cafeteria was barely half-full. Thrasher pushed his tray along the counter and picked up a ham-and-cheese sandwich, a bag of potato chips, and a diet Coke. He noticed that there was no sushi available; Yamagata took a salad and iced tea.

Once they were seated at a table and had unloaded their trays, Thrasher said, "Well, from what my tech people tell me, we're going to need at least nine Delta IV launches."

Yamagata bobbed his head and smiled.

"I'm hoping we can get by with six or seven, but we're willing to commit to nine. What's the best price you can give us?"

Yamagata's smile faded. "Before we can discuss pricing, you will have to obtain permission from NASA to use the launch complex."

"Permission from NASA?" Thrasher snapped. "I thought you guys ran the show here."

Warily, almost guiltily, Yamagata replied, "We do . . . within certain limitations."

"Limitations?"

"International Launch Services is a consortium of several aerospace corporations, and the governments of the United States and Japan."

"I know that. You offer launch services to private companies and government agencies."

With a patient sigh, Yamagata replied, "International Launch Services leases this facility from the United States government. The NASA Kennedy Space Center oversees our day-to-day operations, and NASA Headquarters, in Washington, controls the terms and conditions of the agreement."

"Washington," Thrasher muttered darkly.

"I have been informed that it will be necessary for you to reach an agreement with NASA Headquarters before you will be allowed to lease launch services from ILS," said Yamagata, his expression so stiffly impassive that Thrasher thought his face might break.

"That's not the way you usually do business."

"No, it is not," said Yamagata, almost apologetically. "But my hands are tied. You must get specific approval from Washington."

⚛ 5 ⚛
HOUSTON TO WASHINGTON, D.C.

Linda rode in the chopper to Hobby Airport with him because Thrasher hadn't gotten to the office until past ten a.m. She sat facing him as she ran through his unanswered messages and the day's agenda, while he sipped blearily at black coffee.

". . . and Mr. Reynolds will be waiting at Reagan National with a limo to take you to NASA Headquarters, downtown."

Thrasher nodded. "That's it?"

Linda nodded back. "That's everything, up to the minute."

Glancing out the helicopter's window, Thrasher saw the runways and aprons of Hobby approaching.

"Thanks, kid. Sorry to drag you away from the office."

She made a tight smile. "The office is wherever you are, boss."

"No," he corrected, "it's wherever *you* are. I can go batting around the countryside and everything runs smoothly because you're taking care of things at home base."

"That's my job."

"I appreciate it," he said.

Linda looked into his bloodshot eyes, then said, "It would help if you took it a little easier on your weekends."

He sighed. "I guess it would. But . . ."

"Victoria's come out here three weekends of the past four."

"Yep."

She said nothing, but Thrasher could see the disapproval on her face.

Spreading his hands almost apologetically, he said, "Look, it's just fun and games. Nothing serious."

"Does she know that?"

"Sure she does . . . I think."

"If I were in her place, I'd think that you were more serious than fun and games."

Thrasher fell silent, but he was thinking, Hell, Vicki's a grown-up. She knows I'm not serious about her.

"Tell her," said Linda, quite firmly. "Tell her you're not serious in plain words."

But then she might walk away from me, Thrasher said to himself.

"You've got be fair with her," Linda said.

"I suppose so."

"The last thing you need is a lawsuit."

"Lawsuit?" he yelped.

"Be honest with her," Linda insisted.

"I guess you're right," he grumbled.

"There are other women in the world, you know."

Thrasher sighed. "I suppose so." But Vicki's so damned convenient, he thought.

Reynold R. Reynolds was not waiting for him at the airport. Standing next to a stretch limousine in the hangar as his executive Learjet taxied in was a burly black man in a chauffeur's livery and a cap that perched precariously on his big bush of tightly curled hair.

Before Thrasher could ask anything, the chauffeur explained, "We'll pick up Mr. Reynolds at the office and then swing over to NASA Headquarters."

Thrasher nodded and crawled into the limo. The driver's compartment seemed to be half a block away from the plush seat he was sitting on. Helluva lot of car for two passengers, Thrasher thought. I ought to get Sid Ornsteen to look into the Washington office's budget.

The driver phoned ahead as they crossed the bridge over the Potomac, and Reynolds was standing at the entrance to the office building when the limousine pulled up, wearing a hand-tailored light gray business suit and posturing self-importantly with a briar pipe clamped between his teeth. The pipe was unlit, Thrasher saw. It's a prop, he realized. He looks like a statue to himself.

Reynolds stepped to the curb and waited for the chauffeur to hustle around and open the limo door for him. Ducking inside while Thrasher slid over to make room for him, the Washington rep shook his boss's hand firmly.

"We'll be talking to Franklin Larusso," Reynolds said, without preamble. "He's in the Contractor's Services office of the Mission Support Directorate. He's the pigeon that Yamagata reports to."

With a shake of his head, Thrasher said, "I don't understand this setup. I thought ILS was a private company that leased the launch facilities from NASA."

"Sort of," said Reynolds, keeping his knowing smirk minimal. "ILS has to operate within NASA's regulations for safety, scheduling, and all that kind of crap. NASA can pull the plug on them anytime they want to."

"So it's not really free enterprise, is it?"

"Only for the news media. In reality it's a government-run operation, same as it's always been. But instead of having government employees doing the work, the launch crews are employed by ILS."

Thrasher felt his brows knitting.

An hour and a half later, he was frowning even harder.

Franklin Larusso turned out to be an amiable-looking Latino with a round face the color of tobacco leaf, a thin moustache, and a bright, toothy smile. He was badly overweight, his paunch straining the buttons of his shirt. His office was modest: a government-issue metal desk, two chairs for visitors, bookshelves crammed with thick reports, one window that looked out at another window across the way.

Although Larusso was still smiling, what he had to say was far from pleasing to Thrasher.

"So, to sum up, you'll have to get permission from the safety office for each launch," he was saying, "but before that you'll need to have a detailed agreement with our legal office that gives complete specifications on each payload you want to launch."

Thrasher turned from Larusso to Reynolds, who just sat there with that damned pipe, trying to look knowledgeable but offering nothing in the way of help.

"And from what you're telling me," Thrasher said to the NASA manager, "that kind of paperwork can take months before NASA approves it."

Spreading his hands in a gesture of helplessness, Larusso replied, "Those lawyers aren't Speedy Gonzales. Nothing I can do about that."

"Isn't there any way we can cut through the red tape?"

"Not at my level. You'll have to go upstairs."

Reynolds came to life. "Upstairs? Who?"

"The chief of the safety office."

"Reed?"

Larusso nodded, his smile gone, his eyes suddenly fearful. Thrasher got the impression that he was scared to speak the name aloud.

◎ 6 ◎
HAMILTON REED

As they rode an elevator down to the lobby, Thrasher started to ask, "Who is this Reed guy?"

Reynolds held up a cautioning hand. The elevator cab was empty except for the two of them, but still Reynolds insisted on silence. Thrasher felt impressed. Unfavorably.

Once safely in the limousine and on their way back to the office, Thrasher asked again, "Who the hell is this guy Reed?"

Reynolds sucked on his unlit pipe before replying. "Hamilton Reed. One of the old-timers. Been with NASA since the Stone Age. Very powerful guy."

"In the safety office? How powerful can he be?"

"More powerful than the Administrator, the Deputy Administrator, and most of the people on the Administrator's staff."

Thrasher saw that Reynolds was totally serious.

"Like I said," the Washington rep continued, "he's been around a lot of years. A lot of people owe him favors. He knows where the bones are buried. And as chief of the safety office he can find ways to stop anybody, any program. Just like that." Reynolds snapped his fingers.

"Jesus," said Thrasher.

"I understand what's going on now," Reynolds went on, jabbing the pipe in Thrasher's direction. "Reed's going to do his best to scuttle your program."

"Why? What's he got against—"

"A private program? Go to Mars without NASA? Showing up the space agency? *His* space agency? He'd rather eat rat shit before he'll let that happen."

"Jesus," Thrasher repeated, more fervently. "How do we get around him?"

Reynolds shook his head like a man in mourning. "I don't think you can."

"But we've got to! We can't let some goddamned government bureaucrat stop us!"

Still looking solemn, Reynolds said, "I'll set up a meeting with him." Then he added, "If I can."

Patti Fabrizio said, "Hamilton Reed? Who's he?"

Before returning to Houston, Thrasher had called Patti and asked her to meet him at the Cosmos Club bar. She swept into the darkly-paneled room, wearing an elegant ankle-length black skirt and long-sleeved cardinal red blouse with gold trim, spotted Thrasher in the booth at the far corner, and walked regally to him.

When Thrasher asked her what she knew about Reed, she shrugged her slim shoulders and admitted she'd never heard of the man.

"He's an executive at NASA."

"Oh," said Patti. "The space agency. Very dull people, mostly. A few of the astronauts are interesting, but most of the feisty ones have retired."

"Reed's in the safety office."

"A faceless bureaucrat."

Thrasher started to reply, then thought better of it. If Patti doesn't know Reed, it won't do me any good to explain who he is to her. The less she knows about this the better. Information is like gold and diamonds in this town, I don't want her swapping stories about my problems with her newsroom pals. Or anybody else.

It took three weeks for Reynolds to arrange a meeting with Hamilton Reed. On Friday, July third. Thrasher had to phone Victoria Zane and cancel their plans for the Fourth of July weekend.

In his desktop telephone's screen, Vicki looked hurt. "I was looking forward to the weekend with you."

"Me too," Thrasher said.

With an arched brow, she added, "I thought we could make some spectacular fireworks."

Thrasher gulped. "Me too."

"What's so important—"

"Business in Washington," he said.

"Monkey business?"

"I wish."

Uriah Heep. Thrasher couldn't help staring at Hamilton Reed. *The man looks like Dickens' character Uriah Heep.* Pinched face, thinning hair, watery eyes behind rimless bifocal lenses. Reed was a thin, gray, chalkdust man, wearing a gray suit and a slightly darker gray tie. With a shock, Thrasher realized the man reminded him of his father.

Reed's office was almost sumptuous, by NASA standards: top floor of the headquarters building, big and airy with windows that looked out on the traffic streaming out of the city for the holiday weekend.

Reynolds, sitting beside Thrasher in front of Reed's heavy, dark mahogany desk, started the conversation with a respectful, "I'm very grateful that you found time to meet with us."

Reed smiled thinly and Thrasher thought of a snake, a pit viper, eying its prey.

"I'm just doing my job as a civil servant," he said, in a thin, high voice, so softly that Thrasher had to strain to hear his words.

"As you know," Reynolds said, "Mr. Thrasher here is heading an effort—"

"To send a crewed mission to Mars," Reed interrupted. "I'd be a pretty sorry NASA man if I didn't know that."

Impatiently, Thrasher broke in with, "Saito Yamagata of ILS tells me we'll need detailed agreements on the launches that we want to purchase from his company."

Reed nodded.

"I'd like to explore what we can do to expedite that process."

Reed leaned back in his creaking swivel chair, pursed his thin lips and steepled his fingers, but said nothing. Thrasher glanced at Reynolds, who sat like a statue, waiting patiently while Thrasher felt his blood pressure rising.

"Safety," said Reed at last, "is of paramount concern. We're very

proud of our safety record, and we want to make certain that your
. . . er, private program meets all the standards of safety and prudence
that we have established over the many years of NASA's virtually
unblemished record."

A vision of the space shuttles that had blown up and killed more
than a dozen astronauts flashed through Thrasher's mind, but he said
nothing.

"Safety is of prime importance," Reynolds agreed.

"We must put the lives of your people before all other
considerations, even though they are not NASA employees."

Thrasher said, "Oh, we won't be doing any manned launches from
Cape Canaveral. All our manned launches will be at the New Mexico
spaceport."

Reed's eyes flashed and he sat up a little straighter. "You don't
intend to launch people from our Kennedy Center? Why not?"

Thrasher shrugged. "It's what my tech people figured out. We'll
launch the components of our Mars spacecraft aboard Delta IVs, from
the Cape. Manned launches will be from New Mexico."

Leaning back in the chair once more and steepling his fingers
again, Reed said, "I see. But safety is still of primary importance."

"Of course," said Thrasher, thinking he had scored a point.

Then Reed's wintry smile returned and he said, "I understand that
one or more of the payloads you wish to launch from the Kennedy
Space Center involves components for a nuclear propulsion system.
I'll have to consult with the Nuclear Regulatory Commission about
that."

Thrasher realized this was going to be a long war.

◎ 7 ◎
HOUSTON

Linda's voice came through the intercom on Thrasher's desk, "Jessie Margulis is here."

Thrasher sighed. This isn't going to be easy, he told himself. But it's got to be done.

"Send him right in," he said, with a heartiness he didn't really feel.

Margulis came through the door, happily unaware of what was going through Thrasher's mind. The engineer looked positively cheerful; he was in his shirtsleeves, and carried a rolled-up piece of paper in his right hand. Another blueprint, Thrasher surmised.

"You want to see me, Art?"

Thrasher nodded. "Sit down, Jess. Would you like some coffee? Iced tea?"

"No, I'm fine," Margulis said as he took one of the chairs in front of the desk. Laying the rolled-up blueprint on the floor, he asked, "What's up?"

Thrasher reached toward the mug of ginger beer on his desk, then decided to do without it and plunge right in.

"Jess, we can't use nuclear propulsion."

Margulis blinked at him. "Can't use . . . are you kidding me?"

"It's politically impossible, Jess. Those bastards in Washington will crucify us."

"But we can't change the primary propulsion system at this stage of the game! It'd set us back two years! More!"

Thrasher had never seen the engineer so worked up. His normally placid face was red-cheeked. His eyes blazed. Even his fuzzy little goatee looked bristling.

"But the politics—"

"Screw the politics. You told me to design the best vehicle for carrying seven people to Mars, and I did that. They're building it out in Portales, for god's sake! This isn't a used-car lot, where you can pick and choose. We're building a nuclear-propelled Mars rocket."

Sagging back in his padded desk chair, Thrasher rolled his eyes ceilingward.

"You *told* me nuclear was okay," Margulis went on. "You approved the plan."

"I know, Jess, but I didn't realize how much opposition there'd be to nuclear."

"We're not going to operate the nuke here on the ground," Margulis said, almost pleading. "It'll only be turned on in orbit, four hundred miles up."

"Can't we switch back to chemical rockets, like everybody else uses?"

Margulis started to answer, then checked himself. His flushed cheeks paled. He took a deep breath.

Very reasonably, the engineer explained, "Art, the reason we chose to go nuclear was that it's the best, the most efficient propulsion system. Way better than the best chemical rockets."

"I know. You told me."

"Do you know what specific impulse is?" Margulis asked.

His brows knitting, Thrasher replied, "It's got something to do with a rocket's efficiency. Like miles per gallon on a car."

"Efficiency, right. Specific impulse is the measure of how long a pound of propellant will deliver a pound of thrust. It's measured in seconds."

Thrasher nodded, thinking that he didn't need an engineering lecture. But he knew he was going to get one.

Margulis continued, "The best chemical rockets burn hydrogen and oxygen. They give a specific impulse of about four hundred and fifty seconds, four fifty-five."

"So a pound of hydrogen and oxygen will produce a pound of thrust for four hundred and fifty-some seconds."

"Right. But the nuclear rocket we're building has a specific impulse of nine hundred and thirty seconds! Damned near double the best chemical rockets in the world."

"Yeah, but—"

"No buts! The nuclear rocket is the best way to go. It cuts the trip time to Mars by a third. It does *not* emit a lot of dangerous radioactivity, and even if it did the rocket will only be used in space, so it can't harm anybody or anything."

Intrigued by the engineer's intensity despite himself, Thrasher said, "As I understand it, the nuke just acts as a heater. It heats the propellant, which is then squirted out the rocket nozzles."

Almost smiling, Margulis said. "Right, boss. We use liquid hydrogen as the propellant, heat it up and fire it out the nozzles."

"And the crew's not exposed to any radioactivity?"

"The nuclear reactor is shielded. Hell, the shielding takes up about twenty-five percent of the ship's total mass."

"And chemical rockets?"

"They need more propellant, give less specific impulse, and would require a complete redesign of the Mars vehicle."

"Damn."

"It's a no-brainer, boss. Nuclear's the way to go."

"Except for the politics," Thrasher grumbled.

"Politics is your end of the stick," said Margulis. "My job is engineering, not ass-kissing."

Thrasher sat there and stared at his chief engineer. He wished the task before him were as simple as building a nuclear rocket system for traveling to Mars.

◎ 8 ◎
TUCSON

For a university town, Thrasher thought, Tucson isn't so bad. He had spent the night at the elegant Arizona Inn, an oasis of comfort and desert beauty in the midst of the city. After a substantial breakfast of huevos rancheros and fresh grapefruit juice, he'd picked up his rental car—a Mustang slingback—at the Inn's front driveway.

It was barely nine a.m. and already the blazing Sun was brutal. Summer in the Sonora Desert, Thatcher said to himself as he gunned the engine, grateful that the bellman who had brought the car to him had started the air conditioning on full blast. He wormed out of his summerweight jacket at the first stoplight and tossed it onto the right-hand seat.

The Lunar and Planetary Laboratory was scattered over several locations on campus. Thrasher used the car's GPS to find the Kuiper Space Sciences Building, on Cherry Street. It didn't look like much from the outside, but Thrasher didn't let that bother him.

Vince Egan was waiting for him in the lobby. He jumped to his feet, all nervous energy, as Thrasher pushed through the front door.

"Right on time," Egan said, sticking out his hand. He was wearing a patterned open-necked sports shirt and comfortable slacks. Dressed for the weather, Thrasher thought, although the building was chilly enough that he regretted leaving his jacket in the car.

"How're you doing, Vince? Everything ready?"

111

Egan nodded, then pointed Thrasher to the receptionist's desk. He had to show his driver's license and sign a form, and then the cute little straw-haired student behind the desk dimpled into a bright smile and issued him a plastic badge that proclaimed VISITOR. Egan already had his badge clipped to his belt.

Another student, male, crew-cut, athletic-looking, came through the far door and escorted them along the corridors toward the back of the building. Thrasher felt like a lab rat negotiating a maze. But he knew that the cheese at the end of the labyrinth was a replica of the surface of Mars.

They stepped through a door into a bare, low-ceilinged chamber that looked to Thrasher like a storeroom that had been emptied out. A man and a woman were standing at a bank of electronics consoles set up against one wall. Otherwise the room was blank, empty.

"Professor Winninger," their student guide called. His voice echoed off the blank walls.

The man turned and blinked at Thrasher and Egan. He was in his sixties, Thrasher guessed, sort of bland looking, with a high forehead and a heart-shaped face. But his dark brown eyes had laugh crinkles in their corners, and he smiled warmly as he approached Thrasher.

"Art," said Egan, "this is Professor Peter Winninger, head of the Mars simulation program."

"Peter Winninger," said the professor in a soft voice as he shook hands with Thrasher. Turning, he said, "And this is Dr. Kristin Anders, the one who really makes this lab work."

She was stunning. Tall and blonde, with a swimmer's broad shoulders and taut body, sculpted cheekbones and eyes like sapphires. She wore a sleeveless, pale yellow blouse and tan shorts that showed her long legs to good advantage.

Thrasher gulped as he took her proffered hand. "You must be Swedish," he heard himself say.

She smiled tolerantly. "Danish descent, actually," she said in a low, throaty voice. "We tell jokes about the Swedes."

"My mistake."

Winninger said, "I suppose you want to see what you've spent your money on."

It took an effort to move his eyes away from Kristin, but Thrasher managed to do it. "Yes," he said. "I want to see Mars."

Winninger grinned boyishly. "Right this way."

He walked Thrasher to the middle of the bare room, where a single wooden chair stood, laden with what looked like a biker's helmet and a pair of nubby-looking gloves. To his disappointment, Dr. Anders returned to the consoles and began tweaking the controls.

"This is our beta version," Professor Winninger said, almost apologetically. "You'll have visual and auditory inputs, but the tactile inputs will be for your hands only, not full-body."

Thrasher nodded. At the professor's direction, he wormed on the gloves. They felt fuzzy, almost like Brillo pads.

"No wires?" he asked.

Winninger smiled. "We're completely wireless . . . when it works right."

"Still got problems?"

"As I said, this is our beta version. We've based the simulation on photographs taken from landers on the surface of Mars, but it's not perfect . . . not yet."

Thrasher picked up the helmet. It felt heavy. Must be a lot of electronics built into it, he thought.

The professor instructed, "Leave the visor up until I tell you it's okay to slide it down over your eyes. You'll be in pretty complete darkness for a moment. Don't panic. The simulation will kick in almost immediately."

Nodding, Thrasher settled the helmet on his head. It covered his ears, muffling them. Winninger picked up the chair and carried it away from him, back to the consoles, leaving him standing alone in the middle of the stark chamber.

Then he heard Dr. Anders' smoky voice in the helmet's earphones: "Can you hear me, Mr. Thrasher?"

"Yes." Somehow he felt nervous. He licked his lips.

"Please pull your visor down."

Thrasher did it. The visor was heavily tinted; he could see nothing.

"Starting the sim."

For a few heartbeats Thrasher simply stood there, blind and deaf.

Then the world suddenly appeared around him. Rust-red sand stretching out toward the horizon, strewn with pebbles and rocks, some of them bigger than watermelons. Hills rose off to his right, and what looked like a shallow crater was no more than a dozen yards in front of him, its rim a circle of striated rock. The sky was a sort of butterscotch color, and he heard a soft sighing sound, like distant humming.

"Is that the wind?" he asked.

"Yes," came Anders' disembodied voice.

Winninger broke in. "Walk around a little. Explore the area."

Carefully, almost as if he were on a tightrope, Thrasher stepped across the reddish sand. Raising his hands in front of his face, he saw that he was wearing a pure white spacesuit, his hands in thick white gloves. Looking down, his legs were also encased in white leggings and heavy boots. Turning to look back, he saw his own bootprints in the sand. No one else's. He was alone on Mars.

Laughing shakily, Thrasher crowed, "I'm on Mars!"

"Virtually," came Anders' low voice.

"This is only a simulation," the professor warned, "not the real thing."

"Looks real to me!"

Virtual reality, Thrasher knew. This is the kind of equipment we're going to sell by the millions. People will be able to get into these rigs and *be* on Mars. What the astronauts see and do, ordinary folks in the safety of their homes will be able to see and do.

Eager as a little boy, Thrasher walked around the rim of the ancient crater. Over the sandy ridge he saw a metal object. One of the rovers NASA landed on Mars years ago! He could see the meandering track of its wheels stretching out to the horizon.

"Is that *Sojurner*?" he asked.

"No," Winninger's voice replied. "That's *Spirit*. *Sojurner* is more than a thousand klicks away from the spot you're at."

For more than fifteen minutes Thrasher walked across the frozen desert of Mars, marveling at how real the experience seemed. He bent down and touched the rusty sand; it felt gritty, even through the gloves. Looking up, he saw that the butterscotch sky was bright and clear, except for the thinnest wisps of a few cirrus clouds. A meteor flashed through the sky, making him twitch with surprise.

At last Winninger said, "That's about it, I'm afraid. You've covered the entire area that we've laid out for the simulation."

Before Thrasher could say anything, Kristin Anders said, "Ending sim. When your vision goes dark you can lift up your visor."

Feeling terribly disappointed, Thrasher stood mutely as the world around him disappeared into darkness. He raised the helmet's visor and he was back in the empty, seedy-looking chamber.

Winninger hurried to him. "How did you like it?"

"Awesome," said Thrasher. Back at the consoles, Anders smiled at him.

"Why don't the four of us have dinner this evening?" Thrasher asked.

Vince Egan nodded quickly. Winninger asked, "Er . . . may I bring my wife?"

"Sure," said Thrasher. Turning to Anders, "Will you come, too?"

"I'd love to," she said, "but I don't think I could get a sitter on such short notice."

"Please try," he said, noticing that there was no ring on her left hand. I've been to Mars today, he told himself. It'd be fun to fly to the Moon tonight. With her.

☙ 9 ☙
ARIZONA INN

Vince Egan drove back to the Arizona Inn in his own rental car and met Thrasher by the big swimming pool. Thrasher's suite was on the other side of the hedge that surrounded the pool. It was a very pretty location, although Thrasher had found early that morning that young children yelling and shrieking around the pool were a very effective alarm clock.

He was able to stifle most of their high-pitched screeching by holding a pillow over his ears, but still the deeper *thronngg* of the diving board kept him awake.

The pool was much quieter now, in the late afternoon, as Egan pulled up a lawn chair to sit beside Thrasher, who had pulled off his clothes and gotten into a swimsuit and a hotel-provided robe as soon as he'd returned to his suite.

A college-age waiter took their drink orders, and assured Thrasher that the main bar, inside the hotel, was stocked with ginger beer. Egan ordered a margarita.

"So what'd you think of the simulation?" the engineer asked.

"Impressive," said Thrasher. "It's going to make a mint for us." But he winced inwardly when he remembered that he'd promised Rutherford half of the VR profits.

"Manufacturing costs are higher than we estimated," Egan said. "I've tried to keep 'em down but they just keep going up."

"Who's handling the financial end for you?" Thrasher asked.

"I've got a CPA keeping tabs—"

"No, no," Thrasher asked. "Who's your financial chief, your CFO?"

"Don't have one," said the engineer. "I've never needed one before."

"That's because you've never headed up a manufacturing project before. You've always handed off the manufacturing tasks to guys like Strabowski or Malatesta."

"Yeah, but you said you wanted me to stay with the VR project all the way."

"And I do. But for God's sake get yourself somebody who can handle the finances. You're not a money guy."

Egan looked hurt. "Guess not."

"I'll get Sid Ornsteen to send a couple of his bright people to interview with you."

"Whatever."

Thrasher leaned over and grasped Egan's arm. "Vince, this is important. You wouldn't hire a guy who doesn't have any engineering experience to head up one of your tech teams, would you?"

"'Course not."

"Well, you need somebody who knows what he's doing to handle your financial end. And it's got to be somebody you like and can get along with."

Egan nodded, reluctantly, almost sullenly.

The waiter returned with their drinks, and he actually presented Thrasher with a chilled mug of ginger beer. After scribbling a generous tip on the bill, Thrasher asked him to make a reservation in the dining room for six people.

As the waiter left, Egan said, "You, me, Winninger and his wife . . . that only makes four."

"Kristin Anders might make it," Thrasher said.

"That's five, not six."

"You say five and they'll try to squeeze you into a table for four. You say six and everybody's comfortable, even if it turns out that only four get there."

Egan nodded, then said, "Besides, if she comes she might bring a date. Or a husband, more likely."

Thrasher felt distinctly unhappy at that thought.

Returning to his room, Thrasher phoned Ornsteen. The treasurer's lean, hollow-cheeked face looked more cadaverous than ever in the phone's tiny screen.

"Sure, I can get a couple of my bright young men to talk with Egan," said Ornsteen, grudgingly. "But I'll need a replacement for whoever he picks."

"No bright young women?" Thrasher asked. He was sitting in a comfortable armchair, the room's TV tuned to a financial channel, muted.

"Vince is a married man, Art."

"I'm not trying to play cupid," he told Ornsteen. "I just want to make sure nobody can complain about equal opportunity."

The treasurer almost smiled. "I'll see if I can find a dark-skinned Latina. A three-fer. Will that be okay?"

"As long as she can do the job."

While he was shaving, the hotel phone rang.

They always call when I've got a face full of lather, Thrasher groused to himself. They must have hidden cameras in the rooms.

Grumbling, he stalked into the sitting room and punched the phone's speaker button. "Mr. Thrasher?" a woman's voice asked. "We have a call for you from a Dr. Anders."

Thrasher's grumbles ended immediately. "Put her on!"

Kristin's throaty voice asked, "Mr. Thrasher?"

"Art," he replied. "My friends call me Art. Not that I'm a work of art, like a Rembrandt or something."

She laughed softly. "All right. And my friends call me Kristin. Not Kris. Not Krissy. Kristin."

"Yes, ma'am."

"I found a sitter. Will it be all right if we make it an early evening?"

"Dinner at six-thirty?" he replied. "That's what I told the professor."

"Perfect."

"Okay, six-thirty, here at the Inn."

"I'll be there."

Thrasher smiled as he said, "See you then."

❈ ❈ ❈

The Arizona Inn's dining room was decorated in Southwestern style, like a large, luxurious adobe home. French doors led out to a lovingly tended garden, and the bar was only a few steps away.

Thrasher got a nice round table in the middle of the room, beneath an ornate chandelier. Vince Egan came in as he was sitting down, and Professor Winninger and his wife followed almost immediately behind him.

Mrs. Winninger was an Hispanic, short and plump and altogether pleasant. She was a professor, too, of languages.

Once they had ordered drinks, Mrs. Winninger said, "I understand Dr. Anders will be joining us."

Thrasher nodded, wondering how she knew. Jungle telegraph? Women's ESP?

"Our son is babysitting for her," Mrs. Winninger added.

The mystery is solved, Thrasher thought. As innocently as he could manage, he asked, "Is Dr. Anders divorced?"

"Widowed," Mrs. Winninger said. "Her husband was killed in Afghanistan."

"Oh. I'm sorry to hear that." It wasn't actually true, but it was what they expected to hear.

"It only happened three months ago," the woman went on. "I think this is the first time she's gone out since she got the news."

Thrasher leaned back in his chair. I'm being warned, he realized. Keep my hands off her.

At that moment, Kristin Anders appeared at the restaurant's entrance, wearing a sleeveless black sheath decorated with a slim rope of pearls. Her blonde hair fell softly to her shoulders. Thrasher popped to his feet as the hostess showed her to their table and seated her next to him.

"Are we expecting one more?" the hostess asked.

Thrasher shook his head. "No, there'll only be five of us, I'm afraid." He tried to keep from grinning as he sat down.

Dinner conversation was strictly business.

"The simulation you walked through is based on existing imagery from several Mars landers," Winninger repeated. "Transmitting live from Mars will be a different order of difficulty."

"You can do it, can't you?" Thrasher asked.

The professor hesitated just the slightest bit before he replied, "Maybe you'd better ask Kristin about that. She's handling the transmitting system."

Thrasher looked into those sapphire eyes.

"We'll get the job done for you, Mr. Thra—um, Art."

He smiled happily. "I'm sure you will," he said, suppressing the urge to pat her hand. "I'm sure you will."

He scolded himself, Don't come on to her. She's practically an employee, for god's sake. And recently widowed. You'll have Mrs. Winninger and probably all the female members of the faculty coming down on you. You can't take a chance on lousing up the VR program. Damn!

But then he realized that he had a perfectly legitimate reason to return to Tucson, to see how the VR system was developing. I'll be seeing a lot of her, he thought happily.

In the meantime, he told himself, go take a cold shower.

But he was thinking how great it would be to share a hot tub with Kristin Anders.

❀ 10 ❀
MONEY TALKS

While summer faded into autumn, the Mars project moved ahead steadily. Jessie Margulis spent more time in Portales than at home in Houston with his family, but the spacecraft his team had designed was taking shape, blueprints were turning into hardware. Thrasher still worried about the battle looming over launching the components of the Mars ship's nuclear propulsion system.

Despite his anxieties, though, the former tire warehouse in Portales rang and banged with the sounds of construction; a new annex was being built to house the spacecraft's growing bulbous shape.

But Sid Ornsteen was looking grimmer every time Thrasher saw him.

"This is costing a lot more than we budgeted for," the corporate treasurer complained.

Ornsteen had stalked into Thrasher's office unannounced, just brushing past Linda and marching up to Thrasher's desk, a fistful of financial reports in his hand.

"We're not broke yet," said Thrasher, trying to remain upbeat.

"We're getting close."

"Our stock price is holding steady."

"So far," Ornsteen said glumly, collapsing his gaunt body into one of the armchairs in front of Thrasher's desk.

"We're getting good publicity," said Thrasher. "Did you see the piece in *Aviation Week*? And the Discovery Channel wants to do a documentary about us."

Ornsteen was not impressed. "*The Wall Street Journal* will do a great article on us when we file for bankruptcy."

"Don't be such a wet blanket, Sid."

With a mournful shake of his head, the treasurer said, "You've got to get your backers to put more cash into the pot, Art."

"They've agreed to a billion a year, each. I can't ask them for more."

"You've got to."

Leaning back in his swivel chair, Thrasher saw that Sid was totally serious. "Is it that bad?" he asked.

"It's getting scary, Art. I mean . . . we're cutting it too damn close."

Thrasher mused, "Maybe I could ask them to chip in next year's contribution a little early."

"Rob Peter to pay Paul? That won't work; not for long, anyway. They need to put in more money."

Thrasher said to himself, Which means I have to go to guys like Jenghis Kahn and Gregory Sampson in sackcloth and ashes and my begging bowl in my hand.

He sighed. "I'll see what I can do, Sid."

As his limousine approached Gregory Sampson's mansion, on the beach of one of Long Island's most exclusive communities, Thrasher thought, It goes to show what God could have done if he'd had money.

The place was built to impress people, a pile of gray stones arranged like a castle, complete with round, cone-topped turrets and pennants fluttering in the breeze from Long Island Sound. Thrasher half expected to see a moat with drawbridge and serfs clenching their fists over their hearts and swearing to Sampson, "My liege!"

The trees lining the driveway were ablaze with autumn reds and golds, the shrubs at their bases still bright with asters and chrysanthemums and other flowers that Thrasher didn't recognize.

A liveried doorman was waiting as the limo pulled up at the mansion's entrance. He showed Thrasher to the carved oak double doors, where a butler bowed minimally and escorted him through an entryway large enough to hold a tennis court, then down a wide corridor lined with paintings by masters from Raphael to Picasso and finally to the library, where Gregory Sampson stood waiting for him, wearing prefaded jeans and a gray Dartmouth College sweatshirt.

The far wall of the book-lined room was all glass, two stories high, that looked out on the Sound. A regatta of sailboats was cutting through the choppy water, under a sky dotted with puffy white cumulus clouds.

Gregory Sampson turned away from the tall windows, a crystal champagne flute in one meaty hand, a broad welcoming smile on his bearded face.

"Artie!" he boomed. "Welcome to my humble abode."

Thrasher had to grin at the man's hubris. "Nice of you to invite me. What do you call this place, Camelot?"

"How did you guess?" Sampson laughed as he waved at an oversized leather wing chair. "Sit down. Relax. Have some champagne?" Before Thrasher could reply, he went on, "No, you drink ginger beer, don't you?"

"If you have it," Thrasher said, sitting in the big chair. He felt dwarfed by it.

"Flew in a couple of cases from Jamaica the other day," said Sampson, jovially. He sat in an identical chair facing Thrasher. "I had a feeling you'd come visiting, sooner or later."

Thrasher nodded. He knows why I'm here. But maybe I can throw him a curve, shake him up a bit.

"I need your help," he said.

Sampson's smile grew even wider.

"How well do you know Senator Jacobs?"

"Chuckie?" Sampson looked puzzled briefly, but he swiftly recovered. "I've known Chuck Jacobs since he was running for his first public office, twenty-five years ago. Why do you ask?"

"He's chairman of the Senate subcommittee for space, isn't he?"

Sampson nodded warily.

"I need him to help move some paperwork through the NASA bureaucracy," said Thrasher.

Sampson's shaggy brows knit. "NASA? What're you doing with NASA?"

Thrasher explained his problem, finishing with, "So as long as this little weasel Reed can delay all the approvals we need, we're going to be tied up in red tape."

Absently tugging at his white beard, Sampson asked, "He can really hold you up?"

"He can, and he will—unless we can find some way to put pressure on him."

"Jacobs' subcommittee handles the NASA budget request," Sampson mused.

"If he could make it clear that the Senate is behind us, and he doesn't want us held up unreasonably—"

"'Unreasonably' is a stretchy word, Artie. What seems unreasonable to you might look perfectly okay to a guy like Reed."

"Look, Greg, this is important. The only way I can think of to pressure Reed is to have Congress lean on him."

"Have you tried plying him with women?" Sampson asked, grinning toothily.

Thrasher made a sour face. "You haven't met him. He's not the type to make a move in that direction."

"Not like you or me, huh?"

"Can you talk to Senator Jacobs?"

"Sure. I'm not certain it will do any good, though, if this guy is as firmly entrenched in the NASA hierarchy as you told me."

"Money talks," Thrasher said. "If Jacobs lets Reed know that NASA's budget depends on how he deals with Mars, Inc., I think it will help us. A lot."

Sampson's cold gray eyes stared at Thrasher for a long, silent moment, then shifted away. "I'll talk to Chuckie, see what I can do. Maybe I'll throw a party in D.C. and invite him. More business is done in Washington at cocktail parties than on the floor of the Senate."

"And invite Reed, too?"

"No, no," Sampson said, shaking his bushy white head. "From what you've told me about him, he'd be totally out of place. Besides, you never invite the victim to the arraignment."

"Oh. I see. Well, thanks, Greg." Thrasher started to get out of the chair, but Sampson laid a heavy hand on his arm.

"How's the project going?" he asked.

"Great. Swell. You ought to come out to Portales and see that spacecraft. Its outer shell is almost finished and they're working on the interior wiring now. Miles of wires!"

"You okay money-wise?"

Thrasher hesitated. *He knows about our finances. He knows down to the penny. Jenghis Kahn keeps him up-to-the minute.*

Very carefully, Thrasher replied, "Oh, we could use more cash, of course."

"How much more?"

A vision flashed through Thrasher's mind: a vulture sitting in a dead tree, watching an animal breathing its last.

"A hundred mill should tide us over 'til the next fiscal year."

"A hundred million. That's in addition to our regular contributions?"

"Yes," Thrasher said tightly.

"It wouldn't be deductible as a charitable donation, would it?"

"I don't think so."

Sampson was enjoying this, Thrasher saw. *He's having fun, stretching me on the rack.*

"I won't hand you another hundred million just for old time's sake," Sampson said, deadly serious now, "but I'll tell you what I will do."

Thrasher said nothing.

"I'll buy a hundred million dollars worth of Thrasher Digital stock. From you. Directly."

I should have expected this, Thrasher thought. *He still wants to take over my company. He still wants to drive me out.*

"I own twenty-five percent of the corporate preferred stock," Thrasher said.

"Sell me half of it."

"For a hundred mill?"

Sampson licked his lips and nodded.

"It's not worth a hundred million, you know that."

"I'm willing to be overcharged."

Thrasher was thinking furiously, *I'll still keep twelve and a half percent. He'll have the same amount, but I can outvote him, if the other stockholders stick with me. But he'll be nibbling away, picking up shares wherever he can. Sooner or later he'll beat me.*

But he heard himself say, "Okay. Twelve and a half percent for a hundred million dollars."

Sampson broke into a wide grin. "Done!"

So he'll run me out of my own company, Thrasher thought. But not before we get to Mars. Not before we get to Mars.

◎ 11 ◎
THE WHITE HOUSE

Christmas was only a week away, but it was so balmy in the nation's capital that news commentators were talking about global warming again.

Thrasher felt unaccountably nervous as his limousine stopped at the security checkpoint. After nearly six years in office, the President of the United States had finally invited him to the White House. And why? To make some publicity points about the Mars project. To show the voters that he's not anti-space, after all.

Even Reynold Reynolds, sitting beside Thrasher in the limo, looked on edge, drumming his fingertips on the thighs of his precisely creased trousers.

"This is the big time," Reynolds muttered, more to himself than to Thrasher.

"I guess it is," he said.

Thrasher's public relations director had been wonderfully surprised when the White House staffer called. Thrasher had never seen her so excited.

"You're invited to meet the president!" Francine had gushed. "In the Oval Office!"

And now he felt excited, too. Even though I think he's a blowhard jerk, he said to himself, he's still the President of the United States. He found himself humming "Hail to the Chief" as an aide led him and Reynolds along the corridor to the West Wing.

And there he was, POTUS himself, sitting behind his massive mahogany desk, smiling his brightest, toothiest smile as Thrasher and Reynolds were ushered into the Oval Office.

The Chief Administrator of NASA was sitting on one of the striped sofas by the empty fireplace, together with a couple of other people Thrasher didn't recognize. Two photographers buzzed around like foraging bees as Thrasher walked across the carpet bearing the Great Seal of the U.S. and up to the President's desk. Reynolds quietly sat on the end of the sofa, with the others.

The president was considerably shorter than Thrasher had expected: a swarthy, stocky Hispanic from California with tightly curled salt-and-pepper hair and a photogenic smile. He reached across his desk to extend his hand.

"Mr. President," said Thrasher as he gripped the man's outstretched hand.

"Mr. Thrasher. It's good to see you."

More clicks and flashes from the photographers.

The president gestured to the only chair before his desk; it was angled so that Thrasher could face the NASA administrator and the others on the sofa, including Reynolds.

"How is your Mars project going?" the president asked.

"Pretty well," said Thrasher. "I'd be honored if you'd come out to our headquarters in Portales and see the spacecraft taking shape."

The president glanced over at the only woman on the sofa. "Can we work that into my next western trip, Connie?"

"Certainly, sir," the woman answered.

"Fine." Turning back to Thrasher, the president said, as if reciting by rote, "I want to congratulate you on attempting to show the world that American free enterprise can accomplish great things. Too many people believe that only the government can manage space exploration. I'm delighted that you've accepted the challenge of putting Americans on Mars."

Thrasher smiled. Canned speech, he thought. It'll be on all the news nets this evening.

"Well, it's not only Americans who're going to Mars, you know. Our crew includes a planetary astronomer from South Africa."

"Fine, fine," said the president.

The NASA administrator spoke up. "I understand that you'll be using our launch center at Cape Canaveral."

"For the heavy lifting, yes," Thrasher replied. "Our manned launches will be done from Spaceport America, in New Mexico."

The administrator nodded. Reynolds frowned slightly and shook his head once. The Washington rep had warned Thrasher not to bring up the Reed problem. Going over the bureaucrat's head would only anger Reed and embarrass the NASA administrator in front of the President.

"That's fine, fine," the president repeated. He got to his feet, signaling that the meeting was concluded.

Thrasher got up too, thinking that the president had gotten his photo op; he'd be on all the news shows. In and out, a few clicks of the cameras and off you go.

The others got up from the sofa, as well. As he approached the NASA administrator, Thrasher said, "I wonder if I might talk to you sometime about our launch schedule at the Cape."

"Of course," said the administrator. "Any time. We'll be glad to help you in any way we can."

Reynolds was getting red in the face, trying to warn Thrasher not to go any farther without saying anything aloud.

"I'll phone you if we have any problems," Thrasher said.

"Certainly," the administrator said, with all the warmth and sincerity of a man who knew the cameras were on him.

As they left the White House, Reynolds blew out a heavy gust of breath. "I thought for a minute back there that you were going to upset the apple cart."

Thrasher shrugged. "At least I can phone the guy if I need to."

Reynolds shook his head. "That's the last thing you want to do. That's a card to be played only as a last resort."

"Yeah," Thrasher said. "But it might help if Reed knows I've got an in with his boss."

Shaking his head like a schoolteacher disappointed with a stubborn student, Reynolds muttered a line from an old movie, "Don't shoot Mongo, you'll only make him mad at you."

◎ 12 ◎
COCKTAIL PARTY

True to his word, Gregory Sampson threw a lavish cocktail party the evening after Thrasher's White House visit. The excuse was to celebrate the Yuletide season. The reason was for Thrasher to meet Senator Charles Jacobs, without going to his office for a formal visit that would immediately be broadcast along the D.C. grapevine.

It was a sumptuous affair, held in the main ballroom of the Grand Hyatt Hotel. Half of the District of Columbia seemed to be there, chatting, laughing, clinking glasses, the men in tuxedos or dark business suits, the women in stylish dresses and jewelry, all of them sipping at drinks and nibbling at the canapés spread out on more than two dozen little round tables scattered across the big room.

But as soon as Thrasher stepped into the crowded, noisy hotel ballroom, with Reynolds at his side, he saw Kristin Anders standing in the midst of the throng, holding a stemmed wineglass in one hand as she talked amiably with a ruggedly handsome, athletic-looking blond young man.

She wore a wine-red knee-length dress with a high mandarin collar. Silver choker with a ruby pendant. Ruby bracelet. Or maybe they're garnets, Thrasher thought as he left Reynolds standing at the doorway and shouldered his way through the crowd to Kristin's side.

"Hello!" he said brightly, raising his voice over the babble of the crowd.

Kristin turned away from the handsome youth, her deeply blue eyes widening with surprise.

"What are you doing here?" she asked.

"I was going to ask you the same question," he hollered back.

Pointing to the young man, Kristin introduced, "This is my cousin, Erik Harker. Erik, this is Arthur Thrasher."

Cousin, Thrasher said to himself. He's her cousin.

The blond young man smiled boyishly as he took Thrasher's hand in a strong grip. "I've heard a lot about you, Mr. Thrasher."

"Some of it might even be true," Thrasher joked.

"Erik is on Senator Jacobs' staff," Kristin said.

As innocently as he could manage, Thrasher asked, "Is the senator here?"

"Yes," said Erik. "We came in together, but Mr. Sampson is monopolizing him and I saw cousin Kristin standing all alone . . ."

"What brings you to Washington?" Thrasher asked her.

"Family birthday," she said. "I'll be staying through Christmas."

"How are things going with the VR system?"

"We're moving ahead. Some problems, but nothing that can't be solved, sooner or later."

Make it sooner, Thrasher urged silently. But he said nothing.

Harker said, "You don't have a drink, Mr. Thrasher."

"I just got here. And call me Art."

Reynolds cruised up, with a heavy cut crystal glass in his hand. "Senator Jacobs is over there, with Sampson."

Thrasher sighed. "Business."

"I understand," Kristin said, with a nod.

Looking into her sparkling eyes, Thrasher said, "Please don't leave until I get a chance to get back to you."

"I'll try . . ."

"Good to meet you, Ernie."

"Erik."

"Oh. Yeah. Sorry." Reluctantly, very reluctantly, Thrasher allowed Reynolds to lead him away from Kristin, through the crowd to the corner where Sampson and Senator Jacobs were standing with their heads inclined toward each other in intense conversation.

Charles Jacobs was a pleasant looking man of about fifty, Thrasher judged. Dark hair just starting to gray at the temples. Lean face, almost ascetic, except for the eagle beak of a nose. Although he was slim, wiry, he stood almost as tall as Sampson, who outweighed him by at least fifty pounds. Thrasher forced himself not to smile at the pair of them: Senator Jacobs, lean and dapper in a gray suit; Sampson bulky and shaggy-bearded, looking disheveled even in the tuxedo he was wearing.

Sampson looked up as Thrasher and Reynolds approached.

"And here he is now." Reaching a long arm around Thrasher's shoulders, Sampson said, "Chuck, I want you to meet Artie Thrasher, the man who wants to get us to Mars."

"Mr. Thrasher," said the senator.

"Senator Jacobs. Please call me Art."

"Fine. And I'm Chuck."

Hiking a thumb in Reynolds' direction, Thrasher said, "And this is—"

"R Cubed," the senator said. "I've known Ray ever since I first arrived in Washington."

"Good to see you again, Senator," said Reynolds.

Thrasher glanced at his Washington rep. *If you've known Jacobs for so long, why did I have to get Sampson to line up a meeting with him?*

Senator Jacobs said, "Greg here tells me you're dealing with NASA. I thought your program was strictly private enterprise, no government involvement."

Thrasher made a self-deprecating little smile. "We need a heavy lift launch capability, and NASA has the only facilities capable of handling Delta IV launches."

Understanding dawned on Jacobs' face. "I see. I see."

Reynolds added, "Even though ILS is actually operating the launch service, NASA is still the landlord."

"Which means we have to jump through all their hoops," said Thrasher.

Jacobs' eyes narrowed. "They're not giving you trouble, are they?"

Before Thrasher could reply, Reynolds said, "Paperwork. Lots and lots of paperwork."

"Red tape," Thrasher said.

"Which costs us time and money, Chuck," Sampson chimed in.

"Dotting the I's and crossing the T's," the senator murmured.

Reynolds said, "Did you see the president on the news shows yesterday? He's solidly on our side."

"Well, so's Congress," Jacobs said, almost defensively. "We're all rooting for you."

"Not the Safety Office," said Thrasher. "They're throwing roadblocks in our way."

"Really?"

"Really. And that's slowing our progress."

"Which soaks up money," Sampson repeated.

"The Safety Office, huh?" Jacobs said. "Well, safety's important."

Sampson fixed the senator with a stern gaze. "Chuck, we're getting the feeling that the NASA bureaucracy doesn't like seeing a private program aiming for Mars. They're circling their wagons and doing their best to slow us to a crawl."

"The Safety Office is doing this?"

Thrasher replied, "That's where their stalling tactics are centered."

Stroking his chin slowly, Jacobs said, "Maybe I should have my people look into this."

"I'd appreciate it if you would," Sampson said, with a toothy smile.

"We'd all appreciate it," said Thrasher.

⊚ 13 ⊚
AFTER THE BALL

As soon as he decently could, Thrasher detached himself from Senator Jacobs and Sampson and began searching the crowd for Kristin. Reynolds, though, tagged along beside him. Thrasher didn't want the rep see him with Kristin—not that he saw her anywhere in the crowded, noisy ballroom.

"Do you think we did any good?" he asked Reynolds, while scanning the partygoers for a glimpse of her.

"We did okay," said Reynolds, doggedly staying at his side. "Jacobs' people will start poking their noses into Reed's operation. Reed will have to toe the line."

"He can still wrap us up in red tape," Thrasher said. He caught a glimpse of a woman in a red dress, but it wasn't her.

Reynolds spread his hands. "A certain amount of red tape can't be helped. Especially when there's a nuke involved. You've got to expect it and play the game accordingly."

"I guess."

"That meeting with the president could be very helpful."

There she was! Thrasher saw Kristin standing by the French windows that led out onto the balcony, talking to two other women. No men with them.

"Well, thanks for everything, Ray. You've done a good night's work."

Reynolds looked surprised, almost hurt. He realized he was being dismissed.

"You leaving now?" he asked.

"In a bit. I don't want to keep you, though. Go on home."

Reluctantly, Reynolds said, "Okay. But give me a buzz tomorrow morning. We can debrief. I'll check with Jacobs' people, see if he's making good on his promise."

"Great," said Thrasher. "Fine."

Reynolds left at last, looking a bit resentful, like a pet dog that's been scolded. Thrasher watched him leave, while keeping one eye on Kristin. As soon as Reynolds went through the door, Thrasher made a beeline toward her.

The other two women were leaving, also. The party was beginning to break up. Over his shoulder Thrasher saw Sampson with one heavy arm wrapped around Senator Jacobs' shoulders, heading toward the bar, with Erik Harker trailing behind them.

And then he was standing in front of Kristin Anders, suddenly feeling foolish, tongue-tied.

"Thanks for waiting," he said to her.

Kristin smiled curiously. "Erik seems to be busy with Senator Jacobs."

"I can drive you to wherever you're staying," Thrasher offered.

"It's practically in Bethesda."

"No problem. The driver knows the city."

She looked across the emptying room at her cousin, deep in conversation now with the senator and Sampson.

"Do you have any plans for dinner?" Thrasher asked. "I'm starved."

Instead of answering, Kristin reached into her little handbag and pulled out a cell phone. She pecked at it, and Thrasher saw Erik Harker flinch and then reach into his jacket.

"Erik?" Kristin said. "Mr. Thrasher is going to take me home." She listened for a moment, then said, "Yes, it was good to see you again, too. Say hello to your parents for me. I'll see you all at the birthday party, I suppose."

She clicked the phone shut and dropped it back into her purse. "Dinner sounds good. I haven't had a thing to eat since this morning, in Tucson."

❦ ❦ ❦

The chauffeur didn't know the streets of the American University Park neighborhood all that well, but Thrasher had him drive to a restaurant he knew in nearby Georgetown.

The Blue Crab was far from fancy: its booths had plain wooden tables covered with brown paper tablecloths. The wine list consisted of "red, white, and pink." The waiters wore aprons and tied terrycloth towels around the necks of their customers. But the crabs were marvelous, fresh from the Chesapeake Bay waters, boiled in tangy spices and served with wooden mallets.

Thrasher avoided the wine list. They ordered beer: Coors Lite for Kristin, Negra Modelo for Thrasher. Once the crabs were served, conversation stopped as they banged away happily and tossed the broken shells into a plastic wastebasket set at the table's edge.

At last Kristin looked up and said, "How did you ever find this place?"

Thrasher dabbed at his dripping chin with his spattered towel as he replied. "First time I ever came to Washington, I asked a cab driver where he ate."

She gave him a curious look. "I'd have thought that a multimillionaire would eat in the posh restaurants downtown."

"I wasn't a multimillionaire in those days." To himself he added, and I won't be one much longer, the way things are going.

She smiled and grabbed another crab from the heap on the big serving platter between them.

"How'd you get interested in virtual reality?" he asked.

"Professor Winninger. I was one of his students, and he told us that VR ought to be more useful than just for making porno simulations."

Thrasher almost choked on his crab claw.

Kristin laughed. "Well, that was the major market for VR, you know."

"I'd never even thought about that!"

"You didn't?" She looked surprised.

"No."

"It's a big business."

"I suppose it is. But I've never dabbled in it."

She said, "I suppose you don't need simulations. You don't have any trouble getting real women."

Thrasher heard a voice in his head intone, You have the right to remain silent . . .

"You do have something of a reputation, you know," Kristin added, the corners of her lips curving slightly.

Trying to make it sound offhand, Thrasher admitted, "I've been married twice."

"And divorced twice."

"Yeah," he sighed.

"With plenty of women before, during and after."

He stiffened. "I was always a faithful husband. Completely."

"That's not what the rumor mill says."

"The rumor mill also says we're being visited by extraterrestrials and global warming is a hoax."

Kristin looked at him for a long, silent moment, and Thrasher found himself mesmerized by her calm, unwavering azure eyes.

"It's the truth, Kristin," he said.

She nodded. "I believe you, Art."

"Thanks."

As they left the restaurant, Thrasher realized he'd been outmaneuvered by a very clever young woman. Yet he couldn't feel angry toward Kristin. He almost chuckled aloud.

The chauffeur found Kristin's aunt's house at last, a modest brick-fronted Federalist bungalow, and double-parked in front of it.

"Thanks for dinner," Kristin said, as the chauffeur opened the door on her side.

"Thank you, Kristin. I had a fine evening."

She kissed him lightly on the cheek and whispered, "I'm not ready for you, Art. Not yet. Please understand."

Then she slid out of the limousine and went briskly up the walkway that led to the house's front porch.

Thrasher sat there, feeling somewhere between foolish and elated.

As the chauffeur put the limo in gear and pulled away from the curb, he thought to himself, Well, I still have Vicki. Somehow the thought made him feel like a heel.

☸ 14 ☸
CHRISTMAS DINNER

It looked like a lonely holiday season coming up, thought Thrasher. Most of his staff was taking off the week between Christmas and New Year's. He grumbled to himself that Santa Claus was putting him a week behind schedule.

Two days before Christmas, Victoria phoned, almost apologetic about going up to Taos for the holiday. "My sister and her family live up there, by the ski resort," she said.

"Christmas is for families," he mumbled into the phone.

"Do you want to come up with me?" she asked. "You could stay at the ski lodge, my brother-in-law can get you a room."

Thrasher found that he couldn't work up the enthusiasm for that. "No, thanks." He repeated, "Christmas is for families."

"Well, Merry Christmas, then," Victoria said. She sounded disappointed.

"Merry Christmas, kid." He cut the connection, wondering if he was doing the right thing. The idea of spending Christmas with Vicki's family was scary. They'd get the wrong impression, he told himself. *She'd* get the wrong impression.

Linda came into his office, looking very Christmasy in a bright red sweater trimmed with white fur.

"What are you doing for the big day?" she asked, all smiles.

He cocked his head and answered, "Not much."

"Well, my mother's having the family over for dinner and I'll be the only one without an escort unless you come with me."

"Me?"

"You shouldn't spend Christmas alone, and I don't want to be the only old maid at dinner, so why don't you come with me? You won't have to buy presents or anything like that. It's just dinner with the family."

Thrasher found himself grinning at her. "Okay. Thanks. Sounds like fun."

She looked doubtful. "It's a pretty big family. Be prepared."

"Should I bring flowers or something?"

"Bring earmuffs."

As Linda flounced out of his office, Thrasher wondered if she had listened to his phone conversation with Vicki. He sat in his desk chair for several minutes, swiveling back and forth, trying to make up his mind. At last he fished out his cell phone and tapped Vicki's number.

She answered on the first ring.

"What're you doing New Year's Eve?" he asked.

Even in the phone's small screen he could see the sudden delight on her face.

"The station's throwing a party for the staff and major advertisers," she said, "but I can skip it, I guess."

"Good. Can you meet me in Portales?"

"Sure!"

"I'll book a suite at the Holiday Express."

"Okay. Fine."

"See you there, late afternoon."

"I'll be there," Vicki said, with a bright, happy smile.

Thrasher clicked his phone shut. What the hell, he said to himself. We can watch the ball go down in Times Square and it'll only be ten o'clock in New Mexico. Then he thought, grinning, *Might as well start the New Year with a bang.*

Christmas dinner was a bewildering rush of Linda's family: parents, brothers, sisters, aunts, uncles, at least one grandfather, and hordes of squealing, running, laughing children. Christmas decorations everywhere: the house's windows all had electric candles, a Christmas tree scraped the ceiling of the spacious living room, dripping with colorful ornaments and tinsel, torn wrapping paper littered the floor. Thrasher was dazed by the energy and enthusiasm of all these people.

Linda's mother, portly and gray-haired, smiled genially as he handed her the poinsettia plant that he brought.

"You can plant it in your garden," he said.

"Yes, of course," she replied, all smiles. Then she turned and handed it to one of her daughters, who placed it beside the six other poinsettias already lined up along the sideboard in the dining room.

Dinner was sumptuous, a traditional turkey plus savory Mexican dishes, candied sweet potatoes, and salsa hot enough to burn the roof of Thrasher's mouth. He enjoyed every bite of it.

Over all the noise and confusion, Linda's father—a stocky dark-skinned man with a stern expression on his mustachioed face—sat at the head of the table and watched the proceedings with unsmiling dignity.

The Lord of the Manor, Thrasher thought, watching him. Founder of the feast. Master of all he surveys. Three generations carrying his genes, all sitting around the dinner table together. It's wonderful, in a noisy, hectic way. Like one of those old movies with Lionel Barrymore.

At last it was all over. Feeling stuffed and a little woozy from the homemade wine, Thrasher thanked them all profusely as he said his farewells. Linda's mother even hugged him.

Linda walked him to the front door.

"You'll be all right to drive? I can get one of my brothers to drive you."

"I'm okay," he said. "Thanks for everything. It was overpowering, but a lot of fun."

"Merry Christmas, boss." She pressed her hands against his shoulders and kissed him soundly.

Totally surprised, Thrasher sputtered, "Ulp . . . Merry Christmas, kid."

Linda grinned at him and pointed overhead. "You *are* standing underneath the mistletoe, you know."

Thrasher looked up and saw that indeed he was.

"See you Monday morning," Linda said.

"Yeah, right. Monday."

◎ 15 ◎
INSURANCE

"David Kahn called me," said Sid Ornsteen.

Thrasher leaned back in his desk chair and eyed his corporate treasurer. Sid always looked worried, he thought, but today he doesn't look as gloomy as usual. Maybe he had a good Christmas, too.

"What did old Jenghis have to say?" he asked.

"He wants to talk with you about getting an insurance policy for the rocket launches."

Nodding, Thrasher said, "Does he want me to call him?"

"No," Ornsteen replied. "He's coming out here to see you." There was awe in his voice.

Thrasher blinked with surprise. "David Kahn is coming here? He's leaving New York to come here?"

"That's right. I was kind of surprised, myself. I always thought that people came to him, not the other way around."

"Yeah," said Thrasher. "When is this momentous event to take place?"

"Day after tomorrow."

"Friday." The first of January, Thrasher realized. A holiday for everybody else, but not for Jenghis Kahn. I'll have to get back here from Portales earlier than I'd planned.

"He said he'll be here in time for lunch."

"I'll tell Linda to book a table at the University Club."

145

"Good."

"You come with me."

"Really?" Ornsteen squeaked.

"Really."

"Okay, if that's what you want." Ornsteen stood up and started for the door.

"And once Jenghis gets here," Thrasher called to him, "lock the doors and count the children."

Ornsteen did not laugh.

The University Club dining room was quiet, dignified, and almost empty on New Year's Day. Most of the Texas alumni were home watching their football team on television, or in New Orleans, at the Sugar Bowl. On the top floor of one of Houston's tallest buildings, the dining room's sweeping windows offered a panoramic view of the city. Unfortunately, a driving winter storm was blurring the vista in pelting rain, mixed with sleet.

If the weather bothered David Kahn, he'd given no indication of it. Thrasher had offered to meet him at the airport, but Kahn turned down that idea and insisted he'd be there on time, weather notwithstanding.

"Hope the weather doesn't delay his plane," Thrasher mused, fingering his mug of ginger beer. His own flight from Portales had landed a half-hour late, and he'd taken a taxi to the Club.

"I called the airport," Ornsteen said. "His plane got in about an hour ago."

"Shouldn't take an hour—"

And there was Kahn at the door, in his powered wheelchair, pointing a knobby finger toward Thrasher. The maitre d' led the old man past the mostly empty tables and moved a chair away to make room for him between Thrasher and Ornsteen.

Kahn looked ghastly, his pallor gray, his bald pate mottled with liver spots. His health must be deteriorating, Thrasher thought. He was wearing a dark gray three-piece suit with a red and blue University of Pennsylvania tie knotted carefully at his wattled throat.

"Arthur," he wheezed.

Thrasher gestured toward Ornsteen. "You know Sid, of course."

"Certainly," said Kahn, without taking his beady eyes off Thrasher.

"Something to drink?" the maitre d' inquired in a servile whisper.

Kahn glanced with disdain at Ornsteen's iced tea and Thrasher's ginger beer, then looked up at the fawning man and said, "Jack Daniels, neat."

"Of course, sir."

"Sorry about the weather," Thrasher said.

Kahn mumbled something.

"Good day for soup," Ornsteen suggested as the maitre d' retreated. Kahn glared at him and the treasurer seemed to shrivel in his chair.

"Is the food here any good?" Kahn asked Thrasher. "Hard to find decent food outside Manhattan."

Thrasher made himself smile. "Well, I like it."

"Steak, I suppose."

"Among other things."

A waiter brought Kahn's drink and a trio of oversized menus. Kahn took a sip, then opened his menu, muttering, "Texas. The bigger something is, the better Texans like it."

"I'm from Arizona," Thrasher said. He looked toward Ornsteen, who seemed to be hiding behind his menu.

Kahn grumbled and muttered. Thrasher didn't ask him why he'd flown in; he figured that old Jenghis would bring up that subject when he was good and ready. Instead he talked about the solid progress the project was making. Kahn continued to grumble and mutter.

It wasn't until they were halfway through the soup course that Kahn finally put down his spoon and said, "Have you picked an insurance carrier yet?"

Thrasher turned to Ornsteen. "Sid, who've you been talking to about launch insurance?"

"There's not many companies who cover rocket launches," the treasurer replied. "There's an international consortium that's got most of the business."

"And they set their own prices," rasped Kahn.

"More or less," Ornsteen agreed.

"I'll handle the insurance," Kahn said.

Thrasher asked, "You'll pick a carrier . . . ?"

"No, I mean that I'll get one of my companies to draw up a policy for you. And I'll give you a better price than those Europeans, by damn."

"You will?" Ornsteen blurted.

"Yes, I will. Save you a bundle of cash."

"That's very generous of you, Mr. Kahn," said Ornsteen.

Thrasher said, "I didn't realize your interests included insurance, David."

With an irritated shake of his head, Kahn replied, "They haven't, until now. This Mars project of yours is making me move into new territory."

"I see."

"So I'll handle your launch insurance. And I'll give you a better deal than you could get anywhere else. Just make damned certain you don't blow up any of your rockets."

Ornsteen laughed shakily. Thrasher found himself thinking about Greeks bearing gifts.

YEAR THREE

1
PORTALES

Thrasher was leading a trio of astronauts—two men and a woman—through the cavernous hangar-like shed where the Mars spacecraft was taking shape.

Jessie Margulis had chosen the three, after more than a year of talking with various candidates and consultants. Thrasher had let Jessie take his pick, although he mentally kept a veto power for himself. He didn't want anyone he couldn't get along with to fly out to Mars.

Bill Polk had been Jessie's first choice, seconded by everyone who knew anything about astronauts. Thrasher had heard of Polk, distantly, as a man who had done several tours of duty aboard the International Space Station.

Polk had been an Air Force fighter jock, originally, before he transferred to NASA. He wasn't much taller than Thrasher himself, but solidly built, with sky blue eyes, thinning light brown hair, and an easy smile. Even in a windbreaker and jeans, he radiated competence. Thrasher liked him the first time he saw him.

"So this is the bird," he said once Thrasher stopped them in front of the completed Mars craft.

"This is it," Thrasher said. "Mars One. May it be the first of many."

The spacecraft loomed over them, aluminum skin gleaming in the overhead lights. Across the big, echoing room the backup hardware was being assembled, an exact duplicate of the Mars One spacecraft, ready to be used if any segment of the original article was lost or damaged. Thrasher had already started negotiations with the Smithsonian Institution and several other museums around the world for selling the backup once Mars One had safely made it to the red planet and back.

Thrasher had ordered all the workmen out of the area while he showed off the massive spacecraft to the astronauts. At one end of the bulbous structure was an empty shell, where the nuclear reactor and rocket nozzles would eventually be fitted. Up front was the big circular assembly where the Mars team would live and work on their way to the red planet. It reminded Thrasher of an enclosed Ferris wheel.

"Home sweet home," said Ignacio Velazquez, his soft tenor voice somewhere between admiration and awe.

Velazquez was a string bean, just over six feet tall but skinny as a scarecrow. His skin was the color of adobe brick, his eyes darkly brown; he had a warm, boyish smile on his lean, hollow-cheeked face. He had never been in space; he had joined NASA's last class of astronauts straight out of CalTech, but never got a chance to fly before the space agency cut back its human spaceflight program almost to zero. Despite Velazquez's inexperience, Polk had strongly recommended "Nacho," and Margulis had quickly agreed after one interview.

"It's big," said Judine McQuinn, the third member of the trio. She was tiny, almost elfin, with plain straight brown hair and a waif's wide, curious eyes. A doctor of space medicine, she had done two stints aboard the ISS, then retired from NASA when the human space program was gutted.

"It's got to be big," Polk said. "Got to house seven people for two years."

Pointing to the spindly ladder leading up to the hatch in the spacecraft's side, Thrasher asked, "Want to see her insides?"

He almost had to run to stay ahead of them.

Once they had all ducked through the hatch, Thrasher told them, "This is the cargo bay, where we'll store your food and other consumables." It was a big empty area, like a warehouse that hadn't opened for business yet. A series of green arrows along the deck marked what would one day be a passageway through the bins and shelves that would fill the space.

"Where's the air recycler?" Velazquez asked.

"Up forward." Thrasher pointed. "All the life-support equipment is grouped together."

Polk nodded. "Propulsion system in the rear, right?"

With a nod, Thrasher said, "Behind the shielding."

"Safety guys going to give you trouble about launching a nuclear reactor?" asked Polk.

"I hope not."

The expression on the astronaut's face seemed to say, *keep your fingers crossed, buddy.*

"From what I've seen of the schematics," McQuinn said, "the infirmary's in the wheel."

"Along with all the other living and working quarters."

She headed forward, along the green arrows. Thrasher and the other two astronauts followed her through a hatch, and down a man-wide metal tube with ladder rungs built into its side.

One by one, they squeezed through a hatch at the bottom of the tube and stood in a passageway that clearly curved up and out of sight in both directions.

"This is the wheel," said Thrasher. "The area where you'll spend most of the flight."

"Rotates to give us a feeling of gravity," Velazquez said.

"Yeah."

Judine McQuinn opened the nearest hatch in the passageway's bulkhead. They saw a compact cabin, with a built-in bunk, desk, and drawers.

"Neat," she said, appreciatively.

"Individual lavatories," Thrasher said, with some pride. "The engineers wanted a communal lav, but I figured you guys would appreciate some privacy."

"Six months," murmured Velazquez. "One way."

Polk grinned. "Better accommodations than the ISS."

They walked along the curving passageway, opening hatches and peering into the compartments where they would live and work on their way to Mars. McQuinn found the tiny infirmary and nodded appreciatively at its two beds and row of diagnostic machines.

At last they reached the point where they could no longer stand up straight: the wheel curved too steeply.

"Where's the command center?" Polk asked.

"Up that way," Thrasher replied, pointing.

"Let's see it."

"We'll have to go back outside and get the techies to rotate the wheel."

Polk eyed the other two astronauts, then said, "Can't they rotate the wheel while we're still in it?"

"Sure, but how're you going to stay on your feet with the deck rotating under you?"

"We can do it," McQuinn said, grinning. Velazquez smiled as he nodded agreement.

"Well, I don't know . . ."

"Come on, it'll be fun," Polk urged.

With some reluctance, Thrasher pulled out his phone and called the controllers.

"Rotate the wheel?" the answering voice sounded uncertain. "With you guys inside?"

With a bravado he didn't really feel, Thrasher said, "That's right. Rotate it until the command center's at the bottom. Slowly."

"Mr. Thrasher, are you sure?"

Feeling irritated, Thrasher insisted, "Yes, I'm sure. We'll be okay."

He heard the controllers muttering among themselves. Then a man's deep, stern voice said, "This is Bellows." The chief of the control team. "Are you sure you want us to rotate the wheel, Mr. Thrasher?"

"It won't cause any damage, will it?"

"No, sir, it shouldn't damage any of the equipment. But you might fall down and hurt yourself."

His cheeks flushing slightly, Thrasher said, "I can take care of myself. Spin 'er up. Slowly."

"Right." Another gabble of muttering voices, then Bellows announced, "Starting spin in ten seconds. Nine . . . eight . . ."

Thrasher tensed. He saw that Polk was grinning. Velazquez looked very serious, determined. McQuinn seemed totally relaxed, on the balls of her feet, knees bent slightly, arms outspread. This is like a game for them, they want to see who's going to fall on his face.

Thrasher gripped the frame of the nearest open hatch as Bellows intoned, " . . . three . . . two . . . one . . . initiating spin."

With a groan and a growl of diesel motors outside the spacecraft, the deck began to slide out from beneath Thrasher's feet. He held onto the hatch frame grimly. The three astronauts were nimbly stepping along, calmly keeping their feet like a trio of kids skipping through a barrel roll at an amusement park.

Thrasher did his best to stay upright, but the world was tilting absurdly and he realized that hanging onto the hatch frame was a mistake. The damned hatch was moving upward! He had to let go. The deck was sliding along. He tried to step with it, slipped, staggered, flailed his arms to no avail and finally did a pratfall, landing on his rump with a painful thump, arms and legs flapping wildly.

Polk grabbed one of his arms, McQuinn the other. Velazquez tried to keep a straight face but finally broke into a loud guffaw as they hauled Thrasher to his feet and held him up upright.

"Just get the feeling of it," Polk told him.

"Like dancing," said McQuinn.

Thrasher grinned shakily, feeling totally foolish in their grasp. With their help, though, he managed to step along as the floor rotated beneath them.

At last the spinning stopped. They were in an open area now, consoles on both sides of them and a wide window that looked out on the bare walls and metal bracing of the shed's roof.

Still grasping his arm, Polk led Thrasher to one of the chairs. He sank into it gratefully.

Velazquez could barely contain his merriment. "It's a shame I didn't use my phone to take a picture of you, Mr. Thrasher. I could've used it to jack you up for a big raise."

Thrasher grinned weakly.

More solicitously, Judine McQuinn bent over him and asked, "Are you all right?"

He nodded. "Nothing's hurt except my dignity."

"That's okay," said Polk. "You accepted the challenge without complaining." And he patted Thrasher on the shoulder.

Thrasher felt a warm wave of gratitude flood through him. This was a test, he realized. They wanted to see if I'd go through with it. It was a test, and I passed it! Sort of.

2
TUCSON

I'm becoming a juggler, Thrasher realized.

He was driving through the blazing desert sun from the Arizona Inn to the University of Arizona campus, ostensibly to check on Professor Winninger's progress with the virtual reality system. Actually, he was looking forward to seeing Kristin Anders again.

It was still only May, but the dashboard display showing the temperature outside his rental car was already nearing ninety. Everything's air-conditioned, Thrasher reminded himself. Just don't park in the sun; the car becomes an oven in just a few minutes.

He had dated Kristin several times, just dinner and maybe a film on campus and then a brief goodnight kiss. Nothing more. He found he enjoyed her company, and as she began to tell him more about her life he started to understand and even sympathize with her.

So we don't go to bed, he thought as he entered the cool shadows of the parking building. She's good company and she seems to enjoy being with me. Up to a point.

For sex, there's Victoria. Thrasher grinned happily at the memories of their antics together. She was coming down to the Inn tomorrow night. Plenty of sex then.

He spent most of the morning on Mars. Standing in a bare workroom, wearing the VR helmet and a full-body sensor suit, he walked across the surface of Mars, picked up rocks, listened to the thin, keening wind, watched a dust storm approaching over the hilly horizon.

Kristin's voice said in his earphones, "You're experiencing what our grad student, Tony, is doing over in the next building. He's transmitting what he's doing to you."

"It's really good," Thrasher said.

He felt his right hand fumbling around for something.

"What's happening?"

"Open your right hand."

Thrasher opened his hand and there, in the palm of his spacesuit's glove, was a tiny bar of metal.

"What's this?"

The grad student's voice came through. "It's a bar magnet, Mr. Thrasher. We're going to write your initials in the Martian sand."

Before he could reply, Kristin explained, "The sand is mostly iron ores. A magnet can move them around."

Thrasher felt himself bending down and sweeping the magnet across the sand. "A D T" appeared in the sand.

He laughed, delighted. "I've put my initials on Mars!"

Thrasher had lunch with Kristin, Tony, and Professor Winninger in the campus student lounge. The place was crowded and noisy with students and faculty lined up at the counters, carrying trays to tables, talking, gesturing, calling to people at nearby tables.

"We've worked out the problems with the transmitting equipment," the professor was saying, "thanks to Kristin."

"Tony's been very helpful," she quickly added.

The grad student actually blushed.

Thrasher said, "So we can have one of our team go out on the surface of Mars with the VR rig, and whatever he or she does, our VR users here on Earth will see and feel?"

"That's right," said Winninger.

"There will be a time lag," Kristin said. "The distance to Mars means it'll take anywhere from eight to forty minutes to transmit the signal to Earth, depending on where the two planets are in their orbits."

"But the user on Earth won't notice any lag," said Tony.

"So he'll feel like he's actually on Mars," Thrasher said happily. He thought, Sampson's getting half the profits from the mission, but we'll clean up on sales of the equipment and virtual reality games. And school courses. And erotic simulations. Then he corrected himself: porn.

Professor Winninger's heart-shaped face grew more serious. "Of course, when Mars is in opposition the transmission's going to suffer."

"Opposition?" Thrasher asked.

"When the Sun gets between Earth and Mars," Kristin explained.

"Will that affect our regular communications?"

"Not so much," said the professor. "But the VR transmission is a much higher-capacity signal. It will be seriously degraded, I'm afraid."

Tony offered, "Unless there's a relay station parked along Mars' orbit. Then you could bounce the signals from Mars to the relay and from the relay to Earth."

"A relay station," Thrasher mused.

"Makes sense," said Winninger.

"If we can afford it," said Thrasher.

Thrasher and Kristin had dinner in a little Mexican cantina, on the other side of town from the campus and the Inn. Lots of spicy food, big families crowding around the tables, noise and Latin music blaring from the ceiling loudspeakers. Afterward, as he walked her across the dusty parking lot to her worn old Toyota RAV4, she abruptly stopped and looked up.

The parking lot was so poorly lit that the sky was clearly visible. Thrasher saw thousands of stars glittering in the dry desert air.

"Look." Kristin pointed.

A bright red star hung low over the hills, unwavering, steady.

"Mars?" he asked, in a whisper.

"Mars," Kristin said.

"It's beautiful," he said. "And so are you."

She turned and melted into his arms. He kissed her tenderly, then more eagerly.

But Kristin disengaged. "I . . . I'm sorry. I shouldn't have done that."

"Why not? I enjoyed it. Didn't you?"

"I've got to get home, Art. My babysitter expects me before ten."

"But . . ."

In the dim light of the stars, Kristin seemed genuinely upset. "Art, please . . . forgive me. I can't. Not tonight."

He could see concern and conflict on her lovely face, tears in her eyes.

"I understand," he said, with a wistful sigh. Then he went on, "But the next time you come out to dinner with me, tell your sitter that you won't be home until morning."

She broke into a smile. "It won't be easy to find a sitter that'd be willing."

Thrasher grinned back at her. "Money is no object. Within reason."

3
ARIZONA INN

Reprobate. Thrasher heard Linda's disapproving voice in his mind as he waited in the sitting room of his suite for Victoria to show up. It was early evening, but his stomach was starting to growl hungrily.

He was watching a financial news station on television. The stock market was down again, unemployment was up, the price of petroleum had jumped sixty cents per barrel in the past week. Strangely, though, Thrasher Digital's stock price was holding up, despite the new downturn. Be grateful for small miracles, Thrasher told himself.

Shaking his head at the screen, he wondered why the dummies in Washington couldn't understand that investing in space technology has been the biggest government stimulus to the economy since World War II.

It isn't that they don't understand it, he thought. It's the fossil fuel lobbies. Big oil and big coal has the entire goddamned government bound hand and foot.

I should talk. I'm investing in space technology and it's driving me broke. We'll go to Mars and I'll go to the poorhouse, the way things are running. Our stock price can't hold up forever; sooner or later it's going to go down the toilet.

The phone rang. Thrasher leaned over and picked up the handset.

"I'm here!" said Vicki brightly.

"Meet you in the bar," he said, clicking off the TV and getting to his feet.

Victoria was sitting at one of the tiny round tables near the bar, dressed in a v-necked black blouse and knee-length skirt, also black. Pearl necklace and earrings. Her curly auburn hair was set in a new style he hadn't noticed before. Very sophisticated, he thought.

The piano player broke into "Fly Me to the Moon" as soon as Thrasher entered the room. Got to find him a song about Mars, he thought.

He saw that Vicki had already ordered a tall drink garnished with fruit slices and cherries and a long, flexible blood-red straw. One of the cocktail waitresses placed a mug of ginger beer on the table as Thrasher sat down.

The benefits of generous tipping, he thought as he leaned over and pecked at Vicki's proffered cheek. They remember what you want and bring it right away.

"I have news," Vicki said, her eyes gleaming.

"Well, you're a newswoman, aren't you?" he joked.

"I'm going to Chicago!"

He sipped at the ginger beer. "For how long?"

"I've got a new job! With the Chicago bureau of Global News! Isn't that wonderful?"

He saw that she was excited, elated. But he knew that Chicago was a thousand miles from Tucson, or Portales, or Houston.

"Congratulations," he said weakly.

"You don't seem all that happy for me," Victoria said, pouting. "This is a big step up for me."

"Chicago's pretty far away."

"You've got your executive jet," she said.

"For now."

"What's that supposed to mean?"

"I'm getting strapped for cash. I might have to sell it . . . or at least trade it in for a plane that's less expensive to operate."

"Really?"

He sighed. "Well, anyway, congratulations on the new job."

"I don't suppose we'll see each other as often," Vicki said. Flatly. No sentiment.

Thrasher sipped at his ginger beer. "Maybe—"

"But you won't be all that lonely, will you?" she said, her voice suddenly cold, accusative.

"What do you mean by that?"

"You'll still have your blonde girlfriend here in Tucson, won't you?"

Thrasher sputtered ginger beer. "She's not my girlfriend," he protested. "She's a scientist at the university."

"And you've been dating her. You had dinner with her last night, didn't you?"

"You've been spying on me!"

"I'm a newswoman, Art," she said—smugly, Thrasher thought. "And you're an important man."

"But—"

"We'll still see each other," Victoria went on. "Just not as often." Then she added, "After all, I want to keep in touch with the Mars project. It was my ticket to the Chicago job, you know."

He just sat there, dumbfounded.

Dinner was awkward. Thrasher realized he was being dumped, and it shook him. Victoria seemed oblivious to his discomfort: she chattered away about finding an apartment in Chicago and keeping her contacts with her old compatriots in Albuquerque.

"I'll pop down to Las Cruces to cover your rocket launches, of course. Global's already got a guy at the Cape; he'll cover your launches from there."

Thrasher nodded and mumbled.

Almost automatically, he took Victoria back to the bar for an after-dinner drink. The piano player went through old-time romantic tunes; Gershwin, Porter, the Beatles. Thrasher sipped morosely at his ginger beer.

At last Victoria finished her cognac and smiled at him. "Well, aren't you going to invite me to your room?"

Thrasher nodded.

Dimpling into an impish smile, she said, "After all, I don't have anyplace else to stay tonight."

He got his feet and numbly led her back to his suite. Once he had closed the door behind them, Victoria flung her arms around his neck and kissed him passionately.

"Let's have one for old times' sake," she whispered.

He made a sardonic little smile. "Let's win one for the Gipper."

The sex was very good, very dexterous. Once they started removing each other's clothes, Thrasher forgot about everything except the here and now.

But in the morning, when he woke up, Victoria was gone. She had left a note on the coffeetable in the sitting room:

Thanks for the memories, Art. Have fun with the blonde.

Thrasher felt totally stunned. So this is what it's like to be dumped, he thought. Hell, not even my second wife pushed me out the window like this.

4
HOUSTON

"Are you all right?" Linda asked.

Thrasher was sitting glumly at his desk, staring blankly at the Houston skyline.

"I'm fine," he said automatically.

"You've been in a funk since you got back from Tucson," said Linda. She looked concerned. "What's bothering you?"

"Nothing," he said, with a shake of his head. He sat up straighter in his desk chair. Lord, if it's this obvious to Linda, I must be moping around like a lovesick teenager. And he realized that he had been doing just that.

"I'm okay," he said. "What's on the agenda for this morning?"

"Conference call at ten with Mr. Margulis and the astronauts—"

"Sounds like a pop musical group," Thrasher quipped. "Margulis and the Astronauts."

Linda broke into a grin. But she said, "This is about the launch schedule."

"Right."

"Lunch with Mr. Ornsteen."

"Break out the antacids," Thrasher grumbled.

"And Mr. Reynolds wants to talk with you as soon as possible."

"Get him on the line, will you?"

"Right." Linda started to leave the office, but turned back to him. "Don't forget the board of directors meeting next week."

He nodded. Sampson's going to attend, he knew. Should be interesting. Maybe I ought to wear some body armor.

Jessie Margulis was clearly upset. Thrasher had plugged the phone call into the big flat display screen on his office wall, and now it showed the engineer and the three astronauts in split-screen views. Polk looked nettled, Velazquez worried, McQuinn puzzled. But Jessie—bland, steady Jessie—looked as if he was ready to tear his hair out.

He was actually twisting his goatee in his fingers. "It's going to mess up our schedule, Art! It's going to set everything back by six months, maybe more."

"Just because of a postponement—"

Bill Polk broke in, "This isn't just a postponement, Art. It's a roadblock."

"Reed," Thrasher muttered.

"Reed," Polk agreed.

"It's not Reed," Margulis countered. "The safety office has nothing to do with this."

Polk smiled tolerantly. "The hell it isn't Reed. This has Reed's fingerprints all over it."

Thrasher made a placating gesture with his hands. "Let me see if I've got this straight. ILS has bumped our launch of the first segment of Mars One because they got a priority demand to use the launch pad."

"From the Air Force, not NASA," Margulis pointed out.

Polk said, "There's three working pads at the Cape, plus two more at Patrick Air Force Base, next door."

"So you think that Reed's put up the Air Force to push us off the launch pad."

"Off the launch schedule!" Margulis yelped. "We've lost our slot in the schedule and we're supposed to go to the end of the line."

"And that'll set us back how long?"

"Six months, maybe more."

Thrasher drummed his fingers on his desktop.

Polk said, "This is the way Reed operates. I've seen him stick knives in people's backs for as long as I can remember."

"Who's in charge of scheduling the launches?" Thrasher asked.

"Mr. Yamagata, the ILS chief," said Velazquez.

"But he can't turn down a priority request from the Air Force," Margulis pointed out. "This is supposed to be some top-security national defense launch."

"And it pops up all of a sudden and pushes us off the launch schedule," Thrasher muttered.

"Something to do with the mess in Iran, I think," Velazquez said.

Thrasher realized he was drumming his fingers again. He balled his hands into fists and put them on his lap.

Polk said, "We can't argue against it. National defense and all that."

"When do they want to launch?"

"Six weeks from now," Margulis answered.

"We were scheduled for five weeks from now, weren't we?"

"Yeah, but they'll need a couple of weeks to put their bird on the pad and check it out. Same as we do, Art. You set up the bird and check everything out on the pad: payload, propulsion, guidance . . . takes a couple of weeks."

Thrasher asked, "Could we move up our launch date? Get our bird off before the Air Force moves in?"

Margulis gaped at him. "Move our launch date *up*? We'd have to push everything ahead by at least three weeks."

"So we launch in two weeks instead of five. Can't we do that?"

For several heartbeats none of them said a word. Then they all tried to talk at once.

Margulis outshouted the three astronauts. "You can't push a rocket launch like that! This isn't like playing with Tinkertoys, Art. There's a whole list of things that have got to be done, in their proper sequence, and—"

"From what you told me, Jessie, you need to have the bird on the pad for two weeks. Right?"

"Right."

"So we put the bird on the pad two weeks from now, spend the next two weeks doing whatever you guys have to do, and then fire her off. What's wrong with that?"

"We're not ready—"

"Get ready. Work overtime. Night shifts, if you have to."

Polk made a tight little grin. "After all, it's not a manned launch."

"Crewed," McQuinn murmured.

"I mean," Polk said, "even if the sucker blows up on the pad, nobody's going to get hurt."

Except Sid Ornsteen, Thrasher said to himself. He'll see fifty million bucks go up in smoke and have a stroke.

"The launch is insured, isn't it?" Velazquez asked.

Thrasher nodded. By Dave Kahn's outfit, he recalled silently.

Aloud, he told them, "I don't want to blow up the bird. It'll be carrying the first piece of Mars One into orbit."

"But pushing the schedule ahead like this," Margulis muttered. "I don't know . . ."

Thrasher grinned at him. "I know we'll be taking a risk, Jess. But what the hell choice do we have?"

Silently, he added, So I'm doing a high-wire act without a net. No risk, no gain. It's like meeting a good-looking woman and maneuvering her into bed. If you don't take the chance, you'll never get to where you want to go.

Polk had an expectant smile on his face. Velazquez and McQuinn looked like spectators at a prizefight, wondering who was going to win. Margulis was frowning and mumbling to himself.

"Tell you what, Jess," said Thrasher. "You think it over for twenty-four hours. If you tell me it's impossible, I'll drop the idea. But it's got to be really impossible. Not just difficult. Not just troublesome. I don't care if you and your whole team lose sleep or have to spend the next few weekends away from their families. Unless it's utterly, totally, irreversibly impossible, *I want that bird launched*!"

Margulis nodded, a little sullenly, Thrasher thought. But he nodded. The three astronauts looked relieved.

"Somebody's going to have to get ILS to agree to the hurry-up," said Polk.

"I'll talk to Yamagata," Thrasher said.

Polk's grin grew into a crooked smile. "Reed'll shit a brick when he finds out about this."

"Good," said Thrasher. "Let him split his guts."

⚙ 5 ⚙
KENNEDY SPACE FLIGHT CENTER

"Do you have any idea of how many pieces of heaven and earth I had to move to accommodate you?" asked Saito Yamagata.

Thrasher grinned at him. "I appreciate it. And I'm sure that Santa Claus has marked you down on his good list."

The two men were in the visitor's stands, watching the big Delta IV rocket standing tall and gleaming bright against the cloudy Florida sky. It was early morning, and a cool breeze was blowing in off the ocean. Still Thrasher felt as if he were standing fully dressed in a steam bath.

A small cluster of other onlookers were there, most of them corporate employees or invited VIPs. Each of them had been carefully vetted both by the NASA visitor screening team and Mars, Inc.'s own security group. Sid Ornsteen stood at Thrasher's other side, looking more nervous than usual.

Thrasher half expected Hamilton Reed to show up, maybe with a monkey wrench in the form of some new piece of red tape to hinder the launch. I've got to find a way around that sneaking sonofabitch, he thought.

Reed had refused to okay launching components of the Mars spacecraft's nuclear propulsion system. Not in so many words. Not in writing. But he was holding up approval for launching the nuclear system, claiming that the Nuclear Regulatory Commission was reviewing the application.

There's got to be some other place where we can launch the nuke, Thrasher said to himself, instead of here at the Cape. Someplace where Reed can't strangle us. Maybe the European launch center down in South America.

Jessie Margulis was in the control center with the rest of the launch crew.

"One minute and counting," came the announcement over the loudspeakers.

Standing in the row in front of Thrasher, Bill Polk turned to face him and gave a thumbs-up signal. "Lookin' good," he said.

Thrasher nodded. It had been a hectic few weeks, moving the launch date up, rushing to get everything done in half the usual time.

But there she was, ready to go. The Delta IV's upper stage bulged noticeably where the first segment of the Mars One spacecraft was stowed. The launch crew had joked about the baby bump. Some called it a pregnant bird.

"Thirty seconds and counting."

Leaning toward Yamagata, Thrasher said in a lowered voice, "Seriously, we all appreciate everything you've done to help us. I want to thank you."

His face impassive, Yamagata said, "Hold the congratulations until the bird leaves its nest."

"Fifteen seconds and counting."

Thrasher realized his tongue was clamped between his teeth. He consciously pulled it away. No sense biting it off, he told himself. Still, every nerve in his body tensed as the countdown proceeded.

"Five . . . four . . . three . . ."

The Delta IV's main engines roared to life. Smoke and steam billowed from the launch pad. The noise rattled Thrasher down to his soul.

Then the strap-on solid rocket boosters ignited and the huge vehicle lumbered off the launch stand and began to climb, stately as a skyscraper lifting to the heavens, then faster, faster, torrents of sound washing over the visitors, bathing them in the power and beauty of the accelerating rocket.

The little crowd roared as the Delta IV dwindled to a bright star flashing against the cloudy sky.

"Go, baby, go!" someone yelled.

It exploded. Thrasher flinched as the fast-rising star blossomed into a flash of flame. The crowd gasped.

"Booster separation," Yamagata said calmly.

Thrasher's heart resumed beating. It's okay. Normal. Routine. Everything's on track.

He couldn't see the bird anymore. It was too high, and a rack of clouds was gliding across his field of view. People began to clap their hands, applauding the successful launch.

"Good launch," said Yamagata. "Let's go to the control center and watch the orbital insertion."

His knees still weak, Thrasher followed the ILS executive down from the observation stands, Polk and Ornsteen trailing behind him. They walked through the tropical humidity toward the concrete building that housed the mission control center.

It's like walking through soup, Thrasher thought. He was perspiring heavily, his summerweight jacket feeling sodden, rumpled, despite the breeze from the ocean.

Ornsteen came up beside him, "I thought she blew up," he confessed.

"Just separating the solid rocket boosters," Thrasher said, like a veteran.

Polk said, "Now comes the tricky part, inserting the payload into the proper orbit."

"Does it matter that much?" Thrasher asked as they walked through the soggy heat. "I mean, as long as it gets into any orbit, you'll be able to reach it, won't you?"

"Sure," said the astronaut, "but every move you make up there takes extra energy, which means it costs extra fuel. If she doesn't reach the proper orbit, or if the aero shield doesn't separate, if the payload doesn't deploy . . . there's still a lot that can go wrong."

"Thanks for the cheerful news," Thrasher groused.

The control center was abuzz with quiet intensity, the four-person launch team at their consoles, the big wall screens showing data coming in from the spacecraft's sensors. Thrasher noted the graph that displayed the rocket's planned trajectory and its actual track. The two curves overlay each other snugly.

The launch team chief, a chubby Japanese-American in white coveralls bearing the ILS logo, smiled at Yamagata.

"Everything on track, sir."

Yamagata smiled back at him. "Good."

Thrasher watched, feeling totally useless, as the payload separated from the Delta IV booster and the upper stage engines kicked in.

"Orbital insertion in seven minutes," announced the launch team chief.

"Lookin' good," Polk muttered.

The wall screens all went blank for an instant. Thrasher felt his stomach go hollow. The screens came back on, but no data was flashing across them. They blinked like a man suddenly hit by an overpowering light.

"Anomaly!" shouted one of the controllers.

Thrasher saw that the curve displaying the craft's track had abruptly stopped. The launch team chief scuttled to one of the consoles and bent over the man sitting at it. Yamagata looked suddenly tense, wired.

"What's happening?" Ornsteen whispered.

"She blew up," said Yamagata, his face grim. "The upper stage exploded."

Thrasher's vision went blurry; his eyes were filled with tears.

⓸ 6 ⓸
BOARD MEETING

White-bearded Gregory Sampson looked like a stern, almost angry biblical patriarch. "How much does this set us back?" he demanded.

The meeting of Mars, Inc.'s board of directors was taking place as scheduled, in the corporation's Portales headquarters, two weeks after the disaster at Cape Canaveral.

Thrasher had barely slept the whole long, agonizing time. Whenever he closed his eyes he saw the TV news programs showing the telescope view of the rocket's upper stage blowing itself to bits. Interviews, inquiries, reviews of the launch procedures, discussions with the insurance carrier, with Yamagata's ILS people, with NASA's safety office. Thrasher tossed in bed fitfully, seeing in his mind's eye Hamilton Reed smiling his beady-eyed smile as the accident investigation team reported their findings.

"We shouldn't have pushed the launch schedule ahead like we did," Jessie Margulis moaned, shaking his head mournfully. "We pushed too hard, too fast."

Thrasher appreciated the "we," but he knew that Jessie was blaming his decision, his pushing the launch team.

The blame for the accident was fixed on a faulty fuel valve on the upper stage's main engine. The engine exploded, igniting the liquid hydrogen and liquid oxygen propellant tanks in the blink of an eye. The first segment of the Mars One spacecraft now rested at the bottom of the Atlantic, in a thousand pieces.

Despite all the inspections and safety checks, Thrasher raged to himself, despite our zero-defects procedure, one lousy valve failed and blew the bird to hell.

"We'll go forward," he replied a hundred times to news reporters. "We're going to Mars. This accident won't stop us."

But his own board of directors was not so sure.

Sitting at the head of the conference table, weary and baggy-eyed from lack of sleep, Thrasher replied to Sampson, "It's pretty bad. We have the backup hardware, of course, but it's going to take several weeks before it's ready to launch, and even longer before we can get on the launch schedule at the Cape again."

Still looking like a disapproving grandfather, Sampson growled, "I understand there's also a problem with the insurance coverage."

Before Thrasher could reply, David Kahn answered in his grating voice, "There's some question about whether this accident could be attributed to an Act of God. If that's the finding, then the insurance company doesn't have to pay out." Thrasher thought the gnomish old man looked almost smug about it.

"It wasn't an Act of God," Thrasher replied, as evenly as he could manage. "The investigating team found that a faulty propellant valve on the rocket engine was the cause of the explosion."

"That's just a preliminary finding, from what I hear," said Kahn.

Will Portal, sitting halfway down the table, looked alarmed. "You mean we might not even get insurance coverage?"

"We'll get it," Thrasher said, hoping that it was true.

"If you hadn't accelerated the launch date, Artie," rasped the elder Kahn, "we wouldn't be in this fix."

"And if we grew wings we could fly to Mars on our own," Thrasher retorted.

Charles Kahn, looking every inch the dashing corporate executive in his blue three-piece suit and expensive tan, countered, "The real question is, where does this leave us? Can we continue—"

"We're going on," Thrasher said flatly. "The program continues."

"Does it?" asked Sampson. "Can we absorb this loss and stay afloat?"

"We're going on," Thrasher insisted. "Accidents happen. We'll get past this and move on."

"Throwing good money after bad?" Sampson asked, breaking into a sly grin.

"We'll stay within budget," said Thrasher.

"Even if the insurance doesn't come through?"

"Even if hell freezes over," Thrasher snapped.

David Kahn focused his cold eyes on Thrasher. "Our budget is strained to the maximum, Artie. You know that, I know that, the entire board knows it. Another accident like this and—"

Simmering inwardly, Thrasher said, "It would help if you told your insurance people to stop waltzing around and pay up."

"They're within their rights to see if this falls into the 'Acts of God' clause."

"They're throwing fine print at us," Thrasher complained.

With a boyish smile, Will Portal asked softly, "Instead of trying to dissect the past, why don't we look at where we are and where we're going?"

Thrasher shot him a grateful glance. "Right. We're preparing the backup hardware for launch—"

"And if that blows up?" Sampson asked.

"We're up shit's creek," David Kahn wheezed. "In a leaky canoe, without a paddle."

"So what do you want to do?" Thrasher demanded.

"Cut our losses. Cancel the entire operation."

"No."

"I'm not going to put another cent of my money into this," Kahn said.

Jabbing a finger at the liver-spotted old man, Thrasher insisted, "You signed an agreement for five years' worth of funding. You try to pull out now and I'll sue you for what you owe, plus damages."

"Go right ahead. I have more lawyers than you do. Better ones, too."

Sampson hauled himself to his feet. "Gentlemen, gentlemen," he said, making a calming gesture with both his hands, "let's not fight amongst ourselves. We've had a setback, but Will is right: we ought to be moving forward, not filling the air with recriminations and threats."

Thrasher felt puzzled, but grateful. Greg wants to toss me out on my butt, he knew, but he's telling Jenghis to cool it. Maybe he really wants us to succeed.

Sampson went on, "I move that we offer Artie a vote of confidence in his leadership."

Mumbles and head shaking up and down the conference table.

Then Sampson added, "Of course, if we have one more disaster like this, I would expect Artie to either resign or cancel the project altogether."

I'll die first, Thrasher told himself. And he heard his father's last words again: *Do something you can be proud of, something worth doing.*

Mars. That's something we can both be proud of, Dad.

7
HOUSTON

Thrasher spent the next Sunday walking a real estate agent through his mansion out in River Oaks. The woman was sharp-eyed, her shoulder length hair a shade of golden blonde that came only from the best salons, very stylishly dressed in a cranberry red skirted suit that she described as her "church-goin' clothes."

"It's very impressive, Mr. Thrasher," she said, her voice restrained, well modulated, with only a tiny bit of insistence showing through.

"I was thinking of asking six mill for it," Thrasher said. He knew it was nowhere near enough to help with the Mars project, but at least it would bring him some pocket money and cut off the drain of upkeep on a house he hadn't slept in since Vicki Zane had moved to Chicago.

The woman pursed her lips. "That's a bit on the high side, considering today's market conditions."

"Really?"

"If you want to move it quickly, I'd peg the price around four million, four and a half."

Thrasher sucked in a breath. "Make it five."

"But you said you wanted to move it quickly."

"Five."

"Four-eight. That will attract buyers and offer you some room for negotiating."

"Okay," he said, feeling a little desperate. "Four million eight." To himself he added, I'll invest it in a nice safe CD and live off the interest. For a while.

"I heard about the accident, of course," said Bart Rutherford. "Anything I can do to help?"

Thrasher leaned back in his desk chair and stared at the retired engineer's image on his phone screen. Rutherford was apparently in his home on the Pacific coast, sitting in a big recliner, wearing an unbuttoned flowered shirt. His long blond hair was slicked back, glistening, as if he had just stepped out of a shower, or maybe the surf. Through the window behind him Thrasher could see a clear blue California sky with gulls soaring past.

"The investigating team found the problem," Thrasher replied. "Bad valve on the fuel injector of the upper stage's main engine."

"So I heard," said Rutherford. "Those injectors are usually very reliable."

"This one wasn't."

Rutherford looked perfectly relaxed and happy. But he asked, "Did your investigating team look into the possibilities of deliberate tinkering?"

"Deliberate . . . you mean sabotage?"

With a shrug, Rutherford said, "Just an idea that popped into my mind."

"Who in the world would want to sabotage us?" Thrasher asked, yet in his mind a list of suspects sprang up: Greg Sampson, Hamilton Reed, the Chinese . . .

"I'd start by looking at the people who inspected that valve and okayed it."

"The government investigators have already done that, I'm sure."

"Maybe," Rutherford said. "But have they checked the guys' bank records?"

"That's ridiculous!" Thrasher snapped. But immediately he added, "I think."

"Think about it some more, Art." Rutherford said it mildly, almost as if they were discussing the weather.

Thrasher sat behind his desk, his thoughts tumbling wildly. A saboteur? Somebody working for me deliberately caused the accident?

Rutherford said, "I have a friend who's a pretty sharp private investigator. Maybe she could help. She's not connected with you, so she'll be able to operate pretty freely."

Shaking his head, Thrasher objected, "I don't want to start a witch hunt."

"If you do have a saboteur somewhere in your outfit, he might try to strike again."

"Or she," Thrasher muttered.

"Or she."

"Is this investigator discreet? Can he be trusted?"

"She," said Rutherford. "She's handled several insurance cases. Maybe I can arrange a meeting with her for you."

Still feeling uncertain about it, Thrasher heard himself say, "Okay, Bart. Have her talk directly to me. Nobody else, not even my secretary."

Rutherford nodded solemnly. "Will do."

"Thanks."

"Oh, by the way," the engineer said, his face lighting up, "I've had some conversations with the Astrolaunch people. And Boeing. They're both working on a hypersonic passenger-carrying transport, but at a low level. Just computer designs and simulations. Too big an investment for them to do much more."

Glad to be dealing with something more concrete than sniffing around for saboteurs, Thrasher asked, "And?"

"I've accepted a consulting job with Astrolaunch, to see how their existing orbital launching hardware might be modified to a commercial surface-to-surface transport."

"Good."

"Boeing's tough competition, you know."

"I don't mind having two outfits working toward the same goal. Competition can be healthy."

Rutherford shrugged nonchalantly. "Easy for you to say, Art. No matter who loses this competition, you'll win. Houston to anywhere on Earth in less than an hour."

"Once you get through the airport," Thrasher reminded him.

⊛ 8 ⊛
PORTALES

"I want our own people inspecting the components of the next Delta IV we use," Thrasher said.

Jessie Margulis gaped at him. "What do you mean?"

They were standing in the assembly shed, where the Mars One spacecraft loomed over them, missing the segment that had been flown to Cape Canaveral and lost in the accident. Thrasher looked at the gaping hole in the gleaming flank of the vessel and thought of a badly wounded animal.

The backup modules rested on individual cradles across the cavernous chamber. A team of technicians were clambering around the segment that would be sent to the Cape for launching, their voices echoing off the shed's metal walls and ceiling.

"Our own inspectors," said Thrasher, over the noise from the technicians. "Separate from the ILS team. Zero defects on the launch rocket, just like the stuff we build ourselves."

"But that'll add to our cost and slow down the schedule, Art."

"I know. But that's what I want."

Margulis seemed to have aged five years since the accident. His little goatee was frayed, his eyes bloodshot, his sandy hair noticeably gray at the temples.

Clearly upset, the program chief erupted, "How the hell do you expect me to keep on this schedule when you want to add another layer of delay? I can't do it, Art! This'll break our backs."

Thrasher shouted back, "We can't afford to have another launch failure, Jess. I want our own people inspecting every mother-loving weld, valve, circuit board, wiring assembly . . . every goddamned thing that goes into the next booster."

"ILS won't stand for that."

"Yes they will. I've already talked to Yamagata about it."

"You're killing us!"

"Do you want another goddamned bird blown up?"

"Do you want to stay on schedule or not?"

Thrasher realized the technicians had stopped their work and were staring at them.

More softly, he said, "Jess, this is how it's going to be. Period. End of discussion."

Margulis just stood there, his usually soft brown eyes glaring, his chest heaving.

Thrasher said, "Have our inspection team work on a late shift. I'll authorize the overtime. That way it won't delay the schedule. Put our team in competition with Yamagata's, give them bonuses for any faults they discover. Okay?"

For several heartbeats Margulis said nothing. At last he breathed an unenthusiastic, "Okay."

"Thanks, Jess." Thrasher patted his shoulder.

"You're the boss," said Margulis. Thrasher heard his unspoken complaint, *but I wish you stayed in your office and let me do my job.*

Reynold R. Reynolds had more bad news for Thrasher when he got back to the partitioned cubbyhole he used as an office in the Portales headquarters.

Linda, in Houston, had relayed a phone message from the Washington rep about the Nuclear Regulatory Commission.

R Cubed's fleshy face looked dismally unhappy on the phone screen. "NRC's been up in arms since the launch failure," he said, his voice heavy. "They're dead-set against letting you launch a nuclear reactor."

Thrasher bit back a reply, knowing that he was watching a recording.

"I'm trying to get a meeting set up with the chairman, but his people are trying to duck out of it," Reynolds went on. "I'm pulling some strings with the Senate committee people who oversee the NRC, maybe that'll help."

To himself Thrasher complained, we've gone over the safety procedures with those bean-counters a dozen times. Even if the bird blows up on launch the reactor's so heavily shielded that it won't be damaged, won't release any radioactive material. Like the black box on an airliner: the plane can crash and burn but the black box will stay intact.

Yet he knew that the facts were being overwhelmed by human emotions. The fear of a rocket exploding and showering the landscape with radioactive debris outweighed all the facts in the world.

And if they couldn't launch the reactor, then the nuclear propulsion system wouldn't work and they'd never be able to head for Mars.

"Mother of Mercy," Thrasher muttered to himself, "is this the end of Rico?"

By the time he got back to his office in Houston, Thrasher had another surprise waiting for him.

As he trudged through the outer office, Linda handed him his usual mug of ginger beer and told him, "Victoria Zane called this afternoon. She's coming to town tomorrow."

"Coming here?" Thrasher's face lit up.

Linda's face was totally serious. With a nod, she said, "She wants to interview you. In your office."

"Oh."

"She said Global News wants to find out how you can keep on going, after the accident and all."

"She wants to do an obituary," said Thrasher.

Linda stood in front of her desk, taut with barely-controlled resentment. She said, "Turn her down."

"What?"

"She's using you. She's been using you all along. You're the reason Global hired her."

He shook his head. "It was that article she wrote for *The New Yorker*. That's what got her the attention."

"The article she wrote while you two were sleeping together."

Thrasher saw that Linda was seething with anger. At me or at her? he wondered. Or at both of us?

Linda went on, "God knows who she slept with to get *The New Yorker* to take the piece."

"That's not fair," Thrasher snapped.

Linda's angry expression crumbled. Tears filled her eyes. "I know it's not fair. It's just that when I think of how she manipulated you, used you, I get so . . . so . . ."

She ran out of words, turned on her heel and rushed out of the office, leaving Thrasher standing there with the mug of ginger beer in one hand, his briefcase in the other, feeling totally dumbfounded.

◎ 9 ◎
INTERWIEW

Thrasher slept poorly that night, and when he did doze off his dreams were a wild jumble of Victoria gloating over his naked body, Hamilton Meek smiling his sneaky little smile as Thrasher searched for something that he had lost but couldn't remember what it was, the Nuclear Regulatory Commission looming over him like a panel of judges condemning him to death, Linda smoldering with righteous anger and his father lecturing him about living within his means.

He sprang up to a sitting position, the bedclothes tangled and damp with his sweat. Christ, he thought, they're all pissed at me. Squinting, he saw the bedside clock read 4:22 a.m. Too soon to get up. But he pulled himself out of bed, wrapped a bathrobe around his naked body, and padded out to his study and through the glass doors to the balcony.

Even at this wee hour the Houston skyline was ablaze with light. That's right, Thrasher groused silently, burn away, use all the oil and coal and natural gas for crap like this. Then maybe we'll get smart enough to make the move to better energy technologies.

It was chilly on the balcony in nothing but the thin robe. The sky was covered with clouds that reflected the lights of the city. Kind of pretty, actually, he thought. But no stars showed through the overcast. No way to see Mars.

Then it started to rain. Go back to bed, Thrasher told himself.

Instead, he went back to the computer in his study and pulled up all the reports they'd sent to the NRC, and the agency's approval forms.

A fat lot of good those approvals will do us, he thought. They can pull the rug out from under us whenever they want to. And what can we do about it? Take 'em to court? That'll take years and a lot of bucks we can't afford to spend.

Then a voice in his head reminded him, If you can't go through them, go around them. There's got to be a way around Meek and the NRC and all their goddamned red tape.

Musing on that thought, Thrasher went back to bed and fell soundly asleep.

"You're looking more beautiful than ever," Thrasher said as he helped Vicki Zane into a chair at the little round conference table in the corner of his office.

She was wearing a smartly tailored rose pink pants suit, with a pleated white blouse beneath the jacket. No cleavage, but the outfit was tight enough to remind Thrasher of her agile, sumptuous figure.

Linda was icily proper as she set a plastic cup of coffee before Victoria and the inevitable mug of ginger beer at Thrasher's place, next to Vicki's.

Once Linda marched out of the office, Victoria smiled thinly at Thrasher. "She doesn't like me much, does she?"

Thrasher made a noncommittal shrug. "She thinks you hurt me."

"Have I?"

"Oh . . . yeah, some."

Vicki's smile grew warmer. "Well, I'm here, Art. Aren't you pleased to see me?"

"Sure," he said, with a confidence he didn't truly feel.

Leaning slightly toward him, Vicki said, "I can stay an extra night, if you like."

"Great," he said mechanically.

Vicki straightened in her chair. "But first I have to get this interview down. I have a camera crew on their way here—"

The desk phone buzzed. Linda's voice said, "There's a cameraman and assistant out here, asking for Ms. Zane." The "Ms." sounded like an angry bee's buzz.

"Send them right in," Thrasher called.

Victoria became strictly businesslike as the bearded cameraman and his overweight assistant set up their lights and a pair of cameras. They moved Vicki to Thrasher's other side, lowered the blinds on the office's windows, and took sound levels of both their voices.

The cameraman wormed on a pair of ear buds and finally said, "Okay, I'm set."

Victoria put on a photogenic smile and started, "I'm in the office of Arthur D. Thrasher, head of the Mars, Incorporated group that wants to send a team of human explorers to the planet Mars."

Thrasher nodded pleasantly at the camera.

"I suppose the question that's on everyone's mind," Vicki went on, "is how you can expect to continue your program in the wake of the recent disaster you had with your first attempted launch."

Forcing a smile, Thrasher said, "Rockets sometimes fail. It's all part of the game."

"You think of this as a game?" Victoria snapped. "What if there'd been people aboard that rocket?"

So this is how it's going to be, Thrasher said to himself. A cross-examination. An interrogation.

"The rocket was unmanned. Nobody got hurt."

"Except your pocketbook."

"We're covered by insurance."

"I understand that your insurance carrier is balking at paying you."

She's got good sources of information, Thrasher understood. She's close to somebody inside the Portales office.

Aloud, he replied, "Insurance carriers are always pretty cautious. But I'm sure they'll honor our policy. We'll go on to Mars. This setback isn't going to stop us."

Looking more and more like a prosecuting attorney dealing with a hostile witness, Victoria said, "You want to launch a nuclear reactor into space."

"That's for the main propulsion system, yes."

"Suppose that rocket blows up? Wouldn't that spray deadly radioactive materials all over southern Florida, as far as Miami and Ft. Lauderdale?"

And so it went, for more than an hour. Victoria was out for blood, his blood, Thrasher realized. Keep your cool, don't let her get under your skin. Stick with the party line. We're going to Mars, that's the important thing. We'll do it safely. We're using the best and safest technology that exists. There may be setbacks, but we're going to Mars.

At last it was over. The cameraman pulled off his earbuds, the pudgy assistant turned off the lights and Victoria leaned back in her chair, looking satisfied.

"I hope I wasn't too rough on you, Art," she said.

"Kind of," he replied.

"I couldn't do a sweetheart interview, it wouldn't look right. The public wants tough questions and straight answers."

"Well," Thrasher said, a little weakly, "the questions were tough enough."

"Good! Now why don't you let Global News treat you to dinner tonight."

"Sure," he said. Then he heard himself add, "Let's include my assistant. She deserves a night out."

Victoria looked surprised, but no more so than Thrasher himself felt.

It was an awkward dinner, with Thrasher sitting between the two women. Linda was entirely proper and kept up her end of the conversation with intelligence and some wit, but Thrasher couldn't help feeling that she was acting as a chaperon, an Aztec princess serving as a dueña, protecting him from a predatory woman who wanted to take advantage of him. He almost enjoyed the ludicrousness of the situation.

Victoria did not. Once dinner was finished she bade Thrasher—and Linda—a frosty goodnight in the hotel's lobby and went up to her room alone.

Thrasher escorted Linda to her home. As Carlo opened the limo's door, he said to her. "Goodnight kid. And thanks."

She grinned at him. "Maybe there's some hope for you, after all."

"Even for an old reprobate like me?"

"You're not so old," Linda said. Before he could respond she slid out of the car and, turning, waved him a goodnight.

⦿ 10 ⦿
RAMONA PERKINS

It was two days later that Ramona Perkins showed up.

She phoned from Wichita, Kansas, identifying herself as a friend of Bart Rutherford. Thrasher took her call, after telling Linda it was personal and he didn't want to be interrupted.

Linda looked puzzled. Her expression seemed to Thrasher to be saying, we just got rid of one bimbo and you're already chasing after another one?

But in the phone screen's image, Ramona Perkins hardly looked like a bimbo. She was pretty, but in a young, wholesome, girl-next-door way. Sandy blonde hair pinned up in a style that made her look even younger. Innocent baby blue eyes and just a hint of freckles sprinkled across her pert little nose.

"Mr. Rutherford said you might want to use my services," she said, in a clear, flat Midwestern twang. Thrasher got the impression she might be a singer in a country music group. She certainly didn't look like a private eye. Probably all to the good, in that line of business, he supposed.

"Yes," he said cautiously. "I'd like to talk to you about that."

"I can be in Houston tomorrow."

Thrasher glanced at the appointment calendar on his desktop screen. "How about lunch?"

"I can do that. One o'clock okay?"

189

"Fine. At the airport. I'll meet your flight."

"See you then!" she said, as chirpy as a cheerleader.

Ramona's flight was nearly an hour late, due to thunderstorms rolling through the Houston area. Thrasher sat the gate where she'd come in, bent over his notebook computer, scrolling for information about launch facilities that could handle Delta IV boosters: the European base on the coast of Guiana, the Russian centers at Baikonur and Plesetsk, even the old Woomera Rocket Range in Australia.

At last the commuter jet taxied in and people began trudging through the doorway into the airport terminal. Thrasher closed his notebook, got to his feet, and searched the arrivals for Ramona Perkins' pert young face.

And there she was, looking like a college kid on school break in a pair of faded jeans and a T-shirt that proclaimed LEGALIZE POT. She was taller than Thrasher had expected, just about his own height. Rail thin, but she wasn't scrawny; Thrasher got the impression she was athletic, hard muscled.

She had a small knapsack on her back and a handbag slung over one shoulder. She recognized Thrasher and went straight to him with a big grin and her hand held out.

"Nice of you to meet me at the airport, Mr. Tee," she said.

He couldn't help grinning back at her. "Nice of you to come to Houston."

She had no other luggage, so they repaired to the nearest restaurant, Pappa's Burgers.

Once they were seated in the crowded, bustling restaurant, Thrasher asked, incredulous, "You're a private investigator?"

Ramona nodded. "I worked for the Wichita police force for three years. Mostly undercover, with the vice squad."

Thrasher felt his brows hike up. "Wasn't that dangerous?"

"Some," she replied nonchalantly. "But the paperwork was worse."

He laughed. "I read the resumé you e-mailed, but it's kind of hard to believe."

"You can check with the Wichita P.D. Or with the Drug Enforcement Agency; I've applied for a job with them."

"So this P.I. thing is temporary."

Ramona nodded briskly as she picked up her burger. "I figured I could make a few bucks while I'm waiting for the DEA to check me out."

She took a healthy bite of the burger.

Thrasher watched her chew heartily, wondering if she could do the job, wondering if he needed a private investigator at all.

As if she could read his thoughts, Ramona said, "Mr. Rutherford says you might have a rat in your outfit. That'd be in Portales, wouldn't it?"

He nodded. "I think maybe Bart's being melodramatic. Saboteurs belong in spy movies, not in real life."

"Maybe," she said, attacking the burger again.

"How would you go about finding him—if he exists?" Thrasher asked.

Ramona shrugged her slim shoulders. "Give me a position in your accounting department. Or better yet, human resources. Let me snoop around a little."

"I don't want my people upset."

"Neither do I. I work undercover, remember."

"But how would you work it?"

"Follow the money. If somebody threw a monkeywrench into your rocket launch, it must've been for money, right? Not a personal grudge."

"I wouldn't think so."

"You don't have any enemies?"

Thrasher started to reply, hesitated, then finally admitted, "A few. But they're more likely to try to get at me through my board of directors. I can't see any of them resorting to violence."

"Maybe," Ramona repeated, noncommittally.

"So I'll hire you for our human resources department," he said. "That way you'll have access to all the personnel files."

"Fine."

"When can you start?"

Her blue eyes widened. "Don't you want to talk about my fee?"

"How much?"

"A thousand a week, plus expenses."

"Minus the salary we pay you as an employee."

She giggled. "Okay."

"Okay. When can you start?"

"Monday morning."

"In Portales."

"Sure thing."

Thrasher nodded. "I'll tell my H.R. director you're the daughter of an old friend. That way she won't question a new hire."

"You better tell me who your old friend is if he's supposed to be my daddy."

Thrasher mentally flicked through a list of his old friends. There weren't that many.

"Terry Cassidy. He's been living in Europe since his marriage broke up."

"Good enough," Ramona said. "I can Google him, can't I? Get his background."

"He's on Google, all right. He's our ambassador to the Court of St. James."

Ramona looked impressed. "So he lives in London. I guess I stayed here in the States with my mom."

"You'd better Google her, too. She was an actress on Broadway. Nothing big. Now she's retired on Terry's alimony."

"Nice family you picked out for me," said Ramona Perkins.

❁ 11 ❁
TUCSON

Chance favors the prepared mind, Thrasher said to himself as his leased Cessna Citationjet taxied smoothly toward Tucson International Airport's executive terminal. The plane was smaller, much less luxurious, and a tad slower than his old Learjet, but it was less expensive to operate.

Alan Dougherty just happened to be visiting the Arizona University's virtual reality lab. And the Australian daredevil just happened to be in the United States to find funding and customers for the Woomera Rocket Range.

Dougherty had won international fame with his high-altitude parachute jumps. Lofted almost to the edge of space in huge helium-filled balloons, the Aussie broke Baumgartner's 2012 record of 128,100 feet, then went on to establish new world's records for HALO—high altitude, low opening—jumps, freefalling for more than a dozen miles before opening his chute.

His last stunt had been right here in Arizona, Thrasher recalled as he drove to the lab on the campus. Jumped from twenty-three miles up and didn't open his chute until he was within five thousand feet of the ground. He made it, but not in one piece. His jumping days are over. Now he wants to restore the Woomera range and put it to use.

Dougherty was talking with Kristin Anders when Thrasher entered the virtual reality the lab. It was difficult to judge his height because he was sitting in a wheelchair, but he looked strong, sinewy. The blond, crewcut face of an outdoorsman, lean and weathered. And smiling brightly as he chatted with Kristin.

". . . so with the stem cell treatments, I'll be on my feet quick as two rabbits make twenty," he was saying to Kristin, with a distinct Australian accent.

She looked up as Thrasher approached her desk. "Here's Mr. Thrasher now," she said, getting to her feet.

Thrasher walked past a table full of electronics equipment to reach her and gave Kristin a friendly hug.

Disengaging, she gestured toward Dougherty, "Art, this is—"

"Alan Dougherty, I know." He stuck his hand out to the Aussie. "I'm—"

"Arthur D. Thrasher, I know," said Dougherty, beaming a broad smile up at him. "You're just the man I want to see."

"Funny," said Thrasher. "You're just the man I want to see."

"So let's find a pub and get acquainted," Dougherty suggested.

"Good idea." Turning to Kristin, Thrasher said, "Let us take you away from all this."

She made a sad little frown. "I'm afraid I can't get away. Too much to do."

"I want to put her to work for me, settin' up a VR link from Woomera."

"The lady's already working for me."

"'Bout Mars. I know."

Kristin said, "It won't take much of our time to set up a system for Alan."

"You could come to Australia, y'know," Dougherty said cheerfully. "See the Outback, Ayer's Rock, the Opera House over in Sydney."

Feeling more than a little nettled, Thrasher said, "I hate to sound proprietary, but the VR system is funded by Thrasher Digital Corporation. We own the rights."

Dougherty grinned up from his wheelchair. "Well, we expect to pay for 'em, mate. We're not going to rob you."

Thrasher glanced at Kristin and wondered how true the Aussie's words were.

Dougherty drove his motorized wheelchair through the blazing

June morning, Thrasher working up a sweat to keep up with him. By the time they found Dirtbag's bar and grill at the edge of the campus, Thrasher felt grateful for the cold blast of air conditioning in the joint's dim interior.

They settled in a booth toward the rear of the place, Dougherty sliding onto the wooden bench from his wheelchair, and ordered beers from the young waitress. Dougherty asked for Killian's Red.

"Not Foster's?" Thrasher asked, surprised.

"Nah. That's for export to you Yanks and the bloody Poms. Back home we drink Victoria."

"I like dark beer," said Thrasher, as the waitress placed a bottle of Negra Modelo before him. Somehow he felt he didn't want to tell this Aussie about his preference for ginger beer.

"So you want to go to Mars," Dougherty said, after a healthy slug of Killian's.

Thrasher nodded. "And I hear you want to establish an international launching base at Woomera."

Dougherty nodded. "Got a big open area in the Outback just sittin' there in the bleedin' sun. Seems to me we could use it to launch commercial rockets."

"Could you handle Delta IVs?"

"Can't handle anything right now, but give us a year—and some money—and we'll launch anything you want."

"What about safety factors? You're pretty far inland, aren't you? Isn't there a danger of spent stages falling on a town or a farm or something?"

Dougherty laughed. "You haven't been to the Outback, have you? There's nothing around for a thousand klicks in every direction, just about. Nearest town's Coober Pedy, and that's mostly underground."

"I heard about Coober Pedy," said Thrasher. "That's where they mine opals, isn't it?"

"Right. I'd like to take that Dr. Anders there, let her pick some opals for herself."

Thrasher's chin went up, but he forced himself to ignore the comment. Hunching forward over the scarred wooden table between them, he suggested, "Mars, Incorporated is planning on nine Delta IV launches over the next two and a half years. Could you handle them?"

"Woosh! That's a bit tight."

"International Launch Services will work the launches," Thrasher said, making a mental note to ask Yamagata if that was possible.

"How soon's your first launch supposed to go?"

"How soon can you get ready?"

Dougherty bit his lip, thinking fast. "You'll foot the bill for settin' up the launch pad?"

"We can do that. But what about the other facilities you'll need? Control center, storage, all that crap they call infrastructure."

"Already underway. We've got money for that, but Delta IVs need a bigger launch pad than we've got."

"Okay, we'll pay for the new pad."

"Better make it two. That's what the rocket guys call redundancy."

"Two, then," said Thrasher, picturing Dave Kahn's withered face when he sprang that bill on him.

"Okay, good."

"So how soon will you be able to launch?"

"If we go balls out," said Dougherty, "nine months. Twelve, on the outside."

"I need it ready in six months, nine on the outside."

Dougherty focused his pale blue eyes on Thrasher for a long, thoughtful moment. Then he said firmly, "Six months, then."

"Done." Thrasher extended his hand across the table.

But Dougherty did not take his hand. "There's another part to the price, mate. I want to go."

"Go?"

"To Mars."

Thrasher gaped at him. "In a wheelchair?" he blurted.

"I'll be on my feet, good as new, by the time you're ready to head for Mars. Stem cell treatments, you know."

"But we don't have room for a passenger."

"I'm a pretty decent engineer. I can train up, be part of the crew."

Thrasher stared at the Aussie. The man was dead serious, he realized.

"I'd have to bump one of the crew," he muttered.

"Bump 'im. I want to go. If I don't, the Woomera deal is off."

"That's blackmail!"

Dougherty grinned boyishly. "Naw, it's extortion." Hunching over the table, he offered, "I'll throw in the two launch pads. Find other funding for 'em. Deal?"

"We get the Delta IV pads for free?"

"Right." It sounded like "roit."

Reluctantly, Thrasher put out his hand again. "Okay, deal. But only if the medics say you're okay to go."

"Done!" Dougherty grabbed Thrasher's hand in a powerful grip and pumped it vigorously.

Wringing his hand, Thrasher said, "Now that you have a firm customer you won't need a virtual reality link to advertise your facility, will you?"

Looking suddenly nonplussed, the Aussie muttered, "Maybe not." Then he brightened again. "You just talked yourself out of a paying customer for your VR system, mate."

"That's all right," Thrasher said, laughing. "The important thing is getting to Mars." Silently he added, and keeping your paws off Kristin.

◎ 12 ◎
HOUSTON

"Australia?"

Even in the phone's small screen, Thrasher could see Jessie Margulis' face go white with shock.

"It's the answer to our prayers, Jess," he said to the engineer as he leaned back in his desk chair and planted his booted feet on the desktop.

"But . . . Australia?"

"We can forget about Meek and the NRC and all the goddamned government's red tape. We'll set up a firm schedule to launch those Delta IV payloads and stick to it."

"All the way out in Australia?"

"Jess, we aim to go thirty-some million miles to Mars. What's a few thousand miles compared to that?"

"I didn't think the Woomera range was still operational," Margulis objected.

"It's not. But it will be, in six months. I need you to work up a launch schedule. And set up transportation for the Mars One modules to Woomera."

"ILS is going to handle the launches?"

"Yep. I've got a call in to Yamagata, right after I hang up with you."

Margulis shook his head. "I hope you know what you're doing, Art."

"It doesn't matter if the Mars One components are launched from

Florida or Woomera, does it? We'll still launch the assembly team from New Mexico and they'll put it all together in orbit."

"Different orbit when you launch from Down Under."

"Yeah, I know. You take care of the technical details."

With a grudging grin, Margulis said, "You sound like von Braun. Whenever somebody asked him how he'd get something done he'd answer that it was just a technical detail."

"That's what engineers are for, Jess."

"My wife's not going to like me going to Australia, Art. For weeks at a time, I imagine."

"Take her with you. And the kids. I'll spring for it out of my own pocket."

Brightening visibly, Margulis said, "Gee, that'd be great. She'd like that."

"Fine. Now get off the phone and let me talk to Yamagata."

"Australia?" Saito Yamagata gasped.

"The Woomera Rocket Range," Thrasher said, enjoying the look of utter surprise that overwhelmed the Japanese executive's normally calm, confident expression.

"In six months?"

"That's we agreed on. You can get your crew out there in six months, can't you?"

"And who will operate the launches that we are contracted for here with NASA?"

"Oh, that."

Yamagata looked very troubled. "Art, International Launch Services has contractual obligations—"

"Which include Mars, Incorporated."

"At Cape Canaveral, not Australia!"

"Can't you do it?"

"ILS can't."

Thrasher started to reply, then realized what Yamagata had just said. Subtle. But maybe . . .

"Sai, are you telling me that your employer won't allow you to set up a new operation at Woomera?"

"No, they won't. They would regard it as too big a risk. Besides, it would hamper the jobs we're already contracted for."

Thrasher drummed his fingers on his desktop for several moments as he thought furiously.

"Suppose you left ILS and came to work for Mars, Inc.?"

Yamagata shook his head. "It would be dishonorable for me to jump from ILS to your firm." But then he said, "Of course, I could leave ILS with honor if it was to set up my own corporation."

"In Australia?"

"In Japan. But our first operation could be in Australia."

"Where would you get the people you need?"

"I can find them. The question is, where would I find the money I need to start the corporation?"

"I could funnel the money I was going to pay ILS to you."

"You will have to pay a fee to ILS for defaulting on your agreement."

Thrasher closed his eyes briefly and saw red ink bleeding everywhere.

"So what you're telling me," he said slowly, "is that you could set up your own corporation, hire the necessary personnel, and operate our six Delta IV launches, starting within six months."

"It would be a squeaker, but it could be done. Of course, I'll have other investors, as well. Some of my family would want to come in on this."

"Would you make a public offering?"

"No. Strictly family. With you as our first customer. We'll use your money as our start-up investment."

"And this will be acceptable to ILS?"

"They will accept it, I'm certain."

"Okay. Better get your butt over to Woomera as quick as you can."

Yamagata nodded. "We are both taking a great risk, you know."

"Yeah, I know. But behold the lowly turtle—"

"He only makes progress when he sticks his neck out," Yamagata finished the old saw.

The two men smiled at each other and then said goodbye. Thrasher thought that sticking out your neck was a good way to get your head chopped off.

"Australia?" David Kahn rasped.

Starting to feel weary, Thrasher said to the old man's image on his phone screen, "Yes, Australia. It's the answer to our prayers."

"Where's the money going to come from?"

"We'll manage. We'll even save some, in the long run, not having to jump through all the goddamned hoops that Meek and the NRC want to put us through."

"Are the Aussies okay with launching a nuke?"

"Yes." Thrasher was stretching the truth, he knew. He hadn't discussed the Australian government's safety regulations with Dougherty. *But if the Outback's as empty as he claims we ought to be able to get the reactor off okay.*

"Are you sure you know what you're doing?" Kahn asked.

"I've talked it over with our tech people and they see no reason why we can't launch from Woomera."

"I can see a dozen reasons."

"Take it up at the next board meeting," Thrasher growled.

"Next meeting's not for six months." Kahn grumbled.

"By then we'll be almost ready to launch," said Thrasher. "Maybe we could hold the meeting at Woomera!"

Strangely Jenghis Kahn smiled. Like a snake. "Maybe we could. And if the launch fails, we could bury your body in the Outback."

"With the kangaroos and dingos," said Thrasher.

Kahn's smile widened.

But Thrasher was thinking, *if this goes through I'll have to find a place for Dougherty on the crew. I can't bump any of the scientists, the whole academic world would scream bloody murder. It'll have to be one of the astronauts. But which one?*

Polk was untouchable, he knew. McQuinn was the crew's medical doctor.

With a sigh, he realized it would have to be Velazquez. *The kid's going to go apeshit. I just hope Polk and McQuinn don't go out on strike for him.*

❂ 13 ❂
SYDNEY, AUSTRALIA

December was the first month of summer Down Under. It seemed strange to see the city decked out in Christmas decorations while the weather was so balmy. Like Florida, Thrasher thought. Santa Claus in shorts, riding a surfboard.

He was sitting in his suite in Sydney's Intercontinental Hotel, going over his notes for the upcoming board meeting with Linda, via Skype.

"... then Mr. Kahn gives the treasurer's report," Linda was saying.

"The bloodbath," Thrasher muttered, thinking of the red ink.

Linda was totally focused on the business at hand, but as Thrasher watched her on his computer's screen he thought she looked very lovely. With a pang he realized that he missed her.

"And then you introduce Alan Dougherty to the board."

He thought he saw her face light up at the mention of Dougherty's name. Thrasher knew that the Aussie had flown over to Tucson at least twice in the past six months. But he hasn't even met Linda and she's already interested in him. Sonofabitch!

"He'll have a representative of the Australian scientific committee with him," Linda went on, "to introduce to the board."

Thrasher nodded. He'd come to Australia a week earlier than the board meeting's scheduled date so that he could talk with the Aussie scientists and get their okay on launching the nuclear reactor. They had already studied the details of the nuke's protective shielding and all the safety precautions that Jessie Margulis had built into the launch plan. The meeting was strictly pro-forma.

Still, Thrasher found himself holding his breath until the chairman of the committee—a redheaded man in a sports coat and open-necked shirt who looked too young to be a scientific bigwig— smiled at him and said, "Mr. Thrasher, we see no reason why you shouldn't be allowed to launch your reactor from Woomera."

Thrasher puffed out a sigh of relief. Then the committee chairman added, "Of course, we'll need a formal agreement from the appropriate government agencies, but that should be no trouble."

"That's just fine," Thrasher had said, resisting the urge to cross his fingers.

Now, looking at Linda on his computer screen, Thrasher said, "So we can wind up the meeting and fly out to Woomera to watch the launch the next day."

"Assuming there are no launch delays."

There's always that possibility, Thrasher thought. To Linda, he said, "Okay, fine. That's it, then?"

She nodded. "I wish I was there with you. Sydney looks so lovely."

Nodding back at her, Thrasher replied, "I guess it is. I wouldn't know. I've been up to my eyeballs in meetings."

"Australian women are very beautiful," she said, arching a brow.

"Like I said, I wouldn't know."

"All work and no play?"

"That's me."

"At least you could bring me back an opal," she said.

He broke into a pleased smile. "That I will, kid. That I will."

As soon as he broke the connection with Linda his screen showed an incoming call. From Bart Rutherford.

The Californian seemed to be in a hotel room, from what Thrasher could see.

"How's everything in Australia?" Rutherford said, by way of opening their conversation.

"Fine," said Thrasher. "What's up?"

"I'm down in Mohave, talking with my fellow wizards," Rutherford said. "I think we've come up with something that might interest you."

"Oh?"

"We're going to modify one of our space launching systems for a flight from Mohave to Australia. We need your help in getting clearance from the airport authorities in Sydney for landing our bird there."

"A manned launch?"

"Sure. We've done half a dozen manned launches to orbit. Might's well try a trans-Pacific shot. Kick Boeing's ass."

Rutherford was grinning like a big kid. Thrasher grinned back at him. "How soon?"

"End of this week, if we can get a landing clearance. Thought we'd do it as a Christmas present to you."

"I'll get on the horn to the airport authorities right away," Thrasher said.

But as soon as he cut the link with Rutherford the hotel's front desk called. "You have visitors, sir," said the pleasant-faced young woman.

"Visitors?" Thrasher wasn't expecting anyone.

"A Colonel Polk, Dr. Velazquez," she badly mangled the Hispanic pronunciation, "and Dr. McQuinn."

Thrasher felt his guts somersault. "They're here?" he squeaked.

"Yessir, here in the lobby. Shall I show them up, sir?"

He felt as if he wanted to run away and hide. But Thrasher said, "Yes, show them up."

Then he rushed to the lavatory and relieved himself. By the time he washed his hands, the door chime sounded.

They must have come up by rocket, Thrasher groused to himself.

"Come on in," he yelled as he stepped out of the lav.

Polk led them in, looking grim. Velazquez was right behind him, his lean face set in a dark-eyed scowl. McQuinn followed them, serious, somber.

Before Thrasher could invite them to sit down, Polk said, "We hear you want to bounce Nacho from the mission."

"I don't want to," Thrasher said. "I've got to."

"To make room for the Aussie showboat," Polk said.

Thrasher gestured to the sitting room's chairs. As the three astronauts sat tensely, he explained Dougherty's demand to them.

McQuinn said, "Has it occurred to you that replacing Nacho with an inexperienced man could endanger the safety of the mission?"

"He's not totally inexperienced," Thrasher said.

"Jumping out of balloons isn't the same as piloting a spacecraft," said Polk.

"I know, but—"

Velazquez blurted, "Christ! First I get squeezed out of the NASA program and now you're squeezing me out of the Mars mission? I didn't think you'd stab me in the back, Mr. Thrasher."

The kid looked as if he would burst into tears, Thrasher thought. As calmly as he could, he replied, "Nacho, the important thing is to get us to Mars. I—"

"Us," Polk said. "Not the Aussie."

"Us," Thrasher repeated, "meaning the human race. If I have to bump Nacho to get the job done, that's what I'll do."

"You can't bump Nacho. I need him to co-pilot the landing vehicle. Dougherty isn't a pilot, Nacho is."

"But—"

"Bump one of the scientists," McQuinn said. "Train Dougherty to operate that person's equipment."

"Like they did on Apollo," Polk agreed. "Armstrong, Aldrin, Alan Bean . . . the only real scientist to walk on the Moon was Jack Schmidt, on the last mission."

"Apollo Seventeen," Thrasher murmured.

"Bump one of the scientists," McQuinn repeated.

Thrasher looked at Velazquez again. He was holding himself together, but just barely. He looked like a little boy who's just been told there's no Santa Claus.

It's a helluva Christmas present I'm giving him, he said to himself. Snatching away his chance to go to Mars.

"Look," he said, as reasonably as he could, "I'm stuck between a rock and a hard place. Dougherty's sweat blood for us to get the Woomera facility up and running. His price for doing that was a seat on the mission. If I try to bump one of the scientists there'll be hell to pay with—"

"There's hell to pay right here and now," Polk said. He didn't seem angry to Thrasher. Worse. He was grimly determined. "If Nacho doesn't go, I don't go."

"Nor me, either," said McQuinn.

Forcing a weak smile, Thrasher said, "What is this, a rebellion?"

"Call it whatever you want," said Polk. "The three of us are a package deal. Bump one of us and you bump all of us."

"Like the three musketeers."

"One for all and all for one," McQuinn quoted.

Sucking in a deep gulp of air, Thrasher said, "Okay, you've got me over a barrel."

Velazquez lit up like a Christmas tree. He grabbed Polk's and McQuinn's hands. "Thanks, guys!"

Pointing to McQuinn, Thrasher said, "Judine, bumping a scientist is your idea. You find the one to bump, the one whose job Dougherty could most easily do. Then you get the poor sap to bow out gracefully. Okay?"

She looked doubtful, but nodded slowly and agreed, "Okay. I'll be your hatchet man."

Nice turn of phrase, Thrasher thought.

◎ 14 ◎
LAUNCH

It was hot in the Outback.

Most of the board of directors had flown out to Coober Pedy with Thrasher and spent the night in that town's underground hotel, where it was cool and dark. Most of the town was underground, carved out of the soft opal-bearing rock by generations of miners. There were some buildings up on the surface, and in the center of the town stood a pair of pathetic, wilted trees that the locals called "the jungle."

Thrasher bought an opal ring at a discount jewelry store up on the surface. The stone was milky white, translucent. He had never thought much of opals: diamonds are a guy's best friend, as far as he was concerned. More bang for the buck.

He had been pleasantly surprised by the quality of the restaurant where Dougherty had arranged for them to have dinner. Emu, lamb and Australian wine. Even sour old Jenghis Kahn would have been pleased if he'd made the trip, Thrasher told himself. But he couldn't help adding, *not!*

It was impossible to tell when the Sun rose from the hotel's underground rooms, but they were awakened by the staff, fed a hearty breakfast, and packed onto buses headed for the launch site before ten a.m.

Now, in the sweltering heat of late afternoon, they stood in the shade of the Woomera range's biggest building—the two-story concrete administrative center—and watched the gleaming Delta IV rocket standing on its launch pad nearly two kilometers away.

"How can those people work in this heat?" Will Portal asked rhetorically. "It must be close to a hundred degrees out in the sun."

Alan Dougherty laughed. "It's not high summer yet. That's when it gets really hot."

Portal mopped his sweaty brow with a handkerchief.

Thrasher stood riveted, watching the final few minutes of the countdown. A pair of news reporters—an attractive Australian blonde and a cadaverously thin young man from the States—flanked him on either side. Vicki hadn't come; probably Global News wouldn't pay for a jaunt to Australia, he thought. They'll pick up the American kid's report.

Dougherty had arranged for the range's public relations people to give their camera footage to all the major news outlets, Thrasher knew. Suddenly he wondered if he should have included a reporter on the Mars crew. No, he told himself; we'll have one embedded digitally with the crew, that's good enough.

"One minute and counting," boomed the loudspeakers, in a discernibly Australian accent.

The liquid oxygen hose dropped away from the rocket. Two other lines feeding electrical power to the first and second stages remained in place.

Something wrong? Thrasher felt a pang of anxiety. Then the power lines dropped away and he breathed again.

"Thirty seconds and counting."

"How does it feel, Mr. Thrasher?" asked the blonde reporter. She wasn't bad looking, but Thrasher resented the stupid question.

"Better than sex," he snapped. "Almost."

She blinked at him.

"Ten . . . nine . . . eight . . ."

In his mind's eye Thrasher saw the launch at Cape Canaveral, saw the bird blow itself apart all over again. Haven't heard a thing from Ramona Perkins, he realized. Probably paying her for nothing.

"Two . . . one . . . ignition!"

Clouds of steam billowed from the base of the rocket and it began to rise, slowly, regally at first. Then it smoothly accelerated and climbed into the cloudless bright sky.

The sound came washing over them, a pulsing, thundering roar that rattled every nerve in his body. Higher and higher the Delta IV climbed, while the small crowd sent up a ragged cheer. Out of the corner of his eye Thrasher saw even Greg Sampson raising both his fists and bellowing, "Go! Go!"

He flinched when the bird suddenly flashed flame. Solid rocket booster separation, he told himself. Still, his pulse fluttered.

And then the Delta IV dwindled to a dot too small to see against the glare of the sky.

"Good launch," said Bill Polk, with a satisfied nod.

Dougherty was grinning hugely. One by one, all of the directors standing there began to applaud. They all turned to Thrasher—even Charles Kahn and Sampson—and clapped.

As if I did it, Thrasher said to himself. But he bowed graciously and accepted their applause. It worked, he told himself. The move to Woomera worked. We're on our way.

⚛ YEAR FOUR

1
PORTALES

It was Memorial Day. All across America cities and towns were staging parades, families were having picnics and barbeques, the Yankees were in first place and the Mars One spacecraft was being assembled in orbit by a team of astronauts and tech specialists led by Bill Polk.

We're on our way, Thrasher thought, smiling with satisfaction as he watched the final section of the Mars One craft being carefully, tenderly deposited on a special double-sized flatbed truck for its ride to the airport and thence to Woomera.

Too bad we can't use Rutherford's Astrolaunch rocket, he thought. Cross the Pacific in half an hour. The airlifted rocket had made three flights from the company's Mohave base to Sydney and one to Perth, all without a hitch, but the FAA had refused to grant the firm a commercial license. They wanted more data, more test flights. Goddamned government, Thrasher grumbled to himself. Nothing but red tape. The Australian government seemed much friendlier to the idea of making it easier for people to reach their shores.

He had thought about basing the Astrolaunch operation in Australia, but without an FAA approval the rocket couldn't land legally in the United States without special permission. Goddamned government, he groused to anyone who would listen.

At least the assembly of the Mars One craft in orbit was going smoothly. Mars, Inc. was launching teams of technicians from New Mexico's Spaceport America on a regular schedule. Things there were going so smoothly the news media barely mentioned it when a new launch took off.

Once the final Mars One segment was loaded and the truck's diesel engines rumbled to life, Thrasher headed back to the cubicle he used as his office in the former warehouse.

Linda was still in Houston, minding the store while he was in Portales, but they were in touch by Skype and e-mail.

He noticed that Linda was wearing the opal ring he had brought her back from Australia. It looked good on her finger as she ran through his morning's agenda.

". . . and a Dr. Herzberg wants to see you," Linda was saying. "He says it's urgent."

"Herzberg? Who's he?"

"He's the head of the National Academy of Sciences. He seemed pretty upset."

"Oh-oh," said Thrasher. "The scientists' union."

"Trouble?"

"Big time." Thrasher knew that Judine McQuinn had been wrestling with the problem of which scientist to disinvite from the Mars mission. None of them agreed. All of them wailed bloody murder.

"He wants to talk to you. In person."

Drumming his fingers on his desktop, Thrasher asked, "When's my next trip to Washington?"

Linda tapped at her keyboard, then replied, "End of next month."

He nodded, thinking. "Okay. Call Herzberg and set up a meeting then."

"I don't know if he'll wait that long."

"Then he can come to Houston."

"All right," Linda said. "I'll tell him that."

"Anything else?"

Linda's face contracted into a puzzled frown. "That Ramona Perkins called yesterday. She said she needed to talk with you."

"Okay."

"Isn't she there in Portales? Why did she call the Houston office?"

Thrasher grinned at his assistant. "I don't post my comings and goings on the bulletin board. Down at the level she's working, she must've figured the best way to reach me is in Houston."

Linda looked dubious.

"I'll call her," he said.

"She's pretty young, isn't she?"

Thrasher realized that Linda thought there was a romantic angle. Laughing, he said, "Very young. Too young for me, if that's what you're worried about."

"Really?"

"I may be a reprobate, kid, but I'm not a cradle robber."

"Really?" Linda repeated. But this time she smiled.

Thrasher realized that his reputation with women actually provided a good cover for his meeting with Ramona. Let them think I'm chasing the kid. I can invite her out to dinner and nobody will know what we're really talking about.

But when Ramona Perkins walked into the hotel restaurant that evening, she looked stylish and quite adult in a brown leather mid-calf skirt and short-sleeved white blouse, with her light blonde hair swept to one side of her perky face. With a pang, Thrasher realized that it had been months since he'd had sex.

"I didn't know you were here in Portales," Ramona said as she slid into the booth opposite him.

"I come and go," he said.

Without preamble, she said, "My appointment with the DEA finally came through. I'll be leaving in two weeks."

"I guess I'm glad for you."

"I appreciate the job you gave me. It helped me bridge the gap. Otherwise I'd have a big hole where my savings used to be."

Thrasher waved a hand. "Nothing to it." But he was thinking that he'd paid her for nothing; she hadn't found a saboteur in his team.

Ramona reached into her pocket-sized handbag and pulled out a jewel box containing a compact disc. "I wish I had more concrete evidence to show you, but everything I found is circumstantial."

Taking the jewel box from her hand, he asked, "Circumstantial? You mean you found something?"

With a pert little nod Ramona said, "Just some bank accounts that had a sizable spike in the weeks right before and right after the accident. And a few e-mail messages back and forth."

"Bank accounts? E-mails?"

"It's nothing that would hold up in court," she said, her face very earnest. "But it's got all the earmarks of a payoff."

"Who? How much money?"

A waiter approached their table. "Would you care for a cocktail, or some wine, perhaps?"

Ramona looked up at him with her baby blues and replied, "A club soda, please. With a couple of cherries."

"Does the bar have ginger beer?" Thrasher asked.

"I'll see." The waiter stalked off, obviously unimpressed with their drink order.

"Who?" Thrasher repeated. "How much money?"

"He works for Thrasher Digital, but he's high enough on the totem pole to—"

"Who?" Thrasher demanded.

"His name is Egan."

"Vince?" Thrasher felt it like a body blow. The chief engineer of Thrasher Digital had been with him since the firm's beginning.

Ramona said, "It's nothing concrete. I could be totally wrong."

But Thrasher was asking himself, Why would Vince skunk me? What did I do to him to make him stab me in the back?

The waiter arrived with their drinks. Thrasher absently took a sip, his mind in turmoil. He didn't even notice that it was ginger ale.

2
JEREMIAH HERZBERG

Dr. Jeremiah Herzberg was smiling as he sat before Thrasher's desk in the Houston office. He was short but thick-bodied, barrel-chested, built like a fireplug, his skin dark as burnt parchment with a fringe of white beard that made Thrasher think of an old-time pirate. Despite his affable smile, Herzberg's light gray eyes were cold as ice, steely.

Thrasher had spent the previous evening looking up Herzberg's biography on various Internet sites. The man had been a plasma physicist—whatever that was—at Cornell University and had won a potful of scientific awards and accolades before being installed as head of the National Academy of Sciences.

Once Linda had served them drinks—bourbon on the rocks for Herzberg and the inevitable ginger beer for Thrasher—the two men looked each other over from opposite sides of Thrasher's desk.

"I'm delighted that you found time to come to Houston," Thrasher lied.

"I didn't really have much choice," said Herzberg, in a smooth, deep voice. "The matter we're faced with is quite urgent."

"I agree."

Still smiling, Herzberg said, "Quentin Hynes is an outstanding geologist, one of the best in the world. You can't toss him off your Mars mission."

With a helpless little shrug, Thrasher said, "I'm afraid I've got to."

"He's a former student of mine, you know."

"It can't be helped. There's only room for seven people on Mars One. We need the three astronauts, so that leaves only four slots for scientists."

"And Dr. Hynes is one of them."

Shaking his head, Thrasher said, "I've got to make room for Alan Dougherty. He's been invaluable to us, and he wants to go on the mission."

"You can't dump a man you've already invited," Herzberg said, his voice hardening.

"I've got to make room for Dougherty, that's all there is to it."

Herzberg picked up his glass of bourbon from the folding table beside his chair and took a sip, his eyes never leaving Thrasher.

"You're going to drop a scientist who's in line for the Nobel Prize to make room for a . . . a stunt man?"

"A stunt man who made the Woomera launching center available for us," Thrasher explained. "I owe him, and a place on the mission is the price he asked for."

"It's intolerable!" Herzberg burst. "It's a slap in the face to science in general and Dr. Hynes in particular."

"I'm sorry you feel that way, but there's really nothing I can do about it. I gave my word to Dougherty; he's been tremendously helpful to us."

Herzberg took bigger sip of bourbon. Thrasher could see the wheels in his head spinning.

"I'm afraid that if Dr. Hynes is dropped from the mission, all the other scientists will quit in protest."

Thrasher had expected that. "All the other *American* scientists," he said.

Herzberg's brows knit. "What do you mean by that?"

"There are plenty of scientists from other nations who'd be deliriously happy to go with us to Mars: the Japanese, the Brits—"

"You can't be serious!"

"I am totally, entirely, completely, absolutely serious."

With some heat, Herzberg accused, "You're supposed to want to put Americans on Mars, and yet you're threatening to keep American scientists off the mission? You're a hypocrite!"

"I want to put human beings on Mars," Thrasher shot back.

"Americans, if possible. You're the one who's threatening to pull the American scientists off the mission."

Herzberg said nothing for several heartbeats. He simply sat before Thrasher's desk, the glass of bourbon in one hand, staring intently at Thrasher. Then, strangely, he broke into a grudging smile.

"All right," he said. "All right. You've got the advantage over me. We wouldn't want the first mission to Mars to have no American scientists."

Thrasher leaned both forearms on his desk and grinned back at the older man. "Then you were bluffing."

"I was bluffing."

Straightening up, Thrasher said, "Okay, then. How do we make the best of the situation?"

"Dr. Hynes is going to be very unhappy. *Very* unhappy. I promised him I'd talk to you, one-on-one. I don't usually lose one-on-one confrontations."

Thrasher was thinking furiously. How to make this right? How can I let the guy have his cake and eat it too?

"What if your man can go along on the mission anyway, just not physically?" he asked.

"What do you mean?"

"Virtual reality," said Thrasher, like a man pulling a rabbit out of a hat. "Hynes trains Dougherty to be his stooge: Dougherty will do what Hynes tells him and Hynes can experience it from his own office here on Earth."

"Virtual reality?"

"We're including a virtual reality link on the mission. It'll allow users to experience what the Mars team is doing, in real time—except for the distance lag."

"Train the stuntman to be Hynes' eyes and ears . . ."

"And hands and legs," Thrasher said eagerly.

"If that could be possible—"

"It's possible. Thousands of ordinary people will be linked to the Mars team through VR. Millions of people!"

Herzberg's smile faded a trifle. "Still, it won't be the same as actually being on Mars."

Thrasher jabbed a finger in the scientist's direction. "Look, what does your boy want? Is he in this for the personal glory of going to

Mars, or is he in this to study Martian geology first-hand, to learn, to explore, to discover?"

Nodding, Herzberg said, "I can see how you've been able to bring this mission into reality. You're quiet a conniver, Mr. Thrasher."

"Art; my friends call me Art."

"I think I'll stick with Mr. Thrasher for the present. If your VR scheme works, then we can become friends."

"It'll work, I know it will. You should get yourself over to the University of Arizona and talk with Dr. Kristin Anders."

His brow furrowing slightly, Herzberg said, "Anders. I don't know any Kristin Anders."

"She works with Professor Winninger."

"Ah! Winninger I've heard of."

"Dr. Anders does most of the work that he gets credit for."

His smile turning rueful, Herzberg admitted, "That's not an unusual situation, I'm afraid."

"You talk with Winninger and Anders. They'll convince you that the VR system will work."

"And then I'll have to convince Quentin."

"Take him to Tucson with you. He'll be convinced. He'll even become famous as the first scientist to explore Mars through virtual reality."

Herzberg nodded again. "All the glory with little of the risk. That might appeal to him. And his wife."

3
VINCE EGAN

This isn't going to be easy, Thrasher told himself as he climbed into the Citationjet. Vince Egan was already aboard, he knew. Now to confront Vince with what Ramona found out.

Thrasher wished he was a thousand miles away, or maybe hanging by his toenails on the lip of a seething hot volcano.

The Cessna was cheaper to operate than his old Learjet, but the cabin was so small that Thrasher had to duck his head as he went to the seat facing Vince's.

"Hi, boss," Egan said cheerfully. "What's the occasion?"

"Occasion?" Thrasher asked as he buckled his seat belt.

"Why'd you ask me to fly to Portales with you?"

The plane's engines whined to life as Thrasher tried to find words to start the interrogation.

"How's the VR program going?"

Egan looked surprised. "I just handed you the monthly progress report. Everything's fine. Polk and his flyboys are installing the equipment aboard Mars One, right on schedule."

Nodding, Thrasher said, "Good."

As the plane taxied out to the runway, Egan broke into a crooked grin and said, "Dr. Anders is in Australia, you know."

Thrasher's chin went up a notch. "She is? Since when?"

"Took off yesterday. Dougherty wants a VR system for Woomera after all, and since all the real work's been done on our system, she figured she'd go to the Outback and see what it's like."

"Dougherty," Thrasher muttered. "With a friend like him, who needs an enemy?"

"I think she's interested in him," said Egan. "Personally, I mean."

"Figures."

The plane hurtled down the runway and arrowed into the sky. Thrasher saw Hobby Airport dwindling and the vast flat scrubland of Texas stretching out to the horizon. The city of Houston and its sprawling suburbs were behind them, unseen; as far as the view from his window was concerned, they didn't exist.

"So why're you taking me along on this trip to Portales?" Egan asked again.

Thrasher bit his lip as he looked at the younger man. I've known Vince since he was a kid at MIT, he told himself. I've made him head of Thrasher Digital's engineering department. Why would he want to screw me over?

"Vince," he began. "About the accident on that first Delta IV launch . . ."

"The one from Cape Canaveral."

"Yeah." Thrasher took a deep breath, then blurted, "Maybe it wasn't an accident."

Egan frowned, uncomprehending. "Not an accident? You mean, somebody caused the explosion? On purpose?"

Thrasher nodded.

"I thought about that possibility myself, Art. I went over every detail of the accident report. Couldn't find anything to put my finger on. The damned valve just malfunctioned."

"That valve was inspected at least four different times before the flight."

"Yeah, I now. But sometimes a glitch happens."

"Or is made to happen."

Egan stared at him as the plane climbed to its cruising altitude.

"Who the hell would sabotage the launch?"

"I've had somebody looking into that," said Thrasher.

"He find anything?"

"She. And yes, she found something. Not much, but something."

"What?"

"You made three deposits into your IRA account in the six weeks before the accident, and two more afterward. They total two hundred and fifty thousand dollars."

Egan looked as if he'd been smacked between the eyes by a two-by-four.

"Me? You looked into my bank accounts?"

"We looked into everybody's," Thrasher said, feeling miserable. "You're the only one with such a big jump. Plus a couple of technicians out at the Cape who got ten thousand each."

"And you think I . . ." Egan's mouth hung open but no more words came out.

As reasonably as he could manage, Thrasher said, "We're covering all the bases, Vince. I don't want to believe that you're involved in this, but I've got to get to the bottom of things."

"And you think I fucked you over," Egan said, practically snarling. "I've worked for you for damned near fifteen years and you think I'm a rat, a traitor!"

"Vince, please . . ."

"Go to hell, Art! My parents and Mary-Ellen's grandmother pony up enough cash to keep us from defaulting on our home loan and you think I'm a goddamned saboteur! Fuck you!"

"Is that what it was?"

"Yeah, that's what it was. You know the house we bought; you've had dinner with us, for chrissakes!"

"You were in danger of defaulting?"

"We bought the fucking palace at the peak of the market. Now the mortgage payments are way more than the place is worth."

"But your salary . . . or you could have come to me . . ."

"Three kids in school. And you've got enough problems without me adding to them. Our families bailed us out. I didn't blow up your damned rocket."

Feeling miserable, Thrasher said, "I'm sorry, Vince. I didn't want to believe you were responsible for the accident, but I had to check out all the possibilities."

Egan looked away from him, his face white with anger. For long moments the only sound in the plane's cabin was the muted drone of its engines.

"Vince, I apologize."

"Yeah."

"I didn't want to think it was you, but I had to check out all the possibilities."

"You already said that."

More silence. Thrasher said to himself, I've lost him. He'll never be able to work for me again. He thinks I don't trust him.

Then Egan said, "So how are you going to find out who really fouled up the launch?"

"I don't know," said Thrasher.

"You said there were a couple of technicians at the Cape who got wads of money?"

"Ten thousand each."

"Our guys?"

"No, they worked for ILS. Yamagata's people."

"Yamagata's in Australia now."

"That's right."

"Maybe we ought to track down those two guys and see what they've got to say for themselves."

Thrasher's heart soared at Vince's use of the word "we."

"Maybe we should," he said.

◎ 4 ◎
ASTROLAUNCH

As he walked across the tarmac toward the waiting Astrolaunch plane, Thrasher told himself that this strange-looking hybrid aircraft would take him from California to Melbourne in less time than it had taken him to fly from Houston to Mohave.

Officially, legally, he was not a passenger on a commercial vehicle. The FAA was still plodding through its interminable mountain of paperwork before certifying the Astrolaunch vehicle for commercial operation. Instead, Thrasher flew as a volunteer observer on an experimental flight—after signing dozens of insurance and safety waivers. If I get killed on this flight, he thought uneasily, my estate won't get a cent out of it.

Might be a slick way to get rid of me, he realized.

The Astrolaunch vehicle was a strange sight, sitting in the bright, warm desert sunlight. To Thrasher, it looked like two ultramodernistic airplanes joined together at the wing, all curves and undulating lines. It reminded him of the Spanish architect, Gaudi, and his fantastic houses in Barcelona.

The long wings drooped almost to the ground. A pair of powerful turbojet engines hung beneath each of the wings. Between them, two snub-nosed fuselages extended back to a pair of raked tails. And between the fuselages hung the rocketplane that would carry him to Melbourne.

The strangely ungainly-looking carrier plane would lift its rocket-powered payload to nearly one hundred thousand feet, then release the rocketplane, which would zoom off to Melbourne. Flight time was estimated to be forty-eight minutes from the release point.

It could be even shorter if we crash, Thrasher thought.

Walking toward the craft with him were five people. Four of them—including one woman—were pilots. Two for the carrier plane, two for the rocket. The fifth was Bart Rutherford, looking very serious in zippered flight coveralls. Thrasher, walking beside him, was in his normal sports jacket and slacks.

Squinting up at Rutherford, silhouetted against the bright California sky, Thrasher asked, "You've flown this bird before, haven't you?"

Rutherford shook his long blond locks. "Not this one. I've done two flights in the sister ship."

"This isn't the first flight for this bird, is it?" Thrasher asked, suddenly alarmed, remembering the old adage that one should never fly in an aircraft on its maiden voyage.

Rutherford grinned. "No, Art. You can relax. This bird's flown twice already."

"Not that I was worried," Thrasher said weakly.

"Me neither."

Two of the pilots—including the woman—climbed into the carrier plane's left fuselage while Thrasher followed Rutherford and the two other pilots to the hatch leading into the rocketplane. Its stubby wings looked too small to keep it aloft, Thrasher thought. But then he realized that most of the bird's flight through the atmosphere would be at hypersonic speed.

As he clambered up the ladder and through the hatch, Thrasher told himself he was risking his neck just to have an hour's talk with Saito Yamagata. But it had to be done. He needed Yamagata's help to track down the technicians who had been enriched by ten thousand dollars each at the time of the Delta IV explosion.

The two pilots went up forward to the cockpit and closed its hatch. Thrasher thought the interior of the spaceplane was surprisingly plush: six comfortable reclining chairs and padded bulkheads. The windows were small, but adequate. Rutherford gestured to the middle row of seats. Thrasher took the seat by the left window and buckled the safety harness over his shoulders. Rutherford sat across the aisle from him and did the same.

The takeoff was smoothly normal. "Plenty of acoustical insulation," Rutherford said as they sped down the runway and into the sky. Thrasher looked down at the barren Mohave landscape: nothing but sand and scrub, except for the runway and its buildings. He saw the other Astrolaunch plane sitting in front of a hangar.

If and when the FAA finally gives its okay, he thought, Astrolaunch is going to make a mint out of long-range, high-speed commercial flights. There were rumors that both Boeing and Lockheed Martin were making offers to buy the company. And I won't get a nickel out of it. He sighed inwardly. At least I'll be able to get back and forth a lot faster.

The climb to release altitude was uneventful. Rutherford chattered about airspeed and angle of attack. Thrasher listened with half his attention, worrying about his upcoming conversation with Yamagata. Would Saito help him find the saboteur? Assuming there really was one. One of the technicians under suspicion was Japanese. Would Yamagata try to protect him out of some nationalistic loyalty?

Outside his window, Thrasher saw that the sky had turned dark, almost black. The ocean looked *very* far below, like a sheet of dimpled gray steel, dotted with rows of puffy white clouds.

"Release in one minute," the pilot announced over the intercom speaker.

Rutherford leaned toward Thrasher and said, "Now the fun starts."

The digital display on the bulkhead up front ticked down the seconds. As the number five flashed, Rutherford muttered, "Here we go."

Suddenly they were falling. Thrasher felt his stomach drop away.

"Release on schedule," came the pilot's voice. Then, "Ignition."

Thrasher felt a strong push in the small of his back and heard a thunderous roar. Rutherford gave out a whoop. "Yahoo!"

And they were zooming up, the ocean beneath them falling away speedily, the sky turning absolutely black. Thrasher could see the horizon was curved. The rocket's bellowing howl seemed to diminish but still he felt the acceleration pushing against his back.

"Wow," Thrasher managed to say.

"Cutoff in thirty seconds," the pilot announced, his voice flat, calm, routine.

The push against his back disappeared and Thrasher's arms floated up off the seat's armrests.

"You're in space, Art," Rutherford said, grinning hugely. "How do you like it?"

Thrasher nodded weakly and forced a grin, while trying with all his concentration to keep his stomach from crawling up into his throat.

He managed to gasp, "You didn't tell me . . . we'd be in zero gravity."

"It's only for a couple of minutes, Art. You'll feel some weight once we start our descent and bite back into the atmosphere." Rutherford seemed blithely unaffected by the lack of weight; he was enjoying the ride.

Thrasher remembered the first time he'd ridden a roller coaster, when he'd been five or six. Don't throw up, he commanded himself silently, forcing his hands down to grip the seat's armrests. Don't make an ass of yourself.

"Re-entry," announced the pilot.

The rocketplane began to buffet and Thrasher's stomach settled back to its rightful place. He saw sparks flashing past his window, and then a panel slid over the glass, blocking his view.

The plane shuddered and bucked noticeably. Thrasher thought that zero-gravity wasn't so bad, after all.

"Australia, here we come," Rutherford said, with a chuckle.

Thrasher kept his mouth clamped shut. The shuddering, bumpy ride smoothed out at last and the window panels slid back. He was somewhat startled to see that it was fully night outside; they had left California in mid-morning.

"We're passing New Zealand right about now," Rutherford informed him. "South Island. Christchurch."

"How fast are we going?"

Rutherford pointed to the digital display on the forward bulkhead. It read: MACH 4.8.

"We're slowing down for the landing," Rutherford said casually.

Thrasher remembered the old pilot's adage: Flying is the second most exciting thing a man can do; landing is the first most exciting.

Down below Thrasher could see the lights of the city spreading across the landscape. They were still too high to make out individual buildings; it simply looked like a starscape of bright, twinkling lights beneath them.

The rocketplane descended smoothly, flared out, and touched down on the runway with no trouble. Thrasher saw the runway lights flashing past.

As they rolled toward the terminal, Rutherford asked, "How did you like it?"

Thrasher thought it over for a few heartbeats. "You're going to have to give your passengers a pretty thorough orientation briefing before they fly this skyrocket."

Rutherford laughed. "Yeah, I guess so. Although the younger set might buy tickets just for the ride."

Which means I'm an old fart, Thrasher thought. But as he unbuckled his seat harness he realized, what the hell, I'm here in Melbourne in less than an hour.

Then it struck him. I've been in space! I've seen the curvature of the Earth and flown above the atmosphere. I'm almost an astronaut!

⚝ 5 ⚝
SAITO YAMAGATA

Yamagata met Thrasher at the airport and, with his usual bright smile, whisked him by limousine to a posh restaurant in Melbourne's theater district. The two men were shown to a booth by a fawning maitre d'. They sat facing each other across the crisply creased white tablecloth and gleaming dinnerware. It was nearly one a.m. in Melbourne, yet the restaurant was almost filled with after-theater patrons enjoying a late supper. To Thrasher, it still felt like early afternoon; his stomach was ready for lunch.

As a waiter presented them with outsized menus, Thrasher said, "I really appreciate your taking the time to see me, Sai."

"To what do I owe this whirlwind visit?" Yamagata asked cheerfully.

"We've been investigating the Delta IV accident."

His smile dimming slightly, Yamagata said, "I thought the investigation was concluded. Your insurance carrier paid up, didn't they?"

"Yes, they finally did."

"So?"

"It might not have been an accident."

Yamagata's brows knit. "Surely the insurance company looked into that possibility."

"Not hard enough," said Thrasher. "Two of the ILS technicians working on the launch received lumps of money."

"Lumps?"

"Five thousand dollars one week before the launch, and another five thou the week afterward."

"And you think . . ."

"It sure looks suspicious to me, Sai."

"Two of my technicians." Yamagata's smile was completely gone.

"They worked for ILS. One of them came over here to Australia to work for your company." Thrasher hesitated, then added, "He's Japanese."

Yamagata looked grim. "You believe that this man deliberately sabotaged your launch."

"I'm not certain. But it's a possibility that I've got to look into."

"Sabotage."

"If it was sabotage, whoever paid for it might try to hit us again, Sai."

"I see."

"Can you help me? Can you let me talk to the guy? Question him?"

Yamagata's lips curved into the slimmest hint of a smile. "You are a skilled interrogator, are you?"

"No, but who else is there?"

"Yamagata Corporation has a small but quite efficient security team. Tell me the name of the man you suspect and I will have my people interrogate him."

Thrasher realized that Saito wanted to keep this affair entirely under his own roof. No outsiders. Not even me.

"Are you sure that's the way you want to handle this?"

Closing his eyes briefly, Yamagata explained, "We are a family corporation. Our employees are like members of the family. We try to keep our dirty linen out of the sight of strangers."

And I'm a stranger, Thrasher realized. Not family. Not even Japanese.

Tightly, he said, "All right, if that's the way you want to handle it."

"It is."

"All right."

Yamagata's smile widened slightly. "If the man is a traitor, my security people will find out. They are not inconvenienced by the usual laws that criminals use to protect themselves. They'll find everything there is to know about this man."

Thrasher nodded. "Okay. Thanks." And he thought, I wouldn't want to be that guy. He's in for a rough time.

Thrasher rode a regular commercial flight back to Los Angeles: fourteen hours in the air. He slept most of the flight, then blearily took another airliner back to Houston. By the time he returned to his office he felt jet lagged, tired, irritable, his stomach bloated and his head thumping.

The instant he stepped into the office, Linda handed him a mug of ginger beer and a pair of aspirins.

But she said, "Sid Ornsteen wants to see you."

"Just what I need," Thrasher muttered.

"He says it's important."

"Yeah, sure."

Thrasher shambled toward his inner office as Linda went to her desk to phone Ornsteen.

Plopping into his swivel chair, Thrasher took the aspirins with a gulp of ginger beer, then called up his daily schedule on his desktop screen. As he scanned the schedule, he thought about Yamagata and the technician who might—or might not—be a saboteur.

What about the other guy? he asked himself. He's still working for ILS, down at the Cape. How can I get to him?

His musings were interrupted by Sidney Ornsteen stepping into his office. Sid looked more worried than usual.

"What's up, Sid?"

"They're at it again," said the company treasurer.

"At what?"

"Somebody's buying the company's stock. Nothing big, nothing that would normally stand out."

"So what's the problem?"

Sitting tensely in one of the armchairs before Thrasher's desk, Ornsteen said dolefully, "Whoever's doing this is going to acquire a majority of the shares, sooner or later."

"Assuming they continue buying."

"Oh, they will. I'm sure of that. Whoever's behind this grab wants to have a majority, maybe for the next board meeting."

"How do you know it's one person behind the buying?" Thrasher demanded. "It might just be that people think Thrasher Digital is a good investment."

Frowning, Ornsteen countered, "With our price-to-earnings figures? Come on, Art, this is a takeover bid, pure and simple."

"How much has been bought this time?"

"Damned near three percent."

"That's not enough—"

Ornsteen held up a skinny singer. "Three percent here, three percent there, pretty soon they'll have a majority position, Art."

"That's assuming that some evil mastermind is behind the buying spree."

"It isn't funny, Art. Somebody's trying to take control of Thrasher Digital."

With a sigh, Thrasher replied, "You know, Sid, some days I'm almost willing to let them have it."

"Don't be ridiculous."

"I said *almost*, didn't I?"

◈ 6 ◈
COCOA BEACH

His name was Ulysses Israel. He'd been working for International Launch Services for more than eight years, according to the Melbourne detective agency Thrasher had hired. No hint of illegal activity: he apparently wasn't a gambler, or a boozer, or a drug user. Nice solid little technician in the middle level of the ILS organization. His only hobby seemed to be a fondness for buying old automobiles, jazzing them up, then selling them to car buffs.

Israel had performed the final inspection of the valve that had failed, just before it was installed in the Delta IV's upper-stage rocket engine. His initials were on the inspection certificate.

He made a decent living. No wife or family, but he wasn't a loner. He played tennis regularly and hung out with a bunch of buddies over the weekends. His hobby didn't bring in much money; he usually spent more on buying and fixing a car than he got from selling it.

The only blip on his record was the ten thousand dollars that he had deposited in his bank account: five thousand the week before the launch accident, five thousand the week after.

"There's not enough there to question him," the head of the detective agency told Thrasher, in the man's seedy, musty office in Cocoa Beach's rundown business district.

"I want to meet him," Thrasher said.

The detective was a big man, but aging badly. He was seriously overweight, balding, and wheezed asthmatically. No Sam Spade, Thrasher thought. Not even Miss Marple. The man was in his shirtsleeves and suspenders as he sat behind his dented metal desk, eying Thrasher wearily.

"I don't think your seeing him is a good idea, Mr. Thrasher," he said, his voice heavy, grating like a rusty hinge. "If you come out and accuse him of anything, he could take you to court for libel."

"You mean slander. Libel's when you defame somebody in print."

"Slander, yeah."

"I still want to meet him. How do I go about that?"

The detective shrugged his massive shoulders. "I can give you his phone number."

Thrasher nodded. "That'll be fine."

"He won't tell you anything, you know."

"Maybe not," Thrasher admitted. But he was thinking: money talks. If ten thousand got him to sabotage the launch, maybe twenty thousand will open his mouth.

Back in his room at the beachside motel that Linda had found for him, Thrasher phoned Ulysses Israel and got his answering machine.

When the machine beeped, Thrasher said, "This is your lucky day, Mr. Israel. I have twenty thousand dollars in cold cash for you, in exchange for a few minutes of conversation. Call me when you get in."

It was nearly midnight when the phone rang. Thrasher was lying in the motel's lumpy bed, watching an old private-eye flick on the television screen.

"Sam Israel here," the voice said.

"I'd like to talk with you, Mr. Israel," Thrasher said smoothly.

"You said something about twenty thou?"

"That's right."

"What's this all about?"

"You'll find out when we meet."

Israel hesitated a heartbeat, then asked, "When and where?"

"Right now's as good a time as any. I'm at the New Satellite Motel."

"That dump."

"It's a roof over my head."

"You've got the twenty thousand with you?"

"In my room's safe."

"In cash?"

"Of course."

Another hesitation. Then, "What name should I ask for?"

"No names," Thrasher said. "I'm in room two-fourteen. On the upper tier."

"I'll be there in fifteen minutes."

"Fine."

Thrasher hung up, chuckling to himself. *He calls himself Sam. Can't say I blame him. Ulysses Grant went by the name of Sam, so why shouldn't the money-hungry Mr. Israel?*

Then he realized he had just invited a total stranger to come and take twenty thousand dollars from him. *He could bring a couple of friends, take the money, and split.* Thrasher thought about phoning the detective agency for some protection, but figured there wouldn't be time for them to get to the motel before Israel arrived.

I hope he's alone, Thrasher said to himself.

Thrasher tried to watch TV again, but couldn't concentrate. He flipped from channel to channel, but this late at night there wasn't much on. The motel's cable service didn't include the financial channels.

Then he heard a car door slam. Thrasher jumped to his feet and peered through the window curtain. A sleek fire-engine red Thunderbird convertible sat gleaming in the hotel's parking lot lights. He could see a tall, lanky figure standing by the car, looking around the parking lot suspiciously. *One man. Only one. He hasn't come to rip me off—not unless he figures he can get the money off me without any help.*

Which wouldn't be too difficult, Thrasher thought, considering his own pitiful martial skills.

The man headed for the stairs and Thrasher heard through the room's flimsy walls his footsteps scuffing on the metal steps, then coming down the outside terrace toward him. Finally, a thump on his door.

This is crazy! he said to himself. *I'm all alone here. Nobody knows what I'm doing, who I'm talking to.*

But he swallowed the lump of trepidation in his throat and yanked the door open. Ulysses—Sam—Israel stood framed in the doorway.

He was close to six feet tall, Thrasher judged, slender but well muscled. Wearing a dingy tee shirt and jeans. Dark hair and eyes, his face would have been handsome, except for the crooked nose. Looked like it had been broken some years ago. Maybe more than once.

"Sam Israel?" Thrasher asked needlessly.

Stepping into the little room, Israel said, "Yeah. Who the fuck are you?"

"My name's Arthur Thrasher."

Israel froze. For an instant Thrasher thought he would turn around and leave the room. Instead, though, he carefully closed the door and went to the room's only chair, by the chest of drawers that supported the TV.

"The Mars guy," Israel said as he sat down. His eyes took in the room in a single sweep. Not that much to see, Thrasher realized.

"Right. The Mars guy," said Thrasher, sitting on the edge of the bed. "That's me."

"So what's this about twenty thou?"

Thrasher said, "You took ten thousand to louse up that Delta IV launch; I figured that for twenty thousand you'd tell me who gave you the money."

"And go to jail? You've got to be kidding."

"No jail. No questions asked. I've got a mole in my organization and I need to find out who he is before somebody gets hurt."

Israel pursed his lips, thinking it over. "You're crazy. I never did anything."

"Where'd you get that ten thousand?" Thrasher prompted.

"I sold a car."

"Really? Would that story hold up against my insurance company's investigators?"

"Insurance company?"

"They forked over forty million for the accident you caused."

"You can't prove anything!"

Thrasher saw beads of perspiration on Israel's upper lip. "I don't have to prove anything. I don't even want to prove anything. All I want to know is who gave you the ten thousand. That's worth twenty thousand."

Again Israel hesitated. At last he said, "Let me see the twenty."

Thrasher thought, once I show him the money he can take it from me and walk out of here. But he knows I'd go straight to the police. Not if I were dead, though. Would he kill me for twenty thousand dollars? Maybe I've walked myself into a trap!

"My people back in Houston know I'm meeting you," he lied. "So does the local Pinkerton office."

Israel made a disgusted face. "I'm not a thief. I earn what I make."

Thrasher nodded. "So do I."

He got up from the bed and went to the closet. Pulling back the accordion-fold door, Thrasher tapped out his code on the little safe and its door hummed briefly, then clicked open. He pulled out an envelope.

"Twenty one-thousand-dollar bills," he said, pulling the envelope open so Israel could see inside it.

Israel broke into a satisfied grin and reached out his hand.

"Who contacted you?"

"I don't know his name. He phoned me. No names."

"How'd you know—"

"He knew about the launch. Knew it from the inside. Technical knowledge. I figured he worked for your competition."

"I don't have any competition."

Israel smirked. "That's what you think."

"He called you at home?"

"At my apartment, yeah."

"When? How many times?"

It took half an hour, but Israel at last gave Thrasher a list of four dates and approximate times. "I've got his voice on my answering machine," he added.

"I'd like to have a copy of that."

Israel nodded. Thrasher handed him the envelope of cash.

Israel got to his feet and stuffed the envelope into the back pocket of his jeans.

"I want that voice recording," Thrasher said. Taking out his wallet and flicking it open, he pulled out his card. "Send it to me."

"Yeah. Nice doin' business with you."

Staring at the scruffy little list in his hands, Thrasher nodded absently. "Don't spend it all in one place."

7
HOUSTON

On the American Airlines flight back to Houston the next morning, Thrasher realized he needed professional help. A set of four phone calls wasn't much to go on, but it was all he had. Somebody in his organization had talked to Israel four times, and passed money to him. How to find out who?

Linda was waiting for him with a mug of ginger beer and his daily schedule as he entered the office.

"I need to talk to Frankenstein," Thrasher told her.

She followed him into his inner office. "Larry Franken?"

Nodding as he headed for his desk, Thrasher said, "Yep. This morning."

"You schedule's already pretty full. And you're having lunch with Jessie Margulis at twelve-thirty."

He grinned at her. "Frankenstein. This morning. And get Saito Yamagata on the phone for me."

Linda looked dubious.

"Please."

She made a smile and headed back to her own desk.

The magic word, Thrasher thought. Works every time. Almost.

Lawrence Franken was the head of Thrasher Digital's minuscule security department. As the man settled himself in one of the chairs in front of Thrasher's desk, Thrasher thought that if they were at a party with a thousand guests and he asked any one of them to find the cop, they'd go immediately to Frankenstein.

He was a big, unsmiling former Marine and ex-police officer with wide shoulders, a thick torso, and arms that looked strong enough to lift a Toyota. Squarish head, shaved down to a boot-camp buzz. Small, squinty eyes set in a heavy, blunt face. His natural scowl was intimidating, and he could look positively scary when he wanted to. *Even when he doesn't want to,* Thrasher said to himself.

"What's up, boss?" Franken's voice was low, growly.

"I've been playing detective, but I'm in over my head, Larry." Thrasher never called the man Frankenstein to his face.

"The agencies you hired haven't done the job, have they?"

"You know about that?"

Frankenstein made one of his rare grins. On him it looked almost grisly. "Now what kind of a security chief would I be if I didn't know what the boss was doing?"

"I didn't want to get you involved; I thought it might leak—"

"Nothing leaks out of my office," Frankenstein said, as firmly as a cop thwacking a perp.

"I'm sorry, Larry. I should have come to you first, shouldn't I have?"

Franken shrugged his massive shoulders. "You're the boss. You do what you want to. My job is to make sure you don't get hurt doing it."

With an apologetic grin, Thrasher nodded. "I guess I should have expected that you'd be watching me."

"Like a guardian angel. If that Israel fellow had tried anything on you last night my people would've been all over him."

"You had people following me?"

Frankenstein dipped his chin. "Sure did. On both sides of your motel room."

To himself Thrasher said, *wish I had known that last night. I would've felt a lot better.*

He pulled the crumpled sheet of hotel stationery from his jacket pocket and handed it to Franken.

"Somebody in the company made these phone calls to Israel."

Taking the sheet in a meaty hand, Franken asked, "Somebody from Mars, Incorporated or from Thrasher Digital?"

"Mars, I should think. But maybe not . . ."

"I'll have to run through everybody's phone records. It'll take some time."

"Do it as quickly as you can."

Franken went on, "Of course, your man might not have been dumb enough to use a company phone."

"I'll also be getting a copy of his voice off Israel's phone answering machine."

As if he hadn't heard that, Franken mused, "We can check office phone records. And home phones. Takes a little arm-twisting and some bribe money for the home phones."

"Do what you have to."

"If he used a cell phone, though . . ." Franken let the thought dangle.

"You can't trace cell phone calls?"

"It's more difficult."

"But you can do it?"

With another slow nod, Franken replied, "Unless he used a throwaway. Then we're screwed."

"Do what you have to," Thrasher repeated. "Just do it as quickly as you can. Whoever it is might try to hit us again."

"In Australia?"

"Or New Mexico, where the astronauts launch from."

The twelve-hour time difference in Australia meant that Thrasher didn't get to talk to Saito Yamagata until well past dinner.

Sitting in the study of his apartment, with Yamagata's ascetically lean face on the wall screen, Thrasher told the Japanese executive what little he had learned from Israel.

Yamagata bobbed his head up and down, his expression stolid. "Pretty much what my people have learned from our technician. Several phone calls, no names. The money was sent by Federal Express. The sender's name and return address were fakes."

"Could you send the dates and times of the phone calls to me, Sai?"

"Of course."

"What's going to happen to your tech?" Thrasher asked.

Yamagata's old smile returned. "He has asked for permission to quit Yamagata Corporation. Begged for permission, actually."

"And?"

"He's on his way back to Japan, to try to find new employment."

"That's it?"

"Did you think we would execute him?"

Thrasher sputtered, "Well, no, but just letting him go—is that wise?"

"What have you done with Mr. Israel?"

"Nothing," Thrasher admitted. Silently he added, except to hand him twenty grand.

"They are best left alone," Yamagata said. "It's not them we want. It's the man who bribed them that we must find."

Thrasher muttered, "Amen to that."

◎ 8 ◎
PORTALES

August in arid eastern New Mexico was hot. Even standing in the shade of the Mars, Inc. building, Thrasher could feel the summer heat baking the juices out of him. He thought he understood how a slab of meat must feel when it's roasting in the oven.

The monsoon season was beginning. There'd be thundershowers almost every afternoon for the next several weeks. Not that much rain, actually: maybe a quarter of an inch per day. But the showers helped to break the day's heat, and once the Sun went down temperatures became tolerable, even comfortable.

As he squinted up into the bright New Mexico sky, Thrasher could see that the few clouds building up over the mountains were beginning to drop rain, but the air was so dry that the rain evaporated well before reaching the ground. What do the locals call that? Thrasher asked himself. Then he remembered, *virgas*.

Enough sightseeing, Thrasher said to himself. There's work to do. As he started to head back inside the air conditioned building, he remembered that Thrasher Digital's annual stockholder's meeting would take place next month. If Sid's right and somebody's trying to buy his way into a majority position among the stockholders, he'll probably make his move at the meeting.

The interior of the former warehouse was blessedly cool. Not frigid, like so many buildings back in Texas, but cool enough so that people could work without feeling soggy.

Who's trying to take control of Thrasher Digital's board? Thrasher asked himself for the thousandth time. And for the thousandth time he came up with the same answer: Greg Sampson. That bearded, grinning, loudmouthed sonofabitch has been after my hide ever since I maneuvered him out of grabbing the company all those years ago.

It's Sampson, he told himself. Got to be. He wants to take over the company. He wants me out on my butt.

There were three items on the annual meeting's agenda that could accomplish that. Thrasher had calculated the votes among the directors and figured that he had a slight edge over Sampson's bloc. But if he's corralled enough of the proxy votes he could win. It all depends on the proxies, and from what Sid says, he's been out grabbing all the shares—and their proxies—that he can lay his hands on.

Well, he might get his chance to bounce me out next month.

As he headed down the aisle toward his cubicle of an office, a voice called to him.

"Hey, Art."

Turning, he saw it was Bill Polk, in his usual windbreaker and Levis, striding toward him with a big grin spread across his tanned face.

"Bill. How's it going?"

"Mars One assembly is just about finished. On schedule and a tad under budget."

Thrasher nodded. He knew that from the reports he'd been reading.

"Good work."

"We're stocking the bird with the equipment we'll carry to Mars," Polk went on. "Got to wait for the backup VR system, though; there's some glitch at the university in Tucson."

"Glitch?"

"Dr. Anders. She's in Australia this week."

"Again?"

Polk looked somewhere between pleased and worried. "She's getting married, I hear."

"Married?" Thrasher felt it like a body blow. "To Dougherty?"

"That's what I hear. I wasn't invited to the wedding."

"Damn!"

"They'll be flying back here Monday on one of the Astrolaunch birds."

They had reached Thrasher's cubicle. He went to his desk and slid into the swivel chair while Polk settled himself easily on one of the burgundy faux leather chairs.

"Married," Thrasher muttered.

"Dougherty's due to ride up to Mars One next week for an orientation tour," said Polk. "He wants to take Anders with him."

"What in—"

"To install the backup VR system," Polk went on, his expression almost serious. "I think they might have a zero-g honeymoon while they're up there."

Thrasher glowered at the astronaut.

Oblivious to Thrasher's dark face, Polk continued, "I mean, we haven't spun up the wheel yet, the whole bird's in microgravity. They'll be up there overnight."

"Okay, spare me the details," Thrasher snapped. "I assume the system they'll be installing is for the geologist we bumped from the flight."

"Dr. Hynes, right."

Goddamned Aussie glamorboy, Thrasher fumed inwardly. She fell for him the minute she saw him. And now they're going to be making it in zero gravity . . . aboard *my* spacecraft! It's just not fair, goddamit!

But Polk wasn't finished. Still grinning amiably, he said, "Nacho and Judine and I have been talking it over, boss. We think you ought to go up to the bird, too. For a visit."

"Me? Go aboard Mars One?"

"Why not?" said the astronaut. "You're the man responsible for it's being there. You ought to go see the finished article."

"In orbit? In zero gravity? Me?"

Quite easily, Polk explained, "We'll be spinning up the wheel in a few weeks. You'll have a feeling of normal gravity once you get aboard."

"I've never been in orbit."

"Neither were half a dozen of the technicians who've been putting the finishing touches on the bird, when we started. Now we ride them up and back every week."

"Yeah, I know."

"You ought to do it," Polk urged. "It'll be terrific publicity for you."

Thrasher stared at the astronaut. Is this another one of their initiation rites? he wondered. Or does he genuinely want me to see the finished spacecraft? Looking into Polk's smiling eyes, Thrasher realized, Bill's proud of what we've built and he wants me to be proud of it, too.

"Maybe I should," he said guardedly.

"Damned right you should."

"When do you spin up the wheel?"

"In a few weeks, depending on the final checkout. You'll have to take some orientation sessions, maybe a month or two."

"I can't spare a month or two."

With a careless shrug, Polk said, "Well, we can stretch out the lessons. Take 'em when you can. Learn how to get into a spacesuit, how to handle low g, emergency procedures, that kind of stuff."

"Sounds intimidating."

"You? Intimidated?" Polk chuckled. "We'll run the orientation course at your convenience. But, hell, Art, you *are* the alpha dog in this pack. You ought to see what you've produced."

Thrasher thought it over for another few heartbeats. I won't be there when Kristin and glamorpuss are. Let them have their goddamned zero-g honeymoon first. At last he said, "Okay, I'll do it. I'll start my schooling right after the board meeting."

Polk smiled warmly at him. Thrasher said to himself, if I'm still running this operation after the board meeting.

⚙ 9 ⚙
BOARD BATTLE

Larry Franken rode with Thrasher from the Houston office to the Marriott Residence Inn, where the annual meeting of Thrasher Digital Corporation was to take place.

"So what have you found?" Thrasher asked as his security chief climbed into the rear seat of the black Mercedes sedan. Franken was wearing dark sunglasses, which made him look more menacing than ever.

The Mercedes was far cheaper to run than a limo, but Franken looked uncomfortable, squeezed in, even though Carlo had slid the front seat as far forward as it could go to give Frankenstein more leg room.

"Zilch," said Franken, his expression bleak, morose. "Whoever made those calls to Israel and the Jap technician didn't use an office phone, nor any home phone of one of our employees."

"Must've used a cell phone."

Nodding heavily, Franken said, "We're checking on that, but it's not easy."

"What about the voice recording from Israel's answering machine?"

"Just about useless. The sound's so distorted we'll never get a match, even if we knew who to match it with."

Thrasher realized that between Mars, Incorporated and Thrasher

Digital there were more than twenty-five hundred employees to try matching voice prints. Too damned many, he told himself. Even if we eliminate the women, it'd take too long to get 'em all, and most of them would refuse to stand for a voice print.

"Well, keep at it until you've exhausted all the possibilities," he said.

"I think we're wasting our time, boss. If this guy was smart enough to know how to sabotage the rocket, he's too smart to use a phone we could trace."

"I guess. But what else do we have to go on?"

Franken said nothing for several moments. Then, "We'll check out the cell phones as well as we can. And there's a kid I know, something of a genius with audio technology. I'll get him to work on the voice recording. Maybe he'll be able to pull something out of it."

But from the scowling expression on his slab-jawed face, it was clear that Frankenstein didn't expect much.

As usual, Thrasher arrived at the Marriott's top-floor conference room a good hour before the board meeting was scheduled to begin. No one was there except Linda and a pair of uniformed latinas from the caterer laying out the trays of finger foods on the table at the rear of the room. Plus a Hispanic man in a dark suit, setting up the bar.

Sexism, Thrasher thought. Women handle the food but they assign a guy to run the bar. That's the least of your worries, he told himself.

There were three items on the agenda that could get him thrown out of control of Thrasher Digital. Sampson had insisted on all three.

The first was a motion to spin off Thrasher Digital's virtual reality business—such as it was—to an entertainment company called Tridinamics that had made a modest bid for it. Thrasher had found that Gregory Sampson had recently invested more than four hundred million in Tridinamics. In essence, he'd be selling Thrasher Digital's VR business to himself. Then he'll own all of it, and I'll be out in the cold.

The second motion called for an independent audit of Thrasher Digital's finances, separate from the auditors that the company used in making its annual financial report. Sid Ornsteen was livid over that one. "The bastard's saying that he doesn't trust us," the company's treasurer raged. "He's saying that he thinks we're cooking the books!"

The third motion was the one that hit Thrasher the hardest. Sampson had moved that Thrasher Digital disassociate itself from Mars, Incorporated. Thrasher knew he'd have to quit Thrasher Digital if that one carried. If he wasn't booted out by the first two motions first.

Thrasher greeted the directors as heartily as he could manage as they filed into the conference room, mentally counting their votes. Sampson had built a clique around himself, but Thrasher felt that he had enough loyal board members to beat back Sampson's initiatives.

If—and it was a big if—the proxy votes went his way. If the little individual stockholders who didn't hold enough shares to be on the board of directors voted to turn down Sampson's three items, he'd be okay.

That was the real issue. Sid's worried that Sampson's bought up enough shares so he can win the majority of the proxy votes. Thrasher had to admit that Sid was probably right.

By the time this meeting's over, he feared, the board will have voted to change the company's name to Sampson Digital.

The meeting was tense, testy from the outset. While almost every board member was there, only a handful of the smaller shareholders showed up, as usual. They hardly filled more than half of the chairs lined up along the conference room's side walls. They'll vote their shares in person, Thrasher knew. The others, the shareholders who stayed home, were supposed to mail in their proxy votes. How many of them bothered? How many of them will go along with Sampson's motions? I'm going to need every vote I can get, Thrasher figured.

Once the board members were seated at the long conference table, Thrasher welcomed them as warmly as he could manage.

"We have three pretty contentious issues to discuss and vote on," he said, "once we've finished with the formalities of reading the last meeting's minutes and the treasurer's report."

From his seat halfway down the table Sampson called out, "I move we dispense with the reading of the last meeting's minutes." Grinning through his beard, he added, "We all know what went on last time."

"Second the motion," said gray-haired Uta Gelson, sitting next to him. Thrasher worried about the seating; has Uta gone over to Sampson?

"Opposed?" he asked mechanically.

Silence.

"Okay, so moved," said Thrasher, turning slightly in his chair to nod at Linda, sitting at the wall behind him. She was recording the meeting.

"Now for the treasurer's report," he said.

Again Sampson spoke up. "I move we postpone the treasurer's report until we've decided the second motion on the agenda."

Thrasher saw Sid Ornsteen's face flame red.

"Okay. Let's skip ahead a little and talk about that item," Thrasher said, looking directly at Sampson. "Anybody object to that?"

Absolute silence.

"Okay, Greg. Why don't you tell us why you want an independent audit of the company's books?"

Smiling again, Sampson replied, "Our profit-and-loss figures are so bad that I'd like independent confirmation of them. If the company's financial situation is so precarious, we need to be absolutely certain of exactly where we stand."

Ornsteen snapped, "Our usual auditors have verified my report. I'm not cooking the books."

Sampson looked surprised, even hurt. "Nobody's accusing you of cooking the books, Sid. Hell, would the numbers look so bad if you were finagling them?"

No one laughed.

"Then why should we spend more money to verify the bad news?" Thrasher asked.

Pointing a finger at Thrasher like a pistol, Sampson said sternly, "Because we ought to be absolutely certain of how your mismanagement has brought this company to the brink of ruin."

"And you think selling our VR technology to Tridinamics will solve our problems?" Thrasher challenged.

Smiling his broadest, deadliest smile, Sampson answered, "I think junking this whole Mars fantasy is the solution to the company's problems. I thinking getting rid of you, Artie, is the only way we can save this company from bankruptcy."

◎ 10 ◎
PROXY WAR

For several heartbeats no one spoke. Thrasher looked down the table at his assembled directors. They were all silent, watching like spectators at a prizefight. Who's going to draw first blood? Who's going to get knocked out?

"All right," he said at last. "Let's put all three of the motions on the table. Greg here wants to sell off our VR technology to a company he has a considerable ownership position in—"

"He does?" asked one of the board members sitting toward the end of the table.

"He does indeed," Thrasher said.

"I've got a minor position in Tridinamics, that's true," said Sampson. "What of it?"

"So if we sell our VR technology to Tridinamics," Thrasher accused, "you'll be getting the fruits of our work for peanuts."

"Thrasher Digital could use some 'peanuts,'" Sampson countered. "Your piggy bank is just about empty."

"The hell it is!"

"The hell it isn't. Don't you read your own financial reports, Artie? Or are they too bad for you to face up to them?"

"We *are* in shaky financial condition," said one of the stockholders, a balding, chunky, pasty-faced man in a dark three-piece suit.

Sampson took up, "Your monomania about Mars has just about ruined this company, Artie."

"Once the mission gets underway," Thrasher said, as patiently as he could manage, "and people start tuning in on our VR systems, our profits will start to soar."

"That's a pipe dream."

"Then why'd you buy into Tridinamics? Why do you want to sell our VR work to a company you own?"

Unruffled, Sampson replied, "I buy into lots of companies, Artie—as long as they're well managed, profitable, and have good prospects for the future. Which is not the condition Thrasher Digital is in."

"Our condition will improve once the Mars mission gets underway."

"Poppycock," Sampson barked. "You're running this company into the ground."

"Then why do you want to take it over?"

"To save it!" Waving an arm toward the shareholders sitting along the side walls, he went on, "To save the investment that these people have made. To save them from being ruined by your fantasies!"

Thrasher saw heads nodding up and down the table.

Through gritted teeth he told them, "Look, when we first went into this Mars program I told the board that we'd be facing some lean years. But once the Mars mission takes off and VR sales start climbing, we'll be solidly in the black again."

Almost smugly, Sampson said, "I repeat: poppycock."

"That's a lie and you know it!" Thrasher snapped.

Sampson shot to his feet. "Are you calling me a liar?"

Jumping up from his chair, Thrasher said, "You know the Mars mission will make this company profitable, and if you say differently you're not telling the truth!"

Uta Gerson said, "I didn't come here to watch you two macho he-men engage in a pissing contest."

Several people gasped at her language. A few tittered.

Nels Bartlett, sitting across the table almost opposite Sampson, spoke up. "Uta's right. You two guys could spend the rest of the day throwing hand grenades at each other. Instead of arguing about this, why don't we vote?"

"Yes," said the florid-faced man sitting next to him. "Enough arguing. Count the votes and be finished with this."

Trying to keep a rein on his anger, Thrasher sat down slowly and said, "Do I hear a motion to vote on all three of the agenda items?"

Sampson took his chair, too, his white-bearded face smirking.

"So moved," said Bartlett.

"Second," Uta Gerson said.

"Discussion? Any objections?" No one raised a hand. "All right then, let's vote."

The board members shocked Thrasher by voting in favor of Sampson's motions, fourteen to eight. I'm finished, he thought. The bastard's beaten me.

But then Linda said, tapping on her laptop's screen, "I have the tally of the proxy votes here."

Thrasher half-turned in his chair to face her. "What's the count?" he asked, fearing the worst.

Linda peered at the laptop's screen. "Seven hundred and thirty-eight thousand shares voted by proxy," she announced, in a perfectly calm voice. "For the first motion there were three hundred and twelve thousand votes in favor, four hundred twenty-six thousand against."

Thrasher gulped with surprise. They voted against Sampson! But there were two more motions to consider.

The vote to bring in an outside auditor lost even more badly: two hundred sixty thousand pro, and four hundred seventy-eight thousand anti. The vote to disassociate from the Mars program was closer, but still Sampson lost: three hundred and forty-two thousand for, three hundred ninety-six thousand against.

Sampson sputtered, "What about the preferred stock?"

Linda went carefully through all the numbers. Thrasher's margin of victory was slim, but he carried all three votes.

Sampson's smirk was gone. He sat there glowering with unconcealed anger. "I want an independent count of the votes!"

As sweetly as a flower girl, Linda replied, "The voting was tabulated by our auditors, Mr. Sampson."

"I want outside corroboration!" Sampson bellowed.

With a self-satisfied grin, Ornsteen leaned across the table toward Sampson and said, "You can count the votes until you're blue in the face, Greg. They won't change."

It was the first time Thrasher had ever seen Sid so happy.

Before Sampson could reply, Uta Gerson said, "Come on, Gregory. You've lost. Take it like a man."

Sampson sat there, his chest heaving. Suddenly he pushed his chair back, got to his feet, and stormed out of the room.

Thrasher watched him go, still stunned by the results of the voting. From behind him, he heard Linda offer, "I can provide copies of the voting to any board member who's interested."

Several hands went up.

At last Thrasher said, "The next agenda item is new business. Anyone?"

Nels Bartlett asked, "So how's the Mars program going? When can we expect to see some profits from it?"

Thrasher stammered, "It's . . . it's going well. The spacecraft assembly has been finished. I plan to take a ride up there and inspect it myself."

"You're going into orbit?" Uta Gerson asked.

"Just for a visit."

The board members—even those who had voted in favor Sampson's motions—listened intently as Thrasher told them about his plans for Mars.

Behind him, Linda recorded every word.

⚛ 11 ⚛
EXECUTIVE WOMEN'S LEAGUE

Once the board meeting ended, Thrasher rode with Sid Ornsteen and Linda back to the office, all three squeezed in the rear seat of the Mercedes, Linda in the middle.

"I can't believe it," Thrasher admitted. "The little guys voted for me."

Ornsteen was equally surprised. "I thought for sure that Sampson had bought enough shares to carry the proxy vote."

"So did he," Linda said.

"Did you see the look on his face when the voting went against him?" Ornsteen crowed. "I wish I had a camera!"

"The whole meeting was video recorded," said Linda.

Thrasher's shoulder was touching Linda's. He looked into her face: she seemed delightfully pleased, but not at all surprised.

"You sure the vote count was accurate?" he asked, half joking. "If Sampson gets an independent count, it's not going to change, is it?"

"Not unless he cheats," she said.

She's so sure of herself, Thrasher thought. As if she knew in advance how the voting would go.

"You tallied the votes before the meeting started, didn't you." It wasn't a question.

"I always do, that's regular procedure."

"You might have told me," he grumbled. "Save me an ulcer."

Linda laughed softly. "I wanted to tell you. I wanted to tell you months ago, but I thought it would be best if I didn't get your hopes up."

"Get my hopes up?"

With a nod, Linda said, "Back when Mr. Ornsteen started worrying that Mr. Sampson was trying to buy enough Thrasher Digital stock to outvote you, I started buying a few shares, myself."

Grinning, Ornsteen muttered, "David versus Goliath."

"A lot of Davids," Linda said. "Only, they were all women."

Ornsteen suddenly looked puzzled. "What are you talking about?"

"I started talking to other women in the company," Linda explained. "And then to women outside the company, other executive assistants and employees of other companies. We used the Internet to keep in touch and we bought as much stock as we could afford."

"You're the reason for the second wave of buying?" Ornsteen gasped.

Nodding again, Linda said, "We networked. It spread across the country. We formed a sort of association, the Executive Women's League. Our goal was to acquire enough shares to outvote Mr. Sampson."

"Enough shares to control the company," Thrasher murmured.

Ornsteen objected, "But you don't have enough money to outbuy Sampson!"

"Yes we do. There's lots of us, all across the country. Not only did we buy enough shares to outvote Mr. Sampson, but we kept those shares out of his hands." She seemed utterly delighted with herself.

"Sampson must've thought he'd bought enough shares . . ." Ornsteen mused.

"But we bought more," Linda said happily. "Just a little here and a little there. Spread across the whole country."

Thrasher gaped at her. "A nationwide cabal. Of women."

"The Executive Women's League," Linda repeated. "We're looking at other companies now. Astrolaunch Corporation, for example."

Ornsteen broke into a hearty laugh. "My god, Linda, you're going to become a force in the stock market."

"You saved my neck," Thrasher said.

Turning to face him, she said, "I couldn't let Mr. Sampson throw you out of your own company. That wouldn't be right."

"You saved my neck," Thrasher repeated, almost in a whisper.

"I wouldn't want to work for Mr. Sampson," she said. "I don't like him."

Ornsteen said, "Well, you sure surprised him. The expression on his face!"

Thrasher found himself staring at her. "My god, Linda," he blurted, "*I'm* working for *you* now!"

"Oh, no," Linda said, completely serious. "I only own about a thousand shares."

Chuckling at the way things had turned out, Thrasher mused, "I'm supposed to be hosting dinner tonight for the board. I wonder if Sampson will show up?"

"If he does," Ornsteen said, "have somebody taste your food before you try it."

They all laughed, but Thrasher felt more convinced than ever that Sampson was the man behind the sabotage of the Delta IV launch.

"Dinner's at seven?" Ornsteen asked.

"Right. At the Marriott. Bar opens at six."

Glancing at his wristwatch, Ornsteen said, "I'll have time to go home and pick up my wife."

Looking at Linda again, Thrasher asked, "Linda, would you do me the honor of coming to the dinner with me?"

She looked startled. "You're not going to tell them all what I did!"

"Not if you don't want me to."

"I think it's best if we keep it our little secret."

"Okay. Fine. But will you be my date tonight?"

Linda smiled warmly. "I'd be happy to."

⊚ 12 ⊚
DINNER

Sampson did not show up, although most of the board members who voted his way did. Thrasher sent Carlo to pick up Linda while he showered and put on a fresh suit, then took a taxi to the Marriott. Sid Ornsteen and his wife were already there, at the bar in the hallway outside the banquet room. Sid was waving a champagne flute, laughing with a couple of the board members, while his wife stood at his side in a floor-length gown dripping with sequins, bone thin, frowning disapprovingly.

Miriam doesn't like to see Sid drinking, Thrasher thought as he approached them. But it sure looks good to see him happy, for a change.

". . . and did you see the look on Sampson's face?" Ornsteen was saying to a pair of older men. "Priceless!"

Thrasher inserted himself between his treasurer and the board members. "It was quite a meeting, wasn't it?" he said cheerily. "Short and sweet."

One of the board members, tall enough to be a basketball player, with a leonine mane of silver hair, smiled minimally. "I still think he has a legitimate point, Arthur. We're on the edge of a precipice, you know."

Nodding soberly, Thrasher agreed, "I know. But there's light at the end of the tunnel."

The man harrumphed. "I just hope that it's not the light of an oncoming train."

Ornsteen laughed loudly and his wife tugged at his sleeve. He reluctantly allowed her to lead him away from the bar. I wonder how many Sid's had? Thrasher wondered. Then he realized that for a man who drinks as seldom as Ornsteen did, one glass of champagne could make the world glow.

Towering over Thrasher, the silver-haired board member asked quite seriously, "What happens to the program if there's another launch failure, or some other sort of accident?"

"That won't stop us," Thrasher said.

"But we're running on such a slender thread. Another accident or some kind of delay might push the company into bankruptcy."

As brightly as he could, Thrasher said, "Then we'll just have to avoid accidents and delays."

"Easy to say, Arthur, but—"

Thrasher spotted Linda coming down the hallway toward him, looking elegant in a navy blue scoop-necked mid-thigh cocktail dress adorned with a single rope of pearls. Her midnight-dark hair curled softly around her shoulders.

"Excuse me," he said and rushed to her.

"Sorry I'm late," Linda said.

"No, no, we're just getting started. You look absolutely wonderful."

She smiled brightly. "I haven't seen that suit on you before. It looks good."

Thrasher led her to the bar and ordered two champagnes.

"Not ginger beer?" Linda asked.

"Not tonight. I'm celebrating."

"About beating Sampson."

"About having the loveliest woman in Texas as my date."

For a moment Linda looked startled, almost. Then her smile returned and she said, "You're not trying your reprobate lines on me, are you?"

"No," said Thrasher, handing her one of the champagne flutes. "I've given up on being a reprobate." Placing his free hand over his heart, he said, "I'm sincere."

They clinked glasses.

"Really?" Linda said.

"Really."

At that moment the doors to the banquet room swung open and the crowd began to surge in. Thrasher offered his arm and Linda took it.

"Linda," he said, in what he hoped was a fair impression of Humphrey Bogart, "this could be the beginning of a beautiful friendship."

◎ 13 ◎
HOPES AND PLANS

The dinner went well. The food was uncommonly good, for hotel fare, and the assembled board members seemed to enjoy themselves. Thrasher gave a slide show presenting the progress of the Mars program and the plans for the mission.

"So what do you expect to find on Mars?" someone called out from one of the tables in the darkness.

"Darned if I know," Thrasher answered. "That's why we're going, to see what's there. That's the whole point of exploration, to discover something new. Columbus didn't know he'd find a New World. Einstein didn't realize his work would lead to solar cells and nuclear power."

"Is there life on Mars?"

"We just don't know. Not yet. But the biggest volcano in the solar system is there, Olympus Mons. It's so tall you could put Mt. Everest inside the crater at its top."

"You think Mars will become a tourist attraction?"

People laughed.

But Thrasher answered, "With our virtual reality technology, people will be able to visit Mars, see the sights, climb Olympus Mons, go skiing down its slopes if they want to. All in the safety and comfort of their own homes."

"On to Mars, then!" Nels Bartlett called out.

"On to Mars," Thrasher repeated, fervently.

Thrasher rode with Linda back to her family's home. Sitting beside her in the back seat of the Mercedes, he chatted happily about his upcoming visit to the Mars One spacecraft.

"They're going to spin up the wheel, so I'll be in normal gravity once we get there."

"You'll be in a spacesuit?" Linda asked.

He nodded, then realized she probably couldn't see the gesture in the shadows. "Yep. I'll be like an astronaut. For a day and a half."

"You're going to spend a night up there?"

"Yep."

For a heartbeat, Linda was silent. Then, "Please be careful, Mr. Thra—"

"Art," he said. "You can call me Mr. Thrasher in the office, but I wish you'd call me Art when we're together."

He sensed her smile. "All right . . . Art."

"Thank you."

"For what?"

"For saving my neck. For running the office. For coming to dinner with me tonight. For being such a delightful, charming, intelligent, beautiful woman."

She laughed shakily. "You're slipping into your reprobate ways again."

"I'm completely sincere, Linda. I think you're wonderful."

"I think you are, too. But I worry about you."

"Worry? What for? I've given up my reprobate ways, honest."

"Not that," she said. "This hop up to orbit. If anything goes wrong . . ."

"I'll be with Bill Polk. He's the best in the business."

"Accidents can happen," Linda said, quite seriously. "Accidents can be *made* to happen."

Thrasher stared at her. In the flickering lights from the street lamps, Linda's face seemed grave, intent.

"Like the Delta IV launch," he muttered.

"That wasn't an accident, was it?"

"No, it wasn't. Larry Franken's trying to unravel who was behind it."

"Whoever it was, they'd have a great opportunity to get rid of you when you fly off to orbit."

"Then I'd better find out who it was before I go," Thrasher said lightly.

"It's not a joke," Linda insisted.

"No," he admitted. "I guess it isn't."

The car glided to a stop and Carlo turned toward them. "This the place?"

Linda nodded. "Yes. Home sweet home."

As Carlo opened the driver's door and stepped out onto the street, Thrasher reached for Linda.

"I know there's some mistletoe around here somewhere," he murmured.

"You don't need mistletoe, Art," she said.

He kissed her soundly, ignoring Carlo's opening the door on her side. Linda clung to him for a moment, then moved away.

"Thanks for a wonderful evening," she said, a little breathlessly.

"Thank you, Linda."

"I'll see you in the office tomorrow morning."

"Sure."

She slid out of the car. On an impulse, Thrasher slid out behind her and walked her to the door of the rambling Dutch colonial house. A single porch light was on, otherwise the house seemed dark, asleep. He slid his arms around her waist and kissed her again.

Linda giggled. "My mother, father, two uncles and three brothers are inside, you know."

"Sounds like a posse."

"They're very protective."

Thrasher said, "They're going to have to get accustomed to me."

She looked into his eyes, then slipped out of his arms and said, "Good night, Art."

"Good night, Linda."

She unlocked the door and went inside. Thrasher stood there for a moment beneath the porch light, then turned and hurried back to the Mercedes, where Carlo still stood by the open rear door, grinning.

"Not a word about this to anybody," Thrasher growled at his chauffeur.

"Sure, boss. I know when to keep my mouth shut." But Carlo was still grinning from ear to ear.

As he rode back toward his apartment, Thrasher berated himself: You have a rule about getting it on with your employees. You're putting her in an impossible situation.

Yeah, but she didn't seem to mind it. She seemed to enjoy it, in fact.

Then he leaned back and shook his head unhappily. Damn! If I want to pursue her I'm going to have to fire her!

◎ 14 ◎
VOICE PRINTS

Larry Franken lumbered into Thrasher's office with a rare smile on his face.

"I think we might have something for you, boss," he said, settling his bulk in one of the chairs in front of Thrasher's desk.

For the past two days Thrasher had been stumbling through the motions of running the company. He was strictly business with Linda, their brief moment the night of the board meeting looming like an iron curtain between them. For her part, Linda was smoothly professional, doing her best to pretend that nothing had changed between her and her employer.

Frankenstein's statement—and his unnerving smile—brought Thrasher's attention to a sharp focus.

"Something? What?"

"You got a couple of hours free this afternoon?"

Thrasher tapped his computer keyboard and glanced at his schedule. "I guess I can juggle things a little. What's going on?"

"This kid I mentioned to you," said Franken. "He's an electronics genius."

"He's got something from the voice recording?"

"Could be. We'll have to go over to his place and see what he's come up with."

"Can't he come over here?"

"Not unless he brings a truckload of equipment with him. We go to him."

Thrasher nodded reluctantly. Squinting at his schedule again, he said, "Okay. Three o'clock."

Frankenstein lifted himself out of the chair. "See you then."

As the Mercedes sped along freeway's nearly empty high-capacity lane, passing the heavy traffic in the other lanes, Franken explained, "The kid's name is Tómas Chandrasekhar. Indian father, Mexican mother. Distantly related to some big-time astronomer from a couple generations back. Father's an executive in an import-export firm, mother teaches music."

"And he's an electronics genius?" Thrasher asked.

Frankenstein nodded heavily. "Got interested in pop music, then started studying acoustics. On his own. Put in a year at MIT, then dropped out and came back to his parents. They bought him a condo unit and he's been on his own ever since."

"Doing what?"

"Spending his old man's money, mostly. He does some consulting work here and there, but not enough to pay for his habit."

"Habit? He's a junkie?"

Franken shook his head. "His habit is gadgets. Expensive digital gadgets. Wait'll you see his place."

Chandrasekhar's place turned out to be a penthouse apartment in a downtown high-rise. To Thrasher, the apartment looked like the back room of a poorly-managed electronics shop. Digital equipment was strewn everywhere. Thrasher recognized a half-dozen amplifiers, four laptop computers, and a single man-tall supercomputer console. The rest of the stuff was a mystery to him, although he could make out oscilloscopes and several sets of soldering irons.

Everything was heaped in a seemingly haphazard mess. No furniture. Not a chair or a sofa in sight. The only table held stacks of electronics black boxes. The windows looked out on the Houston skyline, but the view was blocked by heaps of digital gear.

"He lives here?" Thrasher asked as he and Franken stood just inside the apartment's front door. Franken had knocked once and opened the unlocked door without waiting for anyone to respond.

Frankenstein nodded. "I think he's got a bed in one of the back rooms."

"Where is—"

Tómas Chandrasekhar came through a doorway on the far side of the room, zipping his fly and smiling shyly.

He looked like a kid. No more than a teenager. Short and slight, with dark skin, bright white teeth, and big liquid eyes. Thick mop of shiny black ringlets curling over his ears. Looks like he hasn't brushed his hair in a week, Thrasher thought. Grubby, faded T-shirt and stained, rumpled jeans. His feet were bare.

"I'm very sorry I couldn't answer when you knocked. I was on the pot." His voice was soft, with just a hint of Hindu sing-song.

"That's alright, Tommy," Franken said amiably. "We let ourselves in."

"So I see." Chandrasekhar spread his arms. "Well, welcome to the junkyard."

Thrasher heard himself ask, "How old are you?"

"Twenty-three. And how old are you?"

There wasn't a trace of malice or smartass attitude in the question. The kid seemed genuinely curious. Thrasher decided he liked him.

"I'm fifty-five," he answered. "I used to be twenty-three but I gave it up."

Chandrasekhar laughed, a hearty bubbling sound of delight.

"You're here about the voice prints, am I right?"

"Right."

"Okay. Allow me to show you what I've got." He moved toward a small mountain range of black boxes spread across the floor and squatted cross-legged on the carpet before them. As he clicked switches and the dials lit up, Chandrasekhar motioned for Thrasher and Franken to sit on the floor beside him.

"I keep meaning to get some furniture in here, but somehow I never get around to it."

"That's okay," said Thrasher, lowering himself to the floor. "I'm interested in results, not interior décor."

"Me too," said Chandrasekhar.

Thrasher's nose twitched. The kid was odorous, but not from grime. Cinnamon? He realized that Chandrasekhar smelled like a kitchen spice rack.

Frankenstein sank slowly to his knees, as if he were sitting at a Japanese tea ceremony.

Pressing a button on the keyboard lying before him, Chandrasekhar pointed to a bristling, wavy green line on the oscilloscope in the middle of the junk pile.

"That's the voice print from the recording Mr. Franken gave me," he explained.

"No sound?" Thrasher asked.

"We don't need sound. Just the digital print. Sound affects you emotionally, you know. The print is what's important. It's as individual as a fingerprint or a DNA sample."

"Really?"

Ignoring the question, Chandrasekhar lit up a second oscilloscope dial, beside the one showing the voice print.

"All I had to do was to find a matching voice print. Mr. Franken gave me several days' recordings of the telephone traffic from your offices."

Thrasher turned to Frankenstein. "We bug phone calls?"

Franken nodded solemnly. "Interoffice messages, out of office, especially overseas calls."

"I didn't know that."

"Standard routine. We keep the recordings for a year, then dump 'em."

Thrasher recalled several phone conversations he'd rather not have anyone else listen in on. Vicki Zane, for example. "Even my private calls?"

"Not your private line."

Thrasher felt relieved. But he wondered if Frankenstein was being completely truthful with him.

Chandrasekhar rapped a knuckle on the first oscilloscope trace. "So all that was necessary was find a match for this print."

"Out of thousands of phone messages?" Thrasher asked.

The kid grinned brightly. "The more the better. That's what supercomputers are for. It can run an individual phone call in a few nanoseconds and, if it doesn't find a match, go on to the next. A nanosecond is a very brief period of time, you know. There are as many nanoseconds in one second as there are seconds in thirty-two years."

Impatiently, Thrasher asked, "You found a match?"

Chandrasekhar bit his lip, then replied, "It's a pretty good match. Not perfect, sadly, but very, very close."

"Let's see it."

The second oscilloscope lit up with a spiky, waving green line that looked to Thrasher exactly like the first print. He swiveled his head back and forth, comparing them.

"Here," Chandrasekhar said, "allow me to lay them one on top of the other."

The first oscilloscope now showed both traces, one above the other.

"Now we scrunch them together," Chandrasekhar murmured, his fingers working the keyboard.

The two curves slid together. A few edges of red showed where they did not match exactly.

"Better than a ninety percent correlation," said Chandrasekhar. "I believe that would be good enough to hold up in court!"

"So whose voice is it?" Thrasher asked.

Chandrasekhar tapped a couple more buttons on his keyboard.

"Someone named Vincent Egan," he said. And Egan's name appeared in green letters on the second oscilloscope.

🔄 15 🔄
CONFIRMATION

Thrasher sat cross-legged on the carpet, staring at Vince Egan's name glaring at him from the oscilloscope screen.

It can't be Vince, he said to himself. I asked him about it and he told me he was trying to save himself from defaulting on his mortgage. He told me to my face. He got sore that I suspected him.

To Chandrasekhar, he muttered, "You're sure about this?"

"Ninety-two percent correlation," the kid replied. "Out of all the voice tracks we looked at, his was the only one that so closely matches the phone recording Mr. Franken gave me."

"Vince Egan," Thrasher said woodenly.

"It's him," Franken rumbled.

"But why? Why would Vince—"

"We'll have to ask him about that."

"No." Thrasher shook his head. "I'll do it. Myself."

Franken hauled himself to his feet, like an elephant getting up. "Okay. You do it yourself. You're the boss."

"Yeah," Thrasher said shakily as he climbed to a standing position. Rank hath its privileges, he thought bitterly. And its responsibilities.

When you've got to get a needle jabbed into you, Thrasher told himself, do it right away. Don't try to put it off, it just prolongs the agony.

So as soon as he and Franken returned to the Thrasher Digital offices, Thrasher marched himself down the hall, past Egan's surprised secretary, and rapped once on Vince's office door.

"He's not in," the secretary said, from behind her desk.

"Where is he?"

"He's flying in from Tucson," she answered. "Should be here by five-thirty, if the plane's on time."

Thrasher took the flight number from her, went back to his office, and had Linda check the estimated arrival time. Six-fifteen.

The office'll be closed by then, he said to himself. Of course, Vince might come here anyway, he's not a nine-to-five guy. No, he's so dedicated that he took two hundred and fifty thousand bucks to blow up that rocket and put me behind the eight-ball.

Why? That bullshit about his mortgage was a bald-faced lie. Why did he do it?

Thrasher drummed his fingers on his desktop for several moments, then punched the intercom.

"Linda, tell Carlo to meet me downstairs. I need to go to the airport."

Linda's voice sounded startled. "The airport? Now? You have a meeting—"

"Cancel it. Or rather, postpone it. Reschedule it. And get Carlo."

A brief hesitation, then Linda said, "I could get the helicopter for you. It's on the roof, I'd just have to round up the pilot."

Thrasher nodded. "Okay. Good. I'll take the chopper."

He fidgeted nervously at his desk until Linda told him the helicopter was ready.

"Fine. Tell Carlo to get over to the airport and wait for me."

Flying over the teeming city, looking down at the traffic clogging the freeways, Thrasher could think of nothing except Vince Egan's treachery. That explosion might've killed somebody, he thought. If it had gone off a few minutes earlier . . .

He realized he was working himself up into a rage. With an effort he leaned back in the helicopter's seat and tried to force himself to relax. He tried to use the muted roar of the 'copter's jet engine and the thrumming of the big rotor as a mantra to soothe his nerves. It didn't work.

Thrasher was ten minutes early for Egan's flight. He stood at the exit lane of the security area, peering down the corridor for a sight of the people arriving from Tucson. The minutes ticked by slowly.

Then people started coming through. A couple of youngsters, probably students. Businessmen. A grandmother with two kids in tow.

"Are you coming in from Tucson?" Thrasher asked her.

"Yes," she said, hurrying past.

Then he saw Egan striding along, computer bag slung over one shoulder. He looked surprised when he saw Thrasher standing there, waiting for him.

"Art! What's up?"

Thrasher grasped Egan's free arm and said, "We have to talk, Vince. Someplace private."

Egan looked puzzled, not suspicious. "Private? In the airport?"

Without answering, Thrasher led Egan to the toilets. Men and women were filing in and out of their separate entrances.

"This is your idea of private?"

Thrasher went to the third entrance, the one for handicapped persons. He pushed the door open. It was unoccupied.

"In here," he said.

"What the hell's going on?" Egan asked as he stepped into the tiled room. It held a toilet and a sink at a level where a person in a wheelchair could use it easily, with handgrips set into the walls. Egan unslung his computer bag and rested it on the sink as Thrasher slid the bolt locking the door. Hope nobody needs this facility, he thought.

"Art, what is it? You look like the world's about to end."

"It was you," Thrasher said, jabbing an accusing finger at him. "You're the one who set up the accident."

Egan's face went white.

"That story about defaulting on your mortgage was just so much bullshit. You took two hundred and fifty thousand dollars to blow up that Delta IV."

"No, that's not true!"

"Don't try to deny it. I've got enough evidence to send you to jail."

"I . . ." Egan's mouth hung open, but no more words came out.

"Why? Why'd you do it? Why'd you try to screw me?"

"Because you screwed me!" Egan snapped, his cheeks flaming with anger.

"I screwed you?" Thrasher shouted back at him. "I took you out of MIT and made you my chief engineer—"

"The Mars job should've been mine!" Egan's tortured voice echoed off the wall tiles.

Thrasher blinked with surprise.

"I'm your chief engineer, yeah. Big honor. You stick me with this stupid VR job that a trained chimpanzee could handle while you give the Mars program to an outsider."

"Jessie Margulis is—"

"He's an outsider! You didn't even consider me for the job! You never even talked to me about it!"

"There was nothing to talk about! You're not an aerospace engineer."

"I could've done it. You could've hired Margulis and let him work under me."

"And that's why . . ." Thrasher stared at Egan, hardly able to believe what he was hearing.

"I needed the money," Egan said, his voice lower, guilty. "What I told you about the mortgage wasn't a lie. Just the part about my family handing me the money. Fat chance they'd pitch in to help me."

"Then who the hell gave you the money?" Thrasher demanded.

◈ 16 ◈
A RIDDLE WRAPPED
IN A MYSTERY . . .

"I don't know where the money came from," Egan said, his first blaze of anger spent, his voice almost contrite.

But Thrasher's anger was mounting. "Don't bullshit me, Vince. Who the hell's behind this?"

"I don't know!"

"Two hundred and fifty thousand bucks just arrived in your bank account, out of the blue?"

Egan sat on the toilet and sank his head into his hands. "I got a CD in the mail. No return address. Voice recording. Promised me enough money to save my house."

"A man's voice?"

"Computer synthesizer."

Damn! Thrasher thought. Chandrasekhar won't be able to analyze that.

"So this digitized voice just offered you two hundred and fifty thousand?"

"Not the first message. It just said it could help me with my mortgage payments. Whoever sent it must've known I was in a hole."

"How many discs are there?"

"Five, altogether."

"And how were you supposed to answer them? How'd they know you'd go along with them?"

"I sent a CD to a post office box number."

Just about untraceable, Thrasher realized. Sampson—or whoever was behind all this—could have a lackey take out a post office box and then close it when the deed was done.

Egan lifted his head. "Art, I made sure nobody would get hurt."

"Nobody but me."

"I was sore at you. I needed the money. Nobody would get hurt."

Ignoring Egan's whining, Thrasher asked, "Did you keep the CDs?"

"Yeah, but there's no way to analyze the voice. It's all computer synthesis."

"I want the CDs anyway." Then a new thought struck Thrasher. "They've got CDs of your voice. They've got enough on you to blackmail you for the rest of your life!"

Egan's face crumpled. He sank his head into his hands again and began to sob.

It took a while for Egan to pull himself together. Thrasher watched him coldly, without an iota of sympathy for the man. I took him in, I treated him like a son, I made him chief engineer, and he got mad at me because I didn't give him a job he couldn't handle. He sold me out for a measly two hundred and fifty thousand dollars.

Once Egan had washed his face and straightened his suit jacket, Thrasher said gruffly, "Come on, Carlo's waiting outside. We'll go back to the office."

"I'll resign," Egan said, his voice hoarse.

"No, I'll fire you. That way you get severance pay."

As Thrasher unlocked the door, Egan said, "For what it's worth, Art, I'm sorry."

"Yeah. So am I."

Sitting in Thrasher's office the next morning, Larry Franken took the thin stack of CDs from Thrasher's extended hand.

"Vince tells me the voice is a computer synthesis," Thrasher said.

Franken grunted. "No way to get a voice print, then."

Almost smiling, Thrasher said, "Not unless you want to match it against other computers."

Franken sighed heavily. "I'll ask Chandra about it. Maybe he can figure out something."

"Maybe," Thrasher said bleakly.

Once Franken left the office, Linda came in, looking concerned. "I just got an e-mail from Vince Egan. He's resigned!"

"Damn! I told him not to do that."

"Is this about the accident?"

"Yeah," Thrasher said, disgusted. "Vince sold me out for two hundred and fifty thousand bucks."

"Vince?"

"Vince."

Linda sank into one of the chair in front of Thrasher's desk. "He made the rocket blow up?"

"He set it up."

"But why? Why would he—"

"It's a long story. I'll have to find a new chief engineer."

"What's Vince going to do?"

The fury suddenly boiled up inside Thrasher. "He can blow his fucking brains out, for all I care! Stupid, ungrateful son of a bitch."

Linda stared at him. After several heartbeats she asked softly, "He has a family, doesn't he? Three kids."

"Yeah. I was going to fire him, so he could get severance pay, but maybe resigning is the smarter option. Looks better on his resumé."

"You're not going to have him arrested, are you?"

Thrasher shook his head. "What good would that do? It'd just make the whole mess public. I don't want that."

"No, I suppose not."

Thrasher broke into a bitter laugh. "I'll probably get asked for a letter of recommendation from whoever he applies to for a new job."

"What will you do?"

"We have a standard form on file, don't we?"

Linda said, "We just use it as a guideline. We always put in some personal stuff."

"Well, if anybody asks for a recommendation for Vince, just send them the standard form letter, with his date of hire and date of resignation. List the positions he held. That's all. You can sign it for me. I don't want to see it."

She nodded.

"Okay," said Thrasher. He took a deep breath, then asked, "What's on the schedule?"

Linda tapped the PDA in her hand. "You're supposed to go down to the NASA center tomorrow. Something about a neutral buoyancy tank?"

Thrasher made a face. "Part of the training that Bill Polk's set up for me. I get into a space suit and they dunk me in a deep water tank. Simulates the feeling of zero gravity."

"Underwater?" She seemed alarmed.

"There'll be a team of NASA scuba divers with me. They won't let me drown."

Linda smiled at him. "I wish I could see that."

Shaking his head, Thrasher said, "I need you here, running the office." Then a thought struck him. "Although it would be fun to see you in a bikini."

"None of that, Mr. Thrasher."

"We could spend the weekend down by the lake. Take in a ball game, maybe."

"There's a strict company rule against that kind of thing."

"Dammit, I make the rules. I can break them."

"I'd have to resign," she said.

"All right, I'll fire you. Is that what you want?"

"Not really."

"I'll fire you on Friday and rehire you Monday morning. How's that?"

"You're being ridiculous."

"I want to be with you, Linda. I want you to be with me."

"So do I."

"We can keep it secret, just the two of us."

"You don't understand, Art," she said, her voice low. "I come from a very traditional family. We don't go off and spend weekends out of town. We have proper courtships, get engaged and then married. You're not ready for that."

"I am," he heard himself say. "With you."

She stared at him. "Do you mean that? Do you really mean it?"

"We could fly to Reno tonight and get married there."

"That's crazy!"

"No it's not. Happens every day."

Linda jumped up from the chair. "We can't just run off like a pair of teenagers, Art. This is serious! You need to think about it. *I* need to think about it."

She turned and hurried out of his office.

Thrasher sat there behind his desk, musing. She said she wants to be with me. I heard her say that. So I'll have to fire her and start courting her like a proper boyfriend.

Is that what she really wants? Thrasher shook his head. What was it Churchill said about the Russians? They're a riddle wrapped in a mystery inside an enigma.

That's what Linda is.

Then he remembered, so is Vince Egan, and whoever handed him the money to blow up that rocket.

◎ 17 ◎
LAHE TAHOE

Thrasher spent most of the next day at the NASA center's neutral buoyancy tank. Under Bill Polk's watchful eye he clambered into a space suit and stood like a department store dummy while a pair of technicians checked all the seals and connections. Finally he pulled the bubble helmet over his head and slid the catch that locked it to the suit's metal neck ring.

"Can you hear me?" Polk asked, speaking into the microphone clipped to the collar of his sports shirt.

Thrasher nodded. "Loud and clear. Radio works fine."

To the technicians, Polk asked, "Backpack connected?"

One of them made a ring of his thumb and forefinger. "All okay, Colonel."

"All right, then. Let's do it."

Thrasher clumped in his heavy boots to the edge of the tank. It looked like a moderate-sized swimming pool, but he knew it went several stories deep. A trio of scuba-wearing swimmers were already in the water, splashing around like playful dolphins.

"Okay, Art," said Polk. "In you go."

Thrasher gripped the ladder's handrails and started down the ladder rungs. Breathe normally, he told himself. Even if the air hose fails, this suit has enough air for a couple of hours.

Still, he felt nervous as the water closed over his head and his boots reached the last rung of the ladder.

Here I go, he said to himself. Then he stepped off.

He sank slowly downward, the scuba guys close by. Looking up through the bubble helmet, he saw his air line twisting slowly above him. A mockup of the Mars One entry hatch rose to meet him as his sinking stopped. He was floating weightlessly, almost enjoying the sensation.

Until Polk said, "Okay, now open the hatch and get your butt through it."

Thrasher nodded inside the helmet. No time for enjoying the situation, he told himself. There's work to be done.

By the time he got back to his office it was nearly five-thirty. Linda handed him a mug of ginger beer as he cruised past her and headed toward his inner office.

"How'd it go?" she asked.

"Fine. No troubles. You should've seen me. Junior Astronaut Thrasher, that's me."

He went to his desk and sat in the swivel chair. Then he noticed an envelope in the middle of the desk. Unmarked. Unsealed. He opened the flap and pulled out a pair of airline tickets.

Reno, Nevada, he saw. Friday. Tomorrow afternoon. Return Sunday evening.

"Linda!" he bellowed.

She came in, looking somewhere between demure and apprehensive.

"What's this?" he asked.

Very carefully, Linda sat in one of the armchairs. Thrasher noted that she was wearing an ordinary workaday dress, pale green, short sleeves, knee-length skirt. And the opal ring he had given her. She looked beautiful.

When she didn't say anything he waved the tickets at her. "Reno?"

She nodded minimally. "I thought about what you said yesterday. I slept on it."

"And . . . and . . ." Suddenly Thrasher was out of words.

"We can get married in Reno, like you said. I still want a church wedding, for my family and all. But we don't have to wait for that. That is, if you meant what you said."

Thrasher wanted to leap over the desk. Instead he pushed his chair back and came around to her. Linda rose and they embraced.

"You mean you'll marry me?"

"Yes."

"I love you, Linda!"

"I love you too, Art. I've been in love with you for a long time."

"I'll be damned!"

She giggled. "Father Gilhooley used to tell us kids never to say that. God might take you at your word."

"Tell Father Gilhooley to mind his own business." And Thrasher kissed her again.

"I'm resigning from the firm," Linda said, with a mischievous glint in her dark eyes.

"You don't have to—"

"You can rehire me Monday, when we're man and wife. There's no company rule against spouses working for the company."

He laughed and said. "You can't quit. I'm firing you."

Thrasher could barely concentrate on business the next day. He flitted from his office to Sid Ornsteen's for a scheduled conference. Not even Ornsteen's dour report on the company's finances bothered him. Then he had a long Skype face-to-face with Jessie Margulis and Bill Polk, who were in Portales. Thrasher cruised through it like a kid on a jet ski.

At last he and Linda 'coptered out to the airport and flew to Reno, eating lunch on the plane. Linda had already picked out a justice of the peace to marry them. Not one of Reno's flamboyant wedding palaces, but a quiet little chapel. The JP looked like one of Santa's elves in a brown business suit: short, round, with a long sharp beak of a nose.

Then they drove out of the city to Lake Tahoe, and a rambling old hotel by the water. It was just past sunset when they pulled into the parking lot. They could see the rugged profile of the mountains, dark against the still-bright sky.

"There's Mars," Thrasher pointed to a red dot shimmering above the skyline.

"That's Antares," said Linda. "But it's still beautiful."

"So are you," he said.

As he yanked their roller bags out of the rental car's trunk, Linda said, a little sheepishly, "Art, you know I'm not a virgin."

He shrugged. "Neither am I."

They laughed together and, dragging their roller bags behind them, hurried toward the hotel lobby.

❋ 18 ❋
WEDDING DAY

"Do I look all right?" Thrasher asked as he fiddled nervously with his necktie.

"Fine, Art," said Sid Ornsteen. Like Thrasher, he was wearing a dark blue business suit, with a carefully knotted maroon tie.

They were standing in a smallish room just off the altar of the Church of the Holy Epiphany. On the other side of that carved oak door, Thrasher knew, Linda's family was assembled to witness their wedding.

He'd known that her parents wouldn't accept their civil marriage. Catholic for centuries, the family wanted Linda to be properly married in church, by a priest. To please his bride, Thrasher agreed.

Then Linda had told him, "You'll have to ask my father's permission."

He swallowed hard, but went to her parents' house the next evening.

What if they say no? Thrasher wondered. I'm not Catholic. They must know I've been married twice already and divorced each time.

But we're already married, he told himself. Legally, we're man and wife. Legally, yeah. But not in their eyes.

Linda's father was sternly polite when he opened the front door and showed them into the house. Linda went straight to the overdecorated living room and sat next to her mother on the capacious sofa with its splashy flowered slipcover. She looked properly demure in a modest pale green dress. Her mother said nothing; she just sat there, heavyset, stone-faced, in a black dress, like a grim dueña.

Mr. Ursina invited Thrasher to sit in a big wingchair and settled himself in the armchair facing him. He absently fingered his luxurious moustache as he said, "It is good to see you again, Mr. Thrasher."

"Thanks," said Thrasher. "It's good to see you, too." Nodding toward Linda's unsmiling mother, "And you, as well, Mrs. Ursina."

A younger woman came in from the kitchen, bearing a tray of cups and a carafe. She left it on the coffee table and returned wordlessly to the kitchen. One of Linda's sisters, Thrasher guessed. They must all be hanging out in the kitchen.

Clearing his suddenly dry throat, Thrasher began, "Mr. Ursina, I love Linda. I want to marry—"

"I understand you have already married her," said the father.

"That's true."

"But not in the eyes of God."

"That's true," Thrasher repeated. "We were married two weeks ago, in Nevada."

"So for the past two weeks you and my daughter have been living in sin."

Thrasher caught a glimpse of Linda. She was smiling! She seemed to be saying, Don't be scared. Everything's going to be all right.

"I want to marry her," Thrasher said, "in the eyes of God and the whole world."

Her father broke into a brilliant smile. Linda's mother smiled too, and nodded happily. Thrasher saw that there were tears in her eyes.

But Mr. Ursina's smile disappeared. "I understand you have been divorced twice."

"Yes, I have."

"My daughter is not a toy you can throw away when you grow tired of her."

Sitting up straighter, Thrasher said, "Mr. Ursina, I will never grow tired of Linda. I love her. I want to be with her forever."

Turning to Linda, Ursina asked sternly, "Do you love this man?"

"I do, Poppa. With all my heart."

The older man sighed. "Then we must arrange for the wedding."

Before Thrasher could say another word, a horde of relatives burst from the kitchen, laughing and welcoming Thrasher into the family.

Now he stood before the door that opened onto the altar. Thrasher took a deep breath as the organ began to play. The room seemed to vibrate.

"Ready, Art?" Sid Ornsteen asked.

Thrasher nodded. "Let's go."

He followed Ornsteen out into the church. One side of the central aisle was teeming with Linda's relatives: grandfather, mother, uncles, aunts, brothers, sisters, cousins, a small army of family.

On the other side sat a handful of Thrasher's friends. He spotted Will Portal and his wife, several people from Thrasher Digital, Bill Polk, Nacho Velasquez and Judine McQuinn.

As he took his place at the altar, the organ broke into "Here Comes the Bride," and Linda—on her father's arm—started up the aisle. She wore a long-skirted white gown: her mother had insisted on that. Thrasher thought she had never looked more radiantly beautiful.

'Til death do us part, Thrasher said to himself. Happily.

YEAR
FIVE

◎ 1 ◎
SPACEPORT AMERICA

Bill Polk eyed Thrasher like a hard-nosed football coach looking over a new recruit. Standing in his space suit, helmet in hand, Thrasher felt like a freshman trying out for the team. Polk was in a space suit, too, but somehow on him it looked natural.

"Are you ready to go?" Polk asked. His usual easy grin was gone. He was deadly serious. "You can back out if you want to. Nothing says you have to go."

"I want to go," Thrasher said earnestly.

A hint of a smile cracked Polk's stern expression. "Okay then, let's do it."

Side by side, they clumped toward the locker room door. Before they reached it, though, it swung inward and Jessie Margulis stepped in, the expression on his normally placid face tense, almost fierce.

Before Thrasher could say anything, Margulis blurted, "Art, I want you to know that we've gone over every component of the launcher out there. Every inch of it."

"Good," said Thrasher.

"I don't want you to worry. That bird will work fine. There'll be no foul-ups on this flight."

Thrasher gripped the engineer's biceps in a gloved hand.

"I appreciate it, Jess. Thanks."

"I just wanted you to know."

"Thanks," Thrasher repeated. But as he stepped past Margulis, he started thinking, *I wasn't worried about an accident. Until now.*

The moment Polk and Thrasher stepped out of the locker room they were swarmed by a crowd of news reporters and photographers, all asking questions and clicking pictures at once. Thrasher recognized Vicki Zane among them.

She shoved a microphone under Thrasher's chin and asked, "How does it feel to be going into space?"

Thrasher thought the question was pretty lame, but he grinned and answered, "Terrific. I'm rarin' to go."

One of the other reporters shouted, "Isn't it a little scary?"

"I'm kind of nervous, naturally," Thrasher replied. Turning toward Polk he added, "But I'm in the best of hands. I'm looking forward to the adventure."

Vicki asked, "When will you let a reporter to go up to Mars One and experience zero gravity?"

He saw the suggestion in her eyes. *Vicki knows I'm a married man now, but she can't help playing the sex kitten.*

"Reporters will have full access to Mars One through our virtual reality system. You'll experience the mission without having to leave the ground."

"That's not really the same, though, is it?" she said.

"It'll have to do."

Another reporter took up the theme. "Is that for safety reasons? Are you afraid that the mission is too risky for a news person?"

"If I was worried about safety, would I be going up there?" Thrasher countered.

"Yeah, but you're only going up to Earth orbit, and only overnight. The real mission goes all the way to Mars. They'll be out there for a couple of years, all told."

"You just answered your own question," Thrasher said, with a big smile.

Polk made a shooing motion with his gloved hands. "We've got a schedule to stick to, folks."

The news people parted before him like the Red Sea. Vicki Zane called, "See you in orbit!" Thrasher felt his brows knit. *What does she mean by that?*

Thrasher followed Polk out to the white SUV that was waiting to carry them to the launch stand. It was early April, not overbearingly hot yet, but a crisp breeze was blowing dust across the desert. Thrasher saw a tumbleweed roll past.

Two other astronauts were already in the SUV, technicians who were installing some of the equipment for the mission. They had plugged their suits into the oversized air-conditioning unit in the back. Polk and Thrasher clambered in, took their seats, and plugged in their suits as well.

"Damned awkward in these chairs," Polk complained as the driver put the van in gear and started toward the pad. "They weren't designed for guys wearing space suits."

"You should have told me," Thrasher said. "I could've found somebody to design a better seat."

"For a four-minute ride?" Polk said. "That wouldn't be cost-effective."

So the four of them sat precariously, bundled inside the bulky space suits, as the SUV drove out to the launch pad. Through the van's window Thrasher saw the waiting launcher, four big solid-rocket boosters strapped around its base, the slim winged crew module at its top. Looks like a mini-shuttle, Thrasher thought. More streamlined, though. Racier.

They climbed laboriously out of the SUV and up the metal stairs to the deck of the launch pad, then the four space-suited men squeezed into the elevator that lifted them up to the top of the slender rocket and the crew module. Thrasher had gone through this routine a dozen times in his training, but now he kept thinking, this is real. This is the real thing. I'm really going to ride this firecracker and go up to orbit.

More than anything else he wanted to avoid getting sick in zero gravity. He had slapped an anti-nausea patch onto his neck, as the medics had prescribed. Hope it does the trick, he said to himself.

"You okay?" Polk asked as the elevator stopped and its grillwork door slid smoothly open.

"Sure," said Thrasher.

As the two space-suited technicians stepped out of the elevator, Polk eyed Thrasher carefully. "Last chance to back off."

Thrasher grinned at him. "I wouldn't miss this for all the gold in Fort Knox."

Polk nodded curtly. "Let's do it, then."

The two technicians ducked through the hatch, got into their acceleration couches, and began plugging in their suit connections. Just as he had in training, Thrasher squeezed through after them and crawled across an empty acceleration couch into his assigned seat, Polk right behind him. The crew capsule was cramped, narrow, not a centimeter of wasted space. They had to lie on their backs on the acceleration couches. Damned uncomfortable, he thought as Polk settled in beside him. Thrasher followed Polk's lead and plugged in his electrical power, communications, and life support cables.

The mission communicator's voice came through his helmet speaker. "Message for Mr. Thrasher."

"Message?"

"From Mrs. Thrasher: Good luck, darling. Love, Linda."

Thrasher felt his cheeks coloring as Polk and the other two chuckled tolerantly.

"Ten minutes and counting," said the mission controller.

Polk leaned close enough to Thrasher so that their bubble helmets touched and they could talk without using the radio. "This is the toughest part, the waiting."

Thrasher nodded inside his helmet.

"I always feel like I have to pee," Polk confessed. "Just nerves."

Thrasher felt suddenly grateful. His bladder was sending him uncomfortable signals, too.

What did Vicki mean when she said she'd see me in orbit? Thrasher asked himself. Then it hit him. He was scheduled to do an interview using the virtual reality set in the Mars One vehicle. She's wangled the job of doing the interview! he realized. I wonder what else she's been up to?

◎ 2 ◎
LAUNCH

"...seven...six..."

Thrasher realized he was biting his tongue. With a conscious effort he tried to relax. Hard to do, with pumps gurgling and lights on the control panel flicking on. The cramped compartment seemed to be vibrating, humming with electrical currents.

"...two...one...ig—"

The mission controller's voice was drowned out in the sudden bellow of ten thousand dragons. Thrasher felt an enormous fist pushing against the small of his back, and the whole compartment began to shake hard enough to rattle his bones.

Turning his head, he saw Polk eying the control panel intently. The roar of the engines wouldn't stop, and Thrasher felt as if his insides were being mashed into a puree. His vision blurred. His chest felt tight. He was gasping for air. He couldn't lift his arms off the seat rests, they weighed six hundred pounds apiece.

How long does this go on? he asked himself. He knew the answer: Three minutes and twenty seconds to first-stage cutoff, then another two minutes for the second-stage burn.

But we've already been going for six hours, feels like.

A bang and a lurch so hard Thrasher bumped his nose against his helmet's face plate. How long? How long?

And then the noise and vibration stopped. Just like that. One moment he was being pressed flat and shaken like a rat in a terrier's jaws, the next his arms were floating up off the seat rests and his insides were falling down the longest elevator shaft in the universe.

Zero gravity, Thrasher told himself. We made it! We're in orbit!

His helmet speakers crackled. "Don't make any sudden moves with your head," Polk's voice advised. "Stay loose."

Thrasher started to nod, then caught himself.

"How do you feel?"

"Like I'm falling."

"Normal. Your inner ear interprets microgravity as falling, but your eyes are telling your brain you're tucked inside the compartment. The brain gets confused."

"My head feels stuffy, kind of."

"That's normal. Just relax and keep still. You'll be okay. You'll be fine."

"Right."

"We'll be linking up with Mars One in half an hour," Polk said. "Piece of cake."

Relax and keep still, Thrasher told himself. I can do that. Nothing else to do, really.

Except think.

Yojiro Shima. Professor of something called forensic linguistics. Sounds like hoodoo, Thrasher thought. The deeper we get into trying to track down the man responsible for the accident, the weirder everything becomes. Frankenstein picked out Chandrasekhar and the kid finds this Japanese language specialist.

The voice on the CDs that Vince Egan had surrendered to Thrasher was generated by a computer. "There is no way that I can get anything for you from a machine," Chandrasekhar had said gloomily. The kid had actually put on a clean T-shirt and reasonably creased Levis to come to Thrasher's office and admit his frustration. He was even wearing Reeboks; they looked brand-new.

Sitting unhappily behind his desk, Thrasher had asked, "There's nothing you can do?"

Chandrasekhar shook his tangled mop of hair. "It is not a human voice."

"Then we're stumped."

The kid broke into a sly grin. "Maybe not."

Thrasher said, "What do you mean?"

"There is a professor at Georgetown University—"

"In Washington?"

"D.C., yes. He is a specialist in forensic linguistics. A very clever man."

"Forensic linguistics? What the hell is that?"

"He analyzes the words that a message contains. No two people speak or write exactly the same, you know."

"But the messages we've got to work with are spoken by a computer, not a man," Thrasher objected.

"Yes, certainly so. But the words were originally written or spoken by a human being and then transferred into the computer. Perhaps Professor Shima can analyze those words and identify the person who originally wrote them."

It was a very slender thread, but the next time he went to Washington, Thrasher had Linda set up a visit to Professor Yojiro Shima at Georgetown University.

His office was immaculate. Shima's desktop was clear, except for a phone console and computer keyboard. Bookcases lined the walls, each neatly filled with books, although some of them looked well used. The office's one window looked out onto trees and paved walkways that wound through tidily clipped grass and cheerfully flowering bushes.

Shima himself was round, big-bellied, bald and jovial. He doesn't look like a detective, Thrasher thought. Looks more like one of those statues of a fat, laughing Buddha.

"And to what do I owe the honor of this visit from such an illustrious captain of industry?" Shima asked, in a smooth, strong voice.

Thrasher thought he heard a note of sarcasm, but he ignored it and explained his problem.

Shima's smile melted away as Thrasher spoke. His expression became more thoughtful. At last he said, "If the sample you have is large enough, I can undoubtedly establish a pattern for you. Then, if you have samples of individual persons' writings, I can match them to the pattern. Will that be satisfactory?"

"Very much," said Thrasher.

Shima's cheery smile returned. "You see, Mr. Thrasher, no two people speak or write exactly the same way. Their choice of words, the order in which they place the words, the expressions they use—all are as individual as fingerprints or DNA samples."

"So I've been told," Thrasher said, wondering if he actually believed it.

"I have been called as an expert witness in many court trials. I have helped to identify terrorists and kidnappers, extortionists, and even murderers."

Thrasher nodded.

With a chuckle, Shima pointed a chubby finger at Thrasher and said, "I can tell from your choice of words—and from your silences—that you don't believe a word that I've said to you."

Thrasher grinned ruefully back at him. "I'm afraid that's pretty close to true."

Leaning his forearms on the desktop, Shima said, "You are a gambling man, aren't you?"

"I wouldn't say that."

"Oh no? The man who is sending an expedition to Mars is not a gambler?"

"There's a risk, of course. But I wouldn't call that gambling."

Shima tilted his head back and guffawed. "You see? You use different words!"

Thrasher started to reply, then caught himself. "I get it," he admitted. "I understand."

"Let me offer you a proposition," Shima said genially. "If I fail to identify your culprit, you pay nothing."

"Sounds fair."

"But if I do identify the person, then you will sponsor an endowed chair of forensic linguistics at this university."

"An endowed chair?" Thrasher protested. "That could cost a million dollars!"

"Two million, actually."

"That's a lot of money."

Shima pursed his lips. "Very well. Let's say you will establish a scholarship fund for the linguistics department. Say, five hundred thousand dollars?"

Thrasher studied the man's face. *He's playing a game with me. He's enjoying this!*

"Say two hundred fifty thousand," he offered.

"Three?" Shima asked, grinning.

Thrasher nodded. "Three hundred thousand—if you find the guy who wrote those messages."

"Done!" said Shima, sticking his hand out over his desk.

"Docking in three minutes," said Bill Polk.

Thrasher snapped his attention to the confines of the spacecraft's crew module. I'm in a space suit, he reminded himself. I'm in zero gravity. My head is stuffy and my stomach wants to heave but I'm okay. Everything's fine. Almost.

Sitting beside him, Polk was intently eying the control console's displays. There were no windows in the module, so Thrasher focused his attention on the screen in the center of the console. He saw the docking port of Mars One coming closer, closer.

Too fast! he thought. We're going to crash into it!

He sat up straighter and started to reach a hand toward Polk, but a wave of nausea swept over him. His stomach convulsed and he tasted burning bile in his mouth. Don't throw up! he commanded himself. Don't make an ass of yourself!

But he gagged and upchucked anyway.

✦ 3 ✦
IN ORBIT

Vomit spattered across Thrasher's bubble helmet and the smell made him truly sick. Polk glanced at him with a sardonic grin, then turned his attention back to the control console. Thrasher really didn't care if they crashed and died, he felt so miserable. And ashamed.

One of the technicians, sitting behind him, leaned across and grabbed his left wrist for a moment, then let it go. Thrasher's arm floated weightlessly while he fought down another urge to upchuck.

"I turned off your radio transmitter, Mr. Thrasher," said the technician. "The noises you're making are turning our stomachs."

"Sorry, fellas," he said weakly. No response from any of them.

He felt a weak thump, and before he could panic Polk said, "We're docked."

Then Thrasher heard in his helmet speaker the voice of the mission commander, back on the ground, "Confirm docking. Good job, Bill."

"The auto system works fine," Polk said. "I didn't have to lift a finger."

"Everybody okay up there? I thought I heard some distress."

"Naw. We're okay," said Polk, turning to eye Thrasher's vomit-spattered helmet. "We're transferring to Mars One now."

Miserable as he was, Thrasher felt immensely grateful that Polk didn't let the mission controller know that he'd upchucked. The news would be flashed all across the world in a nanosecond, he thought.

With the help of Polk and the two technicians, Thrasher got up from his seat and floated through the hatch that linked their spacecraft with Mars One, his stomach full of butterflies.

"Just a few more feet," Polk said encouragingly as they led him along the passageway that connected with the rotating wheel.

It was awkward getting through the hatch with the wheel sliding slowly past. Thrasher remembered his tumbling, flailing fall back when the vehicle was still on the ground in Portales.

"Careful now," Polk instructed. "We move on the count of three. One, two, *three*."

And they lifted Thrasher through the hatch and deposited him none too gently on the slowly moving floor of the wheel. The sudden feeling of weight made his knees buckle, but he leaned on the bulkhead and stayed more or less erect. Polk skipped lightly through the hatch and reached for him. The other two followed him.

"How you doin', buddy?" Polk asked.

"I've been better," Thrasher said.

"Let's get you down to the infirmary."

"Can I take off my helmet? It stinks in here."

With a soft chuckle, Polk said, "Sure. Good idea. But you'll have to wash it out yourself. That's an unwritten rule."

Thrasher nodded and realized that it didn't make him woozy. He knew the wheel was rotating but he couldn't sense the motion. It seemed he was standing on a solid floor, feeling normal weight. The floor curved upward farther along the passageway, but that didn't bother him. He clicked the lock on the neck ring of his suit and lifted the begrimed helmet over his head.

Polk's nose twitched. "It does smell pretty bad." Turning to the two technicians, he said, "I'm going to take him down to the infirmary. You guys get on with your schedule."

He offered an arm to Thrasher, but Thrasher shook his head. "I'm okay now. I can walk normally."

"Good," said Polk. Pointing down the passageway, he said, "The infirmary's down there. Judine's there, she can look you over."

"I'm all right," Thrasher insisted. "I just feel silly, making a fool of myself like that."

"It happens. You're not the first one. We had a U.S. Senator from Florida on one flight in the old shuttle. He spent the whole damned mission tossing his cookies. And he was on the Senate space committee."

Dr. McQuinn pronounced Thrasher hale and fit for normal duty, then pointed him to the infirmary's minuscule lavatory. "You can wash up in there."

The cold water felt good on his face, and Thrasher even got his helmet scrubbed out without gagging again. Then he clomped back to the locker area and spent nearly half an hour removing his space suit.

Polk showed up to help him disrobe. Once Thrasher was standing in his standard-issue powder-blue coveralls, Polk said, "You're scheduled to do a media interview in twenty-two minutes."

Thrasher nodded. The stuffiness in his head was gone.

"I'll go set up the VR equipment," he said.

"Fine," said Polk. "I'm going to give the guys a hand unloading cargo."

Thrasher looked up and down the passageway. Polk pointed. "VR center's that-a-way."

"Right."

"You're okay now?" the astronaut asked.

"I'm fine. And I really appreciate your keeping my bout of nausea just among ourselves."

Polk's easy grin spread across his rugged face. "We're all members of the team, Art. We look after each other."

4
INTERVIEW

Sure enough, it was Vicki Zane who'd wangled the task of interviewing Thrasher via the virtual reality link.

As Thrasher wormed his arms and legs into the full-body sensor suit, he felt like a caterpillar morphing into a butterfly—in reverse. The dark gray gloves felt nubby against his hands; even through his coveralls he could feel the scratchiness of the sleeve's sensors. It's like wearing a suit made out of Brillo pads, he grumbled to himself.

At last he pulled on the helmet and slid its visor over his eyes. It was blank; he felt blind.

Then a voice from the ground said, "We're receiving your signal loud and clear, Mr. Thrasher."

"Good," he said into the microphones built into the helmet. "How about giving me a picture?"

"Coming right up, on three. One . . . two . . ."

A swirl of colors and then he was looking at Vicki. She seemed to be standing in a few feet in front of him, looking slightly uneasy. Thrasher knew she was wearing a sensor suit and helmet, just as he was, but the image he saw was Vicki wearing a form-hugging cherry-red skirted suit, the jacket cut low enough to show some cleavage, the skirt not quite knee length.

"Hello, Art," she said, beaming a bright smile at him.

"Hello yourself."

"We'll be on the air in less than five minutes. Is there anything I ought to know? More than the briefing your media people gave us?"

He shook his head. "I'm just going to walk you through the wheel, show you the crew quarters, work stations, command center, stuff like that."

"Okay," she said.

A disembodied voice said, "Reception is good. We go live in three minutes."

"It's good to see you again, Art," Vicki said. "I've missed you."

"Good to see you, too."

"I understand you married your secretary."

"Linda's a lot more than a secretary."

"Of course."

"I mean, she runs the office. I couldn't do without her."

With a sly smile, Vicki asked, "Is that why you married her?"

"I love her," Thrasher snapped.

"Uh-huh."

The disembodied voice announced, "Two minutes."

Arching an eyebrow, Vicki asked, "Is she as good in bed as I am?"

Thrasher bristled. "Better," he snapped.

Her eyes went wide, then Vicki laughed. "You poor sap, you really are in love, aren't you?"

"There's a lot more to a good marriage than sex," Thrasher said. And he realized, for the first time in his life, that it was true. Linda was wonderful in bed, warm and willing, but that was only a part of their relationship. They shared their lives, their work, their fun, their interests, their entire existence. That's what marriage is, he told himself. That's what I've been missing—until now.

Vicki was persistent, though. "I hear you can use virtual reality for lots of different kinds of simulations."

Guardedly, Thrasher replied, "That's true."

"Like porno films, only better. Full sensory experience." She was grinning wickedly now.

"So I've been told," Thrasher said.

"Maybe after the interview is over we could test it out?"

"Vicki, I'm married."

"But you're 'way up there in space. It could be a first! A breakthrough!"

Thrasher sighed. "Thanks for the offer, but no thanks."

"Your loss," she said.

Thrasher said nothing, but he remembered the nights he'd spent with Vicki. They were spectacular, and she knew it. But *my reprobate days are over*, he reminded himself. *I've got something very precious with Linda and I'm not going to endanger it, not for anything.*

He made a mental note to send Linda some flowers as soon he got back down on the ground.

He stood there, feeling awkward, saying nothing, until the director started the countdown to the interview.

Vicki smoothed her auburn hair with an automatic gesture, then turned on the full wattage of her smile and said, "Hello. I'm Victoria Zane, and through the wonders of virtual reality technology I'm going to take a tour through the Mars One spacecraft, in orbit nearly four hundred miles above the Earth, without leaving the studio in which this broadcast originates."

And that's exactly what she did. Thrasher walked her through the wheel's central passageway, opened doors to the astronauts' quarters, the galley, work stations and mini-laboratories, the command center from which the spacecraft was controlled. Vicki oohed and aahed in the right places, asked a few questions. Thrasher spent some time in one of the crew's quarters, showing how comfortable the explorers were going to be on their way to Mars, with a snug built-in bunk and compact private lavatory.

He knew that most of the television audience saw what he was seeing, heard what he was saying. But the few people who had access to virtual reality equipment felt as if they were aboard Mars One, walking through the vehicle as if they were actually inside it.

At last the tour was finished; Thrasher stood almost precisely at the spot where he'd started the show.

"How long will it take to get to Mars?" Vicki asked.

"A little more than six months," said Thrasher.

"And your crew of seven men and women will be living in this vessel all that time?"

"Right," he said. "They'll spend another six months on the surface of Mars, and then return back here to Earth."

"What about radiation? Isn't there dangerous radiation in space?"

Thrasher nodded. "The ship's hull provides enough protection from the normal levels of radiation in space."

Her eyes narrowing, Vicki said, "Yes, but aren't there solar storms that can send out a huge blast of radiation, far above the normal levels?"

She's done some homework, he thought. "That's true," he admitted. "We have a storm cellar for that. It's an enclosed space protected by a powerful magnetic field that deflects the radiation particles."

"Will it be safe enough?"

"The best engineers in the world have designed and tested it. It'll be safe enough."

"How long will the crew have to stay in the storm cellar?"

"Until the radiation levels go down. A couple of days. Maybe three or four."

"Can we see the storm cellar?"

Typical newshound, Thrasher growled inwardly. Ignore all the good stuff and concentrate on a possible problem.

"It's in the main body of the ship, down among the propellant tanks and other stores. We can't get to it while we're in these VR suits."

Vicki nibbled at the radiation danger for a few more questions and Thrasher stonewalled her. Come on, he urged silently, wrap it up.

At last she put on her smile again and said, "Well, thank you for a fascinating tour of the Mars One spacecraft, Mr. Thrasher. I'm sure everyone wishes your crew the best of luck."

"Thank you, Ms. Zane."

Looking past Thrasher, Vicki said, "This is Victoria Zane, aboard the Mars One spacecraft, thanks to the wonders of virtual reality."

Thrasher nodded. This ought to start sales of the VR sets climbing. Greg Sampson ought to be happy.

◎ 5 ◎
RETURN

The Mars One galley was a compact compartment just big enough for all seven of the crew to sit and eat together. Since there were only five people aboard the vehicle, two chairs at the circular table remained empty.

"How'd the interview go?" Bill Polk asked Thrasher.

Nodding as he swallowed a bite of sliced veal, Thrasher replied, "Fine. She hammered on the radiation problem, but I think I explained it away well enough."

Judine McQuinn took a sip of fruit juice, then said, "She didn't ask about sex?"

Thrasher's brows hiked up. "No, she didn't."

"Five men and two women living cheek by jowl for nearly two years," McQuinn said. "That's the first question I would've asked."

Polk muttered, "We're all adults here."

"That's what I'm talking about," said McQuinn, with a mischievous smile.

Thrasher stared at her. "The psychologists have gone over this with each of you. You've all been deemed able to control yourselves." Then he added, "Haven't you?"

"Yes," said Polk, sternly.

McQuinn went on, "Of course, as the team's medical officer, I can prescribe medications if any of the crew gets rambunctious."

One of the technicians, Zachary Deevers, young and darkly good-looking, said with a smirk, "If I was locked inside this tin can for six months with you, Judy-girl, I'd need a lot of medicating."

She gave him a rueful look. "Zach, you'd just have to control yourself."

Zachary countered, "But what if I don't want to control myself?"

Polk broke into their banter. "That's why we have airlocks, kid."

Zachary looked shocked. Polk explained, "As captain of this ship, one of my responsibilities will be to maintain discipline."

"Captain Bligh," the other technician muttered.

"If I have to be," said Polk, totally serious.

They finished the meal in desultory small talk, then the technicians headed to their separate work stations. Thrasher got up and, with nothing to do, walked back to the compartment that he was to sleep in.

He sat on the built-in bunk and picked the phone handset off the shelf that ran along the bulkhead beside it. The ship's intercom was linked to its radio, and by relaying its signal through communications satellites, Thrasher could reach any telephone on Earth.

He punched up his own home number. It was almost eight p.m. in Houston. Linda should be—

"Hello?" Linda's voice.

"Hi!" he said.

"Art! I saw you this afternoon. I took the VR tour with you."

"How'd you like it? How'd it come across?"

"Wonderful! It was like being there."

"Good."

A heartbeat's hesitation. Then Linda said, "Ms. Zane tried to scare people about radiation."

"Linda, she's a professional newsperson. They always try to find something to pick on."

"You stood up to her very well."

"Thanks."

"She thinks she's a sexpot, doesn't she?"

Thrasher thought, Vicki *is* a sexpot. But he said, "All part of her TV personality."

"Come on, Art, I know better."

"That was over a long time ago, Linda. You know that."

"Yes, I know," she said, her voice warmer.

Thrasher got an idea. "Do you have the VR rig in the apartment?"

"No, it's in the office."

"Oh. Too bad."

He heard her giggle. "Are you suggesting what I think you're suggesting?"

As innocently as he could manage, Thrasher replied, "A scientific experiment, Linda. A first. A breakthrough."

"The office is just across the hall. I could go to the room where the VR equipment is stashed."

She's calling my bluff, he realized. Shaking his head, he said, "We'd need somebody to operate the system."

"Three's a crowd."

"Yeah. I'll be back home tomorrow afternoon."

"Good." Then, almost wistfully, Linda added, "Although it would be awfully interesting to try it."

"Maybe. But I'd rather be there with you."

"Me too!"

Thrasher slept fitfully, dreaming about having sex in zero gravity. He was floating naked in space with Linda, although now and then she morphed into Vicki and even his first wife. He woke up when the alarm clock built into the bulkhead started to buzz.

Sitting up in the bunk, he rubbed the cobwebs out of his eyes and muttered to himself, "Sex in zero-g. Yeah. With you upchucking all over her."

All through his shower, shave and dressing in the pocket-sized lavatory he thought about the return flight. I'll be in zero-g again for at least half an hour, he knew. I'm not going to make a jackass of myself again. He slapped two of the anti-nausea patches on his neck, one on either side, and went to the galley for breakfast.

Thrasher and Bill Polk suited up for the return flight, with Zach Deevers checking them over.

As they clomped toward the hatch that led out of the rotating wheel, Polk said, "Remember, no sudden head movements. Keep your head still and you'll be okay."

"Okay," Thrasher said, keeping himself from nodding.

"Everybody gets woozy in microgravity. It's normal. If we were going to spend a day or more in it you'd adapt and start to enjoy it."

Thrasher made a grim smile. "If you say so, chief."

Polk chuckled and pulled open the hatch. Thrasher saw the metal bulkhead sliding past.

"When we reach the open hatchway, you step right through. I'll be right behind you."

"Okay."

The hatch appeared and Thrasher jumped through. His stomach immediately started crawling up toward his throat. He squeezed his eyes shut. He was falling, fluttering like a leaf falling from a tree.

Polk stepped through and grasped Thrasher's arm firmly in a gloved hand. "You okay?"

Thrasher opened his eyes. "Yeah," he said shakily. "I'm okay."

"You'll be fine. Come on."

Together they squeezed through the hatch of the spaceplane and settled into their seats. Thrasher tried to keep his head perfectly rigid as he connected his suit's lines to the outlets in the control panel. Polk busily ran through the countdown with ground control, then said tightly, "Disconnect in thirty seconds."

Out of the corner of his eye, Thrasher saw that Polk did not move his head as he spoke. *He's feeling it too!* Thrasher somehow felt better.

Sitting in the acceleration couch, Thrasher watched the display screen on the control panel as Polk disconnected the spaceplane from Mars One. A gentle push from the vernier thrusters in the plane's nose and they backed away from the docking hatch.

"Free orbit," Polk said to mission control.

Thrasher knew it would be half an hour before they fired their main engines and started their descent into the atmosphere. *Thirty minutes. I can handle that.*

"How you doing, Art?"

"Fine," Thrasher said. And he realized he meant it. He was almost enjoying the feeling of weightlessness. *As long as you don't move your head,* he warned himself.

Once Polk lit off the main rocket a feeling of weight returned. The plane bit into the atmosphere and began its jolting, shuddering flight through re-entry. Thrasher knew they were surrounded now by white-hot gases, air heated to incandescence by the speed of their flight through it. He could hear the howling, screaming sound of the air roaring past them.

His stomach felt almost normal now, although the plane was vibrating so hard his view of the control panel was blurry. Thrasher was glad they had no windows. He didn't want to see the fiery hell they were diving through.

Polk sat back and folded his arms across his chest. The display screen showed nothing but a freakish white hash.

At last the ride smoothed out and the screen cleared to show blue-gray ocean. The water looked iron-hard.

"Through re-entry blackout," Polk said.

Mission control confirmed, "We have reacquired your signal."

Now they were flying like an airplane. Brown wrinkled mountains splotched with patches of late winter snow flashed past in the display screen. Polk swung the stubby-winged vehicle around in a series of wide turns, bleeding off velocity, then flared it out for a smooth approach to the runway at Spaceport America.

The wheels hit the ground solidly and Polk lowered the nose. "We're down," he said, breaking into a satisfied smile.

Thrasher felt glad to be back safely but happier still that he didn't upchuck this time. Then he remembered that he wanted to send Linda a bouquet of flowers.

⊚ 6 ⊚
DEATH . . . AND ANALYSIS

It was nearly five p.m. when Thrasher finally got back to his office in Houston. He trotted down the circular stairway from the roof and breezed into the outer office. It was decked with flowers: roses, peonies, carnations, daisies—the room was ablaze with colors and filled with the soft aromas of spring.

But instead of greeting him with a kiss and a mug of ginger beer, Linda was sitting at her desk, her head sunk in her hands.

"Hey!" he snapped. "Welcome home the returning astronaut!"

Linda looked up; her eyes were red from crying. Thrasher rushed to her. "What's the matter, kid?"

She gestured to the phone console. "It's Vince Egan. He's dead. Suicide."

"Vince? Dead?"

Nodding miserably, Linda said, "His brother just phoned. They found him in the garage, in his car with the motor running. Carbon monoxide poisoning."

"But that doesn't mean it was suicide," Thrasher said. "It must've been an accident."

Linda shook her head. "He had stuffed rags along the base of the garage door. To make sure the gas couldn't get out. He killed himself."

Thrasher felt as if he were back in space, weightless. He sagged onto the edge of Linda's desk. "I can't believe it. Vince wasn't the type to kill himself."

"After the mess he made here . . ."

"Yeah, but he was looking for another job. Didn't you get requests for recommendations for him?"

"Three of them."

"He wasn't moping. He was looking for a fresh start."

"But our recommendations weren't much help."

"No," he admitted. "I guess they weren't."

Linda pulled in a deep breath. "I ought to check with the human resources office, see if the company's life insurance policy for him is still valid."

"If it isn't, tell them to reinstate it and backdate the reinstatement to the day Vince quit."

"Is that legal?"

"I'll pay whatever penalty the insurance carrier slaps on us."

She smiled at him. "You're a good man, Art."

"Yeah." He got up and headed for his private office, thinking, I'm a good man alright. I might have pushed Vince to kill himself.

The next morning Larry Franken dropped in to Thrasher's office.

Standing two steps in from the door, Frankenstein said, "I heard about Mr. Egan."

"Yeah. I never expected Vince to go that way."

"You want me to look into it?"

Thrasher shook his head. "The local police are investigating." Then he added, "I suppose you could take a look at what they find out. Keep me informed."

Franken dipped his chin. "Sure thing."

It was hard for Thrasher to get Egan's suicide out of his mind. As he went through his day's routine he kept asking himself, should I go visit the family? Express my regrets? Yeah, the guy who bounced him out of his job. The guy who answered requests for recommendations for him with a form letter. They'll be happy to see me. Overjoyed.

But, dammitall, Vince sabotaged me! He took money to blow up that rocket. He knew he could ask me for the money he needed, but he was too pissed off at me because I didn't give him the Mars job.

And now he's dead. Not a thing I can do about that. Death cancels all debts.

His phone chimed.

Linda's face appeared on the phone console's tiny screen. "Professor Shima, from Georgetown University."

"Put him through," Thrasher said absently. And he pecked at the phone's keypad to put Shima's image on his wall screen.

The professor was beaming a happy smile as he sat at his desk, round and fat and jovial as Thrasher remembered him from their earlier meeting.

"Good morning, Mr. Thrasher," he said cordially.

"Good morning," Thrasher returned, glancing at the digital clock. It was still morning, but just barely.

"I have good news for you, sir."

"Oh?"

Waving a chubby hand in the air, Shima said, "I have concluded the analysis of the messages you left with me, and I believe I have produced an accurate assessment of the man who originated them."

On a devilish impulse, Thrasher challenged, "It wasn't a woman, then?"

Shima shook his head. "Not a woman. A man. Definitely."

"Okay. Who?"

"That I cannot say, as yet."

"Then what good is your analysis?"

Shima laughed, a full-throated chortle of amusement. "One thing at a time, my impatient one. We must learn to walk before we can run."

Forcing himself to remain calm, Thrasher said, "Explain what you mean, please."

"We have a workable analysis of the man who originated the words on the CDs you gave me. We have a picture of his personality. Now, if you can provide me with voice recordings or writings by the men you suspect of being the culprit, I can match them to the analysis and identify your guilty party."

"You can?"

"With great confidence."

Intrigued, Thrasher asked, "So what does your analysis tell you?"

Shima's smile faded. "We are dealing with a dangerous man, Mr.

Thrasher. He is cold, precise, and very determined. His personality reminds me of something Mr. H. G. Wells wrote in *The War of the Worlds*: 'an intellect vast and cool and unsympathetic.' He is dangerous."

Thrasher thought, That doesn't sound like Greg Sampson. Greg's a blusterer and a bully, not cold and precise.

Aloud, he said, "Okay. I'll send you writings and voice recordings from the boards of directors of Thrasher Digital and Mars, Inc. It's got to be one of them."

"Not someone outside your corporations?"

"I doubt it."

"Or one of your workers?"

Thrasher shook his head. "It's a board member, I'm pretty sure."

Shima's cheerful smile returned. "Very well. As soon as I receive the package I will begin comparing its contents to the analysis we have done. We will identify your miscreant, never fear."

"Good," said Thrasher.

"And when we do, you must write a check to endow a scholarship for my department." Shima laughed heartily as he disconnected the phone link and his image disappeared from Thrasher's wall screen.

⊚ 7 ⊚
PORTALES

Watching from the balcony that ran around three of the walls of the cavernous former warehouse, Thrasher felt unaccountably nervous as the news reporters and camera crews began to fill up the area where the Mars One spacecraft had been assembled. The backup components had been moved to one corner of the big, open space to make room for rows of folding chairs and a platform holding a long table where the seven Mars-bound men and women would be seated.

It was late May, almost Memorial Day, and the launch of the Mars-bound crew was only six weeks off.

This news conference would be the media's first introduction to all seven of the astronauts: Bill Polk, Nacho Velasquez, Judine McQuinn, the three scientists, and Alan Dougherty.

Down in the first row of spectators various dignitaries were already seated: the governor of New Mexico, a deputy director from NASA, Professor Winninger from the University of Arizona, and Kristin Anders—now Mrs. Dougherty. Beside her sat Jeremiah Herzberg, from the National Academy of Sciences, and Quentin Hynes, the geologist who had been bumped from the mission to make room for Dougherty. Behind them, members of the boards of directors of Thrasher Digital and Mars, Inc. were finding their places. The reporters filled the rest of the seats, while camera crews were setting up on either side.

Standing beside Thrasher, Linda slipped an arm around his waist and said quietly, "Don't be nervous."

He looked into her lovely, serious face. "It shows, huh?"

"You look pretty tense."

Gesturing to the board members taking their seats, Thrasher said, "One of them is a killer."

Linda look shocked. "What do you mean?"

"Vince didn't commit suicide. I'm certain of that. He was murdered."

"Why? By whom?"

"Why? Because he admitted he'd set up the accident, and whoever paid him to do it was getting nervous about it. The killer was worried that I might go public with the news that the accident wasn't accidental."

"And he killed Vince?"

"To keep him quiet. No loose ends. Made it look like an accident. Suicide."

"But you don't know who did it."

"Not yet."

Linda's expression turned thoughtful. "That means that, the closer you get to finding out who's responsible, the more danger you'll be in."

"Me? In danger?"

"If he killed Vince to keep him quiet, he won't hesitate to kill you, if he thinks you're going to expose him."

Thrasher mulled over the idea for a few moments. Then he nodded. "You might be right, kid."

"You're going to need protection. I'll talk to Larry Franken."

"I don't want—"

Very firmly, Linda said, "I'll talk to Larry. That's settled."

Thrasher grinned at her. "Harkening and obedience," he murmured. And he grinned at the thought that the two most important words in a marriage are "yes, dear."

The news conference was a big success, carried live on all the major networks and cable outlets. Thrasher climbed down from the balcony and took his seat at the end of the table with the Mars team and introduced the astronauts, the scientists, and the VIPs in the audience.

Then he moderated a long question-and-answer period. Most of the reporters' questions were directed at the astronauts rather than the scientists, although one bearded newsman from a science channel asked: "What would be the most important thing you could expect to find on Mars?"

The team's biologist, the other woman among the seven, answered simply, "Life."

"Martians?"

"Martian microbes are the best we can hope for. We know the surface of Mars is a frozen desert, but microbial life might exist below the surface. Or, more likely, once did and is now extinct."

The newsman persisted. "But you think there's a chance some form of life could exist on Mars now?"

"A slim chance," she replied.

"Is there any evidence that gives you hope . . . ?"

The biologist shifted in her chair, then replied, "Satellites in orbit about Mars have detected traces of methane in the atmosphere. Traces that appear in the local springtime and break down within a few weeks."

"Methane?"

"On Earth," she went on, "there are microbes living deep underground that emit methane. They're called *methanogens*; they produce methane gas as a waste product of their metabolism."

"And you think there might be similar microbes on Mars?"

She shrugged. "Something's producing the methane. It just might be bug farts."

The audience erupted in laughter. The reporter chuckled happily and sat down.

Thrasher looked down the table at the biologist's earnest face and pictured the headlines her words would make: SCIENTIST HOPES TO FIND LIVING MARTIANS. He sighed inwardly: well, maybe it'll help to sell VR sets.

Dr. McQuinn fielded the questions about radiation in space.

"Our storm cellar will keep us safe and snug if we encounter any solar storms on our way to Mars."

"How snug?" asked a female reporter.

McQuinn smiled. "Let's put it this way: we'll be living cheek by jowl for several days on end. Like chickens in a coop. Without shower facilities."

Thrasher closed his eyes, picturing more headlines. And cartoons.

The next question was about sex, of course. From Vicki Zane. She got to her feet, smiled brightly, and asked, "What are you going to do about sex for the eighteen months you'll be on the mission?"

Nacho Velasquez grabbed one of the microphones and blurted, "I don't know about the rest of them, but I'm bringing a big supply of blackstrap molasses."

The audience broke into laughter again.

Undeterred, Vicki persisted, "No, seriously. Eighteen months is a long time. Couldn't the virtual reality equipment be used for, er . . . simulations of an erotic nature?"

Bill Polk took the microphone from Velasquez's hand. "All seven of us are mature adults and capable of controlling ourselves. We're going to Mars to explore the planet, not for fun and games."

Vicki looked unconvinced, but she sat down. Thrasher let out a sigh of relief. But he thought that Vicki's suggestion might boost VR sales more than anything else.

☀ 8 ☀
WASHINGTON, D.C.

June in the nation's capital was hot and muggy. Stuffed in the back of a rattletrap taxicab with the massive Frankenstein crowding him, Thrasher asked the driver to turn up the air conditioning.

"Up's far as it'll go," the driver replied, without taking his eyes off the vans and buses and autos and other cabs clogging the bridge over the Potomac River.

Frowning, Larry Franken muttered, "You'd think there wouldn't be so much hot air now that Congress is on vacation."

Humor? From Frankenstein? Thrasher felt his sweaty brows rise.

Linda had been adamant that Franken accompany Thrasher on this trip to Georgetown University. Thrasher gave in to her, but insisted that they shouldn't let Reynolds know he was visiting Professor Shima. R Cubed isn't the type to keep secrets, and Thrasher didn't want anyone to know he was using Shima's forensic linguistic skills. So they flew to Reagan National Airport on a regular American Airlines flight and took the dilapidated taxi from the airport rather than a company car.

Shima's office was as immaculate as ever: everything in its place. The professor rose ponderously from behind his desk as Thrasher introduced Franken, who bowed stiffly in Japanese fashion. Shima seemed delighted by the courtesy and bowed back.

"Mr. Franken heads my security department," Thrasher explained as the two of them took chairs in front of the desk. "I thought he should hear what you have to say."

Thrasher did not want to admit that Franken was actually serving as his bodyguard, at Linda's insistence.

Shima smiled graciously at Franken, then turned his attention to Thrasher. "I believe I have identified the man who scripted the words on the CDs you gave me."

"And?" Thrasher prompted.

Oblivious to Thrasher's impatience, Shima explained, "My students and I went through all the samples of the writing and speaking of your various board members, comparing them to the messages on the CDs."

"Who is it?" Thrasher asked eagerly.

Holding up a chubby hand, Shima went on, "I compared the word choices, syntactical morphology, sentence structure and other facets of the messages—"

"Who the hell is it?"

Shima put up both his hands. "This is not a totally definitive identification, you understand. I would say it is within about eighty-five or ninety percent of certainty."

Exasperated, Thrasher again asked, "Who?"

"Of all the persons we compared to the CD messages, a certain Mr. David Kahn comes closest to a match. Within eighty-five or ninety percent, as I said."

"David Kahn? Jenghis?"

Shima blinked. "He is named after the Mongol conqueror?"

Thrasher sank back in his chair. Jenghis Kahn. A cold, precise, murderous son of a bitch. Yes. It fits.

Franken asked, "Would your evidence hold up in a court of law?"

Shima nodded vigorously. "Men have been sent to jail on evidence such as this."

To Thrasher, Franken said, "You accuse Mr. Kahn of being responsible for the accident and the first thing he'll do is sue your ass for slander."

"Not just the accident," Thrasher said. "There's Vince's murder, too."

"The police have ruled it a suicide."

"It was murder." Thrasher was absolutely certain of it.

Shima rested his heavy forearms on his desktop. "My analysis will hold up in a court of law," he repeated. "I would stake my reputation on it."

Thrasher smiled wanly. "I'm staking my financial future on it, Professor. And maybe my life."

Back in the steaming streets of Washington, while Franken waved and whistled to attract a cab, Thrasher asked himself, Why would Dave Kahn want to cripple the Mars program? What's in it for him? Old Jenghis doesn't do things on a whim. There's something he's after. What could it be?

A bright new-looking taxi pulled over to the curb and the two men ducked in. The air conditioning was a pleasant relief after ten minutes in the sun and humidity.

"So what are you going to do?" Franken asked.

"I want to find out why Jenghis did this to me. What's he after? What does he want?"

Franken pursed his lips, then asked, "And how are you going to find that out?"

Thrasher thought it over for a couple of heartbeats. "If I start nosing around his operation he'll find out about it in ten seconds."

"I know a couple of people who might help."

Like Ramona Perkins? Thrasher thought. Shaking his head, he replied, "No, that'll take too long. If he's trying to stop the program he has to make his move before Mars One breaks orbit and starts on it way to Mars."

"In three weeks."

Thrasher nodded. "In three weeks. If he's going to make a move, it'll be in the next three weeks."

Franken studied his shoe tops for a few moments. Then, "So what do you want to do?"

"Only one thing I can think of, Larry. I'll have to go to New York and brace him, face to face."

Franken grunted. "Good luck," he muttered.

⊚ 9 ⊚
NEW YORK CITY

It wasn't easy to nail down a date to meet with David Kahn.

"He's being evasive," Linda said. "His people claim he's got to spend a week in a private hospital, for a detailed physical exam."

Thrasher said, "Find out which hospital. Put Frankenstein on the task. Let him earn his keep."

Days passed. At last Franken came to Thrasher's office. "Victoria Clinic," he announced. "It's a private facility, very exclusive. Deals with geriatrics."

"When does he go in?" Thrasher asked.

"Day after tomorrow."

Turning to Linda, Thrasher said, "I'm going to New York tomorrow morning. I'll see the sonofabitch before he goes to the hospital."

"But how?" she asked. "You can't just walk into his office."

"Can't I? Watch me."

Bluff and bravado can carry you only so far, Thrasher thought as he faced the dragon lady who was David Kahn's executive assistant.

He had barged into Kahn's office suite in the Chrysler building and bullied his way past a small phalanx of assistants, aides, and harried-looking executives. Now he stood in front of the dragon's desk, thinking, she'll call security and have me tossed out on my ear if I try to bully her. I've got to change my tactics.

"You can't see Mr. Kahn today," said the woman. "His schedule is very full."

"I'm sure it is," Thrasher said, softly, politely. "The thing of it is that we've run into a problem that needs his personal attention right away."

She shook her head. "You should have called for an appointment."

"It'll only take ten minutes. Maybe less."

Still shaking her head, she looked at her desktop screen and offered, "I can fit you in at the end of the month."

"By then it'll be too late," Thrasher said. He wished he'd brought a hat, so he could hold it in his hands and look properly humble.

"There's nothing I can do, Mr. Thrasher. I'm very sorry."

Thrasher bit his lip, then said. "I understand. Would it be all right if I just sit here and wait for him to come out of his office? As I said, I'll only need a few minutes of his time."

The dragon looked uncertain. "He won't be leaving 'til the end of the day. That's hours from now."

"I'll wait," Thrasher said, heading for one of the plush chairs set against the far wall of the office.

Now comes the moment of truth, he thought as he sat down. Either she calls security to throw me out or she calls Jenghis and tells him I'm here.

She picked up her phone and spoke into it in a sibilant whisper, her eyes on Thrasher.

He sat, trying not to show how nervous he felt. She put down the phone. Thrasher held his breath. Nobody from security showed up. She's told Jenghis I'm here, he realized, and the old bastard is going to make me wait until he's good and ready to see me.

More than an hour passed. Thrasher remembered when he'd been a kid and his father brought him to lecture halls on campus because he couldn't find a sitter to watch him. He had to sit very still and listen to the lectures without making a peep. He saw the students squirming in their chairs, whispering to one another, texting surreptitiously, yawning, even giggling. But he stayed perfectly still, like a stone, like a statue, the whole long time.

People went into Kahn's inner office and came out again, eying him as they passed. The dragon's phone buzzed every few minutes. A delivery boy unloaded a basketful of papers on her desk. Still he waited, like a stone, like a statue.

He knows I'm here. He's in there enjoying himself, making me wait. Well, once I see him his enjoyment is going to stop.

As the second hour passed, Thrasher said to the dragon lady, "I understand Mr. Kahn's going into a hospital tomorrow."

A look of alarm flashed across her face, but she quickly recovered. "It's just his annual physical. Strictly routine."

"Oh," Thrasher said. "That's good."

Late afternoon sun was slanting through the office windows when a quartet of young men came out of Kahn's office, talking animatedly among themselves. As they passed Thrasher, the dragon actually smiled and said, "Mr. Kahn will see you now."

Surprised, Thrasher got to his feet and made a smile for her. "Thank you," he said. "Thank you very much."

As he stepped into Kahn's palatial office, he saw that old Jenghis looked even worse than the last time he had seen him. His skin pallor was a sickly gray. He looked more wrinkled than ever. In his shirtsleeves, his face was sheened with perspiration, despite the room's frigid air-conditioning.

"I can give you ten minutes, Art," he rasped. "Talk fast."

Thrasher sat in one of the chairs in front of Kahn's desk and crossed his legs. "You paid Vince Egan to sabotage that Delta IV flight three years ago and now you've murdered him."

Kahn's flinty expression didn't change by a millimeter, but Thrasher heard the beeping sound from the medical equipment on the back of his wheelchair suddenly accelerate.

"If you're trying to give me a heart attack, it won't work," Kahn said.

"I have enough evidence to send you to jail," said Thrasher.

Kahn grunted. "My lawyers can run circles around your lawyers. Or the district attorney, for that matter."

"You had Vince Egan murdered."

"I did not." Kahn hesitated, then went on, "Somebody did, but it wasn't me."

❀ 10 ❀
CHRYSLER BUILDING

"Who was it, then?" Thrasher asked.

Kahn stared at him with red-rimmed eyes for a few silent moments, then rolled his wheelchair back and came around the desk. Thrasher watched as the old man wheeled toward the windows that looked out on Manhattan. The back of the wheelchair was loaded with medical equipment, beeping and blinking away.

Thrasher got up and went to the windows. He sat on the deep sill, facing Kahn.

"Why?" he asked. "Why'd you try to sabotage the Mars program? Why was Vince killed?"

Kahn's wrinkled, blotched face twisted into what might have been a smile. "You have no idea what you're dealing with, do you?"

Thrasher said nothing.

"You're just a little pipsqueak, Thrasher. A nobody, a nothing."

Leaning forward until his nose practically touched Kahn's, Thrasher said, in a murderously low voice, "I'm a nobody who can wring your neck, Jenghis. I can kill you just like *that*." And he snapped his fingers.

Kahn rolled his wheelchair back a few inches. "You haven't got the balls."

"Want to find out?" Thrasher got to his feet.

Kahn looked toward his desk. Thrasher warned, "It's too far away for you to reach before I can grab you. And once I've got my hands around your skinny throat you won't be able to call for help."

The old man was breathing hard. The equipment on the back of his wheelchair beeped faster.

"What do you want?" Kahn asked.

"Why'd you blow up that rocket? Why'd you murder Vince Egan?"

"I told you I didn't kill him!"

"You ordered it."

"I did not!" Kahn was sweating heavily now, his chest heaving. The phone on his desk buzzed.

He rolled the wheelchair back to his desk, Thrasher following a pace behind him.

Kahn jabbed a bony finger at the phone's keyboard.

"Mr. Kahn, are you all right?" The dragon lady's voice. "The medical monitors are blinking an alarm signal."

"I got a little excited, that's all," he replied. "I'll be all right."

"You're sure, sir? I can call the medical team. Or security, if you want."

Glancing up at Thrasher, Kahn rasped, "No need for that. I'll be all right."

He clicked the phone off. Thrasher plopped into one of the armchairs. His hands were trembling. *I came that close to snapping his crappy neck*, he realized. *I could have killed him.*

Taking a deep breath, Kahn said, "So you want to know who's doing what to whom, do you?"

"And why," Thrasher added.

"It involves Greg Sampson, of course. And . . . other people."

"Sampson."

"He wants to break you. He's carried a grudge against you for more than ten years."

"He's a patient man."

"He's a fool. Letting anger rule his judgment. He thought that blowing up your rocket would ruin your Mars program, or at the least drive Thrasher Digital into bankruptcy."

"He came damned close to being right."

Kahn made a cackling laugh that grated on Thrasher's nerves. "He didn't realize what a prize your company could be. He still doesn't get it."

"You mean the virtual reality technology."

With a wheezing nod, Kahn said, "Exactly. The VR technology. It's going to be worth a fortune. It's going to make somebody billions. Greg didn't want you to be that somebody, so he came to me to help him drive you into bankruptcy."

"He bought into Tridinamics," Thrasher said.

"I told him to do that. I own a good slice of that company, through dummies."

"You do?"

"Together with a couple of partners."

"So Greg set up the rocket failure—"

"With my help."

"And bought into Tridinamics, so he could give them the VR technology once Thrasher Digital went down the tubes."

"That's right. But you didn't go down the tubes. Almost, but not quite. You're more resourceful than we realized."

Thrasher frowned in thought. "So the two of you wanted to give my company's VR technology to Tridinamics—which you own."

"With a couple of partners."

"Greg wanted to screw me."

"And I wanted to make money from virtual reality."

"That still doesn't explain why Vince Egan was murdered."

Kahn spread his hands. "He was a loose end. Once he admitted to you what he'd done, we couldn't take the chance that you'd go to the authorities and ask for a full-blown investigation."

"So you killed Vince."

"I didn't. My Tridinamics partners did."

"Your partners?"

Kahn's seamed, ravaged face crinkled into a self-satisfied smile. "Do you know where Tridinamics' main office is?"

"Las Vegas, isn't it?" Thrasher's eyes went wide as he saw what Kahn was telling him. "Jesus Christ! The Mob?"

Cackling again, Kahn said, "Oh, they're strictly legitimate nowadays. Gambling and prostitution are legal in Nevada." Waggling a hand in the air, he added, "But every now and then they have to go back to their old ways."

"They killed Vince."

"For what it's worth, I didn't know about it until after the fact,"

Kahn said. With a shake of his head, he mumbled, "I couldn't control them, even if I'd wanted to. They go their own way."

"They killed Vince," Thrasher repeated.

"And there's not a thing you can do about it. If you push them, they'll kill you."

◎ 11 ◎
DÉTENTE

Thrasher said, "I could go to the police."

With another grunt, Kahn replied, "Who've written off the matter as a suicide. So what would you tell them, that a little bird told you it was murder? These people are professionals, they get away with murder all the time."

"Because they've bought off the police," Thrasher muttered.

"However they do it, they do it. And if I tell them I'm worried about you, they'll get you, too."

Thrasher felt himself smile. "So maybe I should wring your neck after all."

Kahn blinked his rheumy eyes. "Don't bother. I don't have that much longer to go."

Like hell, Thrasher thought. A stubborn old coot like you will hang in there and bury me, Sampson, and lord knows who else.

"So now that you know what's what, and who's who," Kahn said, "what do you intend to do about it?"

Thrasher though it over for a few heartbeats.

"Looks like there's not much I can do," he said. Then he added, "If what you're telling me is the truth."

"It's the truth, absolutely."

Very firmly, Thrasher said, "I don't want any more sabotage. If there is I'll go public with this whole story, I don't care what those wiseguys in Vegas do."

Kahn held up a placating hand. "There won't be. I want you to succeed. I want your VR technology to make billions."

"But I own the technology," said Thrasher. "I have the patents—"

"And I own a company that can market it, much better than your sappy little outfit."

"For porno simulations."

"For the entire spectrum of entertainment. I told you, the Las Vegas people are mostly legitimate. They have ties to Hollywood, the TV industry . . . this is going to be big, Arthur, very, very big."

"And you want in."

"There's plenty of room for us both."

I'd be making a deal with the devil, Thrasher thought. Eying Kahn sitting there, perspiring heavily despite the room's air conditioning, he realized that this particular devil might really be on his last legs. His scheduled visit to the medics is more than a routine checkup. Got to be.

He heard himself say, "Greg Sampson has half the profits from the VR shows we do during the Mars mission."

"Greg's an oaf. The Mars mission will be great publicity for the VR technology, of course. But the real money will start to come in afterward."

"And you want in on it."

"Why not? We can help each other. There'll be plenty to go 'round."

It'll be like buying insurance for the mission, Thrasher told himself. That's the important thing, making sure there's no more sabotage. The money is incidental. Almost.

"But why are so interested in this?" Thrasher asked. "What's in it for you?"

"Money!" Kahn blurted. "What else?"

"Money? For God's sake, don't you have enough?"

"How much is enough, Artie? How high is up? There's always more money to be made. Money is power, don't ever forget that. Power and safety."

Thrasher shook his head. The old man's nuts. A megalomaniac. But it makes sense to do business with him.

"Okay," he said, slowly, reluctantly. "Thrasher Digital will license its VR technology to Tridinamics." Before Kahn could react, he added, "On one condition."

"One condition?"

"You get Sampson out of Tridinamics. Buy him out, push him out, drop him out of an airplane. I don't want him making profits from the virtual reality business."

Kahn's eyes narrowed, but at last he said, "I can buy him out. He'll do what I tell him, especially with the Egan murder hanging over him."

"You said the police wouldn't reopen the case."

"Not for you. They would for my partners from Las Vegas."

"That's weird," Thrasher muttered.

"Politics makes strange bedfellows," said Kahn.

Getting to his feet, Thrasher said, "Have your people draw up a licensing agreement and I'll get my legal eagles to look it over."

Kahn leaned back and smiled thinly. "We're partners, then." He extended his trembling, fleshless hand over the desk.

"This isn't a partnership," Thrasher said. "It's more like a détente." But he reached across the desk and briefly clasped Kahn's hand. It felt cold, lifeless.

Once he'd left the old man's office, Thrasher asked the dragon lady where the men's room was. He felt an overpowering need to wash his hand.

⦿ 12 ⦿
LAUNCH PARTY

The warehouse in Portales was bursting with people. It was late afternoon on the first of July, blistering hot outside, but inside the Mars, Inc. headquarters building the air conditioning was cranked up to maximum and the atmosphere was frothy with anticipation.

A nine-piece band was playing Latino rhythms, although it was difficult to hear the music over the hubbub of the crowd.

Thrasher had announced the launch party to everyone even faintly connected to the Mars program, and to all the news media people, too. It was scheduled to run from four p.m. until eight, because the astronauts and scientists had to get a full night's sleep before launching the next morning to the Mars One spacecraft, waiting for them in orbit.

He was standing on the elevated walkway that covered three of the old warehouse's walls, one arm around Linda's waist, the other leaning on the steel railing, trying to listen to the music while scanning the noisy, bustling crowd. The whole Mars, Inc. work force was down there. They deserve a party, Thrasher told himself. They've earned it.

"Just about everyone we invited has showed up," Linda said, smiling happily.

"Jenghis Kahn's not here," said Thrasher. "Neither is his brother Charlie." But he spotted Gregory Sampson's imposing, white-bearded figure in the midst of the swirling, babbling, laughing crowd. And made a mental note to get to him.

The astronauts and mission scientists were in one corner of the area, besieged by reporters and camera people, including Vicki Zane. Funny how she can look sexy in a business suit, Thrasher thought. Jessie Margulis stood between Polk and Judine McQuinn. They all looked happy, relaxed. The champagne helps, Thrasher thought.

He saw Reynold R. Reynolds holding forth in front of one of the bars, looking important as he lectured a pair of congressmen. Patti Fabrizio stood out in the crowd, tall, slim, regal in a sweeping deep blue dress that Linda estimated must have cost "a mint."

And there was Will Portal, almost ignored off in a corner, nursing what looked like a cola. Will looked up and made eye contact with Thrasher, grinned boyishly and raised his glass.

"Art."

Thrasher turned and saw Sid Ornsteen walking along the steel gridwork toward him, looking his usual dour self. Letting go of Linda's waist and straightening up, Thrasher put on a smile.

"Hello, Sid. Join the party."

Ignoring the invitation, Ornsteen nodded a hello toward Linda, then said, "I just got off the phone with David Kahn's people. I think we've got the licensing agreement with Tridinamics worked out."

Thrasher said, "Good. Nice work. Now join the party."

"They told me Mr. Kahn's very happy with the arrangement."

"That means we're getting screwed," Thrasher said.

Ornsteen's face fell and Thrasher immediately regretted his wisecrack. "I was only kidding, Sid. I'm sure you did a good job."

"I think it's an equitable agreement," Ornsteen said, a little stiffly.

"Fine. I'll read it tomorr—no, not tomorrow. Tomorrow's the launch. I'll read it the day after tomorrow."

Ornsteen nodded.

"Now go down and join the party. Enjoy yourself. You've earned it."

The treasurer smiled tentatively. "Thanks. I think I will."

As Ornsteed headed for the stairs, Linda asked, "And when do we join the party?"

Scanning the crowd for a sight of Sampson's tall, heavy frame, Thrasher said, "Right now."

It took a bit of maneuvering to thread his way through the crowd to get to Sampson. Everyone wanted to have a drink with Thrasher, to have his or her picture taken with the man behind the Mars mission.

At last, though, he stood beside the big, bushy-bearded Sampson, who was chatting genially with Elton Schroeder and Bart Rutherford. Thrasher joined the chit-chat for a while, then said, "People, will you pardon us for a couple of minutes? There's something I have to talk to Greg about, in private."

Sampson looked surprised, but he shrugged and said, "Let me take another run at the bar, and then I'll be all yours, Artie."

Thrasher crooked a finger at one of the waitresses carrying a tray of drinks. "Mohammed doesn't have to go to the mountain," he said jovially.

Sampson grabbed a plastic flute of champagne and Thrasher turned to Linda. "Excuse us for a couple of minutes, honey."

Linda looked uncertain, but she said, "Sure."

Grasping the bigger man's elbow, Thrasher led Sampson through the crowd to a door in the side wall. He opened it and gestured Sampson into the small storeroom. Shelving covered the walls, mostly empty. Thrasher closed the door and cut off the laughing, clinking, chattering sounds of the party.

Sampson cocked a brow. "What's this all about, Artie?"

"How tall are you, Greg?"

"Six-two. Why?"

"And you weigh . . . ?"

"Oh, around two-ten, two fifteen."

Thrasher nodded, as if satisfied. "I'm five-eight, one hundred and sixty pounds, give or take a couple."

"So you're a middleweight and I'm a heavyweight. What's that got to do with anything?"

Thrasher said, "I hear you've sold your shares of Tridinamics."

Looking puzzled at the sudden change of subject, Sampson replied, "Yeah. I'm not that interested in the entertainment business."

"To Dave Kahn."

Sampson's expression turned wary. "So what?"

"Want to sell your half of the profits from our Mars mission broadcasts?"

Sampson shrugged. "Depends on the price. What're you offering?"

"This!" And Thrasher slammed a punch into Sampson's ample midsection with every ounce of power in his body.

The air exploded out of Sampson's lungs, he dropped the champagne flute as he doubled over and sank gasping to the floor.

"That's for Vince Egan, you sonofabitch," Thrasher said, standing over him.

Sampson clutched his middle and groaned. Thrasher left him there and rejoined the party.

◎ 13 ◎
SPACEPORT AMERICA

Promptly at ten the next morning, Bill Polk led the seven Mars-bound crew in their space suits from the spaceport's administration building to the two white SUVs waiting to drive them to the launch pad. Thrasher looked through the building's sweeping window to the launch rocket, standing out on the pad nearly two miles away.

The launch party in Portales had been a huge success. While Polk and the rest of the crew had left promptly at eight p.m. and flown to Las Cruces, most of the guests partied on until well past midnight. The news media people were among the last to leave, although Will Portal surprised Thrasher by dancing with every available woman—including Linda—until the band at last stopped playing.

Thrasher had called an ambulance for Greg Sampson, instructing the EMT leader to come in quietly and take the still-groaning Sampson to the city hospital. Then he phoned the hospital's chief administrator, a man who had gladly accepted Thrasher's charitable donations over the past several years, and asked that Sampson be kept sedated and under observation for the night.

Satisfied that Sampson would be out of the picture for the critical pre-launch hours, Thrasher flew to Las Cruces with Linda and caught a couple of hours of sleep before the launch.

Now he stood in the visitors' auditorium of the spaceport's stylish main building and looked across the bright New Mexico morning at the launch rocket silhouetted against the cloudless turquoise sky, with the spaceplane and its rakishly swept-back wings perched atop it.

Maybe we shouldn't have put all seven of the crew on the one flight, he thought. Maybe we should have split it into two flights, for safety's sake. Twice the expense, but what the hell.

Then he realized that if one of the launches failed, the whole mission would immediately be scrubbed. So send them all together on the one bird, he told himself. Go for broke.

Linda stood beside him, somehow calming his jitters without saying a word. He knew that Jessie Margulis was over in the control center, pacing among the launch team seated at their consoles during the final minutes of countdown.

Will Portal stepped up on Thrasher's other side. "Good luck, Art," he breathed.

Thrasher nodded without taking his eyes off the rocket. The umbilicals that delivered electrical power and topped off the liquid oxygen propellant dropped away from its side and the service tower began to roll back.

"Launch vehicle on internal power," the mission communicator announced. Thrasher knew that more than a hundred people were crowding along the building's wide windows. He had even spotted Hamilton Reed in the crowd, with R Cubed at his side: the Wicked Witch of the East and the humbug Wizard of Oz.

"T minus one minute."

And counting, Thrasher added silently. His mouth was dry. It took an effort to swallow. He could hear his pulse thumping in his ears. Linda squeezed his hand; he turned and smiled at her.

"This is it," he said.

"T minus thirty seconds."

Thrasher closed his eyes and took a deep breath, trying to calm himself. But in his mind's eye he saw the Delta IV explosion all over again. Not now, he begged a deity he didn't really believe in. Not this time. He remembered a line his father had once quoted at him, *There are no atheists in foxholes.* Yeah. Or at launch countdowns, either.

"... five ... four ... three ..."

A flash of light blossomed at the rocket's base. Thrasher knew it was the ignition of the main engines, but he flinched at the sight nonetheless.

" . . . ignition."

The solid rocket boosters strapped to the launcher lit up with a blast of flame and the ship seemed to leap off the launch pad.

"Lift-off!" said the communicator, excited despite himself. "We have lift-off!"

The bird rose into the sky as if it belonged there, not on Earth. Now the bellow of the rocket engines reached them, rattling the windows, shaking their souls. Thrasher's eyes blurred with tears.

Wiping his eyes, he followed the ship's glowing arc across the heavens, gulped when the explosive bolts separated the solid boosters, held his breath until another flare of light indicated the bird's first stage had separated and the spaceplane was on its own.

The spaceplane was nothing but a pinpoint of light now, racing across the flawless blue morning sky.

"They're on their way," Linda said.

Bill Polk's disembodied voice filled the auditorium. "All systems are green. We'll rendezvous with Mars One in seventy-eight minutes."

The crowd began to edge away from the windows. Thrasher knew that there were three technicians aboard Mars One, waiting for the Mars-bound crew to arrive. The technicians would leave on the same spaceplane that carried Polk and his team into orbit.

Professor Winninger came up, smiling broadly. "This is a great day!" he said. "A wonderful day!"

Kristin Anders, at the professor's side, didn't look as elated. Her husband's on his way to Mars, Thrasher knew, and she's worried for him.

Before he could think of anything to say to Kristin, Linda took both of her hands in her own. "He's going to be fine," she said. "He's going to bring you home some Martian souvenirs."

Kristin smiled weakly.

Somehow Thrasher felt almost disembodied, as if his real self were on the spaceplane with the astronauts. Almost like an automaton, he walked with Linda and the rest of the crowd to the tiers of chairs overlooking the command center, eying the giant wall screens that showed the spaceplane's trajectory as it headed toward Mars One. Absently, he took a seat in the front row, his entire attention focused on what was going on inside the spaceplane.

Bill Polk's calm, confident voice kept up a play-by-play report as the spaceplane achieved its orbit and began its approach to Mars One. Like a mating dance, Thrasher thought. They're going to link up with the spacecraft, mate with her, place the seven astronauts and scientists inside her, bring her to life.

And he realized that he was glued to Earth, a spectator, nothing more.

But that doesn't really matter, he told himself. They're going to Mars, and I'm the guy who'd made it happen.

☀ 14 ☀
ON TO MARS

July Fourth. Arthur D. Thrasher was giving America a birthday present. The seven astronauts and scientists of the Mars-bound crew had spent the past two days checking out their spacecraft as it swung around the Earth. This evening they would break orbit and start the long voyage to Mars.

Thrasher stood in the VR chamber at the University of Arizona's campus in Tucson, walking through the Mars One vehicle. Bill Polk was beside him, leading this tour through the spacecraft.

"And this is the command center," Polk was saying, as they stepped into the compact compartment. It had three high-backed seats, surrounded by a bewildering array of control consoles and display screens. Thrasher heard the soft hum of electrical power and the faint beeps of the sensors, saw the lights on the consoles. A single window looked out on Earth, big and blue, flecked with purest white clouds.

Thrasher nodded approvingly as Polk explained the functions of each console. Tapping the round screen in the center of the panels, he said, "This screen can show us what the telescopes outside are looking at. Right now the main 'scope is focused on Mars."

He pecked at the keyboard below the screen and Thrasher saw a red dot appear in the middle of the screen. With a knowing grin, Polk said, "That image is going to get a lot bigger over the next few months."

Thrasher knew that his company had sold one million, seventeen thousand and forty-two VR sets, mostly to private homes and amusement arcades. Plus another couple of thousand they had given away to news media outlets and schools. Chicken feed, he thought. In another couple of months we'll be selling millions of sets. Through Tridinamcs.

The money would be welcome, but it was secondary. The main thing is we're going to Mars. We start tonight.

It had been a publicity coup to time the departure for Mars on the Fourth of July. Strictly a happy coincidence, Thrasher insisted to every interviewer. The mathematics of the launch window simply worked out this way. Inwardly, he grinned. Yeah, the math worked out that way after we spent a few months massaging the numbers.

So now he had an audience of one million, seventeen thousand and forty-two private homes and arcades. Plus every major television network and news cable station and a handful of schools. People were home for the holiday, walking through the Mars One spacecraft with him, courtesy of virtual reality technology. By the time the team gets to Mars, millions of VR users will be right there alongside them.

At last Polk had walked back to the ship's galley, where the tour had started.

"That's it," he said. "This is where we'll be living and working for the next six months. At the end of that time, we'll be in orbit around Mars, ready to go down to the surface and start exploring."

A preselected quartet of news commentators started asking questions picked from viewers who had tweeted them in. Polk patiently answered them, while Thrasher zoned them out of his conscious awareness.

"I'm finished," he said to the technicians running the VR rig. His vision of the Mars One craft disappeared. The world went blank for a moment, then he lifted the visor of his helmet and saw the bare walls of the virtual reality studio.

And Linda, standing beside him, taking off her VR helmet and shaking her long dark hair free of it.

Kristin Anders came up to them.

"It worked fine, Kris," Thrasher said. "Just fine."

Linda said, "You'll be able to be with Alan every day."

She made a rueful little smile. "It's not quite the same."

"But it's better than nothing," said Linda.

Her smile turned a little more cheerful. "Yes, you're right."

Thrasher pulled off his nubby sensor gloves as Linda and Kristin talked together. At last he and Linda left the VR studio, heading for the car that would take them to the Tucson airport and the plane that would fly them back to Houston.

"We'll be home before they leave," Linda said as they climbed into the black sedan.

"Better be," said Thrasher. "I don't want to miss the big moment."

"Why did you turn down the requests for interviews this evening?"

Pointing skyward, he answered, "It's their show, not mine. Not now. It's all theirs."

Linda gave him a disbelieving stare.

Waggling a hand, "I'm tired. I want to get home. I've had enough publicity."

She nodded. "Sure you have."

By nine p.m. they were back in their apartment, sitting in the living room, watching the big wall TV screen.

Curled beside him on the big, deep sofa, Linda suggested, "We could go across to the office and get into the VR rigs."

Thrasher shook his head. "No. Polk and his team have enough on their hands without running another show for tourists."

"You're not a tourist."

"Yes I am," he said. "Just a tourist now."

Linda studied his face. "Art, you look like you're about to cry."

He tried to smile. "Yeah."

"You're sad?"

"I want to be with them."

"Of course you do."

"I know it's silly, but I want to be there, myself, heading for Mars."

She touched his cheek. "If it weren't for you, none of them would be going to Mars. Isn't that enough?"

"No. But I guess it'll have to do."

They lapsed into silence and watched the TV commentator nattering away the final few minutes before Mars One headed out.

Thrasher glanced at his wristwatch. "Come on," he said, getting up from the sofa. "We can see them from the balcony."

Rising to her feet beside him, Linda asked, "Are you sure . . ."

He nodded sharply. "If we can't, I'm going to fire half a dozen astronomers."

They walked through his den and out onto the balcony.

"It's dark!" Linda exclaimed.

He made a little grin. "I worked with the city fathers. They agreed to turn off the damned lights for an hour."

"Without telling me? When did you do that?"

"Last week, while you were getting your medical checkup."

In the shadows he couldn't make out the expression on her face. But her tone was clear: "And here I thought you couldn't do anything without me."

He shrugged. "Just little things."

Linda looked up into the night sky. Plenty of stars twinkled above them.

"Good thing it's a clear night," Thrasher said.

"I suppose you arranged that, too."

"I wish."

A bright, steady light climbed over the forest of darkened skyscrapers. "There they are," Thrasher said, pointing.

From the TV inside the apartment, they heard Polk's voice counting calmly, "Five . . . four . . . three . . ."

Linda leaned her head against his shoulder. He lifted up her chin and kissed her.

The bright light in the sky flared briefly.

"Trajectory insertion complete," came Polk's disembodied voice. "We're on our way to Mars!"

The light still sailed serenely across the sky, but Thrasher knew that soon it would be gone from his view.

"They're on their way," he said, silently adding, without me.

"Don't be sad," Linda said. "You've done a wonderful thing. You should be proud of yourself."

"Yeah."

"You're going to be a hero to everybody all across the whole world."

"I guess."

"You're going to be very rich."

He nodded.

Linda hesitated a heartbeat, then said, "And you're going to be a father."

Thrasher flinched with surprise. "You're sure?"

"My checkup last week. I'm pregnant."

He burst into laughter and pulled her to him, "We're going to have a kid!"

"I don't know if it'll be a boy or girl, not yet."

"Who cares? We'll start astronaut training for him as soon as he can walk. Or her, whichever."

Linda smiled and nestled in his arms while the Mars One spacecraft started its long journey.

❀END❀